1

***

Operation Crossbow

*** The Procreation Instinct ***

A powerful human emotion that drives
every parent to protect its offspring

Dedicated to Shawn Paul Delorey

[1989 - 2013]

AND

To every US veteran that engages
a battlefield or a warzone to defend our country

***

Operation Crossbow

By William Delorey
(c) 2015

Cover Design: J Lacy Coughlan
Copy Editor: J Lacy Coughlan
Cover Image: Bill Delorey

Special thanks always to Genie for her
support and encouragement over the years

Thanks
Professor Luke Wallin and Writer Michael Lee
A little piece of each of you resides in everything I write

www.billdelorey.com

***A Salute ***

A special salute and recognition to all brother and sister veterans who live the sacrifice and keep this country safe from its enemies, and protect its lands for our children and our future generations

A heartfelt thanks to:

Dr. Natalie Mariano; P.A. Joan McTigue;

R.N. Deborah Honnen; Dr. Larry Edwards;

Dr. Mohammad Ayubi; Dr. Julie Applegate;

VASR Cynthia Dunbar

And the Veteran's Health Care network for the respect and medical treatment our US military veterans earn every day defending our homeland.

Additional Fiction by William Delorey

*** *Shuffle an Impulse* ***

A Novel

A psychological suspense and medical thriller

(2015)

*** Predators: A Six-pack of short fiction***

*Some predators are animals. Some predators are human.
Sometimes it's hard to tell the difference.*
(2015)

*** *A Hobo's Revenge* ***

A Novel

Real Estate :: Financial fraud and manipulation

(2016)

*** *Paper Cuts* ***

A Novel

Medicine & Money :: Medical exploitation and organ theft

(2016)

Go to author website for more information

www.billdelorey.com

Published in the United States of America

WordWizard Publications

411 Walnut Street Suite 6317
Green Cove Springs, Florida 32043

Operation Crossbow
A work of fiction

Operation Crossbow illustrates violent behavior in its characters and actions, and depicts sexual situations. Language describing scenes in this novel makes it less suitable for young ages.

www.billdelorey.com

*** Despite the bliss of mortal ignorance - forgive not that betrayal when a man defiles an innocent ***

Operation Crossbow

A WHITE FUR PARKA completely envelops a man huddled beneath a copse of pine trees burdened with fresh snow. A few remaining flakes blow about, settling into the freeze. Chilling winds push the clouds away after three brutal days of blizzards and below freezing temperatures.

Nearly invisible against a colorless landscape, the man called Tracker exhales through a knit scarf and vapor floats before the embankment, drifting unseen amidst snowflakes and dusk. A shotgun painted white hangs in the crook of his arm, its muzzle a round black dot dancing against the frosty background each time he shifts position. Tracker studies a log cabin buried halfway to its eaves and a small woodshed standing nearby.

Smoke hovers briefly above a stone chimney then drifts away, an ethereal wisp haunting the wilderness. Dim firelight flickers behind tapered snowdrifts banked against frost-covered windows and lends an eerie quality to the scene. Eyes as pale as a glacier flick between the cabin and a woodshed beyond.

The shed door bangs open and a man steps out, his face partially hidden in a fleece-lined hood, his arms cupped beneath a stack of firewood. The man stamps along a trail he shoveled earlier through snow three feet deep and pushes his back against the cabin door. The overlaid wooden slab resists, stuck shut. He kicks at it. A dull thump sounds dead in the wintry wilderness.

"Damn it," the man growls, voicing a thick rasp in the chill air. "Open the fuckin' door, Jack." Again Manny kicks at it then bumps his shoulder against the door.

At that exact instant, Jack twists the handle inside. The thick wooden slab springs open and barks his knuckles. Jack yelps and slams it shut again, tipping Manny backward into the snow bank, the firewood scattering beside him. A heavily bearded face appears in a thin slit then the door swings open.

Manny jumps to his feet and snaps a snowball through the gap.

A cold welt turns red in the center of Jack's forehead as he jerks his head backward and grins, brushing his fingertips at the wet spot.

Manny shoves the door open all the way and stuffs another snowball down his younger brother's shirt.

Jack grabs Manny, lifts him off his feet, staggers outside and tosses him into the snow bank, then spins on one bright red sock, races back inside, still grinning, and slams the door shut one more time.

Manny quickly shakes the white crystals off his shirt and pants, and jumps at the door again but nearly falls inside this time when it pops open easily. The men grapple and bear-hug, wrestling and laughing, rolling around on the floor.

"I'll toss your big hairy ass in that snow yet," Manny barks, and struggles with the weight, trying unsuccessfully to push the much larger man off his chest. "All right, all right, lemme up. You tryin' to heat the whole state? Lemme get the wood and shut the door, before we freeze the joint."

Jack grins, cuffs Manny playfully behind his ears, and rolls off his brother.

Manny scrambles to his feet but suddenly has no face. The first shotgun blast takes him head-high and flips him backward over a rough plank table centered in the room.

Two more blasts slam Jack back against the hearth and drop him in front of the flames. Blood splatters the rocks and walls, and drips onto the slate floor. His left shoulder and arm lie in the coals, his hair and beard sizzle, his shirt smolders. Jack twitches and jerks, twitches again, then lies motionless and feels nothing. Manny lies beside his brother on the plank floor, still as a stone.

White fur fills the frame as Tracker steps inside. Sharp odors hang in the room, gunpowder, wood smoke, blood and old sweat fill his nostrils. Tracker pumps another shell into the chamber just as the first slug hits him above the heart and deflects up and sideways off a rib.

Tracker rolls right and drops the shotgun, caroms off the woodstove and twists quickly. A second bullet slams into a log above his head, and a third ricochets off the stove, punctures a teapot and sprays water all over the stovetop. Steaming beads hiss and pop on the hot metal.

A short, thick-bodied young woman undressed to the waist rises above the loft railing and aims once more.

Two quick shots echo a split second apart.

A small red dot appears below her hairline, another two inches below it where her right eye had been a second ago, and both dots dribble slick red wetness down her cheek.

The snub-nose pistol slips from her fingers and bounces twice on the kitchen floor nine feet below. Her remaining eye widens, staring at Tracker, her brow wrinkles in disbelief, resisting her end. The woman struggles, willing herself to remain erect but finally slumps onto the mattress. Her left hand slips between the rails, her fingers extend crookedly as if grasping at her killer.

"Chose the wrong weapon," Tracker observes, his rough, sandpaper voice evaluating the small caliber, short-range handgun the woman used. "Lucky for me," his abrupt cackle fills the room and he grunts at her mistake.

His smile twists a bit as the pain grabs him. Tracker groans. He reaches inside, rubs his chest, and then wipes his fingers clean. Bloody stains streak his parka, the thin splotches bright red against the white fur. Breathing heavily, Tracker tucks his pistol into its pouch and leans his back against the log wall. He retrieves a handkerchief from his pants pocket and stuffs it in against the bullet hole, fingering a stickiness where the blood leaks, clots, and mats in his chest hair.

Pain grips his chest once more. "Damn that hurts!"

He picked up this assignment nine days ago. The package mapped this location and identified the brothers. It had taken him four days just to pack in, hindered by nasty weather and heavy snowdrifts. The woman completely surprised him. Tracker had been watching the cabin since early morning, awaiting this evening and the opportunity to accomplish his chore, but she had never come outside so he never spotted her. He expected no one but the two men, a mission control error that nearly cost him his life.

"Someone's gonna pay for this." A promise to himself he'll keep later. His gritty mutter fades away with the pain, and he groans again.

The rank smell of burnt hair and cotton shirt fill the room. Tracker wrinkles his nose and pushes to his feet, grabs Jack by a foot and tugs the body away from the flames. He locates a small bucket, kneels, and pours water over the smoldering hair and shirt, dousing the burn and washing away the stink.

A wave of nausea rolls over Tracker. He slumps against the stone hearth, eases himself down slowly and stretches his legs out on the floor, resting a minute. His eyes quiver and slide shut, his thoughts dissipate into a thickening fog of ache and shock.

A chill enters the cabin while Tracker sleeps, driving out the heat. The fire burns down to a few coals, the open door drifts back and forth in the quickening breeze, squeaking on old rusted hinges. A feminine hand hangs over the loft edge, stiff, without life.

*

His eyes flutter then open, close briefly, then open again. Unconscious for more than three hours, his shoulder and chest ache, and the bullet hole oozes blood each time he flexes the muscle. Tracker tilts his head, adjusts his focus. Moonlight filters through the treetops and lights up the woodshed roof. Snow reflects back into the darkness, creating odd shadows across the yard and into the cabin interior.

He rolls over, grips the upended table, struggles to his knees then pushes himself erect. Another wave of dizziness nearly knocks him down again and he shakes his head, a mindless error that aggravates the pain immensely. He leans against the table and waits while his thoughts clear.

Later still, clean and disinfected, he tapes a bandage across the hole. The bullet remains inside and Tracker knows he needs a clinic. Infection will cause him trouble if he cannot get to a doctor soon. He whips out a miniature camera and quickly records evidence of his work. He exits the cabin, packs up his gear and enters a trail, aims his snowshoes at an Arctic Cat snow-runner hidden in the trees, a three hour hike lit by a full moon.

Tracker grunts and takes the first step.

1

Intelligence Coordination Division Director George M. Hallingforth III lifts his eyes, removes his glasses, and gazes out the window, massaging the bridge of his nose. A blue folder slips from his fingers, its contents spill out across his desk. "Wish this damn rain'd quit."

A photograph lands face-up on his blotter, its bright colors clearly illustrating a man with his throat slit and his genitals cut away, the rest of his body battered and bruised. Vacant but glaring, two extremely unforgiving eyes stare back at Hallingforth, accusing. A spasm of remorse crosses his face and Hallingforth glances out the window again.

"Well, here's the proof, Henry. They killed John Symington," Hallingforth says, and shakes his head. "We have to begin again."

Uneasy, standing beside the desk, Henry Bates shuffles his feet, but says nothing. His left hand holds four thin files. His right hand squeezes a black rubber ball. Periodically, he switches the ball and the files, exercising the opposite fist.

Seated in his tenth floor office, Hallingforth stares at the panoramic view, sadness straddling his portly shoulders. Wind and rain beats steadily against the glass and beyond the adjoining buildings an occasional spark of lightning brightens the sky.

Heavy and blowing, the storm has been drowning Baltimore off-and-on for nearly a week. The city dwellers constantly beg for sunshine, and once it arrives, immediately complain about the heat and humidity.

"Will you need anything else this evening, sir?" asks Bates, forever locked in his South Texas drawl. Bates often adds the *'sir'* out of respect, though the men have been friends and colleagues for years.

"Still only four, Henry?"

Bates raises the files, waves them at Hallingforth. "No change."

"Well, you read them too. What do you think?"

Bates shifts the ball and the files between his hands once more. "Tracker's the best by far, but won't do it. Says he retired after that last hit, and still pissed about it. We left him hanging when Tactical missed Ramona Pierce. She almost iced him in the cabin when he sanctioned the Dixon brothers a few months ago. Blames it on us, of course."

"Yes, well he's a contract. Can't expect us to do the same background as we do for our internal Spec 909 ops. Too expensive. Should've checked on his own too, for the money we paid him, and his ass on the line. I'd sure check myself if it were my tail hanging out there." Hallingforth replies. "He's got plenty of soft contacts, probably some we don't even know about,"

That screw-up annoys the director a little, although probably not as much as Tracker and the bullet he took based on an agency error. Hallingforth neither accepts nor tolerates screw-ups, but he masks those feelings at present and for this specific project. No sense letting emotion cloud his judgment, and this operation's fundamentally different anyway.

"Run it all by me again, Henry."

"Salvoni and Fountaine are both ex-CIA and work freelance for us, and for other departments and, unfortunately, for other countries as well. Both have an easily traceable record. Course, same thing with Symington, but he's such a renegade it didn't matter. Well, was anyway, he's off the books now for good. Tracker won't even talk about it anymore, just ignores my pings."

"Sergeant Klyne's a loner by choice, excellent in the operational intelligence and extremely physical, but a real rookie at something like this, and may be tough to convince. He's still active military, might get a bit dicey. Besides, he already said 'No' once last time we asked. Currently in Panama for another few weeks. Told me he's tired, finished with it all. 'Taking a discharge and going home,' he said ... but we don't know which home he means."

"He has family in England and Seattle, and in Jersey. His best friend works in Los Angeles, out in the beach area somewhere. A state drug cop. Both did Special Forces ops all over the world, forged a pretty tight bond."

"I can search it again, but won't find anyone else, unless you change your mind. About the qualifications, I mean."

"Can't we force him? We must have something good on him."

"Who? Tracker? Doubt it. You know him as well as I do. Sent Lenny Mathews down to his farm to ask again. Lenny couldn't find him, and woke up the next morning with the middle finger of his glove tacked to a tree beside his campsite." Bates laughs. "I'd call that a statement."

"Could give it one more try, but he'll just disappear again. Might even come for us if we push him too hard. He's crazy enough to try it."

"I'm not worried about that. He'd just bump up against it. Wouldn't ever get in here unless we let him."

"Not so sure about that, George. And we're not always here either. Wouldn't want to be looking behind myself the rest of my life if we piss him off again, good as he is. And, he's a little nuts. Besides, if we push him hard now and he still turns it down, we won't be able to use him later if we find something he likes."

"Nobody retires. Not in our world," Hallingforth reflects absently. The director leans his elbows on the desk and lowers his forehead onto his palms, digs his fingertips into his scalp.

He launched this operation two months ago. The files detail only four remaining men his ICD computers identified with the skills he needs. Five until a couple days ago. John Symington accepted the contract more than a month ago, but lost his way somehow.

"Not careful enough probably. Getting too old for it maybe?" Bates concludes, and shrugs, as if an adversary butchers one of his contractors every week.

Now the favored mercenary is dead, the photos Hallingforth received last night confirm that unfortunate fact. And, the man insisted on his money up-front, which upsets Hallingforth even more. Budget again, even though his operational money never shows up on any federal accounting, and he never runs out.

"This one's a bit different anyway, Henry ... but still, it's annoying to pay and get nothing for it," he said. Hallingforth shakes his head and rubs his eyes again, a perpetual habit.

"Not exactly nothing, George. He got to one of the targets."

Hallingforth glares across the desk. "He didn't finish it. That matters!"

Bates shifts the ball and files again. "Anything else, sir." He feels a bit uneasy with this specific project. Hallingforth has not shared everything on it, an extremely unusual situation after all the years they've worked together. But his Red Ops are often like that. Need to know, and most don't need all of it.

"I think not Henry, just finish up and I'll buzz if I need something. Leave these files with me and you can go as soon as you wrap up. I'll check these again and decide tonight who we send."

"Okay. I'll be here awhile anyway." Bates steps out and shuts the door.

Hallingforth skims the files, scribbles a few notes as he reads. An hour passes. He points a finger and depresses a switch. "Henry, you still here?"

Bates enters immediately, as if expecting the call. "Yes sir?" Brushing his palm back and forth over an inch of thick blond hair above his craggy, unreadable face, Bates stands across the desk and looks down at his supervisor.

"Have we a Spec 909 agent in the Northwest? A young female, attractive, and extremely competent in martial arts."

"A woman, sir?" Bates asks, his eyebrows arch in question.

"Yes, Henry, a woman."

The ICD Specialist 909 operation center controls two hundred and forty-seven agents, but only sixteen women. Bates keeps track of who, what, and where every Spec 909 operative lives and works, and administers all assignments.

Hallingforth does not, at least not until he needs one. Everyone believes that, although it's basically untrue. George Hallingforth recalls every current operation, and all completed operations as well. That makes him unique, that kind of mind-control and memory.

He never learned it or practiced it, it just came to him from birth, and made him an anomaly in high school and college, then among his peers, and later, as he matured and rose through the ranks, created avenues in federal law enforcement organizations unavailable to others. George Hallingforth paved his own road to the top early on in his career.

Bates inspects dots in the ceiling while searching his mind. "No. Not that I'm aware of." Then his eyes glimmer and what passes for a smile creases his face. "Hold on a minute, Nikki ..."

He pauses briefly, reflecting, begins again, a bit more official tone in his words. "Agent Pepperton, she's right here, well in D.C. anyway, and available. Could send her anywhere on short notice. She's assigned to internal investigations temporarily, but operated in Washington and Oregon, a little bit in Canada, and a couple times in California. She usually works the Far East for obvious reasons."

Bates almost restrains the crack in his face, but his lips twitch at the corners despite his normally stoic persona. "About thirty, if I recall, but still looks like a kid. Attractive, yeah too, no doubt. My sons call her a 'stone fox' with a very nice tail."

The director knows that Henry Bates recalls Nikki Pepperton exactly, and that Bates wishes he could undo the lip-twitch that gave him away just now, and why he pretends ignorance whenever her name pops up. Both men know the story and reasons, and both men know the other man knows it.

Hallingforth says nothing about it, just picks up the files and scans each one quickly. The Pepperton history means nothing today, so he ignores it.

"Thought of her, but she's on med-leave?"

"Just back, bullet didn't do much damage. Pretty tough woman. And she's about ready for assignment. You don't like her for this one, maybe use Jacki Granger. She's actually a couple years younger than Nikki, but looks much older." His eyes crinkle and the corners of his mouth bend up once and flatten back quickly, but again, he refrains from actually smiling.

"Don't tell Jacki I said that. She's working an industrial espionage case in London with Trigger Crabbe, but it's just idling. He can watch it alone for now. If it pops open again we can send someone else if he needs back-up."

"But Pepperton's fully fit, and ready for assignment."

"Good ... excellent. Get me her ops files, not the background." The Director works at his thoughts momentarily. "She still capable? Not hurt or ineffective, or psyched out by that weird hit?"

"No, nothing. Nine confirmed kills, most recent in this last one – then she caught that bullet trying to get out afterwards. Pretty lucky actually, could've been worse. Just grazed her lung so she's been rehabbing for a while. Probably about the best we have in unarmed combat. No reason to rotate her out, she's fully recovered. And Annie Newport did her work-up over at psyche and says her head's just fine."

Bates spins on his heel and leaves the room, returns shortly and hands over a red folder. "Might be something I forgot in here, but I doubt it."

"I'll be home all night if you need me, George." The door swings shut behind Bates, a nearly silent puff of air announces the security door sealing itself.

Hallingforth leans on his elbows, presses stubby fingers into his eyes, gently kneading the orbits. He has five files and a decision suddenly urgent with Symington dead and the mission compromised. "Temporarily," the word barely audible under his breath. He shakes his head, rubs his eyes, and groans. He hides his suffering well, but someone may easily discover his secret if this project stalls much longer.

The director lays the open folders in a row on his desk and boots up his desktop. Alternately, he refers to each page one at a time and taps keys with one index finger on each hand, his old school typing method, slow but sure.

Stopping occasionally, he rests his eyes and refreshes his coffee while searching the web and the federal security data base. He reads and makes notes long past midnight, filling a large pad with small, neat script as well as building a new digital file.

Finally, he copies the info into a flash drive he slips in his pants pocket, and then keys in a security sequence. The computer erases everything he entered and shuts itself down. He sticks the files and the note pad in his briefcase and spins the locks.

He opens the bottom drawer, removes a nearly full bottle and a goblet, and sets both on his desk. Lost in thought, he stares at the tumbler a moment then pours two fingers of amber liquid, passes the snifter under his nose, inhales then sips, rolling the aged brandy around on his tongue, savoring its mellow flavor.

Once again, Hallingforth experiences a secret window that opens directly into his soul and a tart tangerine taste that slides across the palette, followed by the sweetly thick honey-rose liqueur and flat coconut strands that delight his taste buds. Relaxing as best he can under the circumstances, the brandy turns his mind inward.

A vengeful sadness follows his thoughts into a satanic lair while the devil cracks a smile and chuckles silently at behavior the director can no longer resist.

Gazing out the slick dark window, Hallingforth leans back and stretches out his short, thick legs. The wind lightens, the rain finally stops, and a bright half-moon hangs behind thinning clouds. His co-workers often call him 'Chunkie' behind his back and think he doesn't know it. He knows it. The ICD Director knows everything.

"I know everything!" He opens the initial interview with each new agent assigned to his unit. *"If I don't know it, I'll find it out long before you do,"* his lecture continues. *"When you know more than I, you'll have my job, and until you do, don't doubt anything I tell you."*

Most recruits express minor disbelief at first, but later learn the lesson, sometimes a harsh one, and sometimes too late. But George Hallingforth is always right and always one step ahead, or two. Well, almost always - an antagonistic enemy nailed Symington this time, and extremely unusual event in Spec 909 operations.

George M. Hallingforth III founded the Intelligence Coordination Division five years ago and rules it with an iron fist. He misses nothing and plays no favorites. Every person in power politics owes him at least something, even if only one favor. And he owes no one. Nice to park on that throne he reflects often, and very convenient.

He sips again, pours another shot. His eyes roam the room, returning time and again to the family portrait sitting on his desk. His thoughts turn inward, as always, to his only daughter, his love, his life, the dark-haired beauty he buried nearly two years ago.

Victoria Hallingforth, her spirit crushed before its time. Brightness, and sparkle, and humor, and gone. His sweetest memory occupies a huge void in his chest whenever his mind stands idle, a perpetual ache that never lets him rest.

He spent a ton of influence, collected numerous favors, and kept the real story from his wife. Margaret still believes her only child died in an automobile accident in New Mexico while developing an advertising contract for her employer, an electronics development firm based in Virginia.

A tear moistens his eye. Once again, and as always when late and alone, he contemplates a different version of her life, how he might have raised her some other way, and protected her from the viciousness surrounding her death. Again, he comes up without an answer. He had done his best, he believes, but chance and choice had chilled her laughter ... Forever.

He shakes his head once more. His reverie slips away. Absently, he fingers the wet streaks on his cheek, rises, switches off the lights and stands in shadow for a moment. A tremendous weariness suddenly overwhelms him and he sags beneath it, its burden riding heavy in his heart.

Hallingforth changes his mind and turns the lights back on, sits at the desk, pours another drink. He opens his briefcase, picks up the files, and quickly reviews the information again as if a new wrinkle emerged while he pondered his child. He taps his fingers on the desk, lost in thought and planning one last time. He jots a few more notes, places the files and his note pad carefully inside his briefcase and locks it.

"Sergeant Jacoby Klyne, your life's about to change." He whispers his words gently into the darkness. "And I'm truly sorry for that." The ICD Director swallows the remaining brandy, rinses his glass, then locks up and wanders a crooked path to the elevator, pushing himself off the wall several times.

Navigating around shallow black puddles that dot the pavement and wrestling briefly with his conscience over the deeds he's about to set into motion, George M. Hallingforth III carefully masks his rage, wraps his arms tightly around his briefcase, and shuffles across the wet parking lot.

2

Steel chains circle his waist, link his wrists and ankles, and rattle each time the prisoner moves. The Marin County sheriff arrested the ex-Army sergeant Jacoby Klyne three weeks ago. Klyne just pled guilty to a felony as part of a plea bargain that dismissed a crime he actually committed and convicts him of one he had not.

Klyne stands before the bench, flexing his fists and rotating his shoulders, easing the tension that cramps his muscles. His slim, but powerful frame looks thin in a blue jail-suit that fits him like a bag. A thick, wavy mane the color of wet sand curls below his ears, and a razor last touched his cheeks three months ago.

Klyne scans a courtroom as old and worn as the people in it. The worldly tragedies and big city happenings chased by news-hungry stringers remain absent from this small rural courtroom.

No one speaks while the judge reviews a document, then looks up, glances at the defense attorney then the prosecutor and finally at Jacoby Klyne.

The defendant locks eyes with the judge, an icy chill dancing along his spine. Perspiration beads his brow, trickles down his arms, his back, and his chest. The hair beneath his collar bristles. Klyne says nothing.

"By the power vested in me," the judge says, "I hereby sentence you to the term prescribed by law." He snaps the gavel twice, punctuating his words.

The deep voice bellows into the room, bouncing multiple echoes into his ears. Klyne loses the voice for a few seconds as confusion dumps into his brain, and then he blinks twice and opens his eyes wide, connecting again with the unexpected words.

The echoes continue. "... life in state prison for the murder of police officer Enrique Martinez." The judge accents this pronouncement with two additional raps of his gavel.

Klyne blinks again then opens and shuts his mouth without speaking. He leans toward his attorney. "So what's that mean?" His voice cracks. "Thought we made a deal, Louise, the cops know I didn't kill him. Supposed to be a year in county for the drugs. Nothing about murder."

Louise O'Brien stares at the judge, disbelief widening her eyes. A muscle knots above her eyebrows and her lips tighten into a thin pink line. She turns her head, her glare targeting Tommy Minton, the newest assistant prosecutor.

His perpetual scowl hides beneath a nest of thick black hair he deliberately streaks with gray and he always needs a shave even after he just had one.

Minton finger-strokes the coarse dark stubble, a genetic default he shares with his father and two brothers, and his cohorts at the office continually rag him about.

Secretly, the brothers have always been glad his mother produced no sisters, although none actually admit it during family events. Mom wanted a daughter too, but her husband stopped at three. *'Can't afford another kid'*, he stated, after the first two. Tommy Minton is the youngest, and grew up glad his father was mistaken about just two kids. Minton cares nothing about no sister, or his brothers. Only himself.

Tommy Minton aims his eyes at the judge, but the corners of his mouth quiver, not quite smiling. The District Attorney agreed to reduce the charges, provided Klyne pled guilty.

Minton already logged this one as a win. A life sentence was not part of the bargain and O'Brien will fight him on it later, but that's the District Attorney's problem. Minton has his plea, adds one more conviction to his tally, and climbs one rung higher on his race up the ladder.

Nasty and tricky never counts against you in the vicious and devious world where he works. He always believes it anyway, as do his colleagues, and he never stands alone when sneaking around the bargaining table with his back-door antics.

O'Brien turns back to Klyne. "Minton read the murder charge into the record. The judge said, 'Law prescribed'. That's life, a seven-year minimum ... and we did deal. The State agreed, unofficially. We plead it out, he's supposed to reduce the charge, and it lightens the sentence."

She shuffles her papers, "Got it right here." She waves the document. "Angstrom's not legally bound by our agreement and he ignores plea bargains occasionally ... but never with me. And you can bet I'll bang on his door after lunch."

The judge clears his throat. "We're going to teach you and others like you a thing or two about drugs and violence in this country, mister. Starting today!" The judge hangs a twist of sarcasm in the air, and bangs the gavel one more time.

Seated in the top row, way back in a rear corner, a tall, gaunt man wearing a patch over one eye and a frumpy brown suit flips open a small black receiver and punches a series of numbers. He whispers, "Get Bates. Pitchman here." He pauses briefly.

"Interrupt him, he'll want this one." Pitchman glances around the room, as if someone might catch him. No one sees it or cares.

"Yeah, it's done. He's gone." Pitchman disconnects and slips the device into his pocket, straightens his coat, then pushes himself out of his seat and limps out the door.

"Bailiff, remove the prisoner," Judge Angstrom barks, then rises and struts out of the courtroom through a nearly invisible door located in the wall behind his throne. His black robes twist and flap behind him.

3

Klyne drags his eyes from the judge exiting and scans the courtroom, observing several law students furiously scribbling notes. A few curious citizens randomly dot the gallery, collecting warm air at no charge in this unusually cold winter. A tall thin man with an eye patch limps out of the courtroom. Three derelicts huddle near a heat grate, threadbare coats and worn-out hats scant protection against the chill outside. The students pay attention. The derelicts hug the warmth.

A Life Sentence! The words punch into his brain. External manipulations beyond his knowledge or control complicate further an already complicated situation.

He stares at his attorney, disbelief settles on his face. Unable to comprehend the reasons he received a life sentence for murder when a federal agent pulled the trigger and a beautiful woman he spent several intimate weeks with disappeared. She blew off into the wind and left no trace.

He pulls up her memory, recalling the five weeks in Seattle he shared with Alicia Diamond, a fiery lover and fun-loving companion. Everyone involved in this case now claims she's imaginary. Klyne knows she exists, alive and breathing. He dined with her, danced with her, laughed with her, and made love with her. A very physical experience he'll never regret, nor forget.

The woman vanished without a trace and took the answers with her. Federal investigators say they cannot locate her, and find no records. They say she never existed, and Klyne lied about her. But Klyne knows the agents lied instead, he was in the redwood house, she was in the redwood house, but he can do nothing about any of it while handcuffed to a sheriff or living in a cell block.

Both Klyne and his attorney agreed to a plea bargain. He knowingly participated in a drug deal set up by Alicia Diamond. Klyne admitted that much, but murder, never. He killed no one. A federal agent shot the drug seller, who was in fact a crooked police officer engaged in smuggling drugs into the states. But, due to a quirk in the laws, the blame falls on Klyne. His entire body shakes and tiny bumps rise on his arms, the hair stands erect on his neck.

The marshal approaches Klyne and abruptly squeezes his elbow, but Klyne jerks it free. "Let's go," the marshal adds a low grunt and grabs the elbow again, tightening his grip this time.

Klyne pulls away once more. "Some kinda deal this is!" He flicks his eyes at Louise O'Brien. Her cheeks red with anger, she argues with Assistant District Attorney Thomas Minton.

She nods toward the deputy briefly. "Leave him here a minute." O'Brien glares at the prosecutor while ignoring his contrite excuses. "Why Tommy? We had a deal. Just tell me why. Who changed it without telling me?"

Minton slides a sheath of paperwork into his briefcase and spins the lock. "Don't ask me, Louise. Nobody said anything about a deal. I just do my job and put as many years between these guys and the public as I can. Got a complaint, take it up with Frank, I've got too much work to do, and not enough time in the day."

Frustration creases her face when O'Brien finally turns to her client. "The numbers Tommy Minton read into the record charge you with murder, not the manslaughter and drugs in our plea bargain. That specific law mandates life in prison, parole possible after seven years. Most felons do at least ten, usually more."

O'Brien says nothing else, and stares at the ceiling. Anger still grates in her voice. She mutters under her breath, "That's bullshit. Seven years to life, and we didn't even fight it. That's no agreement far as I'm concerned and definitely no bargain."

Still upset, unwilling to let it ride, O'Brien barks at Minton and gets his attention again. "We made an arrangement with your boss, Tommy. It's your job to know it."

"Talk to Frank then. He never passed that plea to us." Minton turns away and greets another attorney approaching the desk. Both assistant prosecutors bump knuckles, and head out the door side-by-side, quiet laughter trailing behind. "Charlie's meeting us at the club for a drink first, we can't tee off until two-thirty."

"Right, not enough time in the day to do your job," rattles after Minton, her irritation still apparent.

A rail thin marshal approaches Klyne. A white name tag on his shirt spells 'Higgins' in black letters. Higgins grabs the chain and guides Klyne through a door at the rear of the courtroom. Klyne twists himself loose, but Higgins just laughs and pushes him into the corridor, all respect absent now that Klyne stands as a convicted felon.

"Just get your ass down there." Higgins shoves Klyne through a door, and then through a gate that slides open as both men approach. Higgins grabs Klyne by the arm again. The gate opens into a wider hallway.

Klyne shakes himself free and walks along the corridor past a row of scratched metal doors, a window centered in each. Chains clink against the concrete floor with each stride. It becomes a dance, Higgins grabs an elbow and Klyne shakes him off as both men move along the corridor.

Behind the glass window set in each door along the hall, a few curious faces peek out, observing both men as they pass. A man waves at Klyne, gives a thumbs-up, then sticks one finger in the air and aims it at Higgins, easing it up and down rhythmically. Higgins ignores the familiar symbol, frequently finding himself its target, an ongoing habit no longer annoying.

Another marshal steps through a doorway behind Klyne. Bulging above and below a thin brown belt cinched three holes too tight in wishful thinking, he joins Klyne and Higgins. Both officers wear crepe-soled shoes that squeak on the concrete floor with each step and in tune with the chains. The symphony of incarceration echoes in the stagnant air.

Centered in the corridor, a bucket of soapy sludge sits on the floor. Age, grime, and stale sweat permeate the atmosphere. Klyne wrinkles his nose.

Bubbles and drips trail in through an unlocked cell door hanging open. Old and well-seasoned, a bald-headed trusty pushes a wet mop in random circles, cleaning the empty cell. The trusty aims a broken-toothed grin at the marshal and raises his hand, extending and wiggling his middle finger. Seems Higgins earns a similar signal from everyone he knows. "Tree mo' days mutha fucka," the ancient convict rasps and turns his back, pretends busyness, coughs up a wet chuckle, spits on the floor and rubs it in with his mop.

Higgins ignores the trusty, but after a few steps he glances back, "Yeah, well I ain't worried, Wishbone. You'll be right back here swabbin' my floor again 'fore you git yore first meal ate."

"Ha, in yo' wet dreams, Higgins." Wishbone laughs again and bends over his work as if he means it.

Despite his dilemma, Klyne grins at the old recidivist.

Higgins and Klyne pause beside another isolation grid and wait while the guard beyond it pushes a button. The grid slides open. The deputy adds one final shove and Klyne steps through into the next corridor. The gate slams shut behind him, grating on his nerves for the first time, but not the last.

"Just keep grinnin' asshole. You'll love where you're headin'. Ain't no joyride. Those convicts will slap that fat smile off your young butt and do something else with it." Higgins spins himself around and struts back along the corridor, twirling his keys as he goes.

Klyne restrains his anger and makes no comment. Confused by intricate and complex legal procedures beyond his reasoning or understanding, apprehensive about the predicament in which he now finds himself, and unsure of his rights, he agreed to plead guilty and receive a light sentence. But the judge said life. The deal seems more bad than good as Klyne evaluates it. At least as he understands it now, after the court proceedings today.

Louise O'Brien set it up, said she would act in his best interest. But now, he's no longer sure who he can trust. He wonders now about his attorney, a woman whom he only recently met. She arrived at the jail unannounced and with no referral. That odd factor bugs Klyne as he thinks it through, wonders where she came from and who sent her. The coincidence begins digging into his mind.

"Come on Klyne, gotta lock you up." The gateman keys the cell door. "Don't pay no attention to Higgins. He got a hard-on for everbody ... 'cept his wife." He hides a grin behind his fist. "And, rumor has it she got one for everbody else. Ain't no wonder he grumps."

His grin advances to an outright chuckle as the guard unlocks the restraints and the chains drop into a heap. "Guess that's what gits him so pissed off all the time." The guard stands aside and gestures Klyne into the cell, then bends down and retrieves the chains.

Klyne steps in and the door bangs shut behind him. The lock clicks. He looks around at the empty holding pen, about twelve feet by sixteen. A single entry door contains a square window in its center, exactly like the doors he passed. Faded paint decorates everything in old slime green. The walls and ceiling exhibit random cracks, old patched concrete, and graffiti scratches in a random coordination of artistic expressions. Opposite the door, a stainless steel sink hangs on the wall and beside it, a toilet bolted in place, both in line with the window.

"Guess these pigs like to watch," Klyne breathes his words, a bare whisper in the room. He curls his lips into a tight smile that does not carry to his eyes. He sits on the bunk. Ten minutes pass, soundless but for the clatter of doors locking and men holding muted conversations between adjacent cells. Another minute passes, then another. A noise at the door interrupts his thoughts. Klyne looks at the window. The door clicks and swings open.

"Your delicious banquet." Higgins carries a tray of food and a note of sarcasm in with him, a cup, a pitcher containing some ugly brown liquid, and a paper sack.

"Coffee," Higgins offers. "Here ya' go, a special chalice for our felons." He grinds his cigarette butt under his boot, coughs and spits in the corner, tosses Klyne a bent tin cup.

Klyne catches it, holds it upright and watches the marshal fill it, then picks up the bag and peeks inside.

Courtroom activities revived his appetite but he loses it immediately when he discovers a dried bologna sandwich with a thin coat of yellow mustard, and a dead scaly orange, no juice. Klyne tosses the bag into the corner. Higgins chuckles again on his way out, and the lock once again clicks behind him.

Left alone, Klyne collects his thoughts. An hour passes and Higgins returns, bangs open the door once more, and hollers "Klyne," then looks around inside the cell as if picking him out of a crowd. "Get your ass in gear. You're movin' out ... Now!"

Higgins installs the same chain restraints, propels Klyne down the hall, out a door and into a van then climbs in after him. The van carries Klyne to the county jail attached to the same cell block and custody rooms where he had been held when he was originally arrested. But, instead of returning him to his cell, Higgins sidetracks Klyne and guides him into a small conference room.

Louise O'Brien follows them in and slides her briefcase onto the table, plops down into a chair. Puffs out a breath.

"Don't know what happened. The D.A. won't discuss it. Well, actually he's unavailable. No judge is legally bound by plea agreements, anyway," she begins speaking even before Klyne sits. "But it's almost unheard of to throw it over completely. Don't know why he sentenced on the murder charge. It's like someone flipped a huge tarp over this case. Nothing plays out like a normal proceeding. Everything about it surprises me, and I get little cooperation from anyone, including the Feds."

"Same response to all my questions, 'I don't know,' or 'ask Harry,' or 'ask Jim,' or 'ask Frank'. And they're all conveniently unavailable at the moment, of course. Getting quite the run-around, Jake. I'm sorry, I don't understand it, never happened to me before. But I'll force some answers eventually. That I promise you."

Her comments fail to improve his mood. "What's the sense of it, if the D.A. kicks the deal, I should just go to trial, find a hole in the case. No deal here for me, seems like. Nothing good anyway. Just a bunch of words, don't mean anything. Except me *'Guilty'*, that meant something. Right?" The anger grows, his voice honing an edge into it. "And I didn't even shoot him. The cop did, even admitted it."

"That's right, the Fed shot him. Minton claims he did deal, sort of a deal anyway. The prosecution dropped the 'no parole' bit, and didn't push the hard time – just murder two – with a possible parole after seven years. The D.A. dropped all the drug charges."

"Dropped the drug charges, big deal, and just murder two ... Huh! Sucks!" His anger runs free now and rages. He throws his hands in the air, but the chains shorten his reach and chaff his wrists. Pain briefly shoots up his arms and he drops his hands back along his sides.

"Calm down, Jake. I'll do something, just don't know what yet."

"Easy for them to say ... *'just a life sentence!'* And prison time! No chance of short time county jail." He tries to relax and think. No luck. "So, what do we do now?"

"Right. No county. You begin the prison time, but there are a couple of things I can try. The D.A. didn't hold up his end far as I'm concerned. Minton's more or less a rookie assistant and a ladder-climbing puppet anyway, and won't be around long the way he acts. Someone with the right shoe size will step on him and kick him out the door."

"I'll meet with Frank De Barons directly, as soon as I can find him even if I have to camp on his threshold. You'll transfer uptown anyway, no matter what else happens. I'll do what I can right away, starting this afternoon."

"Saw Jimmy and Sarah in the courtroom, they comin' here?" He's a bit uncomfortable torturing himself, or Sarah, with a visit that now leads nowhere. He left Sarah in Los Angeles several months ago, flew to visit his family in Seattle and never returned. Never explained it to her either. A jail cell's not exactly the best place to reconcile that issue.

"Cops might let them in, not required though. You're a state prisoner now, and they can deny visitors. You'll be shipped out pretty quick. I'll let them both know where you go soon as I know."

Once again, Higgins retrieves Klyne and, while escorting him along the corridor, says, "Seems like you got 'em all, and can't do nothing about it. Sweet young girlfriend sitting in the gallery, pretty lady attorney, could be they'd both like some deputy too, after work one of these nights." He unlocks the chains and the links clink to the floor. Higgins keys the door and it slides open.

Klyne steps into the cell, lies down on the bunk, and stares up at the ceiling. A previous tenant had scratched 'Fuck This Place' in large black letters on the concrete wall beside his bunk. Klyne agrees with the anonymous poet, whoever wrote it. No debate with that line.

Klyne fights off the helpless feeling as stress takes its first small step and begins crushing his spirit. He recalls Sarah and her sweetly bouncing ways, now a distant blur on the endless days strung out before him. A tide of desperate hopelessness emerges, chasing away the last vestiges of a reprieve. Isolated waves of doom and gloom wash in and fill him with despair, forcing him against a black rock of anguish while excavating a hollow pit of depression into which it carelessly tosses his remains. His heart turns to stone.

Discontented thrashing fills a restless half-sleep and Klyne nightmares a recurring vision he often experienced in foreign lands but has not repeated since his return from combat four months ago – the time he spent with Sarah and Alicia gave him a reprieve as well, but he now envisions himself once again locked in a silver coffin so crowded with terror that he lies naked, paralyzed, unable to escape – waiting to die again.

*

In a plush office two floors above the courtroom, a heavy oak door swings shut behind Superior Court Judge Harold T. Angstrom. He hangs his robes on an old brass clothes tree, opens a sideboard, and fills two large snifters with cognac. He hands one to his friend and then relaxes into his favorite antique chair, passes the glass under his nose, then sips and smiles.

"Been a while, George. Too many years between trips lately."

"Thanks, Harry." Hallingforth accepts the drink. "Don't work the field much anymore. Haven't for years. This one's kind of special though. Glad you helped us out."

Hallingforth sips the brandy then swallows half. "Our office will handle it from here on and retrieve our agent eventually."

"Can't figure why you need a man sentenced. Seems you could get the warden to work with you at Quentin if you need Klyne in there bad enough. But I won't ask. You federal boys always do things ass backwards anyway."

Angstrom sips, rolling the brandy around on his tongue. "You like that little snipe about the drugs and the violence?" He flashes his teeth, chuckles, proud of his ad-lib remark in the courtroom earlier.

Hallingforth ignores the question. "Our concern, as usual, security – always. We can't let anyone know, and I mean no one, that he's ours. We can't afford to trust prison security where national security's involved. Christ, Harry, if even one person finds out, the whole yard will know in five minutes. We'd haul him out in a body-bag the same day. And it won't be pretty, not in that pit."

Hallingforth empties his drink, holds up his glass for another. Angstrom stands and obliges. "You should retire George. Take Margaret away, and do a bit of traveling. Relax. Get in touch with the world again. Get away from all that crazy spy bullshit."

"Believe me, it's worth it. Betty and I enjoy it a lot." He hands the refill across the desk. "Doubt anyone else but you could drag me out of retirement, though I still do a case now and again when the regulars get too busy. Only did this one because you asked me personally, and it only took a couple days. I'd sure have passed on a long, drawn out murder trial, even for you."

Hallingforth glances around the room, lost in thought for a moment. "Well, maybe I will. Margaret hasn't been the same these past couple years, and we've been considering it anyway. Might be the right time after this one pops."

Hallingforth suddenly seems distant, reminiscent, or perhaps disturbed by the comments. He'd already begun making plans to retire as soon as this project concludes, but no one knows it yet, not even his wife. The job, the stress, the long hours wear him out lately, can't keep up anymore. And the operations get more and more complex, and more deep-cover ops begin over a shorter time span, and take longer to complete, and even longer to recover. More pressure from the President and Attorney General.

And, he now has this new operation that simply won't cooperate. One thing after another interferes, and back in a corner of his mind he worries that it may upset the balance in his department if word gets out.

Hallingforth puffs out a frustrated breath. "I'd better head out, Harry, my plane leaves in forty minutes."

Angstrom laughs aloud. "Since when does Henry Bates take-off in your jet without you in that seat beside him?"

"Something eating at you George, anything else I can help with? Maybe we should get together soon and take another trip. Take the girls somewhere warm." He chuckles again. "Let 'em shop … we'll find a ball game to watch, and some bar gal to wash your hairy old butt, then turn you over and fix the rest of you."

Hallingforth stands and gulps the remaining cognac in one long swallow, then coughs into his fist. "No, nothing I can't handle. Just a little glitch in the timing, Harry, that's all."

He makes light of the offer. Although Hallingforth often wishes he could accept help here, the complexity drives him into corners, and he occasionally feels threatened. But he says nothing more about it.

"And thanks again for this court time, and the drink, Harry. We must pay you too much, you buying this top-shelf stuff?"

The judge has no way to know that the hollowing thinness in his cheeks, the bleak nervousness, the shuffling gait, and the occasional spasm beneath his right eye began only a few months ago, fed by this operation and the fact he cannot get on track with it. The friendship encompasses more than thirty-five years, back to the trials and tribulations of

Yale Law School when both men emerged as adults, but they had not seen one another face-to-face in more than three years.

Silent, anchored on thick well-oiled hinges, the door swings shut behind him as Hallingforth steps out.

*

Klyne stares at the three-word poem on the wall. Worn out and confused, unable to plan for himself, he lies back and reads it once more. "Fuck This Place." He agrees, and punches the pillow while his thoughts ramble, seeking a clue. *Why me?* He ponders. Klyne takes out a red felt pen and underlines the poetry.

Answers elude him, at least for the moment. He shuts his eyes, but his brain spins free, unable to settle into sleep until he knows, his mind drifts back over the years, fades in and out, sorts through his memories, his life, his entanglements.

While Klyne shuts his eyes and studies his personal history, other lives and activities outside and inside his world circle the drain and affect his freedom in ways Jacoby Klyne cannot even begin to contemplate.

4

Two teenage boys crouched low on a hilltop, staring over a shrub and across a dry creek bed. A few leaves clung stubbornly to a branch above their heads and wiggled in the wind. Each boy breathed vapor into the chill and pulled his jacket a bit tighter, one a mimic of the other, each a mirror of his sidekick's soul. Two sets of lips turned up in identical grins aimed at one another, then two pair of eyes turned back and peered as one across a dried up gully. Best friends, hanging out.

Jacoby Klyne wet his finger and checked the breeze. Satisfied, he sucked in a breath and settled the rifle sights slightly above and to the right of his target, a fuzzy brown head standing rock still and almost too far away, partially hidden below a hanging branch and behind a gently waving bush. A very difficult shot.

Klyne squeezed the trigger. An oddity in the scene briefly clicked in the back of his brain, 'NO!' Too late.

The rifle popped once, a clean head-shot. A hundred and fifty yards across the shallow wash, his prey flipped off a stump and dropped behind it. Grandpa Beans taught Jake well.

Jake shook off the feeling and grinned once more at his best friend kneeling beside him. Benji grinned back and held up three fingers, and rubbed his stomach. "Awesome!"

Both boys jumped up, slid down the bank, crossed the wash, climbed the embankment and wormed through the brush, two rabbits dangled from a cord hanging over Jake Klyne's left shoulder.

Born a week apart on neighboring farms, Jacoby Klyne and Benjamin Taylor grew up reading, writing, hunting and fishing in the rural countryside of New Jersey.

Klyne alternated spring and summers in England, fall and winters in New Jersey, where his father taught medieval history at Cambridge as well as Princeton.

This late autumn afternoon found the boys chasing dinner on the back forty of the Reed farm, closest neighbor and a widow for ten years. The boys liked her, Nana Reed, and helped her with the 'tough digging parts' of her garden and the harvest, and she allowed them to hunt her land and eat her pies.

"Can't beat that bargain," both boys had chirped, explaining the deal to Grandpa Beans a few years ago.

Jake and Benji followed the shot, pushed a branch aside, circled the stump and found a large Burmese cat bleeding all over his collar, its bell forever silenced. Jake sat down hard on the stump and tore his eyes away.

His hands suddenly shook and his knees felt weak and wobbly, his entire body vibrating with emotion. He blinked, spilling tears down each cheek. He wiped his nose and eyes with the tail of his new tee shirt. His entire body shook for several minutes before he gathered himself and stood.

"Shit, Jake. Nana Reed's really gonna be pissed. That's Tobias, and he's her favorite … was anyways, and he's got kittens, too. Well, Popcorn does, just a couple weeks old." Benji raised his eyes. "And remember what Grandpa Beans told you, 'Never shoot nothing you ain't gonna eat'. What're you gonna do Jake?"

"Well, I ain't eating Tobias, that's for sure." Tears ran freely down his cheeks now, and he wiped his face again. "Come on, let's take him home. And don't worry. Popcorn will take care of her babies. Tomcats don't fuss none with kittens, they just make 'em."

They buried Tobias out behind the Reed barn, Nana Reed holding her apron in front of her face the whole time, never saying a word. Benji packed dirt around a red brick he placed on the mound of dirt covering Tobias, wrote a capital T on it with black paint. Then, Jake carried his old bolt-action Winchester Wildcat home, cleaned it, packed it away, and never shot it again.

*

Three years later Susanna Klyne sat in the bleachers above the high school football field and watched her son graduate eleven days before his eighteenth birthday.

Nine hundred miles away at the United States Army training center at Fort Benning, Sergeant Corey Black was teaching a group of recruits the peace-keeping chores in a world filled with violence. The Sergeant held up one fist. "Halt!" Black barked, stopping his platoon beside a large warehouse.

"Di-i-s-s-missed!" Black hollered, "Go eat."

The men broke ranks and hustled away toward the mess hall. The sergeant slid a large steel loading door sideways and stepped into the warehouse, lit a cigarette, and blew a stream of smoke at four large wooden crates stacked inside. Black grabbed a steel bar and pried the lid off one. A dozen brand new M-16 rifles shined up at him. Forty-six days later, Uncle Sam sent Jacoby Klyne a registered letter requesting he come join Sergeant Black and use one.

5

Four years had passed since he completed basic training, and Sergeant Jacoby Klyne sat inside a field headquarters tent in the battle-scarred jungles of Central America. He signed several documents and pushed his second extension across the table toward his commanding officer. "That's it, Colonel," Klyne said, "last time. Two more years. After this one, I'm done. Six years ... enough time out of my life."

The field officer received orders defining his newest mission, and three days later, sent his best Special Forces soldier back into the jungle.

*

On that same day but unbeknownst to Klyne, a celebratory parade began in a rural community a hundred miles south of Bogotá. In the normally quiet Colombian village, a short but boisterous procession wound along the streets. A Ford tractor towed a wooden trailer filled with dry straw and happy children.

A new Jaguar convertible led the procession. A few horse-drawn carts and several teenagers riding burros without saddles followed in the heat. Brown-skinned children scurried about laughing, screaming, waving flags, leading pet goats on a string. Parents, siblings, cousins and the remaining villagers stood at curbside, cheering. Two mutt puppies hid on a porch and yipped. A festive day emerged and smiles blossomed on every face.

Dominic Perez and his brother Chico sat in the white convertible and idled past the crowd, accepting the waves and cheers as if they'd actually earned them. Minutes later, the procession circles in and parked before a medical clinic located on the outskirts of the village beside a small rock-lined pond.

Side-by-side, both brothers climbed a temporary stairway and stood behind a podium set upon staging in front of the new clinic. The brothers accepted a citation, dedicated the building, then turned and pushed through double glass doors entering the reception area. The crowd slowly dispersed amidst a few final cheers and a raised fist or two signaling respect.

Dominic Perez entered an office inside the clinic and dropped into a chair behind his desk. Local villager Benito Juarez peeked into the office and Dominic waved him in. Juarez slid through the door, curling his hat in his hand, subservient but protective. His daughter followed him in, standing shy and partly hidden behind her father, one small fist locked on his rope belt.

Dominic Perez smiled at the girl, ran his eyes over her ripe young body, and glanced up at her father. "Right on time, Benito."

"Please Senor Perez, she's only fourteen. Her mother needs her at home," Juarez pleaded, nearly in tears.

The smile fell off Dominic's face. "But I need a new housemaid." His smile returned and Dominic aimed it at the virginal Maria.

Ricardo Traceda entered the office and stood behind Juarez and Maria. Dominic nodded his chin at Ricardo. The Foreman took Juarez by the arm and led him out, leaving Maria behind.

Perez squirmed on his seat, fingered the tips of his mustache, and grinned. Maria turned her slim brown toes inward, linked her fingers together behind her back, and stared at her feet. Anticipating an early end to his evening chores, Perez ran his eyes over her maturing curves, the friendly smile dropped off his face, replaced by a look of pure lust.

*

A Southwest Airlines jet dropped out of the sky and taxied up to the gate at Los Angeles International Airport. The Perez brothers exited the plane together. An airport employee ushered the men past customs with a minimum of fuss and both headed quickly through the terminal and slid into a limousine. The six-door black Mercedes chirped away from the curb, fought the heavy afternoon traffic and dropped the brothers off at a five-star hotel on Sunset Boulevard fifty minutes later.

After an early dinner in a crowded convention room, Dominic rolled a final sip of Cognac over his tongue and shook hands with his hosts. The brothers left together but separated in the lobby. Chico headed into the lounge. Dominic escorted a young and very attractive dark-haired woman along the hall and into his room. Chico remained at the bar for an hour then followed his brother's footsteps.

Chico opened the door and found Dominic and the woman lying beneath the blankets. Chico entered the room, grinned at the lovers and approached the bed. Naked, Dominic eased himself out and stuck his legs into his pants.

The woman snuggled down beneath the bedcovers and murmured something into her fist, her eyes remaining closed. Then she opened her eyes and smiled at Dominic standing at the foot of the bed. Startled, the smile dropped off her face as Chico began undressing. She sat up in bed, pulled the sheet up and covered her breasts.

She turned her eyes toward Dominic. "Oh ... No ... Please, I'm not that way. You've made a mistake. I just thought we liked each other Dominic." She wrapped the sheet around her body and swung her legs off the bed, grabbed her clothes and started pulling them on.

Chico stepped around the bed and slapped the woman. She fell back and cried out, holding her cheek. "No, please, you have me all wrong," she said again. "I just ..." her words unintelligible behind her fingers as she shook her head. A tear slid down her cheek.

Dominic and Chico each grabbed an arm but she struggled against them. Chico slapped her hard, and slapped her again. She lashed out with a knee, suddenly scared, kicking, biting and scratching. She raked her nails across his face, drawing four bright red streaks on his cheek, fighting like a wildcat. She stabbed at his eyes.

Chico punched her hard, a pink splotch appeared on her chin and she flopped back against the headboard. Both men held her down until she stopped fighting, her eyes dim, but wide with fright. Dominic opened a leather case, extracted a hypodermic, and injected a clear liquid into her vein.

She lay quiet, rubbed her arm, looked up at the men and back at her arm, dazed and frightened. Suddenly, she relaxed. Calm washed over her, a crooked grin appeared. She aimed her smile at each man then blinked. She blinked again, and again, her eyelids fluttering. Then she twitched, she twitched again, and again, her eyes glazed over. Her entire body shuddered and she fell limp on the pillows. Her breathing ceased. Her fingers and toes twitched a few times then she lay still, unmoving.

Chico lifted her head and peeled back her eyelids. He slapped her again, attempting to awaken her this time. He failed. Her head drooped, her eyes wide, green, and staring.

"Fuck this," Chico said, and grabbed her under the arms. He slid into the shower, turned the tap on full cold and held her under it, soaking his clothes. He pulled her out of the shower and forced her to walk. No luck. Her body slumped against his, her legs unwilling. "Help me, damn it." Again, he pried open her eyelids and peered in. He slapped her face once more. No response.

Dominic helped straighten her up. They both looked into her eyes again then released her and she slumped across the bed.

Dominic ran his fingers through his hair, disturbed, angry. "Christ Chico, you're supposed to get her in the mood, not kill her." He whipped out his phone and quickly punched a speed dial.

"We need you up here, right away." He paused and listened briefly. "I don't care who you're doing, kick her out and get up here. Now!!"

*

A vehicle with no lights entered a dark and deserted alley. Creeping between the buildings, it stopped beside a dumpster. Ricardo Traceda and his short muscular companion climbed out, lifted the lid and dumped a heavy object wrapped in a blanket inside with the trash. The men hopped back into the SUV and sped away into the night.

6

Twenty-four months passed quickly, and Klyne engaged his final mission. Awake at sunrise and hungry, multi-colored songbirds flittered from twig to twig. Chirping and chattering, bright feathered heads searched for treats beneath tangled foliage dripping with morning dew. A tepid breeze barely moved the leaves while luminous insects hovered and buzzed, announcing breakfast. One leafy branch scratched against another, scratched again, and again, interrupting the morning activities.

Immediately, the noise ceased. Deafening and hollow, vacant and empty, an unnatural silence echoed into the dawn. Squatting in the shadows behind a thick bush, Sergeant Jacoby Klyne studied the terrain. The jungle was too quiet, far too quiet.

Behind him and above, daylight streaked the horizon. Purple shadows diminished, defining the rich landscapes beneath. Puffy, gray clouds emerged behind treetops rising above the darkness, and an eerie tranquility pervaded the dawn. Klyne sat back on his heels, motionless, his eyes scanning the broken topography. Something felt different, out of place. Something hushed the natural sounds. Something startled the native wildlife into silence.

After a year of intensive training followed by nearly two years operating in the bush, Klyne had grown to hate the heat, and the sweat, and the intense maneuvers in the thick, overgrown rain forests, and the constant complaining.

Finally, three years ago he requested the single-search missions where he worked alone in savage lands filled with violence and deceit. Nearly two years ago he signed his final extension. Klyne smiled briefly, anticipating a ten-day furlough in Mexico City before flying stateside and accepting his discharge.

He told his commanding officer he'd done enough, was tired of the fear, the stress and lack of culture, the absent laughter.

Klyne hugged the shadows and stared through the leaves. The hot breeze barely moved the air, the branches scratched again, lightly. A dark brown object rose into view beyond his right shoulder and Klyne slowly rotated his head, his eyes picking out a man urinating beside a shrub forty feet away. Soundless, Klyne laid his rifle by his knee, reached into his pack and retrieved a weapon. Sucking air deep into his lungs, he held his breath and lined up the sights. The man shook himself off and raised his eyes, staring directly at Klyne.

Klyne released the trigger and the line snapped tight. A razor-edged blade split the air and a short brass bolt penetrated the sentry's throat, puncturing his windpipe and severing his spinal cord. Blood spurted down the filthy shirtfront. The man dropped immediately, his lungs deflating, a slight expulsion of breath the only sound, then muted thrashing. Death arrived. After a moment, the absence of noise disappeared and nature began singing, chirping, and feeding again.

Klyne slid the crossbow back into its sheath, but remained motionless for fifteen minutes, rotating only his head from side to side, seeking a back-up for the dead man. His profound patience and noiseless movement kept him alive these past years. A piece of his recent past invaded his thoughts.

*

Major C.J. Perkins had called Klyne into the command center when he returned to camp after clearing his patrol a month ago. Klyne pulled the canvas flap open and entered the tent. The major introduced Special Agent Henry Bates recently arrived from Washington. The agent wasted no time.

"We're impressed with your work," he said. "We want to hire you. We have a special operation entering phase one. Suits your particular talents. You'll work directly for ICD, that's us, Intelligence, performing top-secret operations. Same as here, except you'll become a civilian, but still work for Defense. Private contractor, more money."

"More drug stuff, or what?"

"That part's classified. At least for now."

"What can you tell me?"

"It involves some infiltration, and jungle warfare. And, yeah, probably drugs, at least some of your assignments."

"What else? Executions?"

"Nothing else. Not until you agree. Then you'll leave with me now, today, and fly to Washington tonight. The director will brief you there and handle your discharge."

Klyne stood at ease, dressed in filthy combat gear, and fresh off the line. A stranger wearing a gray business suit and mouthing a Texas accent in the middle of a combat zone wanted to change his life. Immediately.

"Bit sudden, isn't it."

"That's the way we work. It's urgent, first assignment's a national defense problem. You already have the clearance and training."

Klyne hesitated, briefly looked at this feet, then back at Bates. Recently, he had thought about his discharge, going home, meeting up again with Jimmy Dodds, his friend and ex-sergeant. Last month, he turned down a full commission and declined another extension. He was worn out, ready to leave the violence behind him.

"I'll need a few minutes."

Klyne stepped outside, and dropped the tent flap. Four military jeeps sped past, slipping and sliding through slick, dark mud. A helicopter dropped onto a clear spot near a small tent topped by a ragged flag, its red cross in a white circle flapping in the prop wash. Two medics unloaded a stretcher bearing a man screaming for water as blood soaked into a thick pad taped across his stomach, and raced toward the miniature hospital. Six men packed up, heading back into the field. A missile thumped beyond the treetops. Soldiers straggled past in twos and threes, heading for the mess tent.

Not a smile among them.

Sweat trickled under his arms. His entire body itched and he wanted a bath and a hot meal, city lights and a new movie. The thought of fresh bacon and real coffee made his mouth water.

For five full minutes, Klyne stood motionless, staring mutely into the unforgiving vessel that contained his life. Hollow and empty, devoid of all emotion but fear, his future reflected back at itself. Jacoby Klyne was worn out, beat down, and afraid he might stay forever if he agreed again, either walking the trail or lying beneath it. He lifted the flap and stepped back inside.

"No thanks. Six years is long enough."

Expressionless, Henry Bates stood up, but said no more.

"Going home this time." Klyne nodded at the agent, saluted the major, stepped out, and dropped the flap.

*

Sergeant Jacoby Klyne pulled his thoughts back to the present, and his search for the camp. He stared into the jungle, concerned that the execution, even as silently as he works, might alert others. No one appeared. Satisfied, he circled away from the trail and approached the dead man from the opposite side. Motionless, he waited another ten minutes then stepped out into the clearing and searched the sentry. Klyne found nothing of interest, and retrieved his arrow, wiped it off on his victim's shirt.

He splintered the rifle against a thick tree trunk and poked dirt and mud into the automatic pistol, disassembled both weapons and tossed the parts into the brush. He pocketed the ammunition and two kit knives then searched the area for twenty minutes, finally locating the entrance. He lifted a hidden trap door and peeked inside an underground cavern where the lookouts often hid. He dumped the body into the hole and rigged an explosive filled with nails and sharp stones, setting it to blow when the next unlucky individual opened the hatch. He spun around and disappeared into the rain forest, silent as a snake on the hunt.

Klyne prowled through the steaming jungle, tired and hot, his entire body leaching sweat. His orders arrived with a bright red 'URGENT' stamp across the top, and he pushed hard to locate the camp. Seemed all of his orders arrived with the same reflective stamp urging him to hurry so he could finish one assignment in time to begin the next. The sameness of it all, and the violence, and the lack of success in the political arena that drove his superiors had begun wearing on him. He longed for the farm, what remained of his family, and a hot breakfast, scrambled eggs and a rare steak served with no fright.

He penetrated the thick vegetation, keeping himself off the trail. Deep in hostile territory, he stayed clear of an ambush or an accidental encounter. Six days out this time but he covered only twenty-one miles. The treacherous, uneven terrain and profuse vegetation slowed his pace. Klyne disturbed nothing, left no evidence of his march.

He discovered the camp in late evening. After killing the trail lookout, he traveled east the rest of the afternoon, crested a hill, and crawled under a bush above the encampment. His orders directed him to a prison camp where a State Department representative sat in a cage, held captive for over a month. An emissary direct from the President had been on a mission to negotiate payments for growing legitimate farm products instead of drug producing crops. A cartel soldier trapped the representative and he remained a prisoner.

Klyne received a single direct order, retrieve the federal official and return him to Base Tango unharmed. Assistance none. Method unregulated. As usual, his freedom to operate allowed him to adjust as the situation warranted, and guaranteed no blowback later.

Night settled in while Klyne rested, surrounded by lush vegetation. Stars sparkled in a clear sky with no moon, but rain clouds bunched in the distance beyond a ridge and darkened the sky, threatening. Squatting halfway up the hill beneath lush tree cover and behind a thick shrub, Klyne investigated the camp.

"Intelligence getting a bit slack," he whispered to no one, felt a slight disturbance to his left, turned his head and stared directly into a fuzzy red face. A chill raced down his spine then a grin pushed into his cheeks. A variegated squirrel perched on a moldy tree stump and nibbled a flower it held between its paws. Its nostrils quivered, its cheeks twitched, and two large brown eyes stared up at Klyne.

"Well, my furry-tailed buddy, twenty-three days and a get-up, and you'll be dining alone." The tiny red ball of fur squeaked once and evaporated immediately, leaving its flower behind. Klyne relaxed his grin and, turning back to his quarry, listened again. The background noise had become his friend. Chirps, whistles, and gentle buzzing proclaimed his safety.

Smaller and less active than his intelligence report indicated, the camp was still large enough to complicate any plan to retrieve the emissary. Over the next few hours, he counted fourteen men and four women wearing a variety of mismatched combat garb, four thatched huts, and three tents in what looked like a semi-permanent site. And, an additional complication, there was more than one prisoner. "Damn," Klyne whispered to himself, "Which one?"

Three cages hung in the center of camp, each containing a man, and one had been severely beaten, dried blood encrusting an infected head wound. Turning that new information over in his mind, Klyne studied the situation in detail.

One woman cleaned and oiled a weapon. Several men sat on a bench, each dipped a metal spoon into a plate sitting on his knees that contained the evening meal. Three partially uniformed soldiers shuffled out to man guard positions, and two men and a woman took turns shoveling dirt out of a hole, excavating a new latrine behind a clump of trees. Located way in the back-country and far beyond the need for high security, the camp appeared settled and safe to its occupants. A huge mistake.

Klyne crouched and observed, content to organize a plan during the daylight hours. He leaned back against a tree, opened a meal pouch, and spooned cold ham and peas into his mouth. He scratched a hole beneath a bush and buried his litter, watching the dark clouds roll in, and then shut his eyes. Klyne dozed off and on during the night, a resting but alert state he developed for his own safety.

7

A warm, misty dawn colored the scene. Sunlight slanted through the trees occasionally, the thin sticks of brightness creating a unique setting in the thriving vegetation. Cook pots clanked and banged, and men rattled battle gear. A foreman barked orders, his words crisp and clear in the morning drizzle. A light rain fell intermittently, dribbling off the trees and vines as the jungle awakened and the rising sun played hide-n-seek behind patchy cloud cover. A perpetual chorus buzzed and chirped. The constant struggle for survival.

Sergeant Jacoby Klyne opened his eyes and scanned the camp without moving a muscle. The men climbed from the tents, struggled into slick rain-gear, and swore at the drizzle. Klyne grinned, as he too once cursed weather he now claimed as a friend.

The sergeant inhaled a deep awakening breath. Pungent and well-spiced, the odor of damp, rotting jungle hung in the mist. The men milled around camp completing the daily chores, then three finally separated and marched toward the outposts to relieve the dawn watch. Klyne crawled back under his tree and shook the water from his poncho. Fat raindrops hung off the brim of his helmet, a tiny rainbow blazing in each.

Rain fell harder as the morning edged toward noon. Three guards trudged across the grounds, hunched over, loudly and continuously condemning the weather and the terrain. One man relieved the sentry at the trail leading south and another the sentry on the trail leading north, and one remained in the center of camp. The captors exhibited no fear of the tightly caged, underfed, wet and weakened captives.

The mid-camp sentry wandered, paying scant attention to the prisoners. Klyne assumed the sentries performed the same watch duties every night, and devised a plan subject to adjustment as he observed the routines.

The men remained inside most of the day except when the guards rotated. The camp almost appeared deserted as the rain fell harder, soaking the grounds. Rainwater seeped through the barred but roofless cage-tops and each captive huddled in a corner, warm enough but drenched and uncomfortable.

The rain finally slowed, spitting intermittent bursts of wet drops, and the clouds broke up. Afternoon sun peeked out, shining down on the lone American soldier circling south, reserving a midnight dance with danger.

Klyne waited for darkness. The rain stopped completely and the last fuzzy clouds drifted away. One hour after the midnight watch changed, Klyne pushed to his feet and began his stalk. From tree to bush to tree, he closing the gap, soundlessly placing each boot beyond the next. One false move and the sentry would scream the night awake.

Klyne stepped, once again, then three more times, softly, silent as the night. Twenty feet, two thick trees rose between them, nothing else, no additional protection.

Seated on a large rock, the sentry faced away and toyed with his rifle strap, bored as usual.

Klyne eased his left boot down. Silence ached into the darkness. He stepped again, twice. Ten feet, he maneuvered around the last tree. The near silence threatened his actions. Night noise would help.

Suddenly, across the clearing, a bird screeched startling both men. It screeched again and flapped its wings, interrupting the deadly waltz. Klyne froze and held his breath, exposed for eternity.

The sentry looked up and stared across the clearing. More alert now, he shifted his weight, squirming, fidgeting and stamping his feet. He kicked a pebble and it rattled across the trail.

Five feet lay between the men, two quick steps.

The guard stood, absent-minded, simply stretching his boredom away. Klyne froze in place again. Sweat dripped from his chin and ran down his neck and arms, soaking his shirt. His clothing stuck to his body.

The guard stared across the trail, searching for the bird. Klyne stepped once, silently, then once more and finished the dance.

The sentry stretched, his short arms embracing the night sky, and he angled his eyes over his right shoulder.

Klyne stood directly behind him and the men locked eyes for one second frozen in time.

His eyes popped wide open, a look of terror streaked across his face as comprehension shook the sentry alert. His mouth shaped a scream cut short as Klyne dropped a loop over the man's head and jerked the wire halfway through his throat. The sentry gurgled and spit blood, his alarm cry choked off, only a bare squeak escaping as he clutched without effect at the wire that cut off his breath and his life.

Klyne bent his knee, pushing it hard between his victim's shoulders, stretching and straining. The garrote sliced deeper, nearly severing the man's head.

Kicking and twisting, the soldier finally spilled his soul onto the dirt. Blood soaked thick and black into his shirt and sprayed into the darkness, the last few drops detouring across the executioner's wrists.

The struggle finally ceased, two dead eyes locked open. The body wiggled, jerked, and twitched, denying the death that settled upon it. Easing the corpse to the jungle floor, Klyne stood up, alert and watchful. Silently, rotating his head back and forth, he quickly searched the scene. His eyes and ears recorded no change in the sleeping camp.

He hauled the dead sentry into the brush, took a few precious seconds and jammed dirt into the rifle, pulled his knife out and broke the trigger, then grabbed his own weapons and headed north.

Twenty minutes later, he edged along a finger of bush jutting toward the largest hut. Soaked and muddy, he slithered along the ground, crawling under prickly shrubs that tore at his clothes. Twisted trees blocked his path and he slid sideways between them, finally resting at the edge of the clearing. Klyne watched the second sentry saunter back and forth beneath the cages.

Sweating heavily, afraid his arrow might not stop a warning if the guard cried out. Klyne hunched down behind a shrub and stared. The first guard had wandered. Klyne hoped this one might too, and close the distance. Patient and confident, Klyne settled into position, waiting, watching.

The guard paused beneath the cages and Klyne set the crossbow. Steady. Ready. Slowly, soundlessly, he sucked air deep into his lungs and tightened his finger.

Suddenly, a movement to his left caught his eye, and Klyne held his fire. A man exited the building and hurried toward the bush where Klyne hid.

Klyne angled the crossbow slightly and lined up the man over the sights, tracking as he approached.

The soldier stopped fifteen feet to Klyne's right, opened his pants and splashed urine into the brush, chasing a few insects into the night. Then he walked over and spoke to the night watch. One man broke out tobacco and papers. Both men rolled and lit a cigarette and talked and laughed quietly, sucking smoke. Klyne froze, motionless and tense. Finally, one man crushed the butt under a boot, wandered back to his hut, and climbed inside.

Klyne relaxed, adjusted his aim, and covered the sentry again, waiting fifteen minutes. His muscles ached and sweat saturated his body and his clothing. He squeezed the trigger slightly, then all the way to release.

The guard settled down and drew his last breath. A perfect shot toppled him backward. The man clutched his throat, writhing and bucking, kicking, rejecting the inevitable, but finally died soundless.

Klyne set the crossbow beside his knee, grabbed his carbine, an M4A1, and turned his eyes toward the tent for a few moments. No one emerged and he packed the crossbow, backed out, turned north once again. Ten minutes later he worked along the ravine, unsure exactly where he might find the third guard.

He inched along, eyes and ears alert, but the jungle remained silent, offering no clues. Then, heavy boots squished on the trail nearby, sucking mud, stepping slowly. The sentry stopped, standing near the original guard post. The other guards had been casual and unworried, undisciplined, easy prey, this one no different. Klyne began his stalk.

The third sentry wandered in an irregular circle, swinging the rifle back and forth in one hand.

Klyne hid behind a tree while the soldier ambled nearer, then turned back and gazed up at a few wispy clouds. Klyne slowly sucked in his breath then lunged, digging strong fingers and thumbs into soft throat tissue.

The guard spun and brought up a knee, then an elbow to the chest nearly cracked a rib, then a steel boot-heel stomped his instep and almost broke the hold.

Klyne struggled, surprised by the quickness and defense movements, but secure in his own strength and ability. Extremely well-trained, Klyne feared no one hand-to-hand. Klyne squeezed, straining, stifled a cry, then flexed, grabbing the soldier's shirtfront. His fingers captured soft breast flesh instead of muscle, and he dropped the sentry over his hip. He tightened his grip, nearly strangling the woman.

Klyne slammed her to the ground face up, breath burst from her lungs and she bit her lip, her arms pinned beneath her body, but still she struggled, fighting for her life while Klyne increased the pressure, choking until her eyes rolled back in her head. Klyne eased up and straddled her chest, her tight round breasts pressing against his thighs.

The woman lay motionless.

The sergeant wanted answers.

Klyne stuck a dagger beneath her chin and pushed the hilt slightly. A thin, bloody trickle leaked along her throat. The threat to kill was real. Frightened brown eyes stretched wide as she remained immobile beneath his knees, stark fear glistening on her terrified young face.

"You're dead if you move," Klyne growled, questioning the woman in Spanish, then French, then two local dialects. She offered nothing, no names, no operation, and no information. He threatened her again, pushing the knife deeper. Still nothing. More blood.

Then she offered the one bargain she did have. A sensual smile tickled the corners of her lips, seductive and knowing, oddly more sensual as her split lip trickled blood. She mouthed one word, in French, and pushed her breasts tighter against the thin blouse.

Klyne grunted. The dagger thrust deep and deadly. She opened her huge brown eyes impossibly wider, her neck muscles strained, her head quivered and jerked. The blade pierced her tongue and blood spilled out both sides of her mouth.

"You're dead anyway." Emotionless, his words cut the night, as chilling as the steel shaft he forced into her brain. Klyne wiped the eight-inch blade on her shirt. The jewels inlaid in its handle glittered even in the darkness. Then Klyne slipped back into the landscape and settled down on the ground.

Wet and cross-legged, he sat on the damp jungle floor, vulnerable. His weapons lay beside his knees. The shaking began again, as it always did. Stretched tight, his nerves nearly screamed with pain-filled agony, his entire body shook, and the salty wetness filled his eyes.

Surrounded by the empty night and a jungle filled with life and death, Klyne sat in the muck and raised his eyes, staring at a moonless, starlit sky beginning to cloud up again. Tears streamed down his cheeks, the wet streaks trickling through eleven days of dirt and bristles, dripping onto his shirt, and mingling with the rain and sweat and mud.

Several minutes passed and the trembling finally stopped. Klyne shook himself free of the tragic irony and collected his weapons, then stood and listened, turning a complete circle, staring into the shadows. Silence, then the night noise returned. Easing back into the jungle, he snuck into camp, silently opened the cages, and guided all three prisoners back to the operations center located at Base Tango.

8

Dressed in a clean pressed uniform, Klyne approached the sign-out counter. The major grinned, initialed the discharge and pushed the duplicates across his desk, along with a hundred dollars in cash and Klyne's final government paycheck, and a bonus for a job well done. He grinned at the amount, and at that moment, Jacoby Klyne officially became a civilian again.

"Good luck, Sarge. And thanks for everything you've done for us, all of us, here and back home," the major said. The officer suddenly stood erect and saluted Klyne, an unusual show of respect for all Klyne had accomplished while in uniform.

No civilians and most military personnel would never know or understand the significance of his contributions. But this major served with Klyne as a command liaison a year ago, and signed off on his field reports. The major knew the sergeant's reputation and abilities as well as anyone, anywhere.

"One more thing, Jake." The major handed Klyne an envelope with his name printed neatly across it, nothing else. Klyne tore it open and inside found a business card. A name - Miller Winston - a telephone number printed beneath it, no address or title.

Scribbled in ink across the bottom of the card: *Call if you ever need a favor.*

The name belonged to the emissary he rescued, and the area code was Boston, Massachusetts. Klyne slid the card in his wallet, tossed the envelope in the trash.

*

With an airline ticket to Los Angeles tucked into his shirt pocket, Klyne carried his bag outside and climbed aboard a bus. Dressed in new civilian clothes four hours later, he climbed out of a taxi at San Francisco International Airport. Later still, waiting for his plane, he sipped an Irish coffee and thought about his Army buddy, Jimmy Dodds.

Klyne glanced at the clock. He had been sitting in the airport for a half-hour when his flight number echoed in the background. He drained his cup, and then raced up the ramp. Twenty minutes later, San Francisco Bay fell away beneath the wingtips. His eyes slid shut.

*

Henry Bates watched the jet lift off, and then punched in a phone number. "Bates, here." He listened. "He flew to L.A." Bates listened again. "I thought he'd go to Seattle, too. Matter a fact I'm sure he will, it's his only close family."

Annoyed, Bates drummed the counter, his fingertips tapping a quick rhythm.

"We planned for this possibility, George, it'll still work." Bates listened again. "Okay. I'll follow up." He shut the phone and headed toward the hanger.

*

Fifty-five minutes later large black wheels beneath the jetliner chirped then touched down and rolled toward a Los Angeles International Airport terminal.

Police Inspector James Dodds greeted Klyne at the gate. Both combat veterans embraced then Dodds pushed away. "Damn it, Jake, I'm glad you made it home." A tear filled his eye, but he fought it back.

"Great to have you back. Been worried this past year, without me watching your back." Dodds grinned, over-riding the seriousness of his comment.

Both men smiled, neither one exactly sure whether the statement had more or less truth in it. Each had done a lot of back-watching while completing military operations during a three-year period they spent together as special ops soldiers under the same command.

"Me too, it's great to see you. Been almost two years." They leaned closer, embraced, touched foreheads briefly, remembering the dangers, remembering the uncountable times each saved the other's life.

"Come on Jake, I know a place where a sweet young lady serves ice cold beer and a great sandwich."

*

Drooping green fronds topped tall brown palm trees lining the road. The winter sun shined like springtime and dropped toward the sea. Dodds turned right and drove down a side street, passing cars parked along both sides, and eased into a loading zone. He stuck a blue police signboard with a gold badge emblem in its center on his dashboard. "Keeps the meter-maids off my wheels," he said.

A dark blue musical note hung at eye-level on the thick oak door Dodds pushed open. Both men angled toward the bar and sat, then glanced around the room. A candle flickered inside a glass holder in the center of each table, and thick carpeting covered the floor. Soft, indirect lighting set a tranquil mood for the casual, yet classy, interior.

A long-haired musician dressed in faded jeans and a tie-dyed shirt occupied a bench behind the sleek keyboard isolated in a corner. Graceful and elegant, his fingers wandered back and forth seemingly without purpose, but a sweet soulful melody emerged directly from his heart. Improvising, playing with his eyes closed, he chased the haunting blue notes up and down the keyboard, weaving his magic on the polished ivory keys. Tacked on the wall above him, a cloth sign announced:

"Red Hot Blues"
5 -7 & 9 - 12 Thursday thru Saturday

An overhead spotlight lit a female vocalist swaying in the shadows. Thick dark curls surround a creamy-white oval, dotted with pink and pretty. The singer leaned across the piano and whispered in the man's ear. They laughed quietly, a private joke, and then she snapped her fingers and picked up the beat.

Easing herself in behind the microphone, she shut her eyes, licked her lips, and sang old black blues like she'd been there to write them. A perfect mimic, the green-eyed dreamer captured the moment and Bessie Smith returned from her grave.

The music carried the crowd for a few minutes and then settled into the background. Four attractive women wearing mini-skirt outfits tended the tables. A tall bartender rattled off an unending stream of stories and jokes through a curly red beard while continuously pouring drinks. Three men and a woman huddled on stools beside the cash register, and laughed whenever the bartender hit his punch-line.

This night, it seemed, was particularly jovial and the bartender on a roll. He began a second and third story before he concluded his first, picking up each tale, then bouncing to the next. After a while, he hit one punch line after another all at once and his audience laughed for five minutes while he struggled to keep his face straight beyond the beer taps.

The musicians segued into a personal rendition of the Gershwin and Heyward favorite 'Summertime', a jazz original covered by nearly every singer with a voice, and many more without one. Two couples embraced, and eight barely moving feet circled the tiny dance floor.

"Nice place, Sarge. Nothing like this in Panama," Klyne said, his eyes tracking the hostess as she approached. She hugged Dodds, pecked his cheek, and chirped a greeting, all at once. Her voice sweet as honey, her laughter easy and quick, her lips tipped up at the ends, obviously enjoying her work.

Dodds introduced Sarah Recent. Light brown eyes, dark hair cut short and shaggy, and bright green silk accent a definitive womanly shape that pushed her outfit in all the right directions. His sexual sense awakened immediately, but

Klyne looked at his hands, then at his drink, then back at Sarah.

"Heard all about you Jake. You gonna be a cop too?" A tiny chip in one front tooth accented the smile that hung between two dimples, transforming an impish face from ordinary to charming in a heartbeat.

Klyne could not stop the blush mounting in his cheeks.

Sarah kept at it, flirting, expressing her interest. The woman simply bubbled with the most vibrant personality he'd seen in years. Although he'd been stateside only three months total in the past six years, and spent most of that with family.

Klyne mumbled something incoherent, his mind a blank. He merely stared at the first American woman he'd sat this close to in almost four years. Contact with girls during each military tour was often confined to hookers, hustlers, shopkeepers and barmaids, and a few urchins working the streets. All his military assignments occurred in foreign countries. He'd forgotten how to act here in the states, or maybe never learned. He was unsure of himself and had been a bit shy around local girls when growing up as well, bouncing from the farm in New Jersey to England when his father traveled back and forth to his professional worksites.

"Nope, not unless we can talk him into it," Dodds said.

"Can't speak for yourself?" She winked, her eyes wide, round, and teasing, her dimples flashed once more.

His mouth dried out and the words stuck in his throat. Sipping his drink to wet his lips, Klyne mumbled again, intelligible sounds with no meaning. Sarah spun about and approached a couple entering the club, but tossed a grin back over her shoulder. Klyne watched her bounce away.

"Twenty-seven, divorced, two children, and my wife's best friend," Dodds offered. Klyne looked at Dodds but said nothing. "I told her all about you."

"Thanks a lot Jimmy. Sorta ruins my chances." Both men laughed and tapped bottles.

During the next hour Sarah returned often, chatting and laughing, delivering a sandwich, chips, and another drink each, occasionally sharing a joke. Once, she set her tray on the bar beside Klyne. Reaching across his chest, she pressed her thigh against his hip, stretched her arms out, and placed two glasses in a sink behind the counter. The silky green fabric brushed lightly against his arm, her spicy fragrance enveloped him and a roller-coaster dropped away beneath his seat.

Sarah stood, facing him, nearly touching. Curious, her soft brown eyes captured his evasive blue ones. She glanced down in his lap, then back into his eyes, grinning. Her hips barely brushed his knee, rubbing back and forth in time with the music, a rhythmic capture for which Klyne had no defense. Sarah continued teasing, stimulating, and exciting him, fully aware of her effect. A definite tease, balanced with a light touch of sincerity.

Warmth suffused throughout his body. His face flushed. Klyne still said nothing, intensely aware of her warmth, of her thigh brushing against his knee. He glanced at Sarah then quickly looked away, at the bartender, at the singer, and at the keyboard player, then back at Sarah, and down at his drink, then back at his feet.

She glanced down again, checked her affect on him, and brought her eyes back up and locked with his. Her grin remained.

Dodds finished his drink, stood up, and broke the spell. "We're heading out, Sarah."

After two hours of contact, Klyne finally got one complete sentence out of his mouth. "I'll be back." He looked at his feet again, then slowly at Sarah. She grinned and nodded, well aware that her charm and confidence emerged a clear winner in the first skirmish.

"Hope so." Beyond anything she intended, or could or even would control, her rear end twitched enthusiastically as Sarah hustled back to her tables.

Completely engaged in the most naturally sensual trap in existence, Klyne watched her rhythmic swagger with both eyes.

Sarah glanced back over her shoulder once, and winked.

*

It rained all day, a warm misting drizzle and finally cleared up just before nine o'clock the following evening. Jimmy Dodds got called in to work night surveillance so Klyne was alone for the evening, and just as glad for it.

Klyne pushed the door open and entered the Blue Note. Sarah sat at the bar, an outfit the color of ripe watermelon hugging her figure. Without realizing or intending it, Klyne licked his lips. A dark-haired, stocky man stood beside Sarah, holding her arm tightly, engaged in a heated conversation. She pulled away, pointed at Klyne, and spoke to the man. He looked at Klyne and shook his head. Klyne approached slowly, alert.

Sarah began, "Art, this is a friend ..." But the man abruptly turned and stalked away without acknowledging the meeting. Klyne turned his head, following the angry departure, and then raised his eyebrows at Sarah as the man kicked the door open and stalked through it, obviously unhappy at her rejection.

"It's nothing," she said. "He comes in sometimes when I work. He's asked me out a few times. I'm not interested, he's a bit gruff."

Klyne joined her at the bar and they sat together for a couple hours, enjoying the music and the drinks, and engaging the potential for a new relationship. Neither one had any idea where it might lead. Finally, the band took a break and Sarah slid off the stool. "Come on. Let's walk."

The night was warm but dark clouds still hovered above the city, threatening to splatter the streets again. They strolled along the wet sidewalk side by side until Sarah hooked her fingers through his elbow, led him up the stairway, and unlocked her door.

"Don't wake my kids," she whispered, and paid her sitter. The door swung shut behind the teen-aged girl who lived down the hall.

A curious black cat peeked out over a wicker basket, and blinked at a stranger in his house. Silently, he slunk down and crept out, then staggered, three silent paws and loud thump as the cat worked his way across the floor and rubbed up again Sarah briefly.

"Dog tore off his back leg when he was a kitten," she explained, and poured hot water over two cinnamon-flavored teabags. "We call him Tripod."

Klyne grinned at the name and scratched its ear. "Of course. What else fits?"

"So, you gonna be a cop? Or what?"

"Don't think so, not sure. Got a few options. Army asked me to extend again. Offered me a very fat bonus, up front for another two years. I'm a little worn out and tired of the fieldwork. But that's why the bonus and command won't let me stay stateside for a tour. Said my training's too specialized, whatever that means. And a month before I got out some Feds tried to hire me, but wouldn't tell me what for, unless I agreed first. Seemed a little weird." He sat silent for a moment, not sure what to say, but needing someone to listen. "Guess I'm just looking to take it a little easy for a bit."

"Tired of what? The violence."

"Yes, and the orders, and the structure. I need to find my own way for awhile. One of the things the D.I. said in boot camp, I could learn a trade." He spat out a laugh, with no humor. "They taught me self-defense, survival skills, and how to operate deadly weapons in a kill zone. Not much use for that here. Least not anywhere I'd want to live."

A child whimpered, breaking into the conversation and Sarah hurried down the hall. Klyne sipped his coffee, reflecting on his past. He was confused, unfocused, without direction, had no plans, few job skills. His family was small and spread over three states and two countries, and it seemed his only friend was Jimmy Dodds. His military buddies were stationed all over the world, many still in the armed forces, or buried somewhere. His thoughts turned to his very first patrol with the sergeant who later became his best friend.

*

Sixty-seven months ago, Private Jacoby Klyne huddled in the dirt behind a cluster of trees, hiding for the first time in a battle zone after a firefight. Trembling, he crouched in the bush, his muscles cramping, and sweat drenching his hot, nervous body.

He glanced around and counted six men, those remaining of a ten-man squad that began the patrol nine days ago. Corporal Baggs lay on his left side in the mud, squeezing his leg, grunting in pain. Blood dribbled out of two bullet holes in his thigh. Corporal Aaron Rocho began wrapping a cloth tightly around the wound. "Through and through Baggy, don't sweat it. You'll heal just fine."

The smell of spilled blood and anxious fear hung on the moist jungle air, mingling with the rich fragrance of tropical flowers, fruit, and decomposing wood. Baggs moaned, and grit his teeth, closing his eyes each time the sound escaped.

"Take it easy Hump, I know it hurts." Rocho spoke, calming the soldier and working as well as any medic. "We'll get you out pretty quick." The man chuckled. "You'll be patting some sweet-looking nurse on the butt before lunch you lucky prick."

Rocho slapped tape across the hip. Baggs moaned again and rolled onto his back, easing his injured leg out straight.

Sergeant Dodds circled the area. "It's clear, relax a bit, Rocho and Rats, grab the watch. The rest of you check your ammo and reload, check canteens and your packs. See if you got hit anywhere on your equipment."

Shaffer was sitting on a stump moaning, tears in his eyes, a white cloth clotted with blood draped his left hand. Dodds removed the bandage and examined the hand. Half the smallest finger was missing, and blood leaked out of the stump. Dodds opened his pack and shot a pain-killer into the wound. "We'll fly you out to the clinic in a few minutes, hang it there."

Dodds was temporarily in command. The newest squad leader, a lieutenant, had been in the field only sixty-three days. He tripped a mine yesterday and it exploded under him. Now he was gone forever. Army just can't train field officers fast enough, it seemed.

"Help carry these two guys back to that clearing, and I'll get a dust-off in here quick as I can. Those locals be bringing friends back if we don't get outta here," Dodds growled. Turning, he yelled at the radioman, "Get that chopper down here. Now!"

Eight minutes later a Medi-Evac helicopter hovered above then dropped into the clearing. The squad pushed itself out from beneath the tree cover and hustled across to the landing zone.

Baggs rolled onto a canvas stretcher and flexed his palms, shaping a female rear-end, and then waved to the men, smiling, pushing two thumbs-up at his combat buddies. The pilot kicked out a mail packet then lifted Baggs and Shaffer out after fifty-four seconds ground time.

The squad hiked along the jungle trails for two hours ... leaving the ambush site miles behind. Dodds called a halt and checked every man, passed out the mail, and spoke a few words of encouragement. Frightened half-grins and fear shined on every face, even the combat veterans. Never can tell when another ambush might interrupt the march.

Dodds stopped beside Klyne, patted him on the back like a father. "Good job, kid," he says, quietly. The sergeant was a month short of twenty-one, Klyne was halfway between eighteen and nineteen.

"I'm no longer a kid," Klyne replied, just as quietly. He stared into Dodds' eyes, then glanced around at the squad, and vowed he would never again show this much fear.

In keeping that vow, he failed, but from that day on developed a friendship with Sergeant Dodds that lasted until the sergeant shipped back stateside almost three years later. The soldiers kept in touch, even after Dodds became a civilian and a law enforcement officer in Los Angeles, California.

Each saved the other's life countless times during almost four years they served together. Nicaragua, Panama, Africa, and other countries, quick hits in troubled spots around the world, names all melded into a huge intricate jumble, people and places, scars and battles, and memories that often hurt.

Gladness filled his heart the day Klyne finally flew home, tempered by a sadness as he stood on the dock, waiting. A row of metal coffins shined in the sunlight then slid into the fat-bellied cargo plane poised to carry them home. It had been simply his good fortune and intense training that Klyne rode beside one and not in it.

*

Klyne sipped his coffee. His lips bent down at the ends. Sarah slid back onto her stool, popping his mind back to the present. "So, what do you think about that?" she asked, as if she'd never left.

"According to the newspapers, the only place I need those particular job skills now is shopping in downtown Los Angeles, and I don't get paid for it anymore." A wry smile appeared and he drained the last few drops out of his cup. "I'll probably head for Seattle soon."

She hooked her fingers under his arm, and led him to the door, then stopped and hugged him. As she pulled away, he slipped his arms around her waist and covered her lips with his. She pulled against him and kissed him back, her tongue quickly probing, exploring. Then she pushed him away, grinning, and opened the door.

"Time to go, soldier. See you Monday night."

*

The next morning, Dodds stood in the doorway and woke Klyne. "Stop by the office today. We gotta talk, and there's someone wants to meet you."

Klyne lifted his head off the pillow. "What's up?"

"Tell you then. Coffee's perked, be there before nine."
Dodds disappeared, the garage door banging behind him.

Klyne drank his coffee and a glass of juice, ate a bagel,
showered, and headed for the police station, walking briskly
through the cool, damp morning.

Dotted here and there, grand new high-rise designs
struggled with the aging city. Outdated buildings had been
quietly snatched up and renovated, or demolished and rebuilt.
Decorated with fieldstone and glass and fancy artwork, the
sleek metal framing and curving concrete structures sprang
up almost overnight.

Architects and engineers chased the wealth, as did
developers, builders, and brokers, followed by the blue and
white collars that spent their dreams as the city immediately
began aging again. The never-ending process entered another
cycle, the City of Angles rolling over upon itself one more
time.

Old wooden benches lined a long, narrow park
sprawled at the commons. Stout oaks and tall pines
surrounded dry lawns, brown now but waiting patiently to
sprout lush and green again in the winter rains. Towering
above a rock-ringed pond, a brass fountain sprinkled its mist,
forming a rainbow in the morning sunlight.

Multi-colored pigeons played and fought, danced and
courted on wet masonry walls that edged the brick path
leading toward the main entrance of City Hall. The slick,
metal roof shimmered in the distance as dewdrops
evaporated, misting above the peaks.

An easy three-minute jog over the damp concrete and
decorative brick, Klyne accelerated across the park, down the
walk, and under an arched doorway. Vaporous clouds
billowed out of his mouth as he ran up the steps and pushed
through the doors.

Klyne never noticed a gray sedan following slowly behind. As Klyne entered the building, Pitchman opened his cell phone and punched in a number, spoke into it briefly, then snapped it shut and spun away down a side street leading away from the station.

"Looking for Inspector Dodds," Klyne puffed, bending over, catching his breath, "Should be expecting me. Name's Jake Klyne."

The ancient desk sergeant lifted a roster and squinted down then up. He pointed along the hall. "Elevator to the third floor, turn left, look for the sign CDVU," he grumbled through a dark gray moustache wrapped around the mashed end of a fat cigar. The man disappeared behind his magazine, a thin plume of smoke rising above the fuzzy ears of a Playboy bunny posing on its cover.

Klyne walked toward the elevator, wondering absently what the old fellow would do if his bunny dream came true. "Probably experience cardiac arrest first hand," he remarked, grinning, and stabbed the up button. Klyne found the unit and entered through a door standing open. The sign above it wrapped the words California Drug Violence Unit around a gold emblem shaped like a badge.

Dodds was leaning over a desk, reviewing some information with two clones, each wearing a brown khaki uniform with a silver rookie badge stuck on its pocket.

Klyne thought they resembled high school students, too young to be cops. He'd celebrated his twenty-fourth birthday the same day he'd pulled the emissary out of that stick hut in Panama a few weeks ago.

Dodds looked up and grunted when his friend entered, circled a few items and dismissed the officers.

"Coffee?" Dodds asked, and poured without waiting for an answer.

Steam rose above the cup and Klyne blew on the hot liquid then sipped. "Well, here I am."

"Yeah, I know. My division commander got some background and thought a job might interest you."

Dodds raised his eyebrows but Klyne said nothing. "Usually takes months to put the paperwork together. All that bureaucratic bullshit." Dodds shrugged. "Wants to see you anyway if you like, he's only here for a week, then Sacramento. And he can make it happen practically overnight if he wants you, and you want in."

"So, you give it?"

"Little bit, some background stuff. Thought you'd mostly speak for yourself."

A moment passed while neither spoke. Dodds broke the silence. "Pay's okay and good benefits. And, you seem a bit lost."

"Besides, we can get a quick workout if nothing else. Good gym here, and some mats."

"Let's do the mats first. Haven't worked out in a couple weeks. Then I'll talk to him, see what he's got. No harm in that."

Klyne borrowed a workout suit, and the men played around for thirty minutes.

"Damn. Forgot how quick you are Jake. Seems you haven't lost anything." Dodds puffed a bit, catching his breath.

A door leading in from a lecture room opened and an instructor entered, followed by two rookie police officers. Surprised, Klyne snapped his eyes open then narrowed them. The man who annoyed Sarah at the Blue Note a few nights ago led the young men in and began a training session. Klyne watched the men work. A grim smile stretched across his face.

"Sergeant Art Watson," Dodds said, noticing the look. "Our instructor. Been here eight years. He's pretty good, though he bullies occasionally, especially the new men."

Watson accelerated the lessons, showing off at the expense of his students. He challenged them both at once, dancing around, a cat playing with mice. The rookies were inexperienced, Watson was not, and everyone knew it, so he impressed only himself. After an intense fifteen-minute workout, the men stopped for a breather.

Watson glanced over, grinned, and sent Dodds a mock salute. His eyes opened wider and the grin fell away when he spotted Klyne. He recovered almost immediately and sauntered over, curiosity apparent on his face.

"Training another rookie, Jimmy?"

Dodds began his answer and introduction, but Klyne interrupted. "Nice to see you again Sergeant. Didn't catch the name Friday." Neither man offered a handshake.

"Come for a lesson youngster?" Watson asked, curling his lips into a grin. But his eyes remained sly and wary.

"No thanks," replies Klyne, "I don't teach anymore," returning the stare.

Watson's smile broke-off and lay there in flat little pieces. An intense silence filled the room. Both men glared, eyes fencing, neither man giving.

"Have to finish up with these guys," Watson said, without dropping his eyes. He wanted some action, but he dared not provoke it outright. "Stick around, kid, if you want a fall or two."

"I'll wait."

"What the hell's that all about?" Dodds asked.

Klyne said nothing, concentrating on the workout. Watson finished quickly and dismissed the men, then turned and walked to the center of the mat, hands on his hips.

"Watch his left foot, very quick. He's pretty good Jake, and has three inches and forty pounds on you."

The men circled one another slowly, gauging the opponent, looking for an opening. Watching eyes, feet, hands, shoulders, head, and balance for clues to a move.

The sergeant toyed again, playing, confident, and ready to prove a point, gain a little revenge for the other night. Believing Klyne had little experience, and less training. But after five minutes he'd never touched Klyne once. He intensified his efforts and several officers noticed, then a small crowd gathered. Watson had taught most of them. His style and reputation had no equal on the force. The rookie officers and a couple of staff members began watching, but made no comments.

Kicks, thrusts, parries, throws, lifts, and misses, the accompanying grunts split the air. Soon enough, sweat poured off both men, and heavy panting breaths filled the room.

Both men circled, feinting, threatening, swinging, punching, kicking, sleek maneuvers exciting the audience. The officers remained mute, simply enjoying the match, learning a little self-defense style and technique as they watched.

Watson kicked and Klyne slapped it away. Watson double kicked, spun an axle, and chopped with a right elbow, then punched twice, a left, a right.

Klyne reversed, blocked, reversed again, and double knee-blocked, spun free, and rotated away.

Watson growled and charged.

Klyne grabbed his wrist, hooked his ankle, and tossed him onto the mat.

Watson rolled, bounced up, and charged again, both arms whirling in a blinding series of chops and punches and blocks, his frustration evident.

Klyne side-stepped, tripping Watson again.

An officer spoke, "Your pal better attack. Defense won't beat Art. Can't wear him out, you just gotta beat him flat. And that ain't easy."

Dodds said nothing, but the corners of his lips barely tipped up. Then he nodded and said "Just watch, Barry."

Watson's eyes became slits. He spun again, delivering another blurring series of kicks and punches nearly too fast for an eye. Most missed, but a few connected and staggered Klyne.

Suddenly Klyne attacked and Watson flinched, the move so quick anyone who blinked missed it. Klyne caught Watson in mid-stride, and turned him sideways.

Watson grunted, grimacing in response to a sharp pain at the wrist and climbing up his right arm.

Klyne turned into Watson instead of spinning away, and pulled himself in under the right shoulder, grabbed and pinched Watson's thumb, twisting it backward, vise-like, bent and immobile while he wrapped his left arm behind his opponent's neck, surrounding it and gripping his forearm, then wedged his knee between Watson's groin and thigh.

Watson struggled, his left leg dangling, trapped and useless. Klyne grabbed a handful of hair, stretched the head backwards, the muscles and tendons bulging, tight beneath his chin. Watson hung helpless before his peers, a flush mounting in his cheeks.

Klyne squeezed, flexed, and lifted Watson completely off the mat. Watson struggled, trying to release himself, but failed. Then Klyne released the hold, and tossed Watson again. He struck the mat flat on his back, and lay there a moment before climbing to his feet. He shook himself and walked toward Klyne.

Klyne remained in a defensive stance, poised and balanced. Watson said nothing for a few seconds, and then finally extended his hand. "My apologies."

They locked eyes, and Klyne accepted and shook hands. Watson stepped back and bowed, assuming a posture of courtesy, a gesture of respect. Klyne nodded and bowed in return.

Watson stood at attention, spun on his heel, and walked away but as he opened the exit door, he turned back and gestured. A single thumb popped above his fist.

Klyne clasped his palms together at chest-height, and bowed again.

The crowd drifted away, replaying the bout, suddenly animated, dancing around themselves and mimicking the kicks.

Dodds and Klyne showered, dressed then walked along the hall. "So, you wanna tell me what that was all about?" Dodds asked.

"Nothing much. He just tried to fuck around with Sarah."

"Oh," Dodds said, and hid his grin.

*

Later that evening, once again in spite of the attraction that blossomed between them, Sarah lingered briefly in the doorway enjoying a good night kiss, more than one, but then pushed him out and shut the door. The lock clicked behind him.

After waiting a moment for the unlikely event that she changed her mind and invited him in for the night, Klyne turned and whistled his way down the stairs, bouncing over two at a time, and then headed uptown for the brisk thirty-minute trot back to Dodds' apartment. A light drizzle fell again but had no effect on his mood.

Across the street, Pitchman sat hunched over the steering wheel in a black pickup truck parked at the curb with its engine idling, nearly silent but for a slight valve tick.

Klyne rounded the corner.

Pitchman shifted into gear and followed. As usual, he spoke into a slim black device, snapped it shut, then accelerated down the block. The headlights blinked on after he turned the opposite corner and sped away.

9

Dodds and Klyne arrived at the police station early the next morning. Dodds worked in a department that began operations only two years ago. The California Drug Violence Unit investigated drug-related crime and violence, tracking small-time dealer connections back to the major suppliers.

CDVU aligned with the Federal Drug Enforcement Agency, but has been ineffective up until recently. Takes time to develop connections and a network to exploit, and a budget that can afford it. As usual, a larger budget needs a successful track record. And a track record is harder to achieve without a larger budget. A perfect Catch-22 operating at its finest hour.

Most drug-related violence was family and friend oriented, or involves crime related to the money addicts needed for habits. Drugs became the catalyst, and drove the violence. But the drugs originated somewhere.

CDVU investigates the users, and through them, the dealers and the background, seeking the common bond.

CDVU then tracks backwards from those users and small time connections, seeking major suppliers. The individual players withhold information at every turn, eventually bargaining to get a favor or a short sentence, but climbing that chain remains an extremely slow process.

*

Commander Alexander Paar relaxed in a plush chair and ran his eyes over a folder he held in one hand. Sixty-one years old and very heavy, with a chronic back problem, he carried the fancy chair inside the van he drove everywhere he worked, and he never flew anywhere. A slight flight phobia ruled his actions, but he denied it and claimed he just needed his chair.

Fluorescent light reflected off his hairless dome, black eyeglass frames accented the thin fringe of white hair remaining above his ears, and he spoke around an unlit pipe he rolled continuously across his lips.

His questions indicated Paar already knew a lot more about Klyne than Jake figured he should. He blamed that on Dodds, but made no comment about his guess.

Paar's contacts stretched around the world, and he accessed any data bank he wanted anytime he required information. Reviewing more details of his past than Klyne remembered himself without deeper reflection, Paar's hard black eyes pierced Klyne's soul, seemingly aware of the answers even before Klyne responded.

"What about your drug use?" Paar asked.

"What about it?"

"Did you abandon it now? Less stress maybe, after your discharge?"

Klyne shrugged. His military training included evasive answering, and he was not above distorting the truth anyway when it suited him. That question he simply ignored, as he had others during the session. Paar ignored the fact that Klyne ignored certain questions, and just kept talking and asking.

"We always overlook pot. Everyone's done that. You use anything stronger?"

An Offer? A Statement? Paar finally gave away the fact that his sources are imperfect. Nobody only did pot.

White fluffy eyebrows rose above the same black eyes, looking for denial, or a different truth. Paar stared, wondering if he would get an answer this time.

Klyne said nothing, waiting him out.

"Seems like every person past infancy has tried pot, and of course, no one inhales," Paar laughs. "Except me, of course." Then he laughs again, amused at the way he accidentally worded the response, as if he both smoked pot and inhaled. A simplistic variation of his own truth.

He totally disregarded the times he had smoked at Stanford and tasted a few pills now and then to keep him awake for finals. "Hell, we'd damn near eliminate the world if we count weed. We'd have no agents. Might as well recruit directly out of county jail."

Paar grinned again, as if amused once more by the conflicting values found in his own personal history, and those same conflicts in several of his best agents.

Klyne offered no contradiction. He let the statements sit there, offering neither confirmation nor denial.

"We'll find a spot for you if you'd like. Dodds speaks very highly of you and, of course, your training and military record speaks for itself. You let me know."

"I'll think about it," Klyne replied. The men stood and everyone shook hands, and then Dodds and Klyne retreated out the door and down the hall.

"Don't know, Jimmy, it's a little too quick. Just been out a few days. Some Fed asked me too, about a month before my discharge. He wouldn't give me any information though. Just offered some work if I was interested, he didn't push very hard, but he was dead serious. Seemed so anyway. Wouldn't tell me what it was. I turned him down, but he left it open. Told the major he'd be back after my discharge. Hasn't showed yet, though."

"Yes he has. Tall, cowboy type named Bates if it's same guy. Talks like L.B.J. and tried to pressure Paar. Wanted him and me to help them hire you. Wants us to force you. Paar laughed, told him to fuck off, come back and bring his manners."

Klyne remained silent for a few minutes. "Yeah, sounds like the same guy. Wonder what they want me for? I'm nothing special."

"Yes you are, at least to them. You've executed people Jake, face-to-face. Spooks like that. And we don't. We just investigate, no violence, least not intentional."

"Yeah, well I didn't like it. And that's over, I gave up my stripes." Neither man spoke again until they reached the office.

"I'll think about Paar's offer, let you know later."

*

The moon cast dark shadows across the path as Sarah and Klyne walked back toward her apartment after dinner several nights later. A light breeze blew up the valley, blending the fresh smell of salt air with the charcoal, spices, and herbs of Restaurant Row. Sarah chattered constantly, dancing along the sidewalk, laughing and happy, and hooked her fingers in the crook of his arm.

His throat constricted and roller-coaster dropped out beneath him each time her breast rubbed against his elbow. Klyne experienced that same feeling a lot lately when in her company. Arm in arm, the couple approached the entry to her apartment. Sarah twirled the key-chain on her finger and tipped her head back, gazing at the stars.

"Grandma has my girls. This night is ours." She swung the door open and led him in.

City lights flickered outside the windows and gauze curtains fluttered in the breeze. Breathing a light sign, Sarah skipped into the room. Back-lit by the streetlights, she raised her arms, spun a pirouette, then kicked off her shoes and wriggled her toes in the carpet. "Some wine or a smoke?" She hit the switch on a dim lamp then lit two scented candles and a joint with the same match.

Klyne arched an eyebrow, but said, "Little of each works for me."

Soon, a smoky haze hung in the room and the scent of strawberries and sage tickled his nostrils. Sarah grabbed his fingers, tugging gently, and pulled his head down on her shoulder. She draped her arm around his neck, ruffling his hair. He raised his face, she closed her eyes, her smile touched his, sharing moisture and warmth. She embraced him, pulling him tighter.

Her tongue darted out, flicking between his lips, teasing, tantalizing, playful, an intimate clue to her fire. Klyne ran his hand along her thighs, her hips, and slid his fingertips across her ribs, squeezing her breast, touching, stroking, his fingers and palm caressing. Her nipples sprang erect, poking against the tight fabric, straining, swollen.

Briefly, he fought with the buttons, releasing each one by one, and popping two off completely. His hands shook with the heat and the need. Her blouse fell to the floor, she raised her hips and he slid her bottoms down and off, dropping them in a heap, then rose and shed his own clothes.

He caressed her soft mound, hot and slick with sexual juice and her rising passion.

She moaned, a low crooning, and her desire peaked, her body shifting beside him allowing his fingers access. After a few moments building pleasure, she reached below, stroking and softly guiding him in, rotating her pelvis, thrusting, engulfing him. Penetration. Warmth, all slick and silky.

Captured, a willing victim, helpless, Klyne inhaled her feminine mystique, drowned in her beauty, dissolved in her intimate connection

Her gentle coaxing spurred him on, and two lovers danced the age-old rhythms. Softly purring in his ear, she rocked her hips and began panting, moaning, nearing her orgasm she dug her fingernails into his back and bit his neck then his ear, gently, drawing no blood.

Sarah cried out, "Yes! Yes!" and murmured her release. "Yes," once more as she pulsed and pulsed again. She pulled him harder into her body, and he joined her climax, pushing tightly against her, matching her strength and her whisper. Then both sagged together and he remained locked inside, nibbling a lock of hair that curled beneath her ear.

Slowly, the lovers relaxed, recovering, anticipating that another sexual session will follow soon enough. Settling back on the pillows, Sarah continued nuzzling his neck and ears, and ran her fingernails along his shoulders, ribs, and back.

"Glad I met you," Klyne murmured into a hollow pocket at the base of her throat and the light scent of violets drifted into his nose.

*

Klyne returned again during her early shift at the Blue Note that night and the next. Evenings filled with stories, laughter and tentative touching sparked an intense sexual relationship they both enjoyed immensely. Klyne spent three nights and three days with Sarah, but each one seemed like minutes.

Quickly, a week passed, then another, and another. Casually and with a great love and patience, she inserted her children into the relationship and Klyne suddenly discovered the joy of kids too young to know anything but fun and laughter.

10

On the east coast, completely across the country from the apartment where Klyne spent most of his nights with Sarah lately, George Hallingforth stood in his office reviewing an intelligence document.

Established under a Presidential Order five years ago, the ICD evaluates, coordinates and exchanges information between the FBI, CIA, and other intelligence services throughout state and federal governments. Hallingforth designed, founded, and developed ICD, and remained its sole director.

Three years short of full retirement, gray flecks peppered his short dark hair, age lines creased his face, and his stunted frame carried a stoutness going soft now that he often skipped his daily workouts.

Still strong and fit despite the bulk, he cloaked his thoughts in a placid demeanor betrayed only by his eyes.

Sharp and nearly black, they bored holes in everyone he met. With degrees in Philosophy and Political Science from Harvard, and a law degree from Yale, Hallingforth had been recruited by the Federal Intelligence Department directly out of college thirty-two years ago and accepted the federal posting. He remained with the agency for his entire career, his only employer.

Henry Bates stood at the window and gazed down at intricate traffic patterns the matchbox sized automobiles created while hurriedly vacating the ICD parking lot.

Concluding a busy workday, hundreds of government employees scooted about, jockeying for position at the bottle-necked exits. Elongated black shadows crawled across white-lined pavement as the cloud-draped sun drooped toward the skyline. Random snowflakes blew in and stuck against the glass, a frosty pile building on the sill. Sunrays glistened through the ice and daylight settled into dusk.

"Well, Henry," Hallingforth asked, "you still think he'll head up to Seattle?" Without waiting for an answer, he continued, "Probably will, that's his closest family." He muttered the comment quietly, under his breath, as if promoting its truth.

"Probably. Nearly Christmas. I reckon he'll head up soon." Bates responded without turning, his eyes absorbed in the circus below. "If not, we can always move the operation south."

"Our agent in place?" Hallingforth asked, already sure of the answer.

"Yup. Pepperton hit her contact couple weeks ago, but she's ready to move out if necessary. Report's on the bottom of that last page. Be no problem if he heads north, could get a bit more complicated if he stays in Los Angeles. Might spend a lot of time with that new cocktail waitress he met. Make things a bit tougher."

"Give it five more days. If he sticks there any longer, move Pepperton to L.A.," Hallingforth ordered. "We must get this mobilized again." Then under his breath he muttered to himself, almost as an afterthought, "We can always take the woman out if necessary."

This time Bates looked at him directly, raising his eyebrows at the last statement. As usual, he formally agreed, but this time internally reserved his judgment.

"Yes sir. Pepperton's top-notch. Should handle it either place." He moved away from the window and reached across the desk, collecting the reports.

"Take her out though, George? She's civilian."

Bates almost never questioned his superior. But this was very off the track, and Hallingforth had not shared much of this operation with him, unusual as well.

Hallingforth ignored the question, and Bates moved on, but stuck the idea in a corner of his mind.

"Herbie Pitchman's still watching Klyne. He'll call in if there's any change we need to know about," Bates said.

"Don't bother with these Henry, I'll hold 'em awhile." Bates set the files on the desk and retreated into his office. Hallingforth opened a leather briefcase and carefully placed the documents inside, then locked it, and stared out at the weather.

*

Klyne opened his eyes and stretched. Sarah stuck out her tongue, flicked his ear, and climbed out of bed. "Gotta get to class. See you tonight at the club?"

"Guess not." Klyne looked up at her.

Her smile fell away. "Oh?"

"Time I head up to Seattle. Besides, my sister called again, third time, wondering when I'm coming home."

"Thought you lived in New Jersey or England, you said."

"Was raised there, both places. But after my father died my mother moved to England permanently. My sister and her family live in Seattle." Smiling up at her, he embraced her hips. He nosed her robe open and planted a wet kiss just below her navel. "But I'll be back soon. Gotta do the family thing for a bit."

Her look turned serious and she wrapped her arms around his head. He kissed her again, running his tongue into her navel. She arched her back, pulled his head tighter. Her robe slipped off her shoulders and dropped in a pile at her feet.

"Well, if you're leaving today ..." she smiled at the excuse. Sarah pushed Klyne onto his back and slid on top of him. Klyne wiggled lower, nibbled her erect nipple, still lower he found her slick and moist immediately, and eventually eased inside one more time.

Late that afternoon, Dodds drove Klyne to the airport where he boarded a plane bound for Seattle.

A gold jumbo jet with red accents rolled down the runway, lifted off and aimed itself north. Jacoby Klyne grabbed a travel magazine and settled into his seat for the two and a half hour flight.

Three thousand miles away, a red satellite telephone dinged once. Tiny beads of perspiration stood out on his brow, his palms felt cool and wet. Sweat stained his shirt and ran down his arms as Hallingforth snatched up his private line. The receiver crackled, "Pitchman here. He's headed for Seattle."

The line clicked then hummed when the dial tone returned. The ends of his lips turned slightly upward as Hallingforth let the phone drop back into its cradle, his hand remaining absently upon it, his fingers ticking a rhythm on the desktop beside it. "Finally!"

Hallingforth stared out the window. Behind the tinted window and back-lit by the waning sun, storm clouds pushed at the sky. Fading sculptures, reds and yellows and purples, splashed on the horizon as the sunbeams died.

Embossed upon the darkening glass, pensive sadness stained a weary face reflecting back at George M. Hallingforth III. A nervous tick danced beneath his eye. He grimaced and, dropping his forehead down onto his palms, rocked his thick body back and forth. Eventually, he stopped and looked at his watch.

He got up and locked the door, then settled behind his desk and retrieved his bottle. The director unlocked the briefcase again, removed the files, and selected one. He licked a fingertip, turned a page, scribbled a note, and sipped, scribbled a note and sipped, scribbled a note and sipped.

11

Light drizzle blew about as huge black tires skidded and slipped on the wet asphalt runway. Poor weather and thick fog almost diverted the plane that rolled toward the gate. Dim landing lights barely penetrated the early evening shadows, and swirling mists shrouded the bright rectangular blocks that intermittently peeked out, inviting passengers into the warmth.

Klyne peered out at a dusky, overcast Seattle. What little he remembered seemed the same, always wet and dim. He recalled a few visits when he was a child, and ten years ago when he was fourteen, and two short trips on leave from the Army near the beginning of his never ending deployments.

On his most recent visit, his half-sister Elizabeth had invited the family to celebrate Professor Caldwell Klyne's sixty-fifth birthday and his retirement from the academic world. He had taught medieval history at Princeton and at Cambridge. It was the only time Klyne recalled when his entire extended family gathered in one place at the same time.

Late in his life, Caldwell Klyne married one of his graduate students, Susanna Beckworth. Looking for something to occupy her time, she had returned to study after raising three children and losing her first husband. She and Elizabeth, her eldest daughter, had become pregnant at about the same time, and Klyne's half-sister had given birth to Rachel two months before Jake was born.

Unplanned, but undeniably loved just the same, Jacoby Klyne was the only child born to Caldwell and Susanna, and brought unexpected joy into their later years.

He laughed and cried, climbed and fell, walked and ran. Learning patience from his father, tenacity from his mother, and empathy from both, his childhood education occasionally enhanced by a swat in the pants from either, lovingly given of course, just to get his attention. Klyne grew up in a comfortable home, adored by his parents, both his sisters and his brother, although they were more of an age like aunts and an uncle. Elizabeth eventually married and relocated to Seattle with her husband.

Caldwell Klyne had educated himself at Cal-Berkeley on a Gymnastics and Track scholarship. He completed dual majors in World History and Anthropology then moved on to Columbia University for his doctorate. He gained professorships simultaneously at Princeton and Cambridge, traveling with his family for portions of each academic year during his entire professional life.

During his teen years, Klyne learned much about the ancient weaponry from his father and after his untimely demise, the collection was eventually divided between Princeton and Cambridge. Jake selected several pieces, a wire garrote and a jeweled dagger among the tools that he later carried to work.

Jacoby Klyne inherited his superior balance and athleticism from his father and looked forward to each alternate teaching season at the family home in England and his lessons with the rowdy gentleman next door, a retired Royal Marines Commando.

With his three children grown and gone, Gerry McGee first thought it amusing to teach his six-year old neighbor self-defense and survival skills in his backyard.

Later, the elite forces Commando found it both entertaining and challenging as Jake matured, and eventually the retired sergeant found himself amazed at the extraordinary physical abilities his student exhibited in his late teens.

Upon his recruitment at age eighteen, the United States Army recognized and honed those skills early on, and trained Klyne as a Special Forces Ranger before sending him out on some of the most dangerous missions imaginable.

For the retirement party, on his last visit before the funeral, Susanna's youngest daughter, Annette, had arrived from Maine with her husband and four children. Her only son flew in from the Middle East.

A fluid systems engineer with an oil exploration company and unmarried, David designed and built the crossbow replica, and given it to Caldwell Klyne on that date. A couple of years later, after his father's untimely death, Klyne carried the unique weapon and ancient war-toys from the collection into battle.

Susanna Klyne buried her husband in New Jersey then retired permanently to England. Jake Klyne returned to Africa and completed one of many assignments in the wild and less developed areas of the world where criminal elements thrive.

*

Pulled abruptly from his reminiscence by a squeaking intercom announcing the deplaning, Klyne grabbed his bag and trotted down the ramp.

Two young women stood at the exit gates. A happy shriek and a wave caught his attention, and he spotted his niece and her friend.

He ran through the gates and swept Rachel into a hug and swung her around in a tight circle, her feet flying straight out behind. Elizabeth visited often while Rachel and Jake were growing up, and the similarity of age allowed a strong bond to develop between Klyne and his niece. As children, they always acted more like siblings, and Klyne felt that Rachel replaced the sister he never had as a youngster. His half-siblings were a generation older than himself.

A tall, slim, very attractive young woman stood beside Rachel. Long black hair hung nearly to her waist. Enchanting in its own way, two dark eyes slanted slightly toward high, flat cheekbones, giving a clue to her heritage. She appeared part Oriental and part Native American, and the dual race mixture produced a rare beauty in one engaging package.

"Clinic called mom in for something," Rachel explained, "so we got to come git ya'." She smiled, hugging him again. "Alicia Diamond, my friend from work," she bubbled, "meet my cousin, or brother, or uncle ... Jake. Whatever are we anyway?"

Klyne remained mute, but greeted Alicia with a smile, running his eyes over her tight young body.

Another short giggle slipped out and Rachel said, "Get your stuff, the car's close."

He grabbed his packs, exited the airport, and found the girls outside at the curb "Hey, you folks allergic to sunshine? Seems last time I was here the sun never shined all week."

"It's not always like this, but we do get bunches of wetness." The blue Volvo sped into traffic. "Here, mellow out," Rachel ordered, grinning, and handed over a joint, "and light this."

First Dodds, then Sarah, and now Rachel. Klyne began to suspect everyone in the states smoked pot, and had easy access to it. A match flared in the back seat, and Klyne exhaled a thin stream of smoke. "Just might like Seattle," he said, appraising Alicia again, checking her eyes in the mirror.

Her lips curled up a bit before she turned away, and then Alicia glanced back with an appraisal of her own. Her dark eyes sparkled, a few golden flecks decorating each, and then she faced the front window and watched the road.

The city traffic crawled along then diverged quickly as the drivers separated onto outbound routes. Rachel shot across three lanes, accelerating down a connector spike that entered the northbound highway. Idle chatter occupied her mouth while she raced along the turnpike toward the suburbs.

"See that bank building? That's our wonderful place of employment," she giggled, pointing. "We met two weeks ago when the office gave a party. We found out that we both have the same birthday. Ha, different years though." She grinned again.

"Used to be a factory, but the owners got fined for too much pollution too many times, dumping a bunch of crap into the bay. Too expensive to fix and the company went belly-up. So the bank bought it cheap, gutted it, and renovated. Now, it's worth a big, fat, fortune, new offices all over. Every floor inside, all rebuilt with fancy interiors even though the outside still looks old."

She pointed out various changes and the growth patterns, quickening her pace when the city borders fell behind. The car punched out of the mist and into the suburbs.

Rescued from obscurity, a neighborhood of historic homes sparkled beside the road, newly renovated but historic outside like the bank, but update modern inside.

"New money executives, the fat cats, decided these large old homes were affordable and very comfy. Now they cost a mint, if you can find one for sale," Rachel explained. "Maybe I should have done real estate instead of banking. Course, real estate really dumps sometimes, and banking? Well, people always need a safe spot for greenbacks."

Circling up a slight hill into a driveway, she parked the Volvo beside a flower garden, stone dead and waiting for spring. Klyne climbed out, wide-eyed. Rachel sent him a photo once, while he was still in the Army, but in it, the damaged house his sister originally bought appeared quite unlike the beautiful home in front of him now.

The sprawling, ancient castle, decorated with brick and slate and stone, nestled amidst a grove of sugar pines on a grassy knoll. The sun dropped below the skyline. Bright red and yellow streaks accented the gray and black cloud formations floating above the horizon and drew a weirdly decorated tapestry across the roof, the windows, and the siding. Darkening mountains, magenta in the fading light, stretched above the shipyard across Puget Sound. Struck near motionless by the incredible view, Klyne's breath caught in his throat with the beauty of it all.

"Sellers claimed it was built in the eighteenth century by a wealthy pirate," she rattled on, "and it cost mom and

Aaron nearly two years and lots a bucks to restore it. Still working on parts of it, but mostly it's finished now."

All three walked up a brick pathway, side-by-side. "Isn't it wonderful? There's an old dungeon under the kitchen. Now it's a wine cellar. We don't have any criminals in the family to put in it." She laughed. The house had been bought and the project begun three years ago, right after his last visit.

"You stay in the butler's quarters, Jake," Rachel said. "Don't have one of those either, only a gardener, but he doesn't live here."

They wandered into the kitchen, through the pantry and peeked at his new quarters, a large bed centered in a huge room, a sitting area with a double-door view of the bay, and a private bath. "Damn far cry from a hot tent shared with a bunch of sweaty soldiers," Klyne said. "I'd even settle for being a butler."

Alicia fell backwards across the bed and lay still a moment, tight clothes hugging her body. Klyne resisted the urge to climb on the bed with her, and instead, ran his eyes over her lithe curves. He couldn't stop his thoughts and the sexual twitch bit him hard. He backed out of the room before he gave himself away.

Elizabeth arrived an hour later and launched a welcome home party, paroling three bottles of her best port from the dungeon below. Klyne staggered toward his bedroom when the party ended. He shed his clothes and stretched out on the bed. The pot, the wine, and the weariness stripped his mind. He tipped across the border into light and dark and shadow, and finally drifted off.

*

He awakened slowly, discerning a subtle change in comfort, a gentle persuasion returning him to the tactile world, then, suddenly startled, his eyes flew open. A paralyzing fear ripped through his body. His muscles flexed and his breath caught, squeezing tightly in his chest. The adrenaline rush so often experienced in violent worlds on other continents returned and the woman standing near him will never know how close to death she stood. But, his eyes focused and he calmed himself, barely in time. Awareness swam over him, acknowledging that a caress so pure, so soft and perfect, never offered danger. Strong fingertips and gentle nails traced a gliding pattern over his back and thighs, awakening him, enticing him as he slowly withdrew from his dreams.

Exquisite and luxurious, her massage erased what fear remained and chased the last remnants of his sleep away. Hidden in the flickering shadows, Alicia gazed down at Klyne, her body reflecting dim night patterns blurred by wispy clouds that hid the moon. Demure but penetrating, her dark eyes beckoned. Her hair hung straight and black past her waist, and she wore nothing but a sexual promise.

She breathed the words, "Couldn't wait," her voice husky and sure, "I knew we had to be." Her shyness had disappeared, and she exuded confidence, ready to share, ready to choose, ready to join him.

"I wasn't sure your eyes were telling the truth," Klyne said, "or how to find out."

"Pretty simple," she said, "Just ask."

"I will," he responds. Anticipation rolled in his voice. He spread his arms. "And, I am."

Exhaling lightly, Alicia blew sweet breath past his ear and knelt on the bed. The perfumed bath oil she had rubbed on her skin made her movements slick and fragrant. Her scent assaulted his nostrils, elevating his excitement, hauling him up to a new level of sensual awareness. One slick breast slid along his shoulder, her nipple hardening and tracing a delicate path over his chest, tickling the hairs. Klyne moaned.

He drew them together, his hands busy and his lips wet and searching consumed the passing moments. Passion built. Sexuality sparked, and silently, a ancient desire as old as mankind stretched toward the stars.

Her height and her slim lines had deceived Klyne. And to his pleasure, he discovered a radiating fullness in her body that spurred him harder, and faster, and deeper, and faster. She pulled him tighter, digging her fingernails into his hips. Simultaneously, each exploded, orgasmic, breath mingling and blood racing.

Then they rested, without speaking. Klyne pressed his ear to her breast and listened to her heartbeat. Slowly both bodies awakened and, continuing the lust-filled wrestling, each attacked the other again. After the second bout, Klyne and Alicia lay still, the glow of winter moonlight incandescent, the shadows accenting her womanly curves.

"Well," Alicia murmured, "that was pretty wonderful. Where'd you learn such neat tricks with that tongue?" She rolled over and sank into the shadows.

"Had some Recent lessons." His smile flickered when a dark-haired, dark-eyed beauty asleep in Los Angeles momentarily floated across his mind. The memory of Sarah Recent, her laughter and dimples skipped across the miles, spinning a tiny piece of guilt loose in his brain, briefly. Impulsively, he chased it away with thoughts of his re-discovered family, and one impetuous and exquisite family friend.

*

A week passed. Klyne awoke late in the morning and found a note indicating the girls had gone to work, Elizabeth was at the hospital, doctoring, and he would have to scavenge for himself, but the smell of coffee filled the air. Cup in one hand and a muffin in the other, Klyne relaxed on the deck, watched a tugboat chug across the sound, and planned his day. As usual, nothing in it.

His family welcomed his stay, but he could not remain forever. Inactivity and personal responsibility nagged at his thoughts. After the light breakfast, he ran around the block and forced the impending decisions out of his mind. Alternating sprints and jogs, he ran up and down the grade in a long circle, and approached the house from downhill.

He jogged up the flagstone walkway. A silver Porsche he had never seen before idled in the driveway. Alicia sat on the curb beside it. "Just looking for you Jake, let's take a ride. We don't get many days this nice, especially this time of year."

"Thought you went to work. You sure earned a day off pretty quick for such a new job."

"Quit! Didn't like it much, and have other things to do with my time. Come on, we need some dope."

Alicia stood in tight pants, belled at the calf, with her hips thrust forward and a bright halter-top supporting her breasts. She licked her lips, the wandering pink tongue even more erotic in the bright daylight. The midnight passions jumped back at Klyne, and the sexual restlessness throbbed in his crotch again, bulging against his shorts.

"Unless you've something else in mind," she teased. She ran her gaze up and down his body, the bright golden flecks dancing in her eyes. Her nipples popped erect and pushed at the snug top.

She grinned, embraced him for a few seconds, slipped a wet tongue into his mouth and snaked it around. Klyne guided her toward the house, but she would have none of it this time and pulled away, pushing him toward the Porsche. "Come on, let's go. Got things to do."

Alicia weaved in and out of traffic, and Klyne was lost almost immediately. Passing side streets, alleys with no names, and neighborhood parks, she sped into the heart of Seattle and arrived at a tall, crusty apartment building lacking its general maintenance. She parked on a narrow, one-way street lined with full trash barrels.

Two workers jumped off and on the rear bumper of an idling trash collecting truck and dumped cans into its bin, the driver moving periodically along the street. Ahead of the truck, a black and white mutt tipped a can over and its contents littered the driveway. Another fuzzy friend joined it, both dogs romping in the garbage and rooting for treats. Dodging bits and pieces of trash, Alicia Diamond and Jacoby Klyne walked across the street arm-in-arm.

Neglect, disrespect, musk and old dirt, the biting odors permeated stagnant air as they entered the building together, then an elevator, and Alicia punched five. The door slid open and Klyne followed Alicia down the hall where she knocked on a door with no number.

A bearded face peered out from a six-inch crack secured by a door chain that would stop no one who really wanted in. The chain rattled and the door swung open. Hurriedly, the man tucked his flowered shirt into his striped pants and then greeted them, a huge smile on his face.

"Alicia my love, enter please, and bring your pennies," the man said. "Your call has been answered." The man's overly large smile appeared false and ingratiating, and he wrinkled his forehead in disbelief as if everything he said was a lie and he knew it and his customers knew it, and each knew the other knew it but played the game anyway.

A very pregnant woman wearing a tattered housedress sat on the couch. Two small boys chased one another with plastic pistols, popping caps, both out-hollering the television set blaring in a corner.

The man offered his hand, "Riley White." His curiosity regarding Klyne showed on his face but he trusted Alicia. He turned his eyes back and forth between the two and finally grinned at Klyne.

He removed a large bag from a cabinet and they sat on the floor, surrounding an old wooden table. Riley White opened the bag, removed a gray plastic container, rolled a smoke, took a deep drag, and passed it over. All three shared smoke until the joint became a roach and each face gained a faraway, dreamy look.

Riley White broke the silence, "Panama Gold," he said, pushing lush green plants and lemon-tinted buds around in his palm. "Newest stuff, straight from the Canal Zone," proving he knew nothing about its source. The Canal Zone produces Panama Red with rust-colored tips. The man giggled, lost in euphoria. Not his first hit today it seemed.

"What do you think, and how much you want? And I can git as much as you need, pounds, or kilos, whatever. Got a new connection," he bragged. "Coke too if you need it.

Alicia responded, pure business, her voice unaffected by the drug. "Twelve. Think I'll just pass some of this around, it's been a little dry lately." She accepted twelve clear plastic baggies, each containing an ounce of leaves and buds, then handed across a fist full of wrinkled tens and twenties, a couple of crisp hundreds.

White carefully counted it out, pushes the greenbacks into his pocket. A smoky haze filled the room. The children sat quietly now, watching cartoons while their mother cooked chicken broth, the spicy odor mingling with the sweetly resinous smell of burnt marijuana.

"Probably be back Riley," Alicia said, heading out the door. "I'll give a call."

Stoned from high quality pot, Klyne and Alicia rode the elevator in silence and crossed the street again. The dogs had vanished, but the mess remained.

The silver sports car spun a circle in the alley and sped down the narrow roadway, passing a blue Dodge van idling at the curb, no driver visible behind its wheel.

Alicia glanced at the van then looked away. Klyne ignored it completely. As the Porsche rolled through the red but almost still orange light at the crossroads, the ever present Herbie Pitchman once again popped up in the front seat of that blue van and watched the Porsche run the red light. Pitchman slide away from the curb and spoke into his transmitter, accelerating down the alley in the opposite direction.

*

Alicia and Klyne drove the same route four times in the next two weeks. Each time she purchased the same quantity, explaining once to Klyne that when buying five at once, the sixth was free. The great American system of bulk purchase and free enterprise at work. She sold the original five, got her money back, and saved one for personal use. She kept Klyne stoned for days on end. He lived in a fuzzy daze filled with drugs and sex, but limited comprehension.

Typical Seattle, a light drizzle fell as followed Alicia across the street carrying another sack. "I sold the extras and made enough to buy dinner," Alicia said. "I'll be out of town for a few days. How about when I get back?"

"Sounds okay." He needed time away from Alicia anyway. He was living in a cloud. A thickening haze surrounded his life, while she pushed and pulled, directing his days, inducing a sexual euphoria that lead him head-first down a fleet, bouncing road that ended in a darkened hole contained in a mist-filled vacuum.

His mind simply strayed, fogged and confused, with no plans, no job, and no direction. Jacoby Klyne, civilian, experienced few straight thoughts since his Army discharge. Even those few were wildly turbulent. First Sarah, got him stoned nightly and nearly drowned him with her cheer-filled appetite for sex.

Then Alicia offered the same and more when he arrived in Seattle. He stayed high forever, accomplishing little, his lackluster lifestyle driven by an absence of motivation and cloudy euphoria. A little wine, a little sex, a light buzz, and a great sandwich, what more could an ex-Special Forces soldier want or need?

Weeks had passed and still he made no decisions. Sex and drugs occupied his time, nothing else, and he slacked off on his workouts. The violence he lived and survived the past six years finally withered away into the background.

Mental battles plagued him and he continuously argued with himself about his future but resolved nothing. His options remained few and unclear. He fought the fear that he had fallen into a vacuum that was slowly sucking him dry. The life he was experiencing now was nothing like the thoughts about his home that filled his mind before his discharge.

*

Parked diagonally across the street, a Seattle narcotics officer slouched behind the wheel of a dark blue sedan. He had observed Alicia and Klyne each time they arrived and each time they departed over the past couple of weeks.

The silver Porsche sped around the corner one final time and, as it disappeared, the officer spoke into his radio and then watched two Seattle Police cars ease in against the curb, lights flashing and sirens quiet. Four officers accompanied two narcotics detectives and the six men entered the building where Riley White lived. One officer punched the elevator button.

A white Buick passed the Porsche, heading the opposite direction. A tall, blond, athletic-looking man drove easily through the scant traffic, squeezing a black rubber ball in one fist and steering with the other. Henry Bates approached the site on time and casual. This situation was under control and the responsibility for it belongs elsewhere. Bates was simply observing, assuring proper performance and collecting information for his report. George Hallingforth had remained in Washington, as usual, this phase just peanuts in scope, nothing to get him excited yet.

During the ride home, Alicia remained passive. Bates drove past in the rented Buick and Klyne remained oblivious to the controlled events now affecting his future. Klyne relaxed, spinning into a stoned-out dream-world as the posh leather seat settled comfortably beneath him. The Porsche sprinted down the highways, darting through the lazy afternoon traffic.

Alicia braked into the brick driveway and turned to Klyne. She snatched an almost sisterly kiss, then a motherly hug. She pulled away. Then, just for a moment, emotion clouded her eyes. She looked out the window and then pulled him closer, hugged him again then pushed him out the door.

"Better hurry, Jake. I've gotta meet my cousin across town in less than an hour, family business. See you in a couple of days." Alicia sped away, but the Porsche neglected its route across town to meet the non-existent cousin, immediately plotting a course instead that ended at the airport.

Alicia Diamond carried one small bag, and collected a pre-paid ticket waiting at the check-in desk, flashed the security supervisor her badge and weapons permit, and caught the next plane east.

12

"Excellent report, Nikki." Hallingforth directed his words at the agent sitting across from him in his office. "But, does leave a few questions unanswered. Think he'll accompany you on the trip?"

"Yes, I'm sure of it. He's pretty confused, has no direction, no job. Young, easy to push. The general attitude concerning any military issue sets him off though, makes him moody. Hasn't quite come to grips with it yet."

"He voluntarily entered the mess in Asia, then in Central America, also Africa, and South America, spends years there and in other trouble spots, cleaning up the political mess, completing operations so dangerous the public can't even conceive of them, ops so classified no one knows about but us, and a few big-shots over at Defense. And then he gets called, collectively, at least by a portion of the public and the press once some of it leaks, an irresponsible cowboy for doing the best job he can."

The agent shook her head. "Can't blame him much. The violence really burned him out. That's all he saw. Sometimes other methods work, but he thinks political answers only push at the problem, never offer a solution."

"That's because he never saw other options work, the director said. "DOD only called his number when nothing viable remained. His view's a little distorted."

"Not his fault," Nikki Pepperton replied. "He might not be as easy to push into this as you think at this point, sir."

Special Agent Nichrico Pepperton, covert identity Alicia Diamond, current assignment Operation Crossbow, sat erect in an uncomfortable wooden chair in front of Hallingforth's desk. Dressed in the conservative fashions required of government employees, she waited and listened.

The subdued attire accented the exquisite Asian beauty she inherited from her mother and blended magnificently with genes from a different race supplied by her unknown father. Most guessed Native American, but her mother refused comment to everyone, including her only child. It's ancient history and nobody's business.

Nikki Pepperton watched George Hallingforth scan her brief, secure in the knowledge he would approve her course of action. He needed results and had no feelings one way or the other about how his agents accomplished his goals, as long as the agents followed orders and completed the missions.

Thirty years old, and with Special Forces for eight, Nikki Pepperton lived the word patience. The operation carried the highest top-secret classification and Hallingforth controlled it. Pepperton mentally questioned the unusual nature of this assignment, but kept it to herself. Not her business to question authority, most of the time anyway. She had alternate resources as well, but drew blanks on this operation for some reason.

"What happened to Ginny White?" Pepperton twisted in her seat.

Bates beat Pepperton back to Washington D.C. by an hour and stood at the window, watching a stiff wind blow snowflakes in thick swirls, filling the space between the buildings with white fluff. Nikki aimed her eyes and the question at Bates.

Hallingforth answered, "Neil Sanders is his real name. He took the name White when he started using Ginny's place. The drug boys in Seattle have had an eye on him for quite a few months. They delayed his arrest and worked with us. He's been hanging out with Ginny less than six months, and is not the father, by the way. Ginny delivered a daughter in county jail."

"Seattle dropped the charges against her – which were bullshit anyway – and the welfare department took her over, and her kids. We arranged it, well, helped arrange it anyway. She was in the system already, pretty much. Husband hit by a DUI runaway three years ago, died at the scene. She had nothing then, still struggling with it."

"Sanders will do some time, but the records won't track back to anything you did, Nikki. You won't even testify. He made a deal, gave up his connection and copped a plea. We caught two others with his info, each one a step higher up the chain. He'll get county jail, no prison. And, we get his main supplier, plus the next level up purely by accident. Perfect timing on a trap. Seattle police and the state cops took over. We'll continue surveillance and track the next level dealer as well. Henry's monitoring."

"Yup. Rat copped a plea alright," Bates interjected, chuckling. "Should've seen the look on his scraggly-ass face when I walked in during his interrogation. Dropped all those baggies he sold you on the table while he was busy denying everything. His chin dropped a foot, and I thought his moustache was gonna tie itself in a knot."

A crooked brown slit masquerading as a smile appeared in the middle of his face and Bates actually enjoyed his recollection for a few moments.

Pepperton turned back to Hallingforth, "That's okay for her, seems she needed a break or two. Two young kids, one on the way, and no husband." Her voice leaked bitterness, scorched itself with anger at the situation with Ginny.

Nikki reflected a moment, lost in her thoughts. "Well, three kids now. Trying. Working things out. Suckers for men like Sanders. Flash a fat green roll around and preen a lot, pretend he cares, even a little. Use Ginny up and toss her away."

Hallingforth paused momentarily and glanced out the window, then back at Pepperton. He tried, unsuccessfully, to ease the words out..."You seem to be getting just a little bit involved with Klyne, Nikki. We shouldn't let ..."

Pepperton cut him off. "No rule that says I must sleep with a target. No rule says I can't. My choice, alone." They let the silence work, staring at one another. A few seconds pass, seemed longer. "I just do my job, and sometimes I even enjoy it. But, that doesn't mean I'll compromise our mission."

"Ever!"

She jumped right out there this time, but Hallingforth ignored it and covered his annoyance, tolerating her insubordination, temporarily. His main concern, as always, was this operation, his operation, and he maintained some personal flexibility because of its unique nature. He had to leave her in place ... at least for awhile longer.

"Besides, I nearly took him out anyway. He wound up so tight that first night when I woke him he nearly leapt off the bed. No way I'd have fooled him if he'd jumped at me. Even half-asleep he's way too good. I'd have hurt him and he'd have known it. That would've ended the whole thing, right then."

"Okay ... okay ... take it easy Nikki. You've always done an excellent job. Let's keep this one on track a bit longer."

Hallingforth sat a moment longer, pondering. "Think you'll have any trouble if he does turn on you at some point?"

The fact that Nikki could not believe Hallingforth asked that particular question was apparent in her look. Her eyebrows arched in disbelief. "The target learned military martial arts, sir."

Hallingforth waited for her to continue, and when she did not, asked "So?"

"Special Forces and the military train and exercise physically, but even the best rarely identify with true martial arts."

Hallingforth raised his eyebrows as well. "And?"

Pepperton shrugged. "No insight, no soul, no presence. Strictly carnal."

"What about the games? Our guys beat the world three of the last five years."

She shot a glance at Bates then looked out the window in a private moment before returning her attention to the Director. Her expression remained distant.

"Juvenile at best, sir. Amusing diversions. Pubescent neophytes congratulate physical mediocrity, and then hand out trophies as if to illustrate its truth."

Bates spoke up. "Nikki beat them all here last year, George. Our champions, every one of them. But she didn't enter the games."

Pepperton nods, acknowledging his compliment. "One cannot just practice martial arts sir, one must become the arts. And, no sir, I'll have no trouble with the target."

Hallingforth stood and offered his hand. "Good then. You have a flight out first thing tomorrow morning. Henry will drive you to the airport and fill you in on the next stage. Relax this evening and give my regards to your mother and the congressman." He smiled tightly, but lines of strain creased his brow, and a tiny spasm jumped intermittently and erratically on his cheek.

Pepperton accepted his hand and shook it. "Good day sir. And I will." The door swung shut behind her.

"Well, Henry. It's just possible emotion may cloud her judgment this time. Maybe you should perform the execution yourself, so we don't chance a last minute failure."

"Nikki's a top agent, George. She'll complete any operation she's assigned. She'd never bail out unless she's in danger. And that's pretty unlikely, no matter how difficult the situation. She's the best we've got for this, George."

Hallingforth glanced out the window once more, lost in thought. After a moment his gaze returned to Bates. Beneath his eye, the nervous spasm now jumped continuously. Then his glare turned cold, and with a voice like ice he said, "I don't recall asking for an opinion on that Agent Bates. Set it up so you do it, not Nikki. Then we're sure."

"No sir!" Bates replied instantly. And then followed the Director's comment, "I mean yes, I will." He lifted his eyes and confusion crossed his face briefly, then immediately disappeared.

Hallingforth rubbed his fingertips into his temples and softened his glare. "Sorry Henry, you're probably right and I'm a bit tired. I'll think it over again and detail you in the morning. Report here early, before you meet Nikki."

*

Morning traffic crawled along the avenues, struggling with delays caused by nasty winter weather. The snow had stopped, but the plow trucks worked furiously, banking white powder against curbs and corners, burying numerous vehicles that remained overnight, an expensive oversight the owners will later regret.

Bates pushed the car door open in front of a two-story Victorian structure and Pepperton slid in. Her father retired from government service several years ago, but the congressman still consulted occasionally. The home was located in an exclusive complex on the northwest outskirts of Baltimore.

Nikki's mother was of Japanese descent and, born in Japan as well, Nikki never knew her biological father. Her mother never spoke of him but insisted that Nikki begin Aikido and Karate training at the age of four. Nikki added Chinese Kung Fu and Malaysian Silat over the years, perfecting her own unique blend of physical skills and spiritual discipline as she matured.

Partly for her own self-defense, her mother had cautioned, but of greater importance was the mental discipline and awareness taught by the Masters. Her mother stopped at nothing to further Nikki's education, and eventually met an American accountant, an auditor working for the United States government in a trade negotiation group. Although she grew to love Michael Pepperton, nothing helped her family situation more than marriage to a United States citizen who was eventually elected a congressman from Virginia. Three years after the two met, Monika and Michael married. On her tenth birthday, Michael Pepperton adopted Nikki before transferring his family stateside.

Monika Pepperton insisted that Nikki continue her training even while attending college and beyond, until her subsequent acceptance into Federal Special Services, a branch of the Intelligence Department.

Nikki began her career as a financial crimes investigator, but the agency quickly recognized her physical skills, and within six months she became the lead instructor in the self-defense division. Four years later she requested a Special Services field assignment, trained for undercover work, then, three years ago, transferred into ICD to work under Hallingforth.

She never married, engaged in a few brief affairs that never matured beyond a little fun and personal pleasure, and she was completely and absolutely dedicated to her work.

Her top-secret classification as an ICD Specialist 909 intelligence agent authorized Nichrico Pepperton to change orders in the field when she alone deemed it necessary, or if the success of an operation warranted it. No supervisor approval required. A Spec 909 certification authorized Nikki to take a human life when national security or the completion of an operation required it with no legal or agency blowback.

The Spec 909 classification was extremely difficult to earn, and Spec 909 Red Operations are never assigned without extensive reviews, followed by approvals from the agency director and the President. In a few short years, Nikki Pepperton climbed nearly to the pinnacle of an extremely elite unit in a completely covert high security division of the Department of Defense.

*

"Chunkie seems to be holding back a bit on this one, Henry," Nikki Pepperton said. "Is there something more I should know about this project?"

Henry Bates ignored the question and concentrated on his driving. "Wish this snow would quit. Just December, and I'm ready for spring."

She repeated her question. "Don't ignore it, Henry. Anything more, or what? Something's odd about this one. Everything's need-to-know only on this stuff, always, but we can usually figure it out."

"Nope, don't think so." Bates guarded his reply. "Actually, I'm just not sure." Maintaining his personal security blanket came first, even if it conflicted with other agents. "Don't know much more than you, Nikki."

"That's not good enough, Henry. You always hold something back." She pushed a little.

He concentrated on his driving, as if it were difficult in the slow morning glut. Except for the tires and traffic noise, the interior remained silent but for a few Bruce Abbott sax notes in the background. Bright morning sunshine painted the horizon in shades of red and purple, and reflected off the snow and into his eyes. Bates squinted and pulled the visor down, but still offered no response.

"That's not gonna be good enough, Henry." She pushed harder. "You know more than that." She stared across at him, daring him to deny her information that might affect the operation, or her safety. "You always know more."

"I have the authority to cancel any operation in the field if the circumstances warrant it, or, if I feel any operative is unreasonably endangered, including this one sitting right here in your front seat."

"Especially this one!" She adds, quoting almost verbatim from the Red Ops Specialist 909 manual. "And I'll find a reason if I need one."

Bates glared at Pepperton, his eyes as cold as death. She stared back, eye for eye. His face finally cracked a bit. Her sincerity and her obvious desire for information that might help protect her life motivated her questions. He recalled how difficult it is to conclude an operation successfully when an agent receives incomplete information. A similar situation once nearly cost him his life, a chit he still owed his investigating partner for that save several years ago. Interesting enough, his partner at the time was a Treasury operative named John Symington. Small world. Debt cancelled.

"Okay," he relented. "I'll tell you what I know, which isn't much."

"I'm all ears." She turned her full attention toward him.

Bates looked at her ears, then at the rest of her. His lips tipped up at the ends, just barely. "No you're not."

The corners of her mouth wiggled back at him, a bit of history mutely shared. Her ears were not all of her, and not even close to the best parts. His memories toyed with his mind for a moment. Bates recalled the uneasiness he experienced when he attempted an affair with her years ago when Nikki entered the ICD component. The only affair Bates contemplated in sixteen years of marriage, and Bates dearly loved his wife. But, the incredibly beautiful and exquisitely sensual Nikki Pepperton expressed absolutely no interest when he dropped a few discrete advances her way and the relationship blossomed into a solid friendship instead.

"Two years ago Chunkie began investigating a heavy-duty drug smuggling operation that originated in Colombia and pushed large-volume cocaine and marijuana through the west coast cities, California mostly, and Oregon. Seemed pretty casual at first, we just gathered standard information, coordinating and updating every month or so. No special security on the files."

"About six months ago, the file disappeared, at least from our Central Index, and the computer shows no record. Nothing. Not even a disposal chit. And we're the only agents that have access - the 909 group. That's not many people, and most are in the field, and not even here often."

"Chunkie removed everything and took personal control, under a Class One Presidential Order according to him. That's what he told me anyway, finally. Didn't concern me much at the time. You know as well as I that he can control any and every operation anyone sends over and not even work up a sweat. He's about as heads-up as they come in this line of work. Except for the 909 stuff, the rest is just information coordination and exchange anyway. Computers can damn near do it now without any help."

Bates glanced at Pepperton. Still not enough he realized.

"Chunkie began his own computer runs a couple of months ago. Tried to follow him in once, but he hid his access, printed the search, deleted everything, and carried hard copy around in his briefcase, always locked."

Bates peeked at her again, then back at the traffic. "I can always unlock it and take a peek if things get hairy, but haven't cared enough about it to this point. No sense."

"That's not much, Henry." No push this time.

He offered her a little bit more anyway, cutting off her challenge. "According to Chunkie, the President's concerned about a large amount of drug traffic entering northern California, but the sellers disappear after the sale. No one seems to know who they are, or where they come from. He's worried the money funds internal terrorism."

"Best word, they originate in South America and one agent, John Symington, was executed and butchered in Colombia two months ago working this op. Funny thing,

George was really pissed, not because Symington got killed but because it stalled the operation."

The silence enveloped them again. Pepperton stared out the window, totally absorbed by the information, or maybe by the lack of it. As he approached the departure gates, Bates slipped into a spot by the curb.

"Well, what do you think Nikki?"

"John Symington is ... was ... an ex-agent, a mercenary for sale to the highest bidder. Had nothing left after Defense kicked him out.   Stretch Bennett fired him when he compromised an operation. Symington fell in love with Benishe Murann, code name Anita Morris, a deep cover agent from the Middle East. Didn't believe she was an agent and wouldn't kill her. Wouldn't even try to turn her.

"He was wrong. She was, and still is. Bennett just feeds her fodder occasionally, keeps track of her that way just in case. After that one, she's no use anymore. John should have run away with her and both found a happy island somewhere for all the good each did the service units once that came out. Two of them were last to figure it out, everyone knew all about both sides of that op before John and Anita came up for air the first time."

"According to sit-reps, she enjoyed it a lot, even while burning him for classified info. He still believes it was another agent that stiffed him... well, he either knew or didn't know, wherever he landed ... no matter now, not for him anyway. She's still around, but gone soft. No one trusts her today, even though she did her job completely even while carrying his torch." Nikki stared out the window during her entire monologue.

"Like I said Nikki, the files are unavailable. DEA may have hired a contract. It's not unusual, especially in foreign drug cases where the agent has no back-up."

Bates wrinkled his forehead in surprise at her knowledge of the case history. Symington received a 'no-return' discharge three years before Nikki transferred into ICD. Although that just meant Symington worked private contracts instead, and performed the same operations but for more money, a lot more money, but he took more risks too.

"I can set a trap. Next time Chunkie runs a program I'll pass anything that affects your operation. That's the best I can do, Nikki. You're briefed on the next phase, and as near as we can tell you're finished anyway after one more drug buy and the execution anyway." Bates stared straight ahead.

Both agents sat a moment, the engine purring softly, a perfect idle. Henry Bates watched several planes lift-off, ignoring Pepperton. Nikki suddenly inhaled the clean leathery smell of his new BMW 128i coupe. His information was incomplete, the operational information also incomplete. Pepperton had no recourse but to continue or reject the operation, and she knew no good reason to reject it, and it would come back hard on her if she cancelled.

"Guess I don't like anyone taken out unless I know the reason, especially a civilian." Nikki said.

"We depend on a timely completion of all assignments, Agent Pepperton, without question." His statement almost a demand, Bates finally glanced over at her. "You set."

"Yes," skipped out, her lips clipping the word off. Still uncomfortable with her briefing and the lack of information, Pepperton pushed the door open and slid out. Her short blue skirt hiked up, exposing shapely legs and thighs.

His discipline broke and Bates surrendered without a fight. A few wildly erotic possibilities flicked across his mind, and he allowed himself a brief mental pleasure, then gathered his thoughts, straightened his suit and shifted the BMW into gear.

"Keep me up-to-date, Henry," she said, "and thanks for the ride." She leaned back across the seat and kissed his cheek. "And for the info."

Her delicate scent floated near his face, temporarily drowning the new leather smell and immediately intoxicating Bates. His mental discipline broke once more as he watched erotic hips covered with light blue silk carry Nikki toward the airport entrance. The fantasy played itself out this time, and Bates actually grinned then eased out into the traffic.

Henry Bates knew little more than Pepperton, but always felt completely confident with Hallingforth and his leadership. The director instructed him to pass Pepperton as little information as she would accept, and he always exhibited an unwavering loyalty in his relationship with Hallingforth, forever remembering that his immediate superior - 'Knows all available information about each and every operation and consistently performs in a professional manner'.

*

Still impeccably dressed in expensive but conservative browns, Bates shut the front entry to his home and hopped up the stairway to his second floor master suite where he carefully hung up his office attire and pulled on a raggedy but comfortable pair of boot-cut Levi's and an old Boston College sweatshirt with its sleeves torn-off.

The agent poured a double shot of Courvoisier into a Yogi Bear glass, one of a set his boys gave him as a birthday gift years ago. His wife still kids him about the hard-core secret agent drinking cognac out of a Yogi glass, but he just laughs with her and continues loving his boys, the gift, and the emotion it carries with it.

Bates dropped in two ice cubes, and settled into his favorite chair, reflecting on his personal background. His large and impressive combination den and gun room contained many Old West collectibles he no longer used in his work.

Other agents earn good pay for wet work whenever necessary. No one has challenged his marksmanship in years, but he still practiced frequently and in earnest, caressing and testing the old polished weapons every chance he got.

His collection boasts of three British muskets manufactured before the pilgrims settled America, and his favorite, an 1857 Colt .44 pistol once owned by Wyatt Earp, but he takes great pride in every single piece and remains constantly on the alert for new additions. A multitude of glass-front display cabinets and lacquered gun racks decorate the walls in his study.

A special agent for eighteen years and Hallingforth's assistant director for more than twelve, he helped design and implement the ICD program. An excellent bodyguard, and an accomplished pilot, Bates also has an extensive background in computers. The ICD Director travels unscheduled, and often. And ever evolving computer technology supports the backbone of every solid intelligence network.

Bates sipped cognac and opened a gun magazine that arrived in the mail today.

*

Just before sunrise, Bates parked near the basement entrance. He always believed that his superiors had far greater knowledge than he, more of a 'big picture' mentality, and that valid reasoning stood behind every assignment the director sends into the field. He carried the classification of a Spec 909 agent as well, and obeyed orders with absolute confidence and complete loyalty. That's what he was, a Specialist 909 Agent, and that's what he did. Each time. Every time.

Well ... almost complete loyalty, he backed himself up a moment. He felt just a little bit uncomfortable with the fact that Chunkie failed to trust him completely on this one after all the successful years in service together.

Bates already decided to set a trap in the main computer, just to see what it caught, but was unsure whether he'd share any information he stole with Pepperton. He'd wait, and see what his trap revealed first. Patience was definitely prudent in this line of work.

Before reporting to Hallingforth, Bates slid his key-card into the slot, entered the basement, quickly logged on, and set up an access program. He logged out fifteen minutes later and then punched two keys that erased all evidence of his entry. He caught the elevator to the tenth floor. After meeting again briefly with Hallingforth, Bates grabbed a taxi to the airport and boarded his flight to San Francisco, two hours behind Nikki Pepperton on her return flight bound for Seattle.

13

Resuming her operational character, Alicia Diamond parked behind the Volvo and climbed out of her Porsche. She filled a shimmering, body-length gown that turned heads every time she wore it. Firm and wonderfully rounded, her breasts pushed provocatively against the silky fabric of a low-cut neckline. A multi-colored knit wrap clung to her shoulders, light protection against a chilling breeze rolling in off the bay. A bright orange sunset hid behind puffy gray clouds that gathered above a darkening skyline.

"Come on, Jake," she yelled. "We're gonna get soaked if you don't get a move on."

Klyne sprinted down the walkway and wrapped his arm around her waist. They raced together and jumped into the Porsche as the first fat raindrops splashed down wet and heavy. The tires skidded on the slick blacktop as the car slid out of the driveway and turned toward Seattle.

"Seafood here's supposed to be the best in the city," Alicia said, switching off the ignition. The engine purred to a stop. They climbed out and ran for the entrance. Rain fell heavily now, thunder cracked overhead and thick clouds glowed brightly each time lightning sparked. The air smelled clean and fresh, sea breeze and salt mingled with the sweet fragrance of stormy weather.

*

Klyne sipped a glass of California Chardonnay and gazed across a linen table cloth littered with the remains of an excellent dinner. Relaxed and content, he enjoyed the company, but Alicia remained distant during the meal. She pushed a piece of grilled swordfish around on her plate. Her soft brown eyes glanced up, catching an unusual serenity in Klyne.

"So, what are your plans? You've been here a little over a month."

"Don't know yet. Time just flies by lately. Resting, I guess. Winding down the stress after six years takes a little time."

She forked the last morsel into her mouth and spoke around it. "Let's make some." She swallowed, her eyes turn hard and cold, and she said, "Dope."

The statement roused Klyne and his eyes focused but he said nothing, sipping his wine again.

"That's what bought the Porsche, my clothes, and pays my rent." She paused, waiting for his reaction. Nothing, No response. He straightened in his chair, but remained silent.

"My father was not a race driver, and didn't die on a wall at Daytona and leave me a large life policy. I made that part up." A few seconds passed. "Drug money buys everything. This dinner, the wine, my vacation trips, everything. I make a ton of money, and hired the best protection. Paid him too well and he recently found a sweet young thing that liked his money more than him probably, but convinced him to move her back to Puerto Rico, her birthplace. Of course, he tagged along with her, temporarily. He's back after a month, alone, but I can't trust him anymore."

Klyne sat up then and gave her his full attention. "So, what's that mean to me? And what do you mean 'protection'. Protection from what, and how?" His tranquil mood disappeared. Alicia changed significantly in the last four days, and seemed quite unlike the woman he had grown to know these past few weeks.

"You have to make some plans, you know. Your father's trust won't last forever, especially if you can't supplement it with some extra cash." Ever so slowly, the coldness dissolved and her beautiful brown eyes glowed. The agent flicked a glance across the table, sucking Klyne in.

"Can't stay with your sister forever."

Her words sat awhile, forcing his thoughts. She stared, her eyes cut into his, gave him no chance to think, exactly what she wanted.

Neither spoke while the waiter served coffee then departed with a smile both ignored. Klyne gazed around the room. The casual moment disintegrated and he returned to business, locked on her eyes again.

"Riley White got busted, and I know most of his people. With enough dope, we can both live the easy life. Who wants to work in a bullshit office anyway?" The smile slid back onto her face. "You?" Her tinkling laughter broke free, and set her new mood. "Not hardly."

"And certainly not me! I hated that disgusting bank job with your sister, and that repulsive prick Randolph Atkins ...

'Bring me coffee Alicia, deliver these papers Alicia, could you take this mail out immediately Alicia, and bring our new mail in' ... just so he could feast his beady black eyes on my rear-end while I served his skinny, pot-bellied ass."

Her comical display of displaced temper made them both laugh. "Seems he always had at least one hand under his desk whenever I walked in his office, too."

"Only reason I did it was to meet a contact there that 'supposedly' bought lots of drugs for his buddies. Not happening. False lead." She'd kicked up the thread of her thoughts, reeling him in slowly.

"She's my niece. Elizabeth's my sister, half-sister anyway. Thought we had this discussion once. You and Rachel were born on the same day, which makes you, ancient one, exactly two months older than me." His smile lit up the space between them. "Remember."

"I need your help, Jake. I have no problem selling, just worry about buying a large quantity, alone, with no man to back me up." The toughest, most resourceful Spec 909 agent in the entire United States looked down at her plate, carefully hiding the lie.

"Don't know. I'll think about it." Klyne purchased drugs and consumed plenty and in a variety numerous times the past six years. Except for one trip with Major Perkins, never involved himself in the dealing end. Smoking bent the law a bit, but that never bothered him much. Dealing was something different, and something he might not get away with quite as easily, even with any influence his friend Dodds brings to the table.

"Can't, no time, I need to know now. There's a buy in two days and I'm gonna do it. I've got twenty thousand cash, and we can double it in a month."

She pushed him harder now. "I'm just afraid, carrying that much money, alone, without help." The corners of her mouth curled upward a bit, but gave nothing away. She looked down at her plate again, once again skillfully hiding her lies.

Klyne stared past her shoulder at a framed photograph hanging beside the kitchen entrance. A stallion chased four mares, multi-colored manes and tails flaring behind each horse, his personal harem. Klyne focused on a scene far beyond that image. His eyes glazed over, unfocused, peering into his personal history, seeking a clue, some direction, an experience, struggling with his thoughts, making a decision. A muddled haze, a smokescreen, silky white cloudiness floated in his mental eye. His concentration finally split the fog and Klyne stared into his recent past.

The intended political protectors, the world freedom fighters, clustered beneath bushes and trees, hidden, smoking pot, inhaling cocaine, escaping the harsh reality of warfare carefully labeled police action, but deadly battles just the same, bloody and disabling. Officers and enlisted wore starched, spotless uniforms or filthy, march-worn fatigues and sold maxi-packs of dusty vegetation, or smaller packets of white powder, or brown, depending on the need. Each seller owned one minor rung on a very tall ladder, and fed a fat illegal bank account while pretending ignorance. Military Police hawked clear packages, metal tins, or individual highs while guarding a soldier's back. The same MP's, later, off duty, escaped into another lonely and personal drug-induced oblivion, dismantling the gruesome fears of every day police actions and military war zones.

A combat vehicle carrying Major Viceroy Perkins streaked along the muddy and rutted roadway. The jeep skidded sideways, stopping before the last thatched hut in a pastoral village. The major leaped out, his eyes alert, his head swiveling, his pockets bulging with American dollars. The line officer splashed through puddles and potholes along a worn pathway and disappeared into a grass shanty.

One village leader sitting on a bench alongside the hut rose and ambled after him.

Klyne continued along the slushy ruts, spun the jeep around and parked beyond the clearing, idling. Protected from airborne observation by a thick, bushy canopy, Klyne remained watchful while the major conducted clandestine business with local natives on the wrong side of an off-limits boundary. An imaginary No-Man's-Land.

The major reappeared, carrying a sack in each hand. Klyne accelerated as soon as the major exited the hut, the jeep continuously slipping and sliding through the sticky red muck. Klyne slowed, collected the major and his booty, and then quickly fishtailed away.

The old man returned to his perch beside two elders, sitting once again in ritual sequence. White wispy beards curled in the warm, afternoon breeze, the wooden bench worn thin but comfortable beneath each. All three covered their mouths, ancient brown fingers hiding laughter aimed at crazy American soldiers who sped around filled with fright and spent a fortune buying weeds they could easily grow themselves.

"We should never travel to America if it makes you nuts," one elder whispered, and all three cackled again, hiding mirth-filled chuckles behind vintage paws and nodding gently in profound agreement.

One scene faded, a greenish haze floated before his eyes. Another scene emerged. Inspector Jimmy Dodds, a drug enforcement police officer, secretly bought drugs and smoked with trusted friends in his own home. And Commander Parr, joking about a social organization that allowed small-time but still illegal activities to go unpunished because constituents refused to obey laws they did not believe in, and it was too expensive and time-consuming to enforce them.

A spindly character materialized, superimposed over the scene: An aged politician stood behind a podium, gesturing and speaking weakly. A sparse group of lawmakers fidgeted in their seats ... "Well ... ah ... well .. .ah ...."

The politician shook his grizzled head, feinting disbelief ... "You mean to tell me that there are citizens out there that continue to do drugs, even though we've passed laws against it ... and we don't force them to stop because we can't afford it. Well, ah, then, perhaps we better modify the laws again quickly before we begin to look foolish, or raise more tax money instead and hire more police." He shook his head again and bent toward his assistant and whispered. "Tell me what the voters want."

The scene dissolved. Klyne blinked, but remained silent.

"Won't change our relationship, you know. Just need to know now, I'm leaving tomorrow. Need someone else if you don't go with me." She held her breath.

Klyne struggled with his future.

"Make up your mind Jake, so we can split." Motionless she sat, a sleek predator stalking her unsuspecting prey, then pounced, absolutely certain of her prize. "Just want to get you home so I can jump your bones. It's been four days, you know."

Golden flecks danced in her eyes once more, teasing. A seductive smile eased across her face and his passion-filled memories surfaced, threatening his right to choose.

His insatiable woman returned. His blue eyes wandered, tracking the sleek dark hair across her bare shoulders, paused momentarily and enjoyed the rise and fall of breasts encased snug and comfortable in shiny green silk,. Her nipples protruded slightly, tiny buttons unavoidably accented by the tight green fabric. Klyne inspected the beautiful woman before him, unsure how much he cared.

Young and confused, a novice at loving and mystified about his feelings for the second woman in his life he'd ever made love with and not paid first. His eyes wandered again, pausing at a small indentation in her throat, a hollow pocket gently pulsing in harmony with her heartbeat.

Alicia was here. Sarah was not. And Jacoby Klyne didn't stand a chance.

"Sounds okay, I guess. Both. I mean going with you, and going home after." He grinned and nodded for the check. Sucked into the plot now, Klyne made a decision without a choice, and changed his life. Forever.

"I mean, you're right, it's been four days."

14

Brand new Goodyears hummed beneath the silver Porsche speeding south along the rocky western coastline. Oblivious, Nikki Pepperton ignored the local speed laws and kept the powerful engine working hard. Both riders remained mute for much of the drive. The rain slowed and stopped as the Porsche crossed the southern Oregon border and entered northern California.

Unseasonably warm sunshine burned away the morning fog and crisp, clean air streamed in through the open windows. Towering pines and spreading firs lined the highway and stretched toward the wispy clouds. Ancient cedars spilled sweet, invigorating scents into the swirling breeze and, having shed the summer leaves, stately oaks dotted the windswept canyons and rested, silently embracing the winter chill.

Snowcapped and shining, lofty mountains spread along the distant horizon, frosty and shadowed where jagged peaks rose above the tree line. Occasionally, a grassy meadow split by a cool, clear stream accented the thick forests. Vanishing in the distance, a winding black ribbon wandered the rolling hills and sloping valleys, followed obediently by a white stripe centerline and a racing silver Porsche breaking the speed limit.

"Got about a hundred miles to go and our meeting's set for noon tomorrow. May as well eat somewhere, and find a room. We can cruise in tomorrow morning some time. I'm getting a bit cramped," Alicia said.

After traveling eight hundred miles at eighty plus, tight muscles were no surprise. Gravel crunched beneath the tires as the Porsche slid into a lot and parked beside a brightly lit sign that bragged of home cooking and clean beds. Tiny cabins nested amongst the trees. She dropped her forehead down on her arms, resting it on the steering wheel, rotating her shoulders, an elongated groan escaping.

*

Klyne stretched out on the bed, watching the news. Alicia dropped her towel and crawled in beside him under the covers. He whispered past her ear, "Long drive, you must be tired, and sore."

He slid his fingers and thumbs along her smooth, velvety skin, massaging, stroking, up and down her back, patient and graceful, his casual strength rubbed and relaxed her, easing the cramps. Klyne inhaled deeply. No manufactured essence tarnished her perfection, her womanly fragrance, the clean scent of a freshly showered lover. His sexual excitement reached a new plateau for an odd reason. She had never come to him unscented. He slid his hand along her rib and cupped a breast. Her nipple sprang erect, pulsing in his palm.

Gently, she pushed his hand away. "I'm a bit tired, and not much in the mood," denying him sex for the first time in the brief but physically intense relationship.

He rolled on his back and faced the ceiling, then chuckled. "Well then, what should I do with this?" His erection poked at the blanket.

"You don't want to know." Her tone rang true this time and her voice stung. The bump under the blanket wilted immediately.

A tear built in her eye, but she brushed it away. She obeyed operational orders, explicitly, but against her will and better judgment, she had begun caring for the young man she was manipulating, and suddenly perceived him childlike, innocent and lost, wandering untutored among the blistering hazards of an unforgiving world.

And he'll be gone tomorrow.

*

After discarding her cover identity overnight, Agent Pepperton awakened early, forced herself back into character, and grabbed her bag. "Let's get on the road."

The Porsche traveled south along the scenic coastline. "Sorry about last night, okay? This is business and makes me a little uptight," she said. A hint of sadness softened her voice.

Klyne remained wordless. The Porsche climbed one final rise and broached a hilltop. Below, the Pacific seashore spread before them, the craggy rock-lined beaches, and Bolinas, a coastal town north of San Francisco. An hour early for her meeting, she parked in a dirt cutout and climbed out, stuck her phone on her right ear. After a short conversation, she shut the phone, consulted a map, and then headed back up Highway One.

Eight miles out, she entered a county road, drove west nearly to the beach, and turned left twice, almost in a circle. Pebbles kicked up beneath the fenders as she slowed and turned once more onto another gravel road, passing beneath a weather-beaten sign that claimed Moonshine Acres had the best ocean-view home sites available.

"Wonder if you drink it, or it lights the beach."

"More romantic if it lights the beach," she replied, but did not smile, nor touch him, nor act the least bit romantic. The road circled past beach homes and vacant lots. Windblown trees, stunted bushes, grass and weeds randomly dotted the terrain. Her brakes lit up. She idled across the street from the target residence and said, "That's it there, number eighty-eight."

Weathering itself gray, the redwood tri-level sat deep on the lot, extended over an embankment, nearly groaned in disrepair, and appeared deserted but for a thin wisp of smoke drifting skyward from a rock chimney. An ancient green pick-up truck with two flat tires and its windows broken sat in the driveway beside a new blue van, its glass darkly shaded.

Agent Nikki Pepperton switched off the engine and glanced at her watch. Both examined the building, then climbed out and started across the road, leaving shallow footprints and mini dust swirls following in the dirt. Salt air, dry brush, and winter foliage, each smell hung on the sea breeze independently but melded into an invigorating freshness.

"Remember, stay left, always to my left." Aggressive and alert in her role, she said, "You're working now. Earn your money."

Aged salt and sunshine stained the oak entry door that contained one peephole, but no window. Pepperton donned her Alicia Diamond persona once more, and rapped twice, sharply. The door swung open revealing a short, swarthy individual. His disheveled appearance hinted that he might have been born in a barn, or under a dock.

The man flashed a smile that lit up his face. Thick lips surrounded two gold teeth and completely altered his appearance. Now, he resembled a happy field hand. Field-hand bowed and backed away, toting his golden smile. Nodding his head, he waved them in, but spoke no words.

"Alicia, my dear." A man neatly dressed in a tailored suit rose out of his chair and offered his hand. "Allow me to introduce myself, Enrique Martinez," he said, his voice cultured and refined, but containing the barest trace of an indefinable accent. Flashing a line of even white teeth, he brushed his lips across the back of her hand. "Riley White did not nearly do you justice."

Unmistakably obsequious, his smile turned each corner of a neatly clipped moustache upward and everything about the man rang false and overdone, but powerful and accustomed to giving orders. Almost military in his bearing - the top dog showed his teeth.

Klyne moved with Alicia, but remained standing slightly to her left, as ordered. Everyone ignored bodyguard introductions, and no one examined credentials, business at face value in this makeshift office on the beach.

Klyne quickly evaluated the only other person in the room, a compact athlete wearing a dark suit and standing beside the fireplace. He leaned over and tossed another log on the fire then returned to his post. The bulge beneath his left armpit gave clue to his purpose. The man leaned his back against the wall, but his eyes remained alert. Beside him, glass doors opened onto a deck that overlooked the sparkling Pacific Ocean.

Martinez glanced at the security man who suddenly coughed into his fist and shook himself erect but said nothing. The man's dark suit remained buttoned partway.

Klyne had no doubt he could pin that muscular throat to the wall before the bodyguard unbuttoned the coat and accessed his pistol. The jeweled dagger rested in a beaded leather sheath behind his right shoulder, the only weapon he carried save his quick hands and quicker feet. Klyne gathered confidence from its weight.

Alicia Diamond dropped her hand when Enrique Martinez released it. He took her arm, guiding her, pointing at an antique stuffed chair with intricately carved arms and legs. "Be seated, please. Allow me to serve refreshments."

His fawning behavior clearly translucent, he was ready to make a sale. "Coffee, tea, or something stronger, brandy perhaps?" As moldable as wet clay, he pasted a smile across his handsome but devious face, and his eyes flattened, calculating, reading his audience. "Or, would you prefer business immediately?"

Martinez strutted around the couch and removed a tarp, exposing a pile of blocks. Wrapped in ivory butcher paper and stacked neatly in the corner by the fireplace, each piece weighed exactly one kilo. "One hundred kilos, pure Colombian cocaine, the best quality available anywhere in the world." Martinez spoke matter-of-factly and dropped the tarp.

The federal agent glanced at her watch. "Yes, just coffee's fine, black. Colombian, I presume."

Martinez laughed out loud. "But, of course. Only the best for my associates." He snapped his slim, manicured fingers and Field-hand waddled quickly into the kitchen, obviously trained for more than plant, harvest, and opening doors. Martinez sauntered over and sat on the couch.

"Riley White spoke quite highly of you. Riley's not much of a businessman, but we have a distant family connection." He offered a 'what-can-you-do' shrug. "We generally engage in more substantial transactions, and even this one is a bit smaller than normal, but, well, Riley begged." Martinez shrugged again. "I'm certain we can do more in the future. Once we get to know each other a little better."

Martinez grinned again at the beautiful woman he believed he was charming into his future. "I can assure you our product is consistent, high quality, and available in any amount you desire."

The fawning salesman guise continued, "We also grow our own high quality marijuana as well, if you ever have that need. I brought a few samples of our best buds as well."

"You can take that with you. Consider it an international gift." He nodded toward a small canvas bag in a corner of the room.

Field-hand served coffee and retreated, carrying his own cup to a corner seat, away from the action. Alicia sipped hers and glanced at her watch.

"Perhaps you'll accept an invitation to my plantation in Colombia. The growing operation is quite extensive, and our town is civilized, cultured, and only occasionally barbaric, but never discourteous, nor ungracious, and actually quite beautiful." Martinez couldn't tear his eyes from the woman he thought he would sell now and bed later.

He already set her in his crown, another jewel, another sexual adventure. Wealth and power brought many women into his life and most easily available, eager participants in his grand lifestyle. He wears the suave seductive personality on his sleeve. A supremely egotistical perception of himself declares all women his personal property. The man harbored numerous perverse and self-serving personalities, donning them easily and quickly as his individual desires or needs arose.

"Many wild and scenic areas in Colombia are exquisitely romantic and exciting in the right company," he quietly finished, the prediction of another conquest inherent in his smug, self-assured smile.

Alicia Diamond glanced at her wrist again and vanished. In her place, Special Agent Nichrico Pepperton prepared for action. "Well," she said, and set her cup on the floor, "maybe we should get down to business." She pulled herself up out of her seat.

The drug-dealer dropped his smile, replacing it with a grimace. Unwilling to give up quite so easily, Enrique Martinez implores her again. "Perhaps we might discuss travel arrangements another time." Assuming he need only play his scene a bit longer to seduce Alicia, he rose with her, also ready for business.

Martinez turned away and Agent Pepperton eased over and stood near Klyne. The bodyguard stiffened slightly in response to a movement he suddenly perceived on the deck. Two county sheriffs, wearing chaps, vests, and helmets, and carrying short-barrel shotguns, raced full-stride toward the patio windows.

The glass shattered before the charging sheriffs and Klyne reacted quickly as an offbeat thought blinked across his mind...'*that huge pile of dope stacked in the corner will barely fit in the trunk ... And, he had never seen the money*'.

Klyne reached for the dagger, but Nikki grabbed his arm, applying steady pressure from behind. Confusion emerged inside his brain for a split-second, but his field training and instinct directed his actions and Klyne initiated resistance and defense tactics immediately, almost instinctively no thought involved. He pushed right and twisted, forcing a counter-move, but Nikki kept him turning, increasing the pressure. Rotating him against his will and without much effort, she brought Klyne around face to face.

His eyes popped wide-open and a shock blew through his body as Special Agent Nichrico Pepperton delivered a punch over his heart, freezing him in his tracks, then turned him sideways, and hammered a short palm chop beneath his ear.

Klyne dropped unconscious, and as he fell, a shotgun blast splintered the front door and another sheriff entered behind it. The bodyguard reached for his weapon and, just as it cleared his jacket, his hand and the gun disappeared. Bone and blood sprayed the wall, and the Sig Sauer P226 skittered across the floor.

"That's what you get for body-guarding with a buttoned jacket," admonished the sheriff, cocking the second barrel of his shotgun, "asshole," characteristically completing the sentence.

Enrique Martinez flipped a gold police badge out of his jacket and hung it on its pocket. He drew a pistol out from behind his back and fired one round into the ceiling. He screamed the last complete sentence of his life, "International Police! You're all under arrest!"

Slowly, his head swiveled, surprise widened his eyes, and his mouth fell open. Martinez stared at the front door, blown inward and swinging on one hinge, and the man that stepped through it.

"Riley White … ?" Martinez began his question, but never finished.

With almost reckless indifference, Henry Bates pulled the trigger, twice. The first shot punctured the gold badge and blew it off the breast pocket. The second bullet exactly followed the first and entered the heart behind it. The badge flew across the room, clinked off the bricks, then dropped and rolled against the hearth.

The powerful slugs staggered Martinez. He tipped back against the wall splattered with his own blood. He struggled, forcing his eyes open with every ounce of his remaining strength, while seeking answers with every flicker of his remaining thought.

Never for one instant failing to believe he would one day play host to Alicia Diamond, he cocked a strained smile at her, then slowly toppled over, resisting all the way. He lay in a disjointed pile on the floor, unable to pull the trigger again on the pistol clutched loosely in his fist. Blood stained his perfectly tailored tan jacket, and urine stained his perfectly tailored tan slacks. His eyes fluttered, and slowly clouded over and, finally, Martinez stared sightless at an empty nest hanging from a dry old branch stapled above the mantel. The fire sparked once, spitting its dying embers against the rusting screen.

Bates holstered his hand gun. A single tiny crack and three carved notches marred an otherwise perfectly smooth walnut grip, but he forgave those imperfections when he bought the original Colt .44 Walker Revolver manufactured in 1857 complete with authenticating documents sixteen years ago at a private auction in Fort Worth, Texas.

15

Henry Bates joined three sheriffs standing in the room discussing the arrest. The men spoke in low tones, and watched several officers prowl the grounds outside. Nikki Pepperton stood quietly, while Bates snapped one handcuff on her wrist and connected the other half to his own.

A burley sheriff rolled Klyne over onto his chest and handcuffed his hands behind his back, then unbuckled the dagger in its sheath and held it out.

Bates accepted the weapon and spoke, but kept glancing at Klyne. Watching the man as he lay unconscious, making sure Klyne did not open his eyes and recognize Bates, a slight risk Bates was willing to conclude this operation successfully. After all, he could always lie later, or disappear.

"This woman is my prisoner. The home office will contact you later today, but I'll take her with me now and drive her vehicle."

He tugged the cuffs, dragging Pepperton toward the door. "Thanks again for your help, Sheriff. I'll note your cooperation in my report." Bates glanced once more at Klyne then he led Nikki Pepperton through what remained of the front door.

Two EMT's rolled a stretcher in behind as both agents stepped off the front porch. A shiny black hearse labeled Marin County Coroner idled in the road.

*

Klyne awakened slowly, groggy. A stale, musty smell rose off the rug beneath his cheek. He rolled over and tried to sit up, but discovered handcuffs bracketing his wrists. Shattered glass fragments and wood splinters littered the floor, and his dagger was missing. He pushed himself up and shook his head. An uncomfortable ache banged behind his right ear and his chest felt constricted where Alicia punched him above the heart.

His nostrils twitched. A familiar odor hung in the air. Blood smelled exactly like a new copper penny and at the scent of it memories of violence and death flooded his mind, a different world somehow connected. Klyne shook his head again and focused, swung his feet in an arc, straightening up as best he could, and examined the situation.

The medic propped the bodyguard against the wall, and wrapped his butchered wrist. In obvious agony, squeezing his eyes shut, the man clenched his teeth and moaned. The man suddenly emptied his stomach onto the floor and all over his pants.

The medic stuck a needle into the bodyguard's thigh and injected a clear liquid into the muscle. The moaning stopped and the bodyguard's eyes rolled open, revealing a glazed stare.

A second medic kneeled beside Martinez, probed under his chin and along his throat but, appeared to find no pulse. The man looked at the first medic, raised his eyebrows and lifted his shoulders, shook his head. The medic then pulled a rubber sheet over Martinez's body, covering it completely. The first medic stepped through the shattered glass door onto the deck and lit a cigarette, blew smoke into the sea breeze, his job complete for the moment.

Field-hand sat in silence, handcuffed to the stuffed chair, his jaw slack and his eyes puffy. Tears dribbled down his cheeks. He stared at the motionless sheet as if expecting a sudden movement would deny its truth and his cousin would suddenly rise from the dead.

Inside the Porsche behind the wheel, Bates drove the gravel roads quickly and turned onto the highway before he stopped and unlocked the handcuffs. Nikki rubbed circulation back into her wrists and asked, "What'll happen to Klyne?"

"Not sure. Chunkie didn't brief me. He'll be arrested in the drug deal, and the shooting. That's all I know. Apparently, someone needs Martinez dead," Bates replied.

"Can't imagine who, or why. A simple drug dealer, set up and taken out by our organization?" Pepperton wondered aloud, her eyebrows arched in question.

"And it's against our policy to get local law enforcement involved, much less civilians. This whole thing make no sense."

"Got to be something political. Probably more to the guy than just dealing. Likely he's pretty powerful in his home country, or was, anyway," Bates responded.

"And besides, that badge he stuck on his chest, it's real. He's a police captain attached to an international task force home-based in San Francisco, but he spent a lot of time in Colombia. His department investigates international drug smuggling. Though it appears likely he used his position to power some major drug deals into the northern parts of the state, and maybe other states. Nevada plates on that van in the driveway."

Bates stopped speaking and concentrated on driving for a few minutes. He fought the sharp curves while Nikki studied the line of waves crashing against a sandy beach that ran for miles, dotted here and there with black rocks and steep cliffs. Under a clear sky, white foam edged the shoreline, creating lacy decorations where ocean waves met the land. Miniature people strolled along the tide-line, eagerly seeking treasure.

"And I don't know about Klyne and the law. You'll have to ask Chunkie on that one."

Bates pulled into the motel room he booked the night before, left Pepperton there alone, and continued on to the jail.

16

The deputy sheriff muscled Klyne up on the couch, read him his rights then asked if he had anything to say. Klyne elected to wait for his attorney, any attorney. He said nothing while his head cleared. He groaned, still groggy, he'd been sitting for awhile, watching investigators collecting evidence, removed the body, then smoking and chatting on the deck as if nothing unusual had happened.

"Where'd Alicia go?" Klyne finally spoke.

"We ask the questions around here, hotshot, that's all you need to know. You're in more trouble than you can imagine," the deputy snorted. Another deputy joined them, grabbed the cuffs, and hauled Klyne out the door sandwiched between two officers.

The deputy opened a slider and pushed Klyne in the back of a van then shackled his cuffs to a metal bar. Separated by a wire-mesh protective screen, both deputies climbed into the front seats, turned the van around and drove back toward the highway. Twenty minutes later the van parked behind a red adobe jailhouse that looked much too old to be useful.

The deputy slid the door open, unlocked the shackles, and waved Klyne out. Klyne stepped down. One deputy lead and the other followed Klyne into the building then into a room with no windows where a different deputy took charge and removed the handcuffs. The letters on his name-tag spelled out Mennick, and his voice sounded like sand caught in his throat.

"Strip. Everything off. You won't need this stuff for quite awhile." Mennick laughed, "Not where you're going. The officer peeked inside Klyne's mouth as if mining gold then spun his finger in the air. "Turn around. Fluff your hair."

Klyne turned around and ruffled his hair. Mennick looked in his ears. "Bend over and spread 'em," he barked, continuing his examination.

"Open wide, all the way. Get that finger up there where it belongs. You don't know how yet, don't worry, couple these boys doin' time here'll teach ya' pretty quick."

His stilted laugh degraded the entire process, as if he enjoyed 'bossing the animals', making convicts toe some invisible behavioral mark in the sand. When finally satisfied, he pointed with his night stick, "Shower."

Klyne stepped out dripping. Mennick tossed him a towel and a blue jail suit four sizes too large, and three minutes later, lead him out into the hall. The sheriff punched a button. A steel gate leading onto a corridor clicked open and slid sideways on a screeching metal rail. Mennick followed Klyne and both men passed through the gate and marched along the hall, stopping beside a locked cell. Mennick turned a key, pulled the door open, and motioned.

Klyne stepped in and sank down on the bunk. His head ached. His body entire body felt shriveled and dry, all used up, his energy gone. He lay back and drifted into an uneasy half-sleep, reviewing the past weeks and wondering what happened to cause these crazy events.

*

"Klyne!" The shout pulled him up out of the daze. "Wake up, your lawyer's here." The clouded, raging nightmare spun away. Klyne opened his eyes. The air in his cell felt heavy and stifling.

"Interesting. Didn't know I had one," Klyne muttered. The bedsprings squeaked, grating on his nerves when he pushed himself up. He stretched himself awake and adjusted his baggy jail suit while staring through the thick steel bars. The lock clicked open. A thin guard stood outside with a set of steel waist chains hanging from his hands.

"Let's go, gimme the wrists and no monkey business," the order came, crisp and sure. Old hands with years of practice arranged the restraints once more, and the guard led Klyne down a dingy hall and through a barred gate that locked behind them. Another gate stretched across the hall, blocking the way. It clicked open after the first one locked, and both men continued.

Klyne made no sound, but the deputy wore leather soles and had a strange gait that slapped down, like one leg was shorter than the other, and each shoe landed a little different, echoing off the concrete walls as he keyed another locked door and led Klyne through it.

A scratched wooden table and two metal chairs sat in the middle of a room. Locked shut, barred and screened, a filthy window let the afternoon sunlight pierce layers of gritty dirt. Klyne shivered when they entered, walked to the window, found a view of two other windows and red adobe walls surrounding a small courtyard bare of foliage, then settled on a chair.

Carrying a brown leather briefcase, a woman pushed through the door, and began speaking even before she sat down. "The court appointed me to look after you, at least temporarily. If you can't afford to pay me the court will. I'm here to find that out or help you find another attorney if you so choose." Practiced and professional, her manner was crisp and warm, and efficient.

"My name is Louise O'Brien." She brushed her slim fingers through dark red hair, cut short and, placing her briefcase on the table, offered her hand.

Klyne shook it. "Jake Klyne, but I guess you know that." He looked her up and down. Attractive, dressed well, a little stout and wearing thick glasses inside thin metal frames. She looked much too young to be an attorney. In no position to debate her abilities, Klyne said nothing.

"Tell me about your finances."

Klyne explained his trust account contained several thousand dollars and that his family had money if he needed it, and that he believed he could pay her fees.

"Can this go away easily, or what? I don't even know what happened, exactly. And, what about bail?"

"No bail," she replied, "and it won't go away. And a few thousand dollars won't even begin expenses on a murder beef."

"A murder beef," he blew out a breath, "What do you mean? A murder beef! A murder beef?" His voice rose, expressing denial. "We just bought some drugs. I didn't kill anyone, and didn't see anyone murdered," he almost screamed the words.

"And what the hell happened to Alicia. She must know what's going on." He spoke fast and his voice rose again as stress suddenly grabbed him.

"Settle down, settle down a minute. I'm here to help if you let me. Let's just get the story out, and then I'll see what I can do." Soothing and professional, her voice calmed him down. "And who's Alicia?"

"Isn't she here?" His eyebrows rose in question, his voice squeaking this time. "She drove me down, I mean, we rode together from Seattle. Yesterday, we came to buy pot, I thought. Turned out to be cocaine instead, a lot of it. Pretty weird."

"There's no woman on the arrest report. You, two other men, illegals from Colombia, I think. And the big-shot, the cop, Martinez. He's dead."

"Dead? Dead how? Alicia, somehow knocked me out, I mean, I couldn't seem to stop it." He shook his head in confusion, in disbelief, and raised his hands to rub his forehead, but the chains stopped him. It seemed to settle him and his hands dropped into his lap.

"Tell me everything you can remember. It's the only way I can help," the attorney said.

Klyne remained silent for a few minutes, uncertain what he should tell her, staring at her while she stared back, giving him time. The silence dragged out.

"If I'm going to help, you have to trust me. I'm your attorney. Nothing you say to me can go any further ... even if I'm not your lawyer later."

Klyne glanced around the room, not much patience in his pocket at the moment. He looked her directly in the eye, decided to trust her, at least for now.

"Okay. Alicia. Met her a few weeks ago. She's friends with my niece. We've been hanging together a few weeks and just came down from Seattle to score some pot."

"Alicia set it up, and I came along for the ride. She wanted some help, some protection carrying the cash. I don't know why I did it ... been spending time together. She worked with my niece. We just met. It was a lot, though I don't know exactly how much." He repeated parts, confused, unsure what to say, what to keep private.

"We were going to sell it in Seattle. She brought the cash. I thought it was pot, that we were buying pot. But when we got there, it was a huge stack of cocaine bricks. And a little bag of pot, a gift, the guy told us." His brain rambled, redundant and confusing to him and O'Brien.

"There's no mention of her."

"Well this is getting weirder every minute. No way twenty thousand would buy that pile either. She said she had twenty grand cash. But that coke was worth a lot more, and I never did see any money."

"And, why is Martinez dead, I mean how? And Who?"

"He was shot twice by one of the cops. Heart shots, DOA. A federal agent named Jack Brighton shot him. Claims it was self-defense. Claims Martinez pulled a gun on him."

"Shot! He was shot, and by a cop! And self-defense!" Klyne lost the calmness he'd gained. "And I get arrested for Murder!" His mouth opened and closed a couple of times, but no words emerged. Then he gathered himself. "I mean, what kind of bullshit is that!"

"Take it easy, Jake, I'm just explaining." O'Brien put a hand on his arm, ineffective comforting.

"California law says if anyone dies with a felony in progress, then it constitutes an act of murder. You've been charged with conspiracy to purchase and distribute a Schedule II controlled substance – cocaine. A major felony. So, you're also charged with murder for the death of Martinez."

"Even though I didn't shoot him?"

"Even though you didn't shoot him."

"Even though a cop shot him?"

"Even though a cop shot him."

Disbelief left him speechless. Klyne suddenly realized how serious the situation had become, and the knowledge struck him like a blow, his body flashed hot and began vibrating, his body chemistry out of control. His nerves firing randomly. He glanced around, as if hoping someone would wake him.

He found his voice, tight and weak. "I thought I was arrested for drugs. Only for drugs." Klyne aims his gaze at the floor. A few minutes passed while neither said a word.

Patient and experienced, Louise O'Brien waited until Klyne finally found her eyes again. "You have an arraignment Tuesday morning, that's three days from now. The deputy sheriff's making me a copy of the arrest report, and I'll see what else I can dig up." She watched Klyne, her animated green eyes flashing huge and luminous behind her wire-rimmed glasses.

"I can represent you, at least through the arraignment. Give you time to think." For a moment she radiated sincerity then suddenly changed the subject. "Twenty-five hundred gets me and you through the arraignment and preliminary hearing, and sets you up for a trial or a plea bargain. We'll talk about fees for a trial later if it gets to that."

A pinpoint of light sparked in the darkness, and Klyne relaxed a little. "Okay, at least for now. I'll call my family and have them wire the money down tomorrow. And try to find out about Alicia, will you? And contact my buddy in Los Angeles. Jimmy Dodds. He's a police officer with the CDVU. And let him know about this."

"Okay, will do that today," O'Brien agreed.

The same thin deputy sheriff escorted Klyne back down the hall and locked him in the same cell.

Once again, Klyne lay back on his bunk and surveyed his options. Perhaps Dodds can help, he knew about these things. Louise will contact him, and ask for his help ... Jimmy Dodds, best friend, only friend. Sergeant James Dodds, his combat group leader, Army buddy, Police Inspector J.T.

Dodds. The memories bumped up against the cracked block walls, then wiggled through, floating on the rancid night air that filled the stifling jail cell.

*

Private Jacoby Klyne drew midnight watch on a moonless night following his initial combat contact with the enemy. His first firefight. An hour into the watch, Klyne stood and stretched. A soft tinkle exploded into his ears. In the darkness, beneath the dripping jungle canopy, he heard a fully equipped company marching into his tiny island of the war.

Inexperienced as he was, his legs shook so badly that he almost fell down. The night suddenly filled with fright. Raw carnage raked across his mind, and icy fear claimed his courage. The steaming jungle forced sweat from every terrified pore.

Bits of metal clinked again. His wide-eyed stare stabbed into the night, but inky blackness blinked back at him, impenetrable. A thunderous click shook the stillness when he snapped his safety free and shouldered the weapon. His hands shook all the way down to his toes. He slid a fingertip across the trigger. The tinkling continued.

Footsteps squished in the mud, approaching his rear. Startled, he swung his head around quickly and followed with his weapon. Sergeant Dodds ducked and grabbed the rifle barrel, pushing it away from his head.

"Take those coins out of your pocket kid," Dodds whispered, "before you wake the others. These men need their sleep." He grinned.

Klyne flushed, the heat rising in his cheeks. He looked at his feet, then back at the night. He reached into his pocket, pulled a handful of coins, his locker key and a good luck cat's eye aggie Benji gave him the day Klyne left town for his Army tour.

"Take it easy, you'll get comfortable with it after a few patrols. It's the silence that gets to you. Seems every sound amplifies. It's the ultra-quiet, well as your nerves. Guess those coins sound like a whole platoon coming down on you."

"Yeah, guess you're right, I'm pretty jumpy. Can't get used to sitting in the dark, waiting to get shot at by a soldier I don't even know," Klyne said. "And what the hell am I doing here anyway? I expected to learn a trade, induction center guy told us all that anyway. And the next thing I know I'm out here getting my sweet ass shot." Still tense, his nerves vibrating in the quiet darkness, his words stuck in his throat.

"Tell you one thing kid, don't never let your guard down. If you do, you just may stay. Permanently! Or, ride home in a tin box. Just watch careful and pay attention. Try not to get your nerves so jumpy."

They stood quietly for minute or two until the sergeant spoke again. "Here, try this. It'll relax you without dulling your wits." He reached into his pocket and fished out a hand-rolled joint. "We'll share. It's good stuff."

"Pot? No thanks, Sarge. Not me."

In all his eighteen years on this earth, Klyne never smoked marijuana, and said so. "From what I hear it gets your brain all screwed up." He shook his head no after Dodds lit the joint and offered him a hit. The end sparked on a seed and went out.

"Uh, uh, ain't trying it now, especially not here."

Dodds lit the joint again, cupping the fire under his vest. "It will relax you," Dodds said.

Klyne stared at the joint, fighting a battle with himself. He did not want to offend the Sergeant, but had difficulty overcoming the inhibitions and indoctrinations of his short life. Despite the transition through her first marriage and raising three children, then college, then marriage again and raising Klyne, his mother was dead set against any drug use, even pot. But Klyne remembered the oddly sweet resinous odor in his father's den whenever he smoked his pipe, unlike any tobacco Klyne had smelled in the past.

Finally, he shrugged it off, reached for the joint, took a shallow hit, held his breath, and took another, unconsciously mimicking the sergeant. He handed it to Dodds who took another hit and returned it again. Klyne smiled, took another hit, and squashed the last inch out under his boot.

The sergeant stretched his eyes wide, a stare pinned him for five or six seconds then stretched into a minute as Dodds debated how hard he should push the new guy and his ignorance. Finally Dodds said, "As a rookie, I'm gonna let you get away with wasting a third of that joint, but that stuff's expensive, and you better get used to hoarding it, and smoking it all. Next time, you buy!"

Jacoby Klyne, novice to life and stoned for the first time, stared at the sergeant, but said nothing. He would remember, and the decision he just made to accept the joint and join an affiliation of smokers irrevocably changed the course of his life.

Klyne sat, reflecting, his thought suddenly more alive. An intricate quiet lay lightly on the night, the jungle noise surrounding them, the silence unmarred by either man. He felt good, almost relaxed for the first time since his patrol had been ambushed earlier this afternoon. Significantly more aware of the harshness he always observed in the jungle, he suddenly discovered its hidden beauty.

Klyne peered into the darkness as the Sergeant waited, a million miles away, yet hovering near in case the need arose. His senses sharp and clear, unhampered by historical clutter, yet mildly subdued as a light euphoria drifting across the pleasant horizon of his thoughts. Klyne suddenly realized he was absolutely stoned, loaded, high, and floating in a multidimensional daze for the first time, ever.

His mind wandered, perceptive, alert, but cautious. Softened by the drug, his eyes chased a meandering beetle that scurried about seeking refreshment. Diligent in its pursuit, chasing its daily bread, on the hunt. Beetle feet marched briskly across the damp jungle floor, joining in a ferocious battle with its midnight snack, a smaller bug.

The beetle lost his grip and its lunch skittered away. It plunged after its meal and both insects disappeared under a leaf. A moment later, the beetle emerged the victor, a minimeal clutched in its claw. Klyne thought about rescuing the little bug, but by the time that thought actually transitioned from his mind to his fingertips, it was much too late.

His concentration suddenly intensified, Klyne listened. Vigorously, the moist, aromatic leaves stretched toward the sky, the tall grasses whispered in the breeze, and quietly burgeoned taller, germinating and christening the night. He knew then that he would have no trouble hearing the enemy in the unlikely event that one attempted to slip up on his buddies nodding sleepily on their sacks.

Jacoby Klyne experienced a fresh aliveness that no threat of impending violence could deter, yet he remained aware of deep responsibility held for those men around him, their very lives entrusted to his care. Months later, he would discover how false that sense of awareness was, how costly, and how dangerous.

He muttered to himself, "What a stupid idiot I am bringing those coins. What a moron. Can't buy nothing out here, anyway. Besides, I wouldn't have looked like such an ass in front of the sergeant." He watched Sergeant Dodds, his feelings bordering on worship. Dodds never seemed to sweat the conflict, the combat – never seemed to sweat anything, ever.

Dodds wandered away, checking his men. Returning, he broke into Klyne's reverie once more. "You okay? At least you stopped shaking. Guess that ole' poison weed got to you!" Dodds chuckled. "I'm gonna hit the sack. Stay careful, your first patrol is almost over." Dodds moved off and stretched out atop his bedding in a piece of hollow ground he'd located earlier.

At four hundred hours, Klyne woke his relief. "Time to get up, Rocho," Klyne whispered, "it's your watch." Klyne shook Rocho once.

Instantly, ex-sergeant and now corporal Evan Rocho for the third time in three years flashed awake, fully alert and ready for anything. On his fourth tour, Rocho logged even more combat time than Dodds. The soldier rolled quickly onto his feet, his weapon set.

"Okay," he said. "Guess it's all quiet, huh?" Rocho looked around and stretched, a little more at ease. "Go ahead and sack out, I got the handle."

Rocho reached into his shirt pocket, pulled out a half-smoked joint, and cupped a match under his jacket, drawing smoke deeply into his lungs. "This will keep me awake, and alert." His eyebrows arched in question, his breath squeaking as he held it in and spoke. "Want a hit?"

"No thanks, take a rain check, maybe later."

Klyne needed time to digest this new experience. He walked to the edge of camp and urinated into the bush, his voice whispering back from the darkness, "Was afraid to take a leak until someone else was listening, hate to have them natives slip up on me with my prick in my hand instead of a weapon."

Rocho laughed, and inhaled another mouthful of smoke. "You get caught with your pants down here you'll never use that for anything else."

Klyne generally refrained from admitting it, but he had experienced few sexual adventures in his life, and that inexperience created an uncomfortable reticence during campsite discussions of women and sexual delights. When he finished, Klyne crawled quietly onto his roll, asleep immediately, physically and mentally exhausted.

*

Klyne pulled himself back from his past, experiencing similar feelings now, physically and mentally exhausted. Filled with apprehension for a situation over which he had no control, he hoped Jimmy Dodds could help this time as well. Finally Klyne kicked his memories aside and nodded off to a restless sleep, but his mind remained wracked with turmoil.

*

After meeting with Klyne, Louise O'Brien exited through the same door she entered. Higgins watched her walk, his eyes following the sway of her nicely shaped hips and the soft round curve of her calf.

As much as she may deny it in the business world, she's an attractive woman with no way to hide it. Walking along the short hallway alone, her heels tapped a quick rhythm on the worn gray tiles. She turned right and entered an open door at the end of the corridor.

O'Brien stood by the desk and said nothing.

"Will he let you to defend him?" Henry Bates asked.

"Yes. At least until the arraignment, and he's had some time to think. We'll see after that. I could find another attorney later, if he or his family wishes. Though I don't know why, he doesn't know anyone else in this area."

"Good. Thanks Louise. He'll probably keep you on. And we do thank you for your help," said Bates, leading her back to the door. "We'll be in touch."

"Fine, my office will wait for your call Agent Brighton." She turned back and asked, "By the way, who's this Alicia he's asking about."

"I have no idea," Bates responded, expressionless. "Says she's his girlfriend, and that she was there, at the drug house. But we never saw her."

*

Half an hour later Bates returned and picked Nikki up at the motel. They drove across the Golden Gate Bridge, speaking little during the trip to the airport. And Bates, under orders from the director, was not to discuss the case any more than necessary. Bates actually had no more information, at least nothing more until he peeked into the traps he set in the main frame. Pepperton arranged shipping for her Porsche then boarded the plane an hour later. The agents sat in adjoining seats and, after take-off, ordered cocktails and lunch.

"So what else do you know, Henry," Pepperton pried again.

She always followed Spec 909 orders unquestionably, but this operation bothered her. Limiting information hampers an operative, and there appeared no finality, no reasonable service performed. Unless the end of a drug dealer counted, it was a senseless killing, and spent time, effort and dollars from an organization – ICD – that never became involved in local situations unless those situations had national or international implications. And this death seems so trivial when compared with other missions she engaged in over the years.

"Nothing else. Chunkie ordered you out of this one. You're done as far as he's concerned. Report directly to him tomorrow morning, and then take a week off. Your next operation's based in Tokyo and begins on the tenth. He'll brief you when you submit your report."

"Did you set a trap?" Still not content, she pushed for as much as Bates knew, or is willing to give up. She felt uncomfortable knowing half an operation.

"No, not yet. Had no time, my flight left right after yours." The indefinable look on his face gave no indication whether Bates was telling the truth. A top-notch operative, Henry Bates cared first for himself, then his fellow agents, and last in line, the public. Bates pushed away his tray, slid down in his seat, and shut his eyes, concluding the inquiry.

Pepperton watched the in-flight film, but her attention lapsed throughout. She still harbored concerns about the operation and remained slightly bothered, unable to distance her emotional attachment. Fascinated and minimally enticed by Jake Klyne and his quaint social interactions, the mix of English and American cultures that spawned his character, and the sincerity with which he allowed his personal relationships to evolve around him, Nikki pondered her personal feelings.

Klyne never disturbed the flow, almost as if his training somehow transcended the normal military indoctrination and absorbed the unique mental charisma taught by the Masters -- but not quite. She blames some of it on his naiveté.

Nikki Pepperton, referenced by most male agents in her home office as the unattached, unemotional ice queen, Ms. Special Agent Freeze drifted into a restless sleep and dreamt of Jacoby Klyne.

*

Clear and cool, the night sky draped Baltimore in a darkness breached by noise and bustle, the unquenchable thirst for activity twenty-four hours a day inherent in every city. Bates and Pepperton skipped through light traffic, parked, and crossed the nearly vacant lot. A guard they did not recognize checked both identification cards at the entrance. The agents rode the elevator up and both checked the log. Hallingforth signed out at noon. Bates and Nikki found Hallingforth's office dark and locked.

"You need a lift home after?"

"No, my father left his car for me. My Porsche should arrive within the week. I'll call and double check on it tomorrow."

"Enjoy your time off, and give a call if you need anything."

"Tell me what you find out about this Klyne thing. Okay? Just like to know."

Henry Bates watched Nikki Pepperton enter her office and shut the door. He stepped into his own office and waited five minutes, then opened the door, discreetly peering into the hall. Her door still closed, her light still on, Bates crept down the hall and unlocked another office, looked out the window and located a dark blue SUV parked in her slot.

He returned to his office, fudged around on his computer thirty minutes, and then checked again. This time Bates found her door closed and the light extinguished. Bates slipped out, hurried to the window, and peeked out again, and watched Pepperton climb into the SUV. The lights switched on and she backed out. Bates hurried back, locked his office, and rode the elevator to the basement. He unlocked the main computer room and entered, then locked himself in.

Ten minutes later the printer spit out a burst of letters. Bates tore the message off and flipped it over. "Son-of-a-bitch!" The exclamation jumped out of his mouth and Bates absently rubbed the back of his head.

"What's it say, Henry? And no bullshit." The ice-cold words startled Bates, and he spun about. Pepperton stood in the doorway, calm but undeniable, awaiting her answer.

"Look for yourself." Bates offered the page.

She read the words aloud. "Not A Chance, Henry. And Don't Try It Again."

"Thought you didn't set one." Accusation rang in her voice.

"Sorry Nikki. Wasn't sure I could get anything out. Chunkie's no slouch when it comes to these machines. Looks like maybe I can't."

The agents stared at one another for a moment, each keeping thoughts private until after they locked up and entered the elevator together.

"Can't quite figure the reason Chunkie enacted this insane security. He deviates from the Spec 909 operational procedures as if he's unaware of them, or doesn't care."

"That bothers me a bit," Bates said. "What do you think he's up to?"

"Don't know. You know him a lot better than me."

"Says it's a special op ordered by the President, but he's been acting just a little off for a few months. Nothing I can put my finger on though." Bates knit his brow, and frowned. The exited the elevator and walked across the lot, each agreeing to keep eyes and ears open, and to share any information.

A pair of dark eyes glittered at both agents from behind an unlit tenth floor window covered with frost. Bleary-eyed, George Hallingforth sat quietly and stared at his agents. Unshaven and mussed from two nights and days of waiting, he gulped another slug of whiskey. An inch remained in the bottle. Totally out of character with the rest of his condition, a silly grin split his face. Sloppily, he poured another drink, spilling some on his pants, and muttered, "Two down, two to go."

Hallingforth chuckled. Then short, cackling laughter echoed into the stillness.

*

The next morning Klyne clinked and shuffled into the meeting room, expecting to meet with his attorney again. Jimmy Dodds walked in with Louise O'Brien and Klyne's emotions soared. Dodds arrived from Los Angeles, maybe to pick him up?

"What are you doing here, Jimmy? Good news? Am I outta here?" The questions shot out of his mouth.

"Louise asked me to come up ... help explain. So I flew up last night. Maybe you should begin, and tell him what's up, Louise." Klyne sat down quickly, then stood, then sat again, his nerves jumping.

"Well, I'm pretty damned curious about this. The D.A. pretty much has a lock on this case. Dead guilty he told us, and no way out."

Both men looked at her, a question in their gaze.

Her bright green eyes blinked once. "But, interestingly enough, they still want to make a deal. But that's not exactly unusual. D.A. always seems ready to deal. Big trials cost big bucks. He knows he can win this one easily so he may offer a little deal, if anything. But, I'll check it out and see how much he's willing to bend."

"And if you don't want to go for it when we find out, we'll get on with our trial prep," she said. "D.A. never spends money on a major trial if he can help it. Plea bargain always shows up in the win column and the defendant gets a break. When that happens, defense, that's me, or us actually," she delivers a smile with the comment, "writes it as a win too. It's just the simply business of budget and has nothing to do with enforcing the laws. He knows absolutely he can win this. Although it's never ever truly a lock with a jury, but he's pretty certain here, and I am too. I mean the sheriff busted you pretty cold turkey on these drugs and the cop's dead. No doubt about that issue. And in-field police testimony is pretty tough to beat. Juries just believe cops."

Klyne interrupted, "Yeah, okay, okay. So what's his offer?"

"D.A. guarantees a reduced sentence, maybe the drug beef and manslaughter or something like that. You could get away with jail time instead of prison." She was fulfilling her professional responsibilities as his lawyer now, cutting the best deal possible for her client. All three knew there was too much evidence against him to fight it.

"Won't put any definite time or charge on the table yet, he's just looking to see if something like that might tempt you to plead it out." She paused, waiting for Klyne to speak, but Klyne simply stared at her.

"He's just thinking budget and conviction, and he retires in two or three months. Trial like this could stretch out much longer, easily, and he knows it, especially if we keep filing motions and delay, and can't find witnesses, maybe intentionally take our time looking, for example, and I might have appearance conflicts, or just create them." She briefly flashed a grin at that self-serving strategy.

"That won't bother him enough though. He could have any number of assistants do it, or delay his retirement if he felt like it. Also knows he's got a good case, and we know it too, and he knows we know it. You don't have much going for you. Said the alternative is to push the hard book at you."

"What's the hard book?"

"Murder, all the way, hard time sentence, and he'll probably try for no parole. Death of a police officer, even if he was a crook based on what you told me. That was never certain, and even if we proved it, which would be a very tough sell, so what?"

You still showed up to buy the cocaine, that's a given. And he could get real nasty and claim Martinez died in the line of duty ... then you're really up the creek. And he owns all the paddles."

"What do you think, Jimmy?" Klyne glanced at Dodds, no longer trusting his own judgment. One decision he made lately had gotten him into this mess. And, he knew nothing about the law. "You know better than me."

"The D.A.'s got a solid case, you showed up of your own free will. You know and I know you had nothing to do with the shooting. But law is law, that's the way it's written, and for reasons just like this particular case. The D.A. can push the max on this easy. And, you gotta admit, nobody dragged you into this mess, Jake. You were dealing drugs, and in big-time amounts, no denying that part. Judge can sentence you on that cocaine charge alone up to twenty years. He got the pot too, and possession of weapons at a crime site. He has evidence of the Seattle drug buys too, and he can get narcotics detectives there to charge you as well. It goes on and on."

Dodds waited while Klyne digested what he heard. "Well, that was Alicia, and no one knows where she went." Klyne shook his head, bewildered. "Sheriff says she was never there … what bullshit. This reeks of a trap, but I sure know nothing to give them, and haven't done anything to deserve this set-up even if it is one."

"You can't beat this beef, Jake. Most you can do is spend a lot of money, and try to make a deal … which he's already willing to do. This bust was a set up from the start. We know that, with the feds and local cops. It's pretty air tight. The most you can hope for maybe is a technicality. Pretty unlikely at this point, and then, even if you win, all you get is a new trial and he gets a chance to fix his mistakes.

"You've been a victim of circumstance, nothing more. Accidentally fell into an trap bigger than most, and certainly weirder than you thought." Dodds spoke with a tremble, an air of resignation humbling his voice. He can't help his friend, and his friend can't help himself. And more than once each had saved the other's life in a violent world where friendship counts and soldiers gain brothers.

"Seems I don't have much choice." Klyne accepted the facts. "Jailed if I do it, broke and jailed if I don't." His grim, tight grin expressed no humor. He settled lower in his seat, shaking his head. He finally raised his eyes, looking at Dodds, then at his attorney.

"If I agree to deal, then what happens?"

"Then I take over, and discuss terms with the D.A. You still go to court. You'll plead out, lesser charges and get a lighter sentence. The D.A. won't push. Judge looks at all the evidence, your background, listens to the D.A., listens to me, maybe get some character witness, Jimmy for one, get some of your officers to write letters about your character and service to the country. Then the judge makes a decision." She was working hard again. "Best shot you got, Jake."

"Okay. Guess we better do it. Seems there's no other way."

17

Klyne believed all along he that would eventually do some time. Aside from the shooting, the drug bust alone carried enough weight to get him a pretty stiff sentence, ten years or more easily, even without complications. He reflects upon his own stupidity, comes up short in the brains department on this one.

"It will take about a week to make arrangements. I'll speak with the D.A. today, and let him know you're willing to deal, but won't commit yet. We push him for the best you can get before we agree."

Klyne stood up, "Okay, let me know."

O'Brien headed out the door. Higgins arrived and led Klyne back to his cell. The door clanged shut once more behind him. Klyne fell across the bunk, warn out, confused, still wondering how he got into this fix. The continuous stress over since his arrest a few weeks ago has taken its toll.

He signed a plea agreement and waited almost another week to actually face the judge. Mennick arrived, chained him up and led Klyne out to the hearing.

An hour later, back in the cell, Klyne had no idea the sentencing would go so completely different than he and Louise planned.

Judge Angstrom surprised everyone except himself.

A life sentence, no bargain in sight. Plunged Klyne into a place filled with confusion and despair. The judge said 'life' and for murder.

Klyne held his head in both hands, a headache developing as he realized he'd been had, fooled completely by a system within which he brings no experience to the table. His hands shook, his body ached, and tears ran down his cheeks. Then, he felt the rage beginning to build. I'll never do the time, he promised himself, and meant it.

18

The morning after his sentencing Klyne wakes to a nightstick banging on the bars. The cell door slams sideways. He opens his eyes, confused for the moment, unsure where he is, then glances at the cell wall. He remembers underlining the words 'Fuck This Place' on it a couple weeks ago. He's not changed his mind about its poetic truth, but the sight of it pulls his mind back into reality, and the present.

Recent memories flood his brain. Alicia, his arrest, the crooked deal, the courtroom deceit, the life sentence yesterday, the false deal, and the crazy happenings in Seattle and in the sleepy beach town north of San Francisco, all layered with betrayal and treachery.

"Let's go, cowboy. Your attorney's here again." The deputy holds up a set of steel cuffs, wraps him up and leads Klyne out.

*

Four hundred miles south of the jail cell holding Klyne, Inspector James Dodds drops a thin file on the desk and stares across it at Alexander Paar. "Judge blew off his plea agreement yesterday Alex. I've got two weeks accrued vacation, and am going up to help Jake. Will take a look and see if I can figure out what's going on. Can't just sit here and let this happen. He's my best friend. He saved my life more than once, Alex. I can't let that go."

Paar opens the folder, scans four pages quickly and says, "Yeah, well his thing stinks like old fish. Nothing feels normal about this bust on your buddy. Leave the vacation days alone. Fly up there officially and take a peek at the drug part of it. If that happens to help Jake out, well, that's a good thing too. I can easily justify that, and budget for it. Take two weeks - if you find nothing, we'll revisit it then."

"Thanks Alex. I owe you one." Dodds tips two fingers to his forelock in a mock salute.

"No you don't, we're just catching up. Go on, get out of here. Bring something back we can use. You need anything up there, give me a holler and we'll arrange it."

*

Chained again, sitting in the same conference room where he previously met his attorney and agreed to plead the case out two weeks ago, Klyne stares across the table at Louise O'Brien and his friend, Jimmy Dodds. "So, the judge blew off our deal yesterday, right? What can we do about it?"

Klyne, O'Brien, and Dodds believed the D.A. negotiated and accepted a plea bargain agreement. Everyone associated with the case including Assistant D.A. Tommy Minton showed surprise when the judge ignored the agreement, although Minton faked it well, then he denied making the deal.

Oblivious to why it happened, neither Minton nor the D.A. had any idea that Hallingforth intervened with Angstrom, but Minton had a hard time hiding his delight when the judge ignored the plea bargain and sentenced Klyne to prison for life.

*

Klyne tells his story again as best he remembers. The relaxation evident on his face now, he waits for Dodds to tell him there's some mistake, but that's not what Dodds says.

"There's no mistake Jake. You're definitely in a hell of a fix. But something's odd with this Alicia Diamond thing, and the sentencing. First offense, and with your service record, he should have approved it. Judge just totally ignored it, and we can't figure where Alicia fits, and especially that everyone denies she even exists. Can't believe you made her up, makes no sense." Dodds raises his hands, palms up.

Klyne point his eyes at O'Brien. "So, Louise, how'd you get involved here? I don't know you, or my family. Jimmy either. No one I know sent you."

"I'm on the attorney list for defendants with no representation. We have no country public defender now. He suddenly quit with no notice months ago, and was part-time anyway. The federal agent I spoke with checked in with the D.A., made sure we have you represented properly so we don't 'blow the case' as he put it." O'Brien appears a little ticked at the comment, as if it questioned her ability or ethics. She shook it off, got back to business.

"He wants us to prosecute the homicide first so the feds don't waste funds prosecuting the drugs." She thought a moment. "Actually, we'd prosecute the drugs anyway, not the feds, so I don't know the entire story, but apparently Riley White was under federal surveillance - trying to catch the main guys smuggling cocaine into the country. He was a small fish, but led them to Martinez, a major player as it turns out. Like a guppy going after a shark. But it worked, and the feds caught a big one. Been a bit different if Martinez had not pulled a gun. Now, he's dead and we have no new information."

"But, that doesn't change the charges," she says. "You still tried to buy drugs, not for personal use either, and that involves you in the death of Martinez regardless. Even if this Alicia Diamond woman was sitting right here beside us holding your hand, that wouldn't change much, and the charges wouldn't go away."

"That's the strange part," Dodds says, "nothing changes whether she's real, or fantasy, except maybe some answers. Even if, or when, we find her, it might still change nothing. If this is a frame, it's an extremely well developed and executed plan. Almost diabolical in its complexity. One very smart cookie at the top of this food chain."

"No matter how we look at it, you're guilty for at least a part of this, if not the actual murder itself, technically. We've got some very bright manipulators if that's true. And, it makes sense to look at it with those eyes until we figure something or someone else is behind it."

Dodds pauses a minute, his face a flat mask, hiding the emotions he feels for his friend. It bothers Dodds tremendously that he cannot help.

"By the way, I spoke with Elizabeth this morning. The family's not coming down right away, unless you want them here. Elizabeth's upset, but Rachel's in an absolute rage. She's taking the blame because she set you up with Alicia. Rachel went looking for her, but the manager that runs her apartment building says the place is leased to a foreign corporation. He never heard of Alicia Diamond and has never seen her there. But he doesn't live on-site either, so hard to tell anything from that."

"We'll look at that, but am betting it's a dead end. Paar's checking the lease."

Klyne says nothing.

"I tried to talk it out of her, but she's still pretty upset about it. And Elizabeth says you should make whatever decision you want as far as an attorney goes. She'll help with whatever you need, just let her know."

"No reason to change. I guess. That is, if you're available, Louise, and want to tackle it, try to find out why the judge flipped," Klyne said, aiming his eyes at her and arching his brow, the question evident on his face. "And, you know the basics of it already."

Dodds turned back to Klyne. "I asked Paar for some time off to look into this on my own. He did me one better, got interested in the drug side of it too. Paused my cases temporarily and assigned me to this one for two weeks. Just to see what's up. So, we go fishing. We catch anything, we may look some more." Dodds stands, and Louise shuffles her papers, shuts her briefcase.

"You know, Jimmy, even if you find something, Jake's cooked anyway. He pled guilty. You can't appeal a guilty plea."

"But if we find something weird, or fixed, or some kind of entrapment, we can revisit this with the governor. Right?" Dodds asked. "Or take it back to the judge."

"Well, that's correct. If you find something really out of whack, the governor might listen. Doubt the judge will, he already blew us off."

"I'm heading for Seattle tomorrow, just to see what's there. Will check with Rachel, and the bank once more, and I'll push the apartment manager a little. Alicia must have a history, somewhere. She's the biggest mystery, might as well start there." Dodds turns to the attorney. "If we're done, would you excuse us for a minute, Louise? And please wait for me."

"Sure, I'll wait." She picks up her briefcase and heads out the door.

His eyes follow her walk until she exits and turns left down the corridor, earning his Inspector Dodds title. Then Dodds returns his attention to Klyne. "If there's anything you're not telling me, it'll be harder to help. And, beyond that, I'll really be pissed." His voice rose, expressing the anger he's held in check the past couple of weeks.

"You know you got yourself into one hell of a fix. What's the big idea anyway? Smoking a little pot - that's one thing. But dealing's something else, especially at that level, and coke not pot. This ain't a joke Jake, not even a little bit."

"Turned into a murder beef. Man, you don't need this, and neither do I." Dodds throws his hands in the air, walks in circles behind the table.

"There's nothing I haven't told you. Nothing I can think of." Klyne looks at the ceiling, racks his brain. "I've thought about everything, nothing makes any sense."

He stands up, paces back and forth. "I have no idea what to do. Didn't plan on any violence. Just tried to buy some pot. A little weed! That's it. That's all. Didn't even know it was coke until we got there."

"That was all her doing. Alicia. And she's out there somewhere Jimmy in spite of what the record shows and what these guys say. She exists! And she got me into this, and I don't know why. But she does!" His voice rises again, frustration pushing it. "And, then it turns out to be a cocaine deal … that's even crazier."

"All right. Okay. I'll see what I can do. Paar will see what he can find too. He's got lots of contacts and plenty people owe him favors."

"Thanks Jimmy." Klyne reaches across to shake hands, but the restraints shorten his reach. His hands hang in mid-air, the chains bang against the table.

"By the way, you saw Sarah sitting in court. She flew up with me for the sentencing and asked me to say hello. She'd like to see you and talk today. If it's okay."

Klyne drops his hands. He looks in the air, then at the floor, then at the filthy window. "Don't know. Not exactly set up for entertaining here." He turns his head and glances out the window but sees only the dirt, and then looks back at Dodds.

"Not sure." He shuts his eyes a minute, thinking it through. "Okay, why not. I guess if she wants it. She came all this way. Tell her okay, Jimmy."

Klyne enters the corridor. Higgins returns him to his cell. Dodds heads out the door, a phone on his ear, booking a flight to Seattle this evening so he can follow up on what few leads he has. Sarah will return to Los Angeles alone, after her visit.

*

"Get up Klyne. You got a visitor, a real looker too." Higgins unlocks the cell and escorts Klyne down the corridor. Bound in the habitual chain costume over his baggy blue jail-suit, Higgins and Klyne enter the conference room that also serves as a visiting room and apparently, an every other user room.

Sarah stands in the doorway for a few seconds, watching Klyne, almost shy in her unsure mental state. Her peach-colored jumpsuit splashes a blossom of brightness on the drab surroundings. She radiates a beauty Klyne had not remembered clearly due to the drug-induced haze he'd experienced the past two months. He simply stares, transfixed.

A sweet, delicate flower blossoms into the room, spilling an enticing scent into the stagnant air. The exquisite vision expunges his remorse and leaves him numb. Struck motionless by a portrait of innocence but finally driven to action by the vision of her dimples unsuccessful in an attempt to remain detached from her smile and a voice he recalls as the sweetest he's ever heard says two simple words.

"Hello Jake." And his brain implodes.

Jacoby Klyne stumbles, catches himself, and shuffles across the room, forgetting for the moment his linked steel uniform. His joy and excitement flutters away, embarrassment emerges, and he stands with his hands chained to his waist by a six-inch leader that suppresses his agility and thwarts his embrace. The chains clink as he drops his arms.

"The guard says one kiss and no continuous contact, or he'll terminate the visit." Her words float across the void, and the sound raises the hair along his arms and his neck, sparking his memory. His heart thumps, his head swims, and he stares again, then blinks without responding.

A guard sits at a counter in the hall, observing them through a small window Klyne never noticed on his previous visits to this room.

"So, how are you, soldier?" A lilting tinkle in her voice reminds him of cheerful mornings bursting with infectious humor, memorable evenings filled with fun and children and games, and then, finally, the lustful nights of uninhibited passion that always ended with serenity and warmth. He cannot now imagine why he ever left Los Angeles.

Sarah leans forward and puckers her lips, waiting for a single kiss, the one the guard ordered. Uncomfortably shackled, Klyne bends toward her, and for one primitive second stolen from eternity, a solitary taste of the warmest, sweetest nectar ever gathered engulfs him completely. Transcended by an intimate taste of honey in that single instant, he remembers again what he had forgotten. Rising joy and comfort settle within a soul he always denied existed. His heart races and sweat breaks out on his body, the skin on the back of his neck tingles. He looks deeply into her eyes and wishes himself a different life.

"Fine." He answers without thinking, and then adds, "Well, not so fine actually. Good to see you. Guess I got troubles that won't go away. Glad you could make it. Should've called, I mean, from Seattle. So, have you heard from Jimmy? Yeah, guess so, he brought you."

The words tumble out all at once, his patience gone, his thoughts rambling, disjointed, floating, unattached. Klyne suddenly realizes how much he misses Sarah.

"Take it easy, Jake." Sarah reaches across the table and takes his hand, then glances back at the guard still watching them through the window. She jerks her hand away. Her fingers shake, but then she giggles, "Is holding hands continuous contact? Don't want to get thrown out."

Klyne shrugs, but takes her hand squeezes her fingers again. The chains clink against the table. "Jimmy's doing what he can. He's gone to Seattle and is coming back in a few days." Klyne says. "Guess you know that already. Did Jimmy find anything in L.A.?"

"Don't know. He won't share that stuff with me. Just tells me to be patient. I didn't know what was happening with us anyway," Sarah says, and looks away briefly. Her smile frees the dimples again, but she appears unsure how to continue.

The guard stares continuously through the barred spy-hole, suppressing the reactions that Sarah and Klyne feel at the moment.

"Don't know either. Should have called, I guess. Just got caught up," Klyne says. Unspoken emotion floods the room, but the lovers remain apart, four eyes linked across the table. "Remember the shopping," he said, making simple conversation to break the uneasiness.

Each recalls the laughter they shared when Sarah had taken a nearly full shopping cart and hidden it at the far end of the market. A woman continuously and thoughtlessly placed her cart in the center of crowded supermarket isles while she dawdled and browsed, blocking the busy Thanksgiving Day shoppers. Sarah simply moved it all the way to the other end of the store.

"I couldn't stop laughing at that frantic look on her face," Klyne says. "She thought she'd have to shop all over again."

They had both giggled like teenagers at the crowd of city hunters that filled the isles gathering goodies for the annual November feast. Klyne and Sarah followed the harried woman, who ended a fifteen-minute search when she finally located her missing cart hidden behind the last row of chilled vegetables.

"And you kept laughing, and made me laugh harder," Sarah says, giggling again at the memory.

Klyne spoke of Tripod, dressed in slick black fur and wrestling the tasty remains of a plump turkey leg, sliding and thumping across the spotless kitchen floor. His stalk finally ended with a hilariously awkward, three-legged pounce. Then he gorged himself.

"Lost a leg, but gained a bunch of character," Klyne says. "I miss him. And you, and the kids. More than I realized, and more than you know."

Then, subtle and silent, but apparently never absent, feelings each thought the other forgot rekindles and grows, encompassing the room. Grins and memories, and searching eyes, evokes the passion again. The lovers lock eyes, wide-open and willing.

The look of intimacy that shoots between them electrifies the room, and Klyne grabs her hands again. Her slick, damp palms grasp his in return, her grip strong and need-filled, eyes and hands bound tightly in emotion. The arousal clearly visible, they struggle to remain apart.

Erect nipples strain, fat buttons pulsing against her tight blouse. Klyne wills himself to remain seated, throbbing partial tumescence quivers inside his baggy jail-suit. Mute clues hint at the passionate emotions obvious only to each other.

The suspicious guard, squints through the steel-barred window, perceives nothing of the covert sensual by-play engaged in by lovers sheltered from spying by a cloak of motionless communion.

Slowly, Sarah rocks her hips gently against the seat, softly, rhythmic, nearly imperceptible. Enraptured, but with no recourse, Klyne remains motionless. Her erotic movements stoke his passion to a level he never believed possible. In response to the tinge of rising heat that deepens her color and flushes her cheeks, the blood surges in his veins. A few moist droplets form above her lip and her wandering pink tongue flicks between her teeth, stealing a taste of its sweetness. Relentless, the mutual desire scorches both souls. Erotic, oblivious, silent and certain, one captivating moment pauses for eternity.

Sarah pouts her lips, runs her hand inside the elastic band and down between her thighs. The faint mewing sounds escape as she embraces the flow of her passion. Her eyes mist with pleasure, one silver tear twinkling in the corner of each. Small and white, her teeth nibble her lip, then bite harder, nearly drawing blood, responding, as a single pulse of primal ecstasy shakes her body.

Klyne responds immediately. Her muffled purring tickled his ears in the past and spans with no effort the space between them. Unwilling or unable to control his own release, it follows hers, and he groans into the silence. Klyne ignores the spot of dampness spreading across the cloth and staining his jumpsuit. And, in the heat of his passion, Klyne acknowledges nothing save the beauty before him and the memories within him stirred by her presence.

"U-m-m, a little like riding bare-back on Uncle Barney's old mare," Sarah murmurs and lies back in her seat, a dreamy look on her face.

The guard blinks twice, yawns, then lights a cigarette and exhales, contorting his lips widely. The floating gray rings break apart on the steel mesh, and smoke filters into the room, contributing the odor of burnt tobacco to its neglected staleness.

Finally, reaching across the table and grabbing Klyne by his fingers, Sarah says, "Guess holding hands is no prolonged embrace." They sit for the remaining minutes, fingers and minds locked in tragic intimacy.

"Please come back to me," Sarah murmurs, "when this is over," unconsciously predicting that someday it will be. "I miss you, Jake." Her sweet breath warms his cheek.

"Then I guess we miss each other," he confesses, realizing its power again.

Minutes later Mennick and Higgins enter. "Time's up." Mennick nods and leads Sarah out. Higgins motions Klyne toward the corridor and his cell.

"Nice lookin' lady Klyne ... she yours?" Leering, the spindly deputy sheriff stares after Sarah while escorting his prisoner back into the hallway. "Too bad they don't stick around long once you get locked up. Always need someone to poke 'em regular when they look that good, and you ain't gonna be available for a long, long time."

A degrading cackle follows his comment and Higgins curls back his chapped lips, exposing an ugly brown patchwork of decaying teeth. His chuckle surrounds a dead cigarette hanging from his jaw.

An hour later, Higgins returns to the corridor carrying a metal food tray. Picking up his obnoxious comments right where he left off earlier, he opens with, "Think I'll go look up a lonely lady-friend tonight when I go off shift."

Higgins blows a cloud of rancid, alcoholic breath through the bars, drowning the odors of grease, baked chicken, and coffee that waft above the tray. "Maybe she'd like a nice piece a deputy tonight." Then Higgins makes a huge mistake. He opens the cell door, and serves Klyne the evening meal. Klyne rolls off the bunk and approaches the door as it swings open.

"Fuck you, Higgins!" Klyne growls, his fear and his future gone now, absorbed fully and completely by a life sentence. Only his rage remains.

"Ha!" retorts Higgins, "you'd never go back to dogs."

Grinning around misshapen brown teeth and spouting the historical response, Higgins glances up at Klyne.

Both men lock stares, but enlightenment suddenly engages Higgins normally dull mind, the rage and anger darts hit the guard right between the eyes, unexpectedly scaring Higgins and he backs away two steps quickly.

Klyne narrows his eyes. "Get away from me. Don't ever come near me again, and if you ever say another word about my friends or my attorney you'll be dead before you hit the floor." His stare alone nearly knocks Higgins down.

The blood drains from his features, the smile drops off his lips, sweat breaks out on his body, and Higgins staggers backward another couple of steps, jerking his arms in a half-hearted attempt to ward off the fury that Klyne burns directly into his brain.

A flatulent bubble squeals out behind him and Higgins stretches his neck, looking over his shoulder and down at the rear of his pants. He stands alone in the corridor, and Klyne remains unchained and within easy reach outside the cell. Higgins jerks backward again and his arms pop up defensively as if deflecting an attack. Klyne releases his glare and backs into his cell, lies down on his bunk.

A breath bursts from Higgins, so loud it can be heard the length of the hallway. He slides the meal tray onto the floor and drops his keys twice before he twists the lock shut and, wobbling back through the isolation gate, he approaches his desk and slumps into his chair. He curls his upper lip and wrinkles his nose, and reaches under his buttocks, pulling at the seat of his wet, sticky trousers.

The attitude Higgins carries everywhere kills Klyne's appetite and preys upon his mind, straining his patience. But, in spite of it all, he remains silent and stares at the ceiling. A portrait of Sarah spreads across the jail cell wall, and he envisions her smile and flushes the jailer from his thoughts.

Sweeter memories from now and then jog across the pain and chase the hurt away. A vision of her simulated innocence and passionate free-spirit rises up before him, forming a paradoxical display reminding Klyne again of what he misses.

Fragments of Alicia, the fun and games, her flaming passion mixed with hours and days of hide-n-seek, and sometimes mental absence, pokes into this thoughts and chills his trust. His mind ices over, abandoning the sentiment he thought he felt for Alicia. Absently, Klyne wonders if he will ever know the truth about her, or if he cares.

Following the lack of drugs and alcohol, his memory and logic clears. Bits and pieces of his relationship with Alicia surface, but nothing the two had done together explains her total disappearance. His patience finally thins and he wearies of the wait.

He lies back on the bunk and carefully removes a red marker from his pocket and reaches up. Klyne sticks the pen back in his pocket and the words 'Fuck This Place' now have two additional bright red lines beneath them, accenting its truth.

19

Two days pass uneventful, and Klyne enters the meeting room with spirits high, hoping Dodds found some answers in Seattle.

Dodds strangles that elation with two words, followed by his name. "Dead end, Jake."

The smile drops off his face and Klyne stares at the floor. "At least for now," he continues, "we're checking with D.C. to see if we can find any work records around somewhere under Alicia Diamond from Seattle, or anywhere else for that matter. Don't have much to go on, just the name, and that's probably fake."

"What, no luck at the bank either?" Klyne frowns.

"The bank shows no records, no payroll, nothing. Two paychecks sent to the temp agency, in her name but never picked up, and the agency never heard of her. When I spoke with Atkins, the assistant manager, the first time anyway, he was pretty evasive. Told me regardless of anything else, he'd stand by the bank records, even if subpoenaed. Apparently, once the question came up, he and the other employees were advised to refer everything to their attorney. No one else will even talk to me."

"Atkins says they use temporary personnel from various agencies around town occasionally, and she probably came from there. Told me he didn't remember her particularly, but he did speak with me for some reason. Probably just to get information for the higher-ups in that branch. See what we're after, maybe?"

"He's lying. Well, at least Alicia told me he kept trying to get in her pants, but she thinks he's an asshole. Says he's one of the reasons she quit. But, I keep getting confused. The story keeps changing, seems different than I lived it. Besides, I can't be sure about anything Alicia said anymore."

"Right, gets better from here. Turns out, Atkins tries to screw around with the ladies a little, especially any he can pressure, ones that work under him. Anyway, after I talked to Rachel again, I went back and leaned on Atkins a bit more. Threatened him with me showing up at his house when his wife was home too. Told him I'd ask about Alicia and the others he'd tried to screw around with. Cause him a little trouble on the home front."

"He got a little nervous, but still wouldn't give it up."

"Then I told him I'd also push it with his supervisors, all the way up if I had to. That rattled him a lot more."

"Guess he's more worried about his job than his wife, but he finally admitted 'maybe' remembering Alicia. Said she showed up at his office claiming she'd been sent by Brakeman Temps, one of the temporary service agencies. Said he knew they hadn't ordered one that week, but that she came on real strong and talked him into some work. He gave her something to do. Figured he'd hit on her, see if he got lucky, and then release her. Also says she continued with the big come on for a week or so and kept working then one day just never came back."

Dodds shrugs and looks away, uncomfortable with his news.

"I drove out to his house, talked to his wife. Explained it in detail. She got a little upset, but implied she knows about his 'pets', as she calls them. Got the impression she would kick his butt about it now that it's out in the open and part of an investigation. Serves him right, I hope she plants a point right where it belongs. But, she knows nothing about Alicia. Never even heard the name."

Klyne says nothing, and withdraws. He wraps a shell around himself, a dark comfortable shell where he spends a great deal of private time lately.

"Spoke with the bank attorney too, or rather, sat for twenty minutes listening to a one-sided conversation that divulged absolutely nothing. Law school must teach lawyers specifically how to talk in circles that long without taking a breath. Nobody else I know can do it." His attempt to lighten the day fails.

"So we still have nothing." Klyne stares at the floor.

"Right, so far." Dodds appears uncomfortable again, but had nowhere else to go. "Paar says it won't change things anyway. Even if we find her, you still do your time. It'll only change the circumstances if we find out something about her. He's not willing to spend too much time or funding on a loose possibility either, unless something more on the drug end kicks loose. Not likely though at this point. Cops got that wrapped up as much as possible now, it appears."

"He's got no stake in you Jake. He's only doing this for me now, and I owe him one. Maybe if we find something more about the drug imports, might get CDVU interest. But nothing happening there at this point.

"Dodds pauses for a moment." And, Paar's returning me to other duties Monday. We broke something on another case, and I gotta get on it. He reneged on the second week. What time I do have I'll spend with Louise."

"What about the cop who shot Martinez."

"The guy's a federal agent, name of Jack Brighton out of D.C. Claims the operation was a joint surveillance on the drug smuggling operation. Says Martinez pulled a gun, which he did, and that he acted in defense of his officers."

"Turns out Martinez is a real San Francisco cop, well was one, involved in international drug issues but also a crook, and a naturalized citizen originally from Colombia. Apparently, he was involved in high-level smuggling - cocaine and marijuana. The Feds claim you were one of his contacts, said you used the name 'Riley White' and bought quantity in the past."

Klyne says, "That's bullshit. I never met those guys before that day."

"What's he say about Alicia?"

"Said no one knows anything about a woman with you. Claims there was no woman on the scene. Records back it up, and all three deputies stand by the records. They claim everything got spinning so fast they lost track. Seems a little fishy from our end, but everyone wants to stand on written records. No skin off their butts and they all support one other, Ttalk with the state attorney', all spout the same thing."

"By the way, the two Colombians are scheduled for deportation, and won't say a word. Got some high-powered drug lawyer up from San Diego helping them out, wrote a release order. It's possible those two could back you up, at least as far as Alicia being on the scene, but the Feds don't want them, California don't want to spend money on a big trial, and I've got nothing to offer. They're heading home pretty quick, and so far, are keeping their mouths shut tight."

Klyne says nothing, staring past Dodds at the filthy glass.

"Problem is, I keep coming back to the same situation, and it doesn't change. You were there, buying drugs. A cop was shot and killed. That's the bottom line, even if you are my best friend." Dodds pauses, uncomfortable, bothered by his inability to help. His eyes wander around the room then back to Klyne.

"I gotta go, due back in L.A. tonight, but I'll keep in touch with Louise. She'll see what she can do tomorrow. But we got nothing to help you yet."

Dodds stands and reaches across the table. Both men shake hands and rattle the chains. "I won't let this get away Jake, I promise. I will keep after it when I can."

20

Klyne strains his ears, interpreting the sound that woke him. He slowly rotates his eyes, seeking a point of reference, and then recognizes the barred end of his jail cell. Realization floods his mind. The springs squeak every time he moves. He stares at the empty bunk above, and the red comment he underlined on the wall, his eyes wide open but unseeing. He lives alone, but no rest comes while he struggles with complications that now inhabit his life. Reconstructing every detail, evaluating each a different way, another way, then another, but he understands nothing. And still, no one admits knowing Alicia except his family. And no one official acknowledges that fact.

He reviews it again. Alicia exerted tremendous force and defeated him, knocked him out, without effort. It leaves him confused, never before had his skills been so useless. He searches his memory for reasons why she would, let alone that she could, get involved in styled combat at such a high level. She dropped him, over and done before he could react.

No one had ever done that before, never in practice, never in competition, and especially, never in combat. For a brief moment, complete amazement overcomes his frustration, but ultimately gives way to curiosity as he ponders again Alicia Diamond, her amazing martial arts skills, and his relationship with her.

Sharp, flapping footsteps stop at his cell and a shadow falls across the bars. With a dimly lit corridor behind him, a deputy opens an access slot in the door and slides a dented metal tray filled with food into the cell. Apparently, Higgins must have better things to do this morning.

"Breakfast served," Mennick grouches," and make sure we git all the silverware back. Two pieces, count 'em both. Don't even need all yer' fingers. And keep the cup for later."

Similar routines and different deputies fill the next two days. Louise O'Brien stays absent, and Klyne receives no other visitors. Housed alone in a barren cell on an equally barren corridor, Klyne waits with no options. His cell faces an eight-foot wide hallway to a mirror image on the opposite side, a hall lined with identical empty cells. Screwed tightly to the ceiling, two dim recessed fixtures light the hallway. With no future to plan, Klyne passes the time in retrospect, but spends most of his waking hours trying to understand how he had gotten into this predicament. The puzzle remains unsolved, the answers baffling.

Tuesday comes and goes. Higgins removes Klyne once for a discussion with Louise O'Brien regarding the deal the District Attorney failed to honor, and returned him to the cell. Higgins learned his lesson well though, and says nothing about Klyne's friends. Matter of fact, says nothing at all while he does his job.

An assistant District Attorney named Minton that Klyne had never seen before had accused him of numerous malicious acts and spoke as if he personally watched Klyne perform each one, and read penal code numbers assigned to every charge. The judge sentenced Klyne to life, and reneged on a deal the defense thought agreed on both sides.

Louise O'Brien appears twice but offers little additional information. Each deputy denies knowledge of Alicia

Diamond. Her name appears nowhere in the records and the official mouths remain mute. Louise contacted Dodds, and Dodds said he will arrange time and get up again as soon as he can.

21

The jailer returns Klyne to his cell after another fruitless visit with O'Brien. He crawls on his bunk and lays back, a standard position he assumes frequently since his incarceration began. A recollection of fun and cuteness spars briefly with the harsh darkness of other recent memories, and then pushes itself through into his thoughts, uplifting Klyne for a few moments, but the stress and tension wear him out and he eventually drifts off into a restless sleep.

The guard tosses a tattered novel on the bunk and Klyne jerks awake, back to reality. Occasionally, the jailers share novels with him, saving him from total boredom. He devours the reading, supplementing the books with close-in workouts between chapters. The novels offer a diversion from the monotonous routine. Klyne cherishes the few hours of relief from tedious conversations and sedated mentality inherent in his keepers.

Other than on his alternate day showers, only once had he been removed from the cell while he awaits his transfer to the state agency. After the cops shot an additional mug-shot, and printed his fingers again, Klyne returned to his cell and lay back once more, remembering his last days with Sarah. Cherishing each memory, wondering if he would ever see her again. The memory pushes into his thoughts, the pleasure she exudes, the conflict that later developed in his life. Memories flood his mind.

*

The sunrise chased away the shadows, brightening the bedroom walls and ceiling. Barely awake, Klyne stirred. Sarah snuggled against his shoulder, her wandering fingers tickling the matted hair around his nipples. Klyne rolled onto his chest and mumbled into the pillow, "Not again, you'll have to bury me."

She slapped his buttocks, sprinkling laughter amongst the sunbeams. "Okay wimp, breakfast it is." She climbed out of bed and stretched, running her hands over her body, sensuous, rotating her hips, teasing him, her nipples reacting. She worked hard keeping her body fit and, even after the strain of child-bearing twice, she maintained an extremely enticing shape. Finally, she slipped a robe over her shoulders and bounced into the kitchen.

Klyne watched her sashay out. "Too bad then, you lose," she giggled. "Gotta leave soon anyway to get my kids. Only grandchildren my mother's got, and she loves having them, but I love them too. Besides, they live here."

Sarah bustled at the range, and the smell of bacon and toast filled the room. "Kids gotta be at school by eight then I've got a class." Sarah spent three days a week in an art class taught by Stephanie Dodds at the local college. She had met Stephanie five years ago, and met Dodds after he had returned from the Army. Dodds and Sarah dated once, and then Sarah introduced Stephanie and Jimmy. Her best friend matched with Jimmy from the first night they met, and were inseparable after that. They married within six months.

Paar and Dodds offered Klyne the job again. But, Klyne had saved his leave pay and other benefits. His savings from the Army and a trust fund from his father fattened a small bank account. The time had come to visit his family, and then figure out what to do with his life.

He spent several more days and nights with Sarah. Her cheerful exuberance, the whys and whats her children shared, and Tripod's antics, smothered his uncertainty, temporarily. But in the end, he had flown to Seattle, and Rachel, and Alicia, then driven back to California, and finally landed in a jail cell.

22

Jacoby Klyne lives alone in a four unit cellblock. Three exact replicas adjoin his and houses other inmates awaiting trial, sentencing, or transportation, or serving local misdemeanor time. For some unknown reason, Klyne lives in a vacant cell unit. Alternately, he stares at the ceiling, or the walls, or the bars. The corridor remains dimly lit, empty and silent, except when the guards deliver his meals.

Three days pass that seem like a month. A beefy inmate hums his own version of *'Here comes the Sun'* and swings into the cellblock, pushing a cart filled with cleaning gear. He swishes a mop around, scrubbing the old concrete tiles. Bright red letters sewn across the jail-suit back read *'Trusty'* and an ancient New York Yankees cap covers his shaved head. Pausing in front of the cell, he looks up and speaks from the side of his mouth, "Not supposed to talk to you, just keep it low. Jailers mostly deaf and blind anyways. And lazy. Fat son-of-a-bitch told me not to talk to you, won't even walk down here to make sure."

The trusty giggles as if getting away with something. He peeks back over his shoulder. "Dumb ass, what's he think I am anyways, law abidin'?" The trusty has no teeth. A wet chuckle slips out beneath his bushy moustache. A short, plump cigar hangs unlit between his lips and he gums its stub.

Klyne lies on his bunk, unresponsive.

The trusty removes the cigar, points its end toward the cell. "Hear you gotta bad-news beef, killing a cop. Lucky they ain't kicked your butt in here already. The cops, not the cons. Cops don't like nobody that do in their own, no matter if a cop, a sheriff, patrol, whatever. Maybe they didn't 'cause he was crooked ... might a liked his kind even less'n you."

The trusty peeks back over his shoulder then speaks again. "Story is, some Fed was investigating him already too, well, someone was anyways. Another story is, he was crooked as a bent nail."

"I didn't kill him. Another cop did."

"Don't matter. Don't take no idiot to figure out you get big time just for being in a spot when somebody git killed like that ... 'specially a cop. Fuckin' laws all rigged against us common folks."

The man sticks the cigar between his lips and dips the mop, splashing soapy water on the floor and spreading it around. "Never can get this floor clean, but gives me something to do." He scrubs at a spot, but it remains a spot, etched into the concrete.

"O'Brien. She's young, but a good lawyer. Don't let it fool you none, her being a lady. She does her job ... you was going up, no matter."

Klyne asks, "You know so much, when am I getting out of here?"

"Gettin' bored, are ya?" He drops a ragged-page paperback on the floor and kicks it into the cell. "Con's best friend. My man Louie Lamour." The trusty grins, "Trouble with his stories, white hat always wins. Just leave him when you go, I'll get him back next time through."

"Am I going somewhere?"

"Day after tomorrow, down the pipe to San Quentin. Be a lot better when you get outta here. Nothing to do in this place but lay around. Least there you got stuff to do, and ain't locked up twenty-four hours a day." He sweeps the mop back and forth, rigorously and ineffectively cleaning the same spot.

"You'll like it there," he predicts, incorrectly.

"How do you know, you been there?"

"Three times, and twice in Soledad." The man moves forward a few feet and attacks different dirt. "Got food every day, and a soft bed with a pillow. Gives me a nice vacation from the streets once in a while." He dips again and drips gray water in a circle as he swings the mop out once more.

"Kinda miss the pussy though." The trusty straightens up and flares a match, then puffs on the cigar. It goes out almost immediately, and he chews on the end again. "Don't like punks much, always want a commitment. Want you to hurt your ass protecting hers just so only you can have it."

"What're you doing here then, instead of back in the prison?"

The trusty glances around once more, hiding from no one his next comment. "Only trade I got on the streets is burgling and robbing, selling a few drugs once in a while. Keep getting caught. 'Sides, it's tough work. All those rich folks wantin' to keep what they got. Gets harder and harder for us to make a decent livin'."

Again the convict looks around, paranoia leaking out of his actions, as if sharing a secret no one else knows, but with no one else to hear it.

"Did six months county this time. Small beef. Found a bunch a radios just sittin' in back of a delivery truck ... seem like nobody want 'em. Course, I didn't want such fine electronics to waste, so took 'em home. Accidentally sold 'em to a cop riding the fence."

"Neighbor three doors down from my baby sister, but he never told me he was a cop. An' that's cheatin', not telling no one. How we gonna know to stay away from him if no one tells on him – least he gotta tell his neighbors – like the cops make those sicko sex deviants tell if you're a neighbor, so cops outta have the same rules. Leastways be up front to the relatives of his neighbor's kids. Right?"

He chuckles again, knowing he's floating ideas on the wind. "Ha, sixteen regular days plus one git-up, which don't hardly count." The convict spits brown juice onto the floor then swabs the mop over it, concealing it briefly, but sharing it with anyone that later touches the mess he leaves.

"And don't ask that to no one when you get to the big house. Just ain't considered polite. Man's own personal business ... why he's on our side the bars."

The jailer yells down the corridor. "Taking too long down there, let's get a move on." The deputy stands behind a set of double-locked barred doors, staring into the dim hallway.

The trusty ignores the order at first, then changes his mind and waves his middle finger. "Piss off Harris, just doing my job," he hollers.

Lowering his voice again he says, "They skippin' your classification and sendin' you straight up. Somebody got lots a pull and don't like you much. You got no chance to try for one of the easy joints without classification." Then he lowers his voice to a conspirator whisper, "No one even mentions classification. They got you pegged already. Nothin' you tell 'em gonna change nothin'. No matter what you say or do."

He moves off down the hall, swabbing the floor quickly. Looks back over his shoulder. "Take it easy, Klyne, name's Garrison ... this time anyways. And watch yourself, Quentin's a bad-ass prison. Don't trust no one. Run into Danny James on the yard, tell him ya' know me. Might git you a pass on somethin' light. Course, might not too. Depends."

Two more days pass while Klyne waits. The shell he curls around his thoughts becomes his constant companion and, at regular intervals, he crawls inside and dwells in his past. The deputies leave him alone and even Higgins remained distant and passive since the day Klyne threatened him.

*

Klyne wakes to a sound he knows well by now. Waist chains clink, a nightstick raps along the bars. An abrasive voice that Klyne easily recognizes as Higgins breaks into his sleep. "Get your ass up, Klyne. Your chariot's waiting and the chauffeur's getting impatient. Let's jump on the stick."

"Where you taking me?"

"Ain't tellin' you nothin'." Higgins laughs and jingles his keys. "What the hell, you'll find out soon enough. You're headin' a little bit south. San Quentin. You'll love it." Still chuckling, Higgins blows smoke and stale breath into the cell. A cigarette butt hangs from his lips, wet tooth marks denting its filter.

Seems Klyne should believe the convicts sooner than the judges. Convicts are correct, even if he doesn't like the answers. The system seems to lie pretty regular, and convicts know it before anyone else.

Higgins becomes the third person in as many days that tells Klyne he will like a place he probably will not. Maybe they like it, but Klyne has his doubts and would rather take the chance he can find meals and a bed on the streets, and he doesn't like punks much either.

*

Gold letters stenciled beneath a badge decal on the side of the green van that rolls in and parks beside the gate spell out the word Marin County Sheriff. Two men climb out dressed in state officer brown, the public servant fashion statement.

Across from the irregular shoreline of Marin County, the waters of San Francisco Bay edge San Quentin State Prison. The ancient, dungeon-like structure houses the most vicious state felons and carries a record for violence challenged only by Folsom. A panoramic view above the southern walls overlooks the bay. Steel struts and concrete pillars and the paved alleys of Richmond Bridge rise above the sea. Treasure Island hovers beneath the fog, and the Oakland Bay Bridge glints in the distance.

Breeze-blown sailboats, sleek racing yachts, pug-nosed tugs, and monstrous commercial vessels, pleasure and toil in strong harbor winds. The budding flower children of America's rebellious generation call it home, and a hodge-podge of humanity circle the streets, deposited haphazardly and often from distant seaports around the world. The city skyline sprouts into sight across windswept seawater capped with white froth.

San Quentin sits on the shore, aiming its grated windows south and east toward another institution surrounded by choppy seawater and clouded by thick fog beginning to blow away. Perched on a pile of rock in the middle of the bay, the old federal prison now sits deserted. Alcatraz Island, decrepit and broken, an institution formerly reserved for federal prisoners of the most heinous reputations. Closed several years ago, the federal government now provides guided tours on Alcatraz Island promoting the public fascination with infamy for a nominal fee.

Klyne climbs out of the van. Two correctional officers take custody and escort him through an archway into a concrete room protected by doubled entry gates.

"Strip." The officer orders. Klyne removes his clothes, stands for the standard custody exchange search. The officer tosses Klyne a set of white coveralls, boxers, and slippers. Klyne pulls the prison uniform on. The same guards guide him along the corridor. Concrete cells with barred doors rise triple-tiered on both sides. Inmates dressed in dungarees sit at a small desk or lie on a bunk in each cell, watching him pass.

From inside one cell a razzing voice yells, "New Fish," and follows the label with laughter. "Piss up a rope, Easterling," one officer yells back, "and quit harassing the fish. You'll find yourself in the hole again."

Inmates awaiting indoctrination and a permanent cell assignment wear white jumpsuits with the words 'state prisoner' stenciled in large red letters on the back, the general prison population wears blue dungaree shirts and pants. Same stencils.

Klyne walks between and slightly ahead of the officers and glances up. Armed guards patrol multiple catwalks that hang along the upper tiers, and watch the movement below. Locked steel doors at the end of each catwalk allow the only access.

Built more than a hundred fifty years ago, concrete, rocks, bricks, and steel rises above a sand and rock base grade. Despite its prime source building materials and state of the art design in the eighteen fifties, the prison decays daily, escalating as the years pass. Minimally maintained and moldering foundations degrade into the dirt. Chipped paint and cracked walls, patched and plastered only when necessary, surround the convicts and the prison staff.

Like an ancient musty tomb, San Quentin exhales a dead bouquet mingled with the unmistakably living odors. Stale sweat, dirty socks, and peeling paint saturate every breath. Intimidation, anger, fear, hate, demonic ferocity, and madness electrify the musty atmosphere.

Motionless, but vibrating into every darkened corner, a synthetic peacefulness permeates the vaults. Armed with threats and backed by law, prison guards wear green uniform jackets over brown shirts and patrol the grounds, dominating the artificially constrained violence. Tight-fisted tyranny enforcing the peace.

Klyne and the guards enter another hallway, traverse a cellblock containing only white-suited inmates, and stop before a locked grate. North Block, cell twenty. Klyne will call it home until the indoctrination period ends. The barred door slams open and Klyne enters a concrete cell equally as bare as his last and observes double bunk beds, a toilet, and a table bolted to the floor. A sink with push-button water taps hangs in one corner. The sight greets him now as an old friend, repetition breeds comfort even under these nasty conditions.

California hustled up a price break ages ago, a large volume deal on a multiple purchase of identical haciendas. All the comforts of home. A replicate cement box measures six feet by ten, fully furnished, and ready for personalized decor.

Catered meals arrive three times daily and no nasty between meal snacks spoil your diet. And, for those lonely nights at home without a mate, a personal library cart delivers your favorite authors twice a week. As an added incentive, each individual palace maintains a complete security system, guaranteed. No one allowed in or out without a thorough strip search and a delightful peek into each body cavity. Playboy, Penthouse, and National Geographic available by special order only. Local judges reserve each convict a private condominium and the supply appears infinite and the list of residents endless.

Klyne frowns, steps into his new home and sits down, then eases back and rolls his legs up on the bunk. His head drops onto the pillow. His mouth twitches when the bunk does not squeak, but he finds no happiness here. Having had plenty of practice lately, he lies motionless without effort. Angry, disappointed, disturbed, and vengeful, he reviews his private collection of yesterdays, and immediately begins planning his escape.

Infrequently removed from his cell for a variety of physical and mental probing, Klyne composes his daily routine. Jogging in place, push-ups and sit-ups, reading, eating, and restless sleep passes the time. Counting the days never matters, for the present his tally reaches infinity. His parole board hearing dots a microscopic light, a pinpoint of brightness at the farthest end of the longest, darkest tunnel he ever imagined.

A Life Sentence stares back at him. Seven years minimum. Fat chance!

*

The next morning a short inmate dressed in dungarees pushes a book-cart along the corridor. "Want a book?" The man stops and peers through the bars.

"What've you got?"

"Take a look." He rotates the cart and Klyne reads the titles. "You can only take two, but I come twice a week. About three weeks you can get 'em yourself."

"How's that?"

"They'll take that long figuring you out. Check your health, and your risk, then classify you."

"Then what?"

"Then get a job. If you get a work assignment, you get out. You're free. You can roam around during the day, work out, run the track, use the library. Otherwise you get lockdown."

Silently, Klyne disputes how this man defines the term free. But eventually, each inmate earns the ability to move about in a larger, but equally confined area, observed constantly by the cat-walking guards, each one armed and vigilant.

The book clerk accurately predicts the future. Following three weeks of questions and answers, prods and pokes by an indifferent staff, Klyne stands before a cell in East Block. The cell door bangs open and, dressed now in a blue cotton shirt and dungaree pants like everyone else on the yard, he carries his new wardrobe and bedding inside. A toothbrush and a bar of soap sit in his pocket.

Klyne observes various decorations. Personal effects hang on the walls, sheets and a blanket stretch military tight across the bottom bunk.

"Guess I live upstairs," Klyne decides, tossing his clothes and personal effects on the top bunk. Sequestered out of sight and reach, unseen hands bang the door shut, and the lock clicks behind him. Klyne climbs up, lies back, and shuts his eyes.

*

Pulled from his fantasy by the never-ending clank of a cell door sliding open, Klyne opens his eyes. An older man, thin and tan, crosses the threshold and tosses a book on the lower bunk. Intelligent eyes as deeply blue as his own mirror back at Klyne from beneath thick black eyebrows and a full head of pure white hair cut military short. Klyne peers down at the man and a portrait of himself in forty years sends a chilling tingle along his spine.

"Mr. Klyne, I presume." A voice too deep and resonant for such a slight frame emerges. "Conroy MacKlain," he says, offering his hand. "Call me Mac if I like you, Mr. MacKlain if I don't. And, if I don't, you won't live here long, so don't get too comfortable yet."

"Hello Mac," Klyne says, shaking the old convict's hand, aware of a tight strength in his grip. "Call me Jake if you like me and Mr. Klyne if you don't. And I don't care if I stay or not if you're that hard to get along with."

The healthy resonance emerges again as the mimic triggers Mac's throaty chuckle. "Least you got a sense of humor. Let's try Jake for now, and see if you change my mind."

Mac splashes water in the sink and washes. "Better get ready for dinner. Cell door only opens for about a minute then you're outta luck. No free delivery on this block, gotta hike to eat."

A loud bell no one can sleep through rings three times. A guard marches along the corridor, stops before each cell and counts every convict. The routine inmate count occurs four times a day at specified hours, and then adds the outs – the men in the medical clinic or still working odd-hour jobs elsewhere in the prison. If the tally equals the convict population the daily routines continue, if not, every cell-block remains locked down until the guards account for any absentees.

Apparently everyone's home tonight and the bell rings once more. The cell doors bang open, shattering the quiet, and the inmates step out. Shouts and laughter echo along the halls, home-boys chatter, released after a strenuous day on the job, doing time.

Klyne and Mac exit the cell together and walk toward the cellblock gate. Mac points at a bulletin board hanging beside the exit. "See that board? That's the movement sheet. Check it every day. It'll tell you any appointments you got, job changes, whatever. But, you'll never read the best one. Your name comes up in that last column the day after you leave. Parole or dead." Mac says, grinning. "Unless you get busted again, same day. Then you can read it."

Klyne reads the sheet and finds his name. "Looks like I clean the weight-yard, twice a day."

"Not a bad job," Mac says. "Do it right, and don't lose it. Otherwise, no movies, no library, no yard, no nothing. No job means lock-up all day." Both convicts turn away together, heading toward the mess hall.

"You got that particular job 'cause I don't like gettin' woke up early. Don't fuck it up. They gave you a mess hall job first. I changed it. Mess hall jobs get you up at four. You get that one again, you move out the same day. I don't shine that early."

Klyne glances at Mac, but says nothing.

"Small pay number, eight bucks, but we'll see about that after you been here awhile. The warden controls the pay numbers, and I just happen to work for the warden." Mac grins again.

"There ain't enough pay jobs to go around. Tough to get 'em, too. Unless you know somebody." Mac grins again. "Like me!"

Klyne has family and can get what little additional money he'll need. He's satisfied with the job and the fact he'll spend solitary time outdoors. That's good enough for now.

He balances his daily routine and escapes into his mental shell after meals, workouts, and yard clean-up. He loses himself in his memories, embellished significantly by passing time. Except for a tenth run catalog movie each Friday, providing the inmates are nice all week and don't kill anyone, every day matches exactly.

Thirty-five days pass and, except for incidental violence between convicts, one stabbing death, and one escape attempt by an inmate serving life, remain uneventful for the rest of the prison population. A few parole out, and few arrive, but not much changes from day to day. Routine turnover, social recidivism hard at work.

Mac accepts Klyne, and Klyne keeps his job and remains in the same cell. They develop a loose friendship. Mac has been incarcerated thirty-seven years, but Klyne does not know why and has not asked, a courtesy he incorporated into his introductions once that Trusty in country lock-up explained the concept after Klyne received his life sentence.

Mac knows everything about everybody Klyne included, and uses the information to his best advantage whenever he can. Mac works as the warden's assistant and gains certain benefits, not the least of which is an in-house track on useful information, and he continuously polishes his ability to manipulate each and every situation.

Mac maintains a regular monthly income from his pay number, and supplements it with favors he grants and tidbits he sells. Sometimes ten dollars, sometimes a hundred, occasionally only a pack of smokes, whatever the traffic will bear, but always a charge. Some inmates have more money than others, and a small charge always better than no sale.

First Interstate Bank in downtown San Francisco carries an account with Mac's name on it, and it gets fatter every month. A convict strikes a bargain inside, a relative feeds dollars into Mac's account, and mysteriously, a few days later the convict finds his wish granted. And Mac never works C.O.D.

*

Mac sits in his usual spot astride the stainless steel throne, reading a book. He constantly reads law books, and successfully appealed many cases for inmates over the years. He loses a lot too. That figures. Most convicts receive a prison sentence for reasons they can't dispute. The appeal process merely prolongs hope, until time completes the sentence in spite of conditions. Mac runs a lucrative practice, relatively speaking, as a jailhouse lawyer, and one of the best San Quentin has ever housed.

A cold wind blows east beneath and through the Golden Gate Bridge and in off the choppy bay. Rain pours from thick black clouds and soaks the prison walls and grounds. Protected from the weather by thick concrete walls, his eyes flutter then open at six o'clock Tuesday morning. Klyne sits up and drops his legs over the edge of his bunk.

On the first day, Mac informed Klyne that this morning event, his rites of passage to the new day between five forty-five and six-fifteen, never varies. Interfere with Mac's morning routine and garner instant expulsion from the cell, and new quarters immediately. Mac turns a page and sips coffee he brews in a miniature percolator first thing. Every morning he drinks two cups while reading the law.

"Morning Mac."

"Be done in a couple minutes, breakfast ain't until six-thirty." Mac's ritual greeting wraps around the rim of his coffee cup. The routine introduces the day, each a replica of the day before. A habit etched in stone. Mac spreads his book on the table, and looks up. "Guess you can have my spot here the next four mornings. I'm going on vacation."

His tight, white teeth cut a slit in his normally serious face. "Wife and son be visiting, celebrating my son's birthday. He'll be six this Sunday."

"Six!" pops out, and Klyne looks quickly at Mac. No offense taken.

Klyne learned bits and pieces of Mac's story, exchanging casual conversation with the reticent convict, but never asked about Mac's conviction. The marriage and a young child definitely surprise him.

"Right, six. Been married nearly eight years. Every three or four months we spend time in the old trailers reserved for conjugal visits. Sure nice to get away. Met Emily by accident actually. Wrote to a bookstore in St. Louis that specializes in out of print titles, mostly law books. Had a tough time ... but she finally found one I'd been trying to get for over a year. We wrote a time or two, then a lot more times, and she came to visit twice a year. After three years she moved to Mill Valley and began visiting regular. We got married after another year, but our minds married up long before that."

Klyne raises his eyes and wrinkles his brow. Mac's life term carries no parole. His wife intentionally married her own life sentence.

"Feeling a mite generous this morning, so I'm gonna give you a piece of information free of charge ... and also because you'll be looking after my stuff while I'm gone."

Mac grins. Klyne fidgets. In an unusually good mood this morning, Mac watches Klyne dangle awhile. Even free tidbits carry a price, and Mac enjoys his cellmate's discomfort for a few minutes more until Klyne can no longer resist asking the question.

"Information about me?"

"Yeah, about you. Seems some federal officer's interested in you and coming out from Washington in a few days. Ain't got no name, but you better put on your best suit and say '*yes sir*', because according to what you told me, those Washington boys must have answers you don't."

Klyne jumps down so quickly he barks his elbow on the bars, his mind racing. "What else you know?" He rubs the arm.

"Nothing yet."

Klyne sits on the stool, a tight smile on his face. Nothing can be worse than this cell. Anything the agent from Washington offers has to be better. It has to be.

"Maybe could get a name, find out what he wants." Mac pauses, as if debating. "Cost you though. Cause I gotta pay first," he baits the hook, "I'll let you know."

Klyne frowns at the lie. Nothing cost Mac, and Klyne knows it. Mac just gathers and sells. Only the bait comes free. Mac will try harder for the name and the reason, but only if the price fits his effort.

Mac finishes packing and sits down on the bed. "Make sure your lawyer knows about this guy, and don't give nothin' up. Every one of these bastards worse'n a rat's ass when it comes to us convicts. Don't believe nothing he says, and don't give him no information he don't already have. Never trust no one," he says. "Never! Not anyone, especially cops or cons, or government men."

Mac looks Klyne in the eye. "Or women."

The cell door bangs open. Mac pushes up from his bunk. "That's free advice, no charge. Believe it." Mac scoots out and heads for breakfast, leaving Klyne alone with his thoughts.

Dressed in civilian clothes and reborn for the moment into an imaginary world inside his shell, Klyne imagines himself, step, step, step, and pass through a double-gated archway. Silently, he walks out and discards the chains, then dances arm in arm with a handsome stranger whose face he cannot see. "How much?" he hears himself whisper, but the stranger ignores him. Klyne shakes his head, then opens his eyes and stares at the ceiling, unable to imagine an offer he will reject, nothing he will decline.

"No price to high," he whispers aloud. But even his craziest guess, his wildest imagination could not prepare Klyne for the games he was about to engage.

Klyne contemplates the news, finally stands and takes two steps forward. The cell door bangs shut, locking him in. Klyne slaps the bars, upset with himself that he'll miss breakfast this morning.

23

Mac returns and collects his bag. Whistling and singing, nearly prancing around the room, totally abnormal behavior for the old convict. Mac fills the cell with his chatter while Klyne lies brooding.

Mac floats back and forth, four steps at a time, the length of the open space. His family visit begins in a few minutes, but Klyne shares none of Mac's upbeat attitude.

"MacKlain," an officer barks, "your family's here." The lock clicks.

"Fourteen, stepping out," Mac sings the words way off key and gritty, but doesn't care nor correct it, even though he could.

Klyne lies on his bunk, day-dreaming. Waving meadows, breeze-blown trees and silky flowers fill his mind. A single flaming blossom surrounded by fleeting dimples in a field sparking with color. Patient again, his passion stymied for the moment, but he's destined to quench the fire in his visions. Sarah Recent holds his hand, but only in his dreams.

The cell door bangs open and Mac steps out. Klyne opens his eyes and stares at the disgusting, contemptible hole within which he barely maintains his existence. He never counted the days until now, but reverses his habit immediately, breaking the time into minute fragments, three days, six clean-ups, nine meals, seventy-two hours, forty-three hundred twenty minutes until the equation solves itself. Next Monday morning Mister Washington will arrive and open the gates, and a tall government agent with no face, dressed in a gray suit, will enter and answer, and put a period on this chapter.

The cell door bangs shut.

Suddenly impatient, Klyne watches the clock, but every hour drags and each minute takes a week. Sleep eludes him, he cannot eat and, for the first time, escape within his shell fails, as does its healing memories. A repetitive phrase, Monday morning ... Monday morning ... Monday morning ... rings in his head. The tension tweaks his nerves. A venomous balloon threatens to burst and desecrate his mind. Using every mental discipline he ever learned, he wills himself to rest and finally sleeps, mentally exhausted.

Klyne stays alone in his cell all weekend. As soon as he arrived at the prison, he began planning his escape. He has no intention of spending the rest of his life here. Now, this surprise visit suddenly breathes new life into his future, whatever the man brings. Maybe his departure might be easier than he anticipated.

Dodds flew up once to visit, but offered no new information. Alicia remains a mystery and, even though Atkins admitted her existence, no clues to her identity have been uncovered. Klyne informed neither Dodds nor O'Brien of the visit he expects from Mister Washington, whoever he is. He decided to wait now and get that information first.

Monday morning ... Monday morning ... Monday morning ... ultimately arrives.

Klyne lies awake, impatient. Two hours pass. Clothing rustles, a nightstick raps on the steel bars and a guard squawks. "Wake your ass up Klyne, and get dressed. I gotta message for ya'." The cobblestone voice grates in the stillness.

Klyne sits up immediately, fully alert, adrenaline surging through his body. He fights the rush and calms his mind. "I'm awake," his voice croaks, surprising himself.

"You got an official visitor. Report to the shakedown room after breakfast." The officer hands Klyne a pass chit and saunters away. The count bells reverberate throughout the building, breaking the morning silence, then the release bell rings and Klyne steps into the corridor, barely restrains himself from running out the gate, and maintains a brisk pace through the cell block gates.

He by-passes the meal and heads straight for the visiting room. He shows his pass and slides between the bars of a metal detector then stands for a visual search. The guard pats down his body, then chains him, and escorts him to a room.

The walls and ceilings are the same adobe-like concrete, but maintained better than the cellblocks, workshops, and other confining areas. New paint and no cracks set it apart, and a single window overlooks the parking lot. The office contains a desk, three wooden chairs, and two gray metal filing cabinets. A wooden door across the room remains closed, and the guard stations himself inside the metal door through which the men entered and spins his key, locking them inside. Neither man speaks.

Klyne peeks out the window and finds a view of the octagonal watchtower perched along the shoreline, guarding the main entrance and the parking lot. In the distance, Richmond Bridge looms behind it, shrouded in thick, gray fog tumbling against itself in the light breeze. On this dim and dingy morning, Klyne controls his feelings, barely. He sits erect on a wooden chair, concealing his impatience.

Thirty minutes pass. Forever. But finally, two sharp raps on the door break the silence and interrupt his thoughts.

The officer unlocks the door then exits through it. The tall, gray-suited government agent does not appear. Instead, a short, stout man with graying hair, dark eyes, and a light brown cardigan enters the room. The door swings shut and the lock clicks behind him.

"Mister Klyne, my pleasure, Jonathan Wings here," George Hallingforth says as if he really means it, extending his right hand in greeting. "I represent the United States government." Hallingforth removes a leather wallet, produces fabricated proof of his identity, allows Klyne a quick look, then sits behind the desk and places his briefcase upon it.

Klyne says nothing.

Hallingforth watches Klyne a moment. "You're probably wondering why I'm here."

"Who's Alicia Diamond?" His voice grates, brittle, intense, his emotions barely under control. Klyne sits stone rigid. Every nerve in his body vibrates. Nearly hysterical, he fights the desire to reach over and throttle the government man, and force the information from him immediately.

"I've never heard that name."

"Aren't you here about my conviction?" His voice still tight and so intense it nearly squeaks.

"No, certainly not. I'm here about your release."

Klyne waits again, the confusion and tension build, producing a mental condition capable of anything or nothing. Unconsciously, he leans forward, balanced at the edge of his seat and at the brink of his sanity.

"Well, let's go then. There's nothing I need from the cell, I'm ready. Do we just walk out or what?" His voice finally cracks and a crooked grin splits his face, frozen, conveying only grim humor.

"Well, it's not quite that simple. We want to make an agreement with you. I'm actually from the intelligence branch of the federal government, and we need you to work for us."

Suspicion, mistrust, and wariness creep into his demeanor, and Klyne says, "Again? No way. Made a deal already, a couple months ago. Look where that one got me. Think I enjoy this joint – what a deal, huh?" Alert, he eyes the agent, challenging every word. "And how do I know you're real. That fake I.D.'s probably easy to make, especially when I can't test it here anyway."

Military specialists supplied anything and everything Klyne needed for his military intelligence operations, and he correctly assumes this man can get any documents he needs with even greater ease stateside, whether he's legitimate or a fake. Awareness creeps into his consciousness, and Klyne suspects a trap.

"You a friend of that Bates guy, that Texan? He keeps showing up and asking the same thing. Panama then California. Don't know who he is, and don't care. Won't care about you much either unless you get me released pretty quickly."

"Don't know anybody named Bates. This is a special operation, direct from the President."

The government agent rises and walks to the door, knocks once and pushes it open. Klyne raises his brows when the warden looks up from his work and smiles at the government agent.

"Would you excuse us a moment?" Hallingforth asks. "We need your phone."

"Certainly Agent Wings." The warden responds respectfully as he stands and walks around his desk, retreating through another door and closing it behind him.

"Come with me." Klyne follows and both men enter the room, Klyne shuffling a bit with his chain halter still engaged. Hallingforth stops at a table beneath a window that looks out over the bay and picks up a telephone.

"This phone is not monitored. It's a direct outside line, no recorder. Do you recall the area code for Washington?"

Klyne nods, and the agent hands him the phone. "Dial it, and this number." Handing Klyne a slip of paper, he says, "Ask for me."

Glancing at the paper, Klyne dials it and memorizes the number. He listens. The line rings twice and a female voice answers, "Federal Services, Intelligence Division. May I direct your call?"

"Jonathan Wings, please." A series of clicks rattle in the background. A telephone receiver lifts off its hook.

"Operations, Jonathan Wings office," a gruff male voice that sounds exactly like Henry Bates disguising his voice says, "Agent Billings here, may I help you?"

"Jonathan Wings, please," Klyne requests again.

"He's out for a few days, may I be of service?"

"Do you know where he is?

"California. Can I help you?"

"No."

Klyne drops the phone on its cradle and follows the agent back into the original room. Hallingforth shuts the door behind them and both sit again. The agent unlocks and opens his briefcase. He extracts a sheath of papers clipped together. "Take a look," he says, handing them across the desk.

Klyne reviews his original military operational files, in his own handwriting. A shock punches through his brain and he nearly loses control, his mind races, dreamlike and violent, carrying his thoughts backwards across a swirling carousel filled with passions and fears. His full military history lies before him in grueling black and white.

His mind thrashes, disjointed, a wooden marionette bouncing uncontrollably, enters a dream-like state, seeking a reason, any reason. *Why Me!* A stranger plucks the strings, a mysterious tune he never heard before vibrates inside his skull.

Kaleidoscopic and multifarious, his memory paints a vision in his mind's eye. Psychedelic reds and blacks, the portraits of his peacekeeping violence flash before hm. His hands shake, sweat beads his brow, his body twitches, and Klyne barely restrains the urge to scream.

"Those should prove conclusively that I'm whom I say."

The words pop Klyne back to the present. He drops the papers back on the table. His temples throb in tune with his elevated heartbeat. He shakes his head to free his mind.

"No other way I can get originals," Hallingforth remarks, convincingly. "We've reviewed your military file quite extensively and, obviously, discovered that you've successfully executed our enemies in the line of duty, and in the defense of your country."

Hallingforth pauses, waiting for a comment. Klyne stares, offering no reply. Hallingforth continues, "We are asking you to do it again, and are willing to release you from this life sentence as payment for your services."

An execution. Every hair stands up on the back of his neck and along his arms. The realization strikes him and Klyne blinks once. His heartbeat increases, blood races through his veins, his skin warms, hot and dry, and his palms sweat, cold and clammy.

An incomprehensible enigma stares back at him across the old black desktop. Someone he doesn't know killed a man to get him in here, he'll have to kill a man he doesn't know to get out, and he thought he was done with all that.

Klyne sits, motionless, absolutely amazed. The price of freedom higher than he ever considered. A price he could never imagine. A price he will pay without question, and is prepared to initiate at once. A serene calmness washes over Klyne instantly.

His nerves quiet, his pulse slows, his mental alertness returns. He understands an operation, something tangible, something real, a physical event. The tension floats away. Immediately, Klyne becomes a soldier again, relaxed, assured, and awaiting orders. He gathers his control and hides his emotions.

Klyne stares at the stout government man, confident he now holds his freedom in a suffocating grasp that will not be released until he is.

The same transformation occurs frequently in similar situations with other government agents. The relaxation, the stress release, and the mental and physical preparation for an assignment always appear the same externally. Identical observations occur nearly every time Hallingforth assigns a dangerous operation. It's the nature of undercover work.

Hallingforth watched it hundreds of times in the past and will observe it again in the future each time he assigns a Red Op to his team. He looks away and heaves a quiet sigh of relief, nearly indiscernible, in recognition of the well-known responses that precede the acceptance of an operation.

As if to punctuate the scene, Klyne finally speaks, his voice completely under control now. "What do I have to do?"

Hallingforth clears his throat. "We require the execution of two individuals in the interest of our national security. One lives here in this prison, in a cell exactly like yours. Your method of termination unregulated, we don't care if it looks like an accident. You'll receive no weapons, nor help. We'll deny involvement if you're caught."

"You'll need to hide your work here, at least temporarily until we get you out. If the authorities find out before we can release you, then we probably can't. And, should you attempt to involve our agency if you're caught, we'll deny it, and your incarceration here will become permanent. The life sentence."

"We can guarantee that as quickly as we can your release. You won't receive information regarding our second target until after you successfully eliminate the first and we've retrieved you. The second target is not incarcerated and lives in another country."

"Why me?"

"Simple, basis for this execution, national security on a need to know. You don't in this case, but you happen to be the only individual presently in this prison with the operational training and ability to complete this operation and the following one. You also have the clearance. To your benefit, however unfortunate, you happen to be in the right place at the right time. It's that simple."

"What are my guarantees? I want assurances I'll not be ignored afterward, like last time. Made a deal with the D. A. once. Here I sit, fucked! Great deal."

"You have none. I couldn't order the warden from his office, and use his phone unless I have that power. Wouldn't be carrying your military files in my briefcase if I couldn't do this. Believe it. You have only one chance."

"Choose now."

Klyne says nothing. Hallingforth stares, immobile. "Right now."

Klyne stares back, unflinching. "The target?" He had chosen long before he met the government agent. "And how do I contact you?"

"Once you've set your operation, send the warden a message. He'll contact me. He believes you may become a federal witness, and you'll have made up your mind when you ask to see me. You'll then have twenty-four hours, so be certain before you tell him."

"We'll extract you the following evening, the same day you execute. Otherwise, someone may figure it out and hold you here. If you fail, we ignore you and modify our operation." Hallingforth stares again. "No second chance."

"Money," Klyne says, his blue eyes glacial, his voice rigid, containing no fear. "Got no money when I get out. It cost me everything for a lawyer, and then some."

"What did it cost, how much did you have?"

"Eight thousand dollars." Klyne bluffs. He cares nothing for the money. But, he bluffs anyway.

"Done. In an account as soon as you leave here." A thin smile barely cracks the agent's face. He quickly controls the twitch but gave himself away.

Klyne already named the amount, expressing his own ignorance. Entering the high-stakes game, Klyne requested a pint-sized bankroll. Recognizing his mistake immediately, he continues almost without pause. "That's for the initial target. We'll negotiate the second fee when the information becomes available to me. And I retain the option to abort if it's not set right at the beginning, and redesign the operation myself in the field."

Hallingforth pauses, as if undecided, but knows he's been had this time, fakes thinking about it a moment and then says, "Agreed, but we retain the option to re-set an alternate if you abort, conditioned on your input."

Klyne nods his head. Typical operations control, abort, plan again, abort, plan, adjust and execute. With his skills and field experience, child's play.

"It's agreed. Raise your right hand." Hallingforth falsely swears Klyne in as a deputy special agent.

"A name," Klyne demands.

"Rafael Alphonse."

Klyne eases back on his chair, envisioning a small office with books piled everywhere and an extremely unfortunate library clerk dressed in convict garb, sitting behind a wooden desk. Dungaree pants cover his thin legs, his spit-shined shoes resting comfortably on top of a blotter. The clerk nods his head against his chest, dozing as often as not.

A smile tickles the corners of his mouth. Klyne frequently spends time in the library and sees the library clerk asleep at the desk frequently. He now envisions the man dead. The rudiments of a plan form behind his gaze immediately. Klyne blinks away the vision as the agent speaks again.

"If there's nothing further, knock twice on that door and the guard will return you to your cell. You must be operational in ten days. I'll expect your contact prior to that. Otherwise, we chose another method. We're in hurry, as usual."

"Traditional," Klyne remarks. "The Red Stamp." He knocks twice and steps out. The door swings shut behind him.

Hallingforth reaches into his briefcase, removes a half-pint flask and swallows half the whiskey. He coughs and wipes his mouth. Sweat breaks out on his brow and the nervous spasm returns beneath his eye. His dark eyes sink further into their sockets.

"Time," he mutters, "no time, no time. It's time." He managed to remain complacent and official for the last hour, but beneath the stress-filled wreckage of his face, a special smile suddenly stretches slowly across his cheeks. George M. Hallingforth III rises, straightens his tie, wipes his brow, and gathers himself and his briefcase, then pushes the door open.

*

Klyne returns to his cell, tormented. His country calls again, though he does not understand the reasons. But, he had known little about his military assignments either, at least not the grand strategy. Mutely, obediently, and continuously, he followed his orders while other men determined the long-range needs and goals, and evaluated his success.

His depression disappears and in its place grows a plan. A different future exists now and, in the tiniest corner of his mind, Klyne nurtures a bright smile with dimples hanging beside it. The smile belongs to Sarah Recent. But that's later, first the soldier begins designing his strategies, and he knows he'll spend a lot more time in the library.

Mac will return this evening, his family visit ends today. Klyne opens in his locker, finds two full cartons and two packs, three Snickers bars, and two granola bars, and three soft plastic water bottles. Wonders if that's enough to pay Mac a fee.

*

The lunch bells ring. The gate bangs open and Klyne jumps down off his bunk. His clean-up job begins at ten in the morning and again at three in the afternoon. Usually he carries his books back to the cell, but he'll change that routine immediately. He'll read in the library and observe his target.

The soldier feels no negative emotions. In the past, he executed men in the name of his country and will do so again. The hardship of moral judgment falls to others and he effectively excuses himself by ordained reasoning.

Apparently, a greater social need exists than the value of one unfortunate life, according to a high-level representative of that same government.

Barred doors clang open along the tiers. Klyne steps outside his cell and marches through the cellblock, out the steel gate, and into the corridor, mingling with the other inmates. Another bang as the doors slam shut. Quietly, he moves along the concrete floors, cleaned and shined by daily sweat, but old, cracked, and dingy nonetheless. His steps make no sound, a soldier on the prowl, stalking his victim.

Klyne enters the mess hall and stands in line behind a huge inmate who spends all day in the weight-yard. Thick dark muscle stretches his shirt-sleeves and the man owns no neck. A short, curled, afro crowns a bullet head that attaches directly to shoulders that seem to end just beneath his ears. The convict walks with an exaggerated swagger that keeps his muscular thighs from rubbing together.

Without delay, Klyne kicks his plan into action. He reaches up and punches the huge weightlifter lightly in the back. "Hey, Lil' John, what's for lunch." Klyne cleans the weight-yard every day and knows every inmate that pushes iron.

"Greasy chicken, doncha know? Monday. Trade your chicken for my cake again?" It sounds almost like an order, but not quite. Klyne and the big convict nearly always trade on Mondays. Many inmates often trade a portion of each meal.

Some like sweets, some like vegetables, and Lil' John eats all the meat he can get. He always stands at the head of the line whether he arrives first or not. He served eight years this time with six more to go. His second time down, he buffs iron every day, rain or shine. Not an inmate here can bench-press more weight than Lil' John, nor do any challenge him for head of the chow line when he arrives, or for second helpings, or even thirds whenever that opportunity occurs.

"Yeah, okay," Klyne agrees without thinking, his mind absorbed, evaluating schemes and tactics. He needs more information before his plan materializes, and wonders, if he kills Alphonse, 'No', he reminds himself – when he kills Alphonse, will the government agent honor his part of the curious bargain?

His memory of the distorted deal the Marin County prosecutor promoted stings his throat, but Klyne swallows the bitterness and promises himself that if Wings fails to release him, he will escape anyway and find the agent, whatever it takes. He made up his mind long ago that he will not stay in prison and serve his sentence regardless, even before the federal agent offered the 'get out of jail free' card.

"Might need something from your shop, Lil' John."

"Everything got a price." The huge man curls his lips in anticipation. A 'gimme' always brings a little extra to the repair shop foreman.

"Okay. Let you know." Klyne eats quickly, wanting to investigate the library today.

The lack of activity makes him antsy. A new future lies before him and he's anxious to participate. And, tucked away in a secret corner of his mind, dark-haired beauty awaits his release. Pushing his tray and silverware through a slot into the dishwasher, Klyne hurries along the passageway and crosses to the next building.

He glances up, reminding himself that armed guards follow every move of every inmate when the cellblocks slide open and the inmate population moves about the facility. The guards stand above, staring into the courtyard. Nooks and crannies are non-existent in corridors, passages, or the yards.

Every cellblock hosts piercing eyes, and leaves nothing invisible, nor hidden. Supposedly.

Klyne steps through the gate into his cellblock. One inmate stands against the wall, one guard watches the convict while another searches cell number fifteen, a random shakedown hunting contraband. Happens a lot, officials seeking weapons, drugs, or cash money select a cell for no specific reason and search it top to bottom, stripping sheets and pillow cases off the beds, open lockers and dump everything out. Flip pages in the books and pull clothing inside out, check cuffs and pockets.

But convicts scheme continuously, preying on the lazy habits and the diluted mental attitude of the guards, carefully shifting illegal paraphernalia, home-made alcohol, and drugs into the cells the officers most recently searched. A never-ending cycle emerged over the years. Seek-then-hide, the sufficiently reversed variation of a well-known childhood game keeps the contestants busy with entertainment carefully labeled work.

Klyne stops and backs against the wall as well, waiting until the shakedown ends and he's allowed into his cell. He grins at his neighbor. Willy Cable shoots Klyne a thumbs-up, shakes his head, grins and mouths 'Nothing'. Klyne continues planning a way to gather and hide the equipment he needs.

The shakedown finds no contraband. The officers release the hold, the gates slide open and several inmates waiting in the hallway file into the cells. Klyne steps into his own house, finds Mac sitting on his bunk. "Looks like Willy gets the pruno wagon today," Mac says. "He's off the list now, won't get another shake for at least a few weeks." The cells gates slam shut.

Klyne laughs. "Yup, shake Willy today, safe Willy tomorrow."

After the count, Klyne quickly eats dinner and heads down into the library, examining the layout, paying careful attention to details he ignored in the past.

The library opens into the hallway through two wooden doors. Yellow with age and historical dirt, an unbarred window stares across the yard toward the visiting room. Shelves bursting with books line the room and five inmates huddle around four scratched-up old tables. Klyne recognizes all but one. "Must be a new guy," he whispers to himself, identifying all factors that may affect his plans.

A Dutch-door open at the top and another door beside it lead into a pair of offices. Beyond one open door, the librarian sits at his desk checking magazines the mail clerk just delivered. The remaining room contains a desk, a small table, a stack of bookshelves, and Rafael Alphonse. Unfortunately, he's still breathing.

"Not for long," the thought pops into his mind as Klyne opens the bottom half of the Dutch-door and enters. Short, skinny, and brown, he clerk sits at the desk labeling new books. He combs black hair straight back above round steel-rimmed glasses, a pencil moustache, a thin protruding jaw, and thin lips. His face resembles the rodents inmates routinely see scurrying around the buildings. He earned the nickname 'Rat' for his facial structure, not because he snitches, and no one calls it to his face. Alphonse lights a cigarette and leans back in his chair, ignoring the no smoking sign hanging behind him.

"Not supposed to be in here, library's out there," the clerk says, running a thumb along the crease in his denims. He strokes his moustache and speaks, exhaling a thin stream of smoke through both nostrils. "Beat it."

"Sorry." Klyne makes his way back into the library and examines it again. He looks out both windows. A tower rises above the wall beyond the exercise quad and sunlight winks back at Klyne when the guard sweeps his binoculars across the yard, stopping at each window in each building, a quick peek inside. Klyne checks the line of sight and discovers the guard cannot see into either office, even with the glasses.

Klyne leaves the library and hurries along the corridor. Approaching the weight-yard, he circles the chain-link barrier and enters through the gate, nodding. Two convicts spot heavily-laden weight bars above two others sweating and straining beneath the iron. Lil' John stands with his feet spread and holds a weight bar above his head, dropping and lifting, dropping and lifting, a quick rhythm behind his neck.

"Need something." Klyne says. Lil' John looks down at him but says nothing, the iron rising and falling in a steady cadence. "Need two eye-hooks big enough to hold twenty or thirty pounds each."

"Trade your dinner meat every day for a week."

"Kind of expensive."

"Can't afford it, don't ask. Just git the fuck outta my sweat."

Klyne shrugs. "Okay, done."

Klyne races through his workout, sweeps the yard and stores his tools, then stacks several weights on the storage racks. Thirty minutes remain before the four twenty bell rings, recalling each convict to his cell. Each one then stands at the bars, and waits for the count to clear before the night feeding.

At three-fifty Klyne enters the library, grabs a book, and finds a seat. He peeks into the office. Alphonse sits hunched over his desk, writing. The same short black inmate Klyne met the day he arrived runs the cart in and stacks the books he collected back onto the proper shelves. At four o'clock the Freeman taps each remaining inmate on the shoulder and points at the clock.

Klyne sits, quiet, pretending he's engrossed in his book until the librarian taps him. Klyne looks up.

The friendly smile on the chubby face makes it a request, not an order. "You gotta get out. We close at four on the button so you guys get home for count."

Klyne steps out, but dallies in the hallway long enough that he suddenly fears he might miss count. Alphonse and the cart man remain inside. Finally, the door opens, and both inmates rush down the hall. Klyne trails directly behind them, past the cellblock the men enter together and cycles into his own. A grim smile betrays his thoughts. MacKlain returns tonight and both clerks stay twenty minutes beyond closing.

24

"Fourteen, stepping in," Klyne yells down the hall.

Conroy MacKlain lies on the lower bunk, his eyes wide open, staring back at the weekend. He blinks as the cell door slams open and Klyne enters, and blinks again as it bangs shut. "Howdy Jake. Looks like nothing's changed," observes Mac.

Klyne climbs up on his bunk and Mac slides out and sits on a stool beneath a small writing table bolted to the wall between two personal storage lockers.

"How was it?" Klyne asks. The thought of Sarah Klyne arriving for a conjugal visit if he fails in this mission sends a chill down his spine. Not anxious to discover what such a visit might be like, he shudders, chasing the idea away.

"You need to ask?" Mac says.

The bell rings three times and a guard walks along the rows, counting heads. Mac begins his own tally, counting and replacing tiny plastic chips with a hole in the center. He strings them on a thin leather thong.

Each morning since his arrival, Klyne watched Mac remove a chip and place it in a Band-aid box, but never asked about them.

Mac looks up. "Ninety-four." He stops counting and stringing. "Ninety-four days until my next vacation. Rather see the pile get smaller each day. The fewer chips, the closer my wife and boy." Mac signed up immediately for the next available opening, as does every inmate when each returns from a family visit. Mac lives for the visits, and his law books.

Nine days remain, and Klyne kicks his plan into gear. "Need a job change, Mac." The statement lies there, naked as a thorn. Mac begins counting again, but says nothing, finishes, and puts the remaining chips away, "How come? Thought you liked the outside air and the job." And, almost without a pause, "Probably cost ya," Mac says, already plotting another sale.

"Want a bigger pay number, got no money and looks like I'll be here awhile. Need as much time in the library as I can. Maybe get myself out on something technical the D.A. missed. Got to read up on the law books, like you." No sense wasting time, in San Quentin State Prison and you pay for what you get. Period.

"No sense pussyfooting around Mac, I want the library clerk's job."

"No can do. Alphonse, rat that he is, got too much money and power. Was a big, big timer on the streets. Accidentally caught one by the DEA. One of the narcotics guys bought it during a drug smuggling operation he was running and the feds kicked his ass, made the state put him inside. Couldn't even buy his way out. But, that won't last. Imagine he'll spring himself soon as he can get at his money. He's been here 'bout eight months. Seems like his partners ain't helping him out none."

That makes sense. Alphonse must've stepped on some pretty big federal toes and been involved in some top level activities to get Wings attention. And Jonathan Wings must be a pretty powerful individual just to authorize the hit.

"No. I want the cart job, delivering books. What about the little black guy." Klyne wants to work with Alphonse in the library, not replace him. Replacing him will just add more complications.

"Cost you. A lot. He's getting out on parole, be gone in four months. But there's a waiting list for big pay numbers and you ain't even down on it. Besides, library job's a cush job, everybody wants it."

Klyne says, "How much, Mac?"

Conroy MacKlain smiles, the grin indicating his fat bank account is about to get fatter. "Fifty bucks and you got it when he leaves." A voice as thick as a file rasping on the jail cell bars wipes the grin off his face.

"How much for right now. Immediately. Or do I go to somebody else?"

"Can't. No one else can do it. Everyone else just charge you a pack or two for information then tell you to see me." Mac chuckles. "Even if we wasn't cellmates. Least I can save you two packs." The smile slides back onto his face. "You really want a pay number don't you, or is it the law books?"

Mac glances up at Klyne. "Or is it something else?"

Klyne pushes hard now, completely in control. Mac never passes up a sale. And if Mac can't do it, it can't be done, and Klyne needs that knowledge now.

"The price, Mac," he waits a few seconds, "the price by breakfast bells in the morning or I withdraw the offer and figure out something else."

Mac turns his smile to the wall.

Klyne hides his relief, rolls over and faces his wall too, bunches a fist. *Yes!* Silently pops into his brain.

*

Mac remains out after dinner, returning ten minutes before the final lock-up count. "Fourteen, stepping in." Mac's voice echoes down the corridor and the gatekeeper releases the lock. Mac enters. Klyne lies on his bunk, staring at the ceiling even after Mac sits down.

"Pay number's eighteen a month, the price is one year's pay. In advance." Mac speaks matter-of-factly, tosses his cap on the locker and unbuttons his shirt.

Peanuts. The price, peanuts. Klyne would pay thousands. Jonathan Wings gave himself away when Klyne named a price too low, but recovered and will raise his ante for the second job. He stares at the bars, composing himself. He won't give Mac the same opportunity.

"How do I pay? You can't fit that many packs in your locker?" Both men laugh aloud at the absurd thought. Each inmate locker measures about three cubic feet. Inmates never carry money, it's against the rules. Convicts barter work, food, favors, protection, sex, drugs, or packs of smokes. Cash in hand gets confiscated and an additional penalty an inmate would rather not pay. Cigarette packs act as currency inside the walls, the going exchange rate equal to one package at the central store on the yard where inmates purchase candy, tobacco, and other snacks.

"Easy, I'll give you my bank account number, when your family or your attorney makes the deposit the deed's done. Simple as that. Wife monitors it, lets me know."

"How about we do it now and I'll have my family send the money." Klyne decides he'll send Mac the money personally, from outside. No reason to cheat the old convict, Klyne just wants to implement his plan without delay.

"No way. Don't do C.O.D ... let alone credit. Do I look like a bank teller? This here cell ain't no credit union. Cash in advance. Period."

Klyne shuts his eyes and racks his brain. Dodds and O'Brien he disregards. They'll ask too many questions, and his family's too far away, and complicated. He'll have to explain it too.

Klyne has more than enough money in his own prison account, but the prison bookkeeper will ask questions. The staff always refuses a transfer of money from one inmate account to another anyway unless the warden approves it, and it needs a very good reason.

He rolls off his bunk, retrieves paper and an envelope, writes a brief note, and addresses the envelope to the warden. He'll contact Wings. If Wings told the truth, the government intelligence expert he claims, he'll recognize the note as a request to talk, and won't pull him out yet. He places the note under his pillow and sleeps on it.

*

Two days later he sits at the black desk and greets Jonathan Wings. "Pretty quick response. Glad you didn't pull me out."

"Pretty obvious you wanted to see me. Don't do it again, and this better be good." The agent appears nervous or angry, a cheek twitches. Klyne doesn't know him well enough to guess or care about it.

Klyne explains his need and how Wings can accomplish it. Handing the agent a scrap of paper with the bank account number on it, Klyne says, "No deduction from my fee. Seems a legitimate operational expense to me." Without waiting for a reply, he turns, knocks twice, the door swings open. Klyne steps through it without glancing back.

*

Klyne naps each day before his afternoon job, cleaning the weight yard. Mac shakes Klyne awake two days after he had met with the government man. His eyes blink open and Klyne looks down at Mac.

"You gotta job change coming out tomorrow. Appears our friend Mister Brown got tapped today. Cops pulled a random shakedown in his cell, found a little baggie a heroin tucked under his bunk. They rolled him up and sent him off to the hole for a few weeks. That happens, ya' always lose the pay number. Just the rules.

"Funny thing. He killed his wife for screwin' around on him, caught her in his own bed with some cowboy. Guy jumped out the window barefoot and slipped on the fire escape. Broke an ankle. Dumb rodeo clown forgot he was on the second floor."

"Then the little dude beat her to death with her lover's boots ... metal heels. Never touches drugs, not even on the streets. He'll sure be after somebody's butt if he gets outta the hole before his parole." Mac lies down and shuts his eyes, his smile reflecting a larger pile of dollars and cents.

The bells ring three times. The night count begins and ends. The lights dim twice then blink out and darkness engulfs the cellblock.

*

The silence edges away. As light as Klyne sleeps, Mac wakes him each day while beginning his morning chores. Living together in tight quarters induces an intimately courteous relationship similar to marriage, including sexual activities as often as not, but usually lacks the arguments. Verbal battles often turn violent in the prison environment, and an inmate will move before taking that chance. If you can't get along, you don't live together.

Klyne rises immediately. A purpose motivates his actions and he assumes Mac received confirmation of the payment. "Guess I'll check the sheet before chow and report to my new job afterwards."

"Won't be disappointed," The response climbs from darkness atop the throne. He skipped his session of legal investigation this morning, the cell light remains dark. "You paid and you got it ... s'all there is to it."

Klyne stands inside the bars. When the door slams open, he steps through and hurries down the walkway, stopping before the movement sheet. His eyes roll down the lists, reading quickly.

Inmate assignments, activities, and appointments line two columns. The third column names men paroled the day before, or died before they could gain a discharge. Interesting how the two equate.

Klyne finds his name atop the fourth column and lists his new job as library book clerk. The soldier relaxes, the operation now completely under his control and, in that instant, his freedom run begins.

After breakfast, he heads straight for the library where he finds two inmates seated at the tables, reading. The Freeman loafs behind his desk, sausage-shaped fingers surrounding a cup of creamy coffee that warms his hands. Klyne enters and gives his name.

"Taking Brown's place, I gather." The librarian sips and nods at the book cart. "You'll run the cart three days a week, bring books to the lock-up cells, and then re-stack everything you bring back. Aside from that, Alphonse tells you what he needs."

He blows on the coffee and sips again. Steam spirals above the white ceramic cup and Klyne detects a slight coffee odor mingling with the sickly sweet cologne the man always wears. A large chrome percolator stands in the corner, reflecting a distorted picture of the library and the assortment of unmatched cups stacked beside it.

"Have a cup if you like," he offers. "My name is Gregory Packard, and mister isn't necessary. Gregory will be fine." Packard works as a freeman employee, not a guard or correctional officer, and believes he has an easier time with the convicts if he deletes the mister, a correct assumption.

He slurps more coffee and dips a sugared donut, stuffs it into his mouth. White powder drifts down, settling on his tie and shirtfront. He licks his lips and his fingers. More than a Packard, he reminds Klyne of a happy toad with bulging eyes. A wide slit of a mouth aimed at Klyne turns up at the corners and a sagging triple chin shakes each time Packard moves or speaks. "Have you any experience with the Dewey system for stacking books?"

"Not a lot," Klyne responds, "except I can find any book I need and put it back." He grabs a cup, pours, and sips the brown liquid, much better and hotter than mess hall coffee.

"Well, that's a start. Work with Alphonse when he arrives and he'll show you what to do. I open every day at eight, but you inmates start at nine. You'll alternate weekends with Alphonse, too, soon as you know the routine." Packard waddles over and refills his cup.

"We close at four, get you back for count. Alphonse opens evenings Monday and Tuesday, and Thursday and Friday from seven until nine. Wednesdays we're closed. You guys can trade off the evenings too, once you know how to operate things. It's a lot of hours, but it's a big pay number and though you have to be here, time's your own after the work's done. You'll earn your money."

"Yes, I'll earn my money," Klyne predicts, and a grim smile spreads across his face. The big, fat eighteen-dollar pay number will never be drawn this month, at least not by him. But there remains no doubt in his mind he will definitely earn his pay.

"Wander around if you like, Alphonse will be here shortly."

Packard proves correct. The short, thin clerk in meticulously pressed jeans and shirt arrives at the stroke of nine and enters the library, walks directly into the office. After a few minutes speaking with Packard, Alphonse returns carrying a cup of coffee and approaches Klyne, introducing himself.

"Come in my office and I'll tell you about procedures." He speaks in precise wording that sounds as if he learned English from a language course, but his voice hangs heavy with a Spanish accent. "My procedures," he emphasizes his authority.

Alphonse sits behind an ancient wooden desk retired from an elementary school classroom a thousand years ago. The clerk pushes his chair back against the wall and surveys the office and the main book section through the door. Satisfied his castle is safe, he rips open a pack of cigarettes and throws the wrappings into a dented green trash can lined with a white plastic baggie. The can overflows with paper scraps and book wrappings. The clerk fires up a match, inhales then blows smoke.

Alphonse says, "Take the cart each Tuesday, Thursday, and Friday and deliver books to the fish tank and the locked down security cells. Come back and re-shelve the books you pick up. Other days you catalog new arrivals, the rest of the time do what you want, just don't leave the building unless you tell me."

"This is a cush job," Alphonse repeats Mac's appraisal of the paid position, "for both of us. Don't screw it up, for you or for me. Especially me. There's too many rules in this prison already, but I'm adding a few of my own, right now. Don't do no drugs in this building. Ever. And don't hide pruno, or brewing either, because if I find out you jeopardized my spot here you'll wish the warden has locked you in the hole and melted the key."

Klyne notes the imperfect English, but ignores it. No reason to correct a dead man or to speak in the man's native tongue, even though Klyne could correct him in either language.

Alphonse blinks once and squints. "Senor-r-r-r." His sarcastic intent inherent in the way he rolls the last word off his tongue and shows his teeth. He speaks precise English, but his accent bounces in and out and he points his glare directly at Klyne as if it frightens him. He tightens his accent more than normal, as if proving he means every word as an order. "Remember, we work together here and it's much easier if we both understand my rules."

"Don't do drugs anyway." Klyne lies, unafraid. He smokes marijuana twice a day, three or four times a week while walking the track. And, dead men never scare him. Alphonse just doesn't realize that fact, and hasn't fallen over yet.

"And don't like pruno much," Klyne lies again. He often drinks the alcohol brew inmates ferments from mashed grain, vegetable juice or fruit the wine-makers secretly retrieve from the mess hall.

Hidden from a prowling shakedown crew randomly searching the cells and prison grounds in an easily predictable pattern, the pruno stills move from one cell to another daily, and each team steps up to the bar immediately after an exquisite aging period that lasts several days. In an amazing feat of ingenuity, inmates steal vegetables or fruit, sugar, and yeast then mix it with water and pressurize it with a chlorine-based siphoning tube that kills the brewing odor while the mixture percolates.

A vintner's wet dream? Not exactly, but an extremely creative and very simple processing system. One that works quite effectively and efficiently in a captive social system, and produces the wine many convicts crave.

*

Klyne continues his exercise routine, running twenty laps daily around the track, then walks the last two. He avoids smoking pot, and curtails his alcohol. He throws off the cloudy, euphoric escape the drugs allow, and begins planning his departure.

Changing his daily routine this morning, Klyne heads out the cell door and hits the track immediately after breakfast then pushes iron in the weight yard, working up a healthy sweat for an hour. No alcohol, no drugs from here on.

He rolls off the weight bench and heads toward his library job. As often as time permits during the day, he sits quietly at one of the tables, reading and observing.

Klyne stares over a law book, his relentless blue eyes stalking his prey. Alphonse usually remains in his office, relaxing, reading, occasionally even doing his job. His other assistant performs most of the actual work, a carryover from the typical power structure in the American workplace.

When not in his office, Alphonse often leaves the library, but appears at four o'clock every day, without fail, and closes up. He tidies his office and prepares for the evening hours. Packard never works nights, or Wednesday afternoons. The staff and supervisors meet every Wednesday and nearly every employee attends – the staff eats, drinks coffee and heads home early. No sense returning to the job and wasting time working, even if the meeting ends before the normal punch-out.

During every spare moment, Klyne hides behind his law books, designing his lethal operation and banking heavily on the continuity of prison routine. He backs it up with his ability to adapt in the field, and gains confidence hourly as his plan matures. He exits the building, seeking Mac.

Mac lies on his bunk, eyes closed, breathing lightly when the cell door slams sideways. His eyes flick open, but he says nothing when Klyne enters. Mac shuts his eyes again when the door bangs shut. Mac took the day off today and awaits the bell announcing the evening meal.

"Need string Mac, where can I get it?"

Mac's awake. No one sleeps through the pandemonium when the count bells ring and a hundred cell doors bang open at the same time, then slam back into a steel cradle. He answers without opening his eyes. "We get boxes tied with it instead a tape. How much you need, and what for?"

"Want to weave a headband, tired of sweat dripping in my eyes when I run and workout. Don't like a hat." Klyne manufactures a reasonable need, and keeps his secret.

He made a deal with Lil' John, too. Trade the weight-lifter his dinner meat for a week in exchange for two metal eye-hooks, a very high but reasonable jail price under normal circumstances. Lil' John will have to smuggle the metal out of the workshop and through the detectors, a difficult chore.

Klyne cares nothing about the price or his meat. He knows he'll be gone. A journey home engages his mind full-time now, and nothing stands in his way, least of all money or food, especially prison grub.

"Leave two packs on my bunk. I'll bring string home tomorrow." Mac never opens his eyes during the entire transaction.

*

Deft fingers weave back and forth, in and out, slowly giving birth to a thirty-six inch braid. Klyne sprawls across his bunk, making quick work of the white cotton headband. He winds it once around his forehead and knots it. The ends tickle his neck. He hid two metal eye-hooks in a law book earlier. Lil' John earned his extra meat today.

Emotionless, Klyne stares at the scratched concrete ceiling and waits for tomorrow. The faceless gray suit in his dreams disappeared, as will the endless days and nights of his miserable confinement. The rat-faced library clerk will take his final breath, and a short, fat government agent will release Klyne from the redundant banging steel. Klyne rolls over, faces the wall and shuts his eyes. The anguish that filled his last few months disintegrates.

25

Tuesday morning, as usual, Mac wakes Klyne while performing his residential chores. A smile creases his face as Klyne jumps down from his bunk. The bells ring and he races out of the cell, clutching an envelope addressed to the warden. He passes it to the gate guard. He looks forward to breathing free air tomorrow night.

*

Klyne enters the library and helps himself to hot coffee. He checks his request list and fills his cart with reading material for the lock-down blocks, and checks his metal eye-hooks. His tools remain safe, and he adjusts the cotton sweatband. The rear wheel squeaks goodbye when the book cart rolls into the hallway. Alphonse sits behind his desk marking new books and ignoring the rest of the world.

Klyne completes his rounds in two hours and returns with the cart. Lunch hour approaches. At eleven-fifteen, Alphonse stands up, shelves his books, and saunters out the door for lunch. Klyne fiddles with the books, killing time, and watches the last inmate leave at eleven-fifteen. He carries the law book into the clerk's office immediately. Keeping one eye on the door and the other on his work, he screws both eye-hooks into the underside of the desktop in front of where Alphonse sits, and hurries back outside.

Klyne wanders the grounds, examining potential escape opportunities in case Wings fails to honor his agreement. Klyne began planning his own way out as soon as he arrived, but moved it into a back-up mode when Wings offered Klyne a job. But the longer he wanders the yard, the more apparent it becomes that he will need patience, time, and probably a lot more money than what's currently in his bank account if Wings abandons him.

Patience and time he has plenty and, engraved on his memory, a phone number leads the way to Wings if the agent fails to perform. Klyne spends the remaining hours plotting an escape and his back-up strategy, just in case. The workday ends and he returns to his cell, but his eyes remain open long past lights out. Finally, mental exhaustion and the late hour claims him and he succumbs to the darkness, sleeping heavily and dreamless.

*

At zero four-thirty Wednesday morning Klyne listens to silence, his mood restless and anxious. His eyes ease open, bare slits, searching the dawn, and he strains his ears. He shakes himself alert and peers out at motionless shadows beyond the bars. The prison sleeps as a ghostly graveyard. A muffled cough or a burst of flatulence puncture echoes through the bars occasionally. Stale and musty, the odor of wasted humanity permeates the stagnant atmosphere.

Ruthless, the executioner waits, certain he will gain his freedom before it ends. Minutes pass, stirrings and mumbles below indicate Mac survived the night. Klyne greets his final day in prison and climbs out of bed, still fully dressed from the day before. He chases the gloom away and a grim smile crosses his face.

Klyne and Mac step across the threshold, but Klyne wants no conversation today and lags behind. He walks into the mess-hall alone and surprises Lil' John. Klyne places a full tray beside the weight-lifter without a word, slaps him on the shoulder, and walks away before the convict can respond. Shiny white teeth and a large black grin follow Klyne out.

*

Heavy gray clouds hide the sky and light raindrops sprinkle a chilling wetness over the prison grounds. Klyne wanders, reflecting absently on his past military missions when departure occurred immediately after his assignment. The delay creates more disruption in his mind, influencing his mental state, and the unproductive waiting taxes his patience. He enters the weight yard, lies on the bench and starts pumping iron. A heavy workout reduces the stress, kicks up the endorphins, calms the brain.

The minute hand ticks zero nine hundred. Klyne steps into the library and looks into his work tray. Unfortunately, it contains a short stack of papers and ten new books, an easy work day much lighter than he hoped. The day will pass slowly, but he has a date at sixteen hundred, a dance with the devil. Klyne collects his papers, approaches his table, drops into his chair, and peeks inside the office. His eyes fall on an empty chair where Alphonse usually sits.

A jolt of energy rocks his body and he quickly places his work aside and enters the main library office. He grabs a cup and fills it. Barely controlling his voice he asks, "Alphonse absent today?" deathly afraid Packard will say yes.

"Not feeling well this morning and went to sick call. Might not make it back." The librarian responds casually to the most important question Klyne ever asked. "He's got some kind of recurring viral infection and sometimes misses several days in a row. You'll have to tend checkouts this afternoon if he goes back to his cell. But I'll be around if something comes up you can't handle."

This new information certainly would have influenced his plan if Klyne had known it. The nasty coincidence unsettles him. A hot rush rages inside his skull as he realizes he might not see Alphonse today. He struggles, barely remains passive, using every ounce of his skill. "Oh," sounds flat in the air.

Klyne staggers back to his worktable. *No! No! No!* He screams silently into the hollow space inside his mind that most recently contained his plan. *Wings will pull me out tonight, and then put me back forever.* The words echo in his brain, threatening his sanity. He must find a way, he must find the clerk.

Klyne forces open a law book, gaining time, thinking, staring blankly at the print. A few troubled moments pass. His mind blanks out until he feels a presence behind his chair. Gregory Packard reaches over Klyne's shoulder and turns the law book right-side up.

"Pretty good trick, if you can read upside-down. But I'll bet day-dreaming won't help you beat your sentence," the librarian says, chuckling as he walks away.

The morning hours drag and, after finishing his work, Klyne remains in the library and controls the book checkout. Unable to leave and find Alphonse and then adjust his plan, his eyes follow Packard approaching the desk again.

"You'll have to return this afternoon and work checkout again if Alphonse takes the day off," Packard says. "Staff meeting this afternoon and I'll be gone. And we're closed this evening anyway." He reminds Klyne, "We're never open Wednesday night."

Three off-hand statements steal nearly all the time that remains. If the plan fails, a life sentence bounces back at him out of nowhere and once again hovers on the horizon, beckoning, embracing his soul with its arms stretched wide, 'Come on back to me', it sings, the words harsh and bitter in his mind.

"You can eat lunch at eleven-thirty, be back by twelve-thirty. The staff meets at one today," Packard says, producing an hour. Klyne cradles the gift. Sixty minutes.

Containing his urge to run, which always aggravates the guards, Klyne walks quickly toward the mess hall. He searches the room, eyes roaming, hunting, checking every inmate, then he turns and scans those still in line. No Alphonse.

Klyne continues his search into the next building, but discovers sick-call locked and empty, with everyone gone to lunch. Worried, unable to locate his prey, Klyne prowls the dingy corridors, the mud-soaked weight yard, and tracks across the open quad, oblivious to the drizzling wetness blowing about.

He examines every face and gets some odd looks in return, some even threatening. Finally approaching Alphonse's cell block, located one corridor beyond his own, he stops at the gate. Prison rules forbid any inmate to enter a cellblock unless he lives inside it, no exceptions.

Klyne asks, "Alphonse in his house? Need to ask him a question about library checkouts and Packard left early." Klyne prepares a frivolous question, but only wants the information ... If he is, the plan collapses. Absolutely no way can Klyne enter this cell block.

"Nope," replies the guard, "checked out for sick-call early. Ain't seen him since." Klyne receives that good news with relief, except now it makes him worry that Alphonse has been referred to the prison hospital, equally as inaccessible as his house.

Twelve twenty, the minutes tick off quickly. His brain races much faster than his feet, Klyne hurries back and enters the library, forming and rejecting plan after plan as he searches his brain. If only he can locate the target.

And, recognizing one final option for a confirmed atheist, just like his father, Klyne almost prayed he will find Alphonse today. Klyne actually looked up at the sky once while searching the yard, but then shook his head.

Appearing reserved and busy at his worktable, he covers all his options, building a new plan, pushed hard by seconds disappearing too fast. All of his backup strategies dissolve in a flood of uselessness if he cannot locate The Rat.

Klyne never imagined a sickly Alphonse would fail to appear at work. No alternative remains but to explain when Wings arrives tonight. If the agent really wants this operation completed bad enough, which he obviously does, then he must adjust like any other agent in the field. You have orders, but you modify in the field if the situation changes or endangers an operative. That's pretty classic decision-making process in any military operation, and should hold true in federal security operations as well.

Alternately staring at the law book and glancing at the clock, Klyne watches the hands tick up to eleven and four, the final minutes. A slight movement catches the corner of his eye, and Klyne glances at the door. His lips curl into a deadly smile as Klyne watches The Rat saunter in through the door and enter the room waving an envelope. The clerk tosses two pills into his mouth and bends over the water fountain.

Klyne nearly leaps from his seat to embrace the reed-thin body and kiss the mousy lips. He can almost feel the carefully creased seams squeeze against his chest. Thank you Doctor Deane. Restraining himself, Klyne sits immobile. Now the wait.

Sixteen hundred hours, straight up, time to dance. He hustles a few remaining inmates out the door, then returns and enters the office.

Rafael Alphonse finishes labeling a book. He pauses and asks, "What do you need?" A brief smile cracks beneath his moustache. He glares at Klyne poised inside the door, and then opens his eyes wider. Awareness creeps across his face, his smile dissolving slowly when he recognizes a confrontational development. Alphonse has been involved in killing often and immediately recognizes the look of death that stares across the room.

Alphonse slowly rises. "Who sent you? Those lousy Colombians that won't help me," answering his own question incorrectly. "I can pay you more," he offers, the smile returning but now unreal, forced, insincere. "Much more."

Klyne says nothing, takes two steps forward and waits, confident. A retired elementary school desk stands between Jacoby Klyne and a disappearing life sentence. The doorway stands open directly behind him, the only exit out of this room. Klyne will not be denied.

"How much?" Slowly, Alphonse rises, his eyes dart about, seeking a way out. None exists. "Thought that was kind of strange, you getting this fancy job so quick. Should have known something was slick. How'd you do that, anyway?"

The question remains unanswered. The smell of raw fear accents the mustiness, filling the tiny room. His hands shake, and sweat drips off his chin, and Alphonse narrows his eyes. Suddenly, The Rat bends over and wrenches the wooden leg from his desk. The desk tips sideways, its rear corner dropping. Papers and books slide free and land in a jumbled pile on the concrete. The desperate, terrified look slowly transforms and frightened but vicious cunning stretches across his features in its place.

Alphonse pulls a steel shank from the hollowed out desk leg, sliding his finger into a welded grip. Holding a knife in his right hand and a club in his left, he faces Klyne. The weapons chase away a bit of his fear, but his brow glistens and wet stains quickly darken the shirt beneath his armpits.

Klyne stands his ground, unworried by the amateur challenge, concerned more with the passing time. He must finish quickly and return for the count. Retreating one step, as if fear pushes him away, Klyne baits the target.

Alphonse, showing more confidence now that he's armed, steps sideways and slides around the desk, working toward the open door.

Klyne backs up and sideways another step, letting Alphonse believe he fears attack, and inches away, just beyond reach.

Sweat rolls off Alphonse as he moves cautiously toward escape. Nearly there, he takes two quick steps, easing himself toward the door and freedom. Alphonse clears the edge of the desk and his executioner pounces.

Klyne kicks once. The desk leg flies against the shelf and several books fall on the floor. Quick as a snake, he grabs the knife, nearly crushing the spindly fingers holding it.

Twisting easily, Klyne breaks the wrist and the knife clatters uselessly to the floor. His other hand clamps a chokehold across the clerk's throat and shuts off his air.

Weakly, and with no chance to escape, Alphonse struggles. His eyes bulge and finally roll back in his head.

Klyne now wraps both hands around the clerk, twisting the scrawny neck and crushing the esophagus.

Alphonse kicks out, his ankles thumping weakly against the old desk, and his arms flap uselessly at this sides. A wet crunch punctuates his strangled breathing, and Alphonse coughs blood onto the floor, evacuates his bladder, and settles into death.

"Eight seconds," Klyne whispers with no emotion, and settles the twitching body down onto the concrete floor. "A thousand dollars a second. Beat football players and politicians, and probably most defense lawyers."

Klyne sinks to his knees and blows out his breath ... waiting for the shaking, and the tears. It always comes. But, for reasons beyond him, neither does this time, and after a few minutes Klyne shakes himself alert and begins covering his tracks.

He examines the desk leg, hollowed out and slotted to accept the knife, then anchored beneath the desk, unglued and accessible. He retrieves the shank, replaces it and, lifting the desk corner, installs the leg under it, then gathers and organizes the books and papers into new piles atop the desk.

Klyne unbuttons the dead clerk's shirt and tears off his undershirt and swabs up the blood. He sits Alphonse upright and sticks his hands inside his pants pockets, then grabs the plastic trash can liner. He turns the corpse and places his feet inside the can and quickly wraps the liner around the dead man's head and ties the closure, trapping body fluids that may soon began draining.

He pulls the chair away and bends Alphonse over, stuffing his body inside the cavity beneath the desk. Quickly untying his headband, Klyne knots it to one of the eye hooks he screwed into place the day before and strings it around the body, and then ties it to the other eye-hook screwed into the opposite panel. The woven rope supports the bent-over corpse upright beneath the desk.

Klyne marches quickly to the doorway and looks back at his work. The desk appears old and used, and sits in its normal spot. The swivel chair butts against the wall and only the lower half of the trash can appears beneath the wooden skirt surrounding the desk. No piece of The Rat shows. The desk skirt completely hides Alphonse, his feet balanced in the trash can, the headband holding him upright inside the knee slot.

Satisfied, Klyne turns, in a hurry to make the count and nearly bumps into the guard coming in. "Everyone out? I'm locking up," the guard says, peering inside, a vacant look on his face.

"Just me Holland, Packard's gone to the meeting." Klyne stands inside the door, his entire body vibrating.

Swinging his keys, Holland enters and looks around, then walks into the office.

"Where's Alphonse?" No suspicion in his voice, just curiosity, he backs out and wanders into the opposite office, glancing around.

Klyne follows Holland, prepared to strike instantly. His orders say nothing about the guard or collateral damage, and Klyne prefers that the man live, but nothing will stop him now. At all cost, he'll protect himself and his operation, and his release.

"Alphonse checked into sick call today, and left early. Don't know where he went after," Klyne says, "probably in his house already."

"Okay. You better hurry and make count." Holland jingles the keys behind him as Klyne blows his breath out and quick-steps down the corridor, heading for his cellblock. The guard locks the library doors, wiggling each knob twice, but gently. No suspicion.

*

Mac stands at the gate, staring through bars, awaiting the count. Klyne lies on his bunk, certain the release bell will ring late, if at all. Several times since Klyne arrived, the count tally came up short. Once, an inmate hid himself in a laundry basket, attempting an escape. More than two hours passed that day before the guards found him under the dirty linens. The meal bells rang very late that evening. Only Klyne and the cooling library clerk hidden beneath an ancient desk know that Rafael Alphonse will fail the count today. An inevitable delay.

An unarmed guard carries the tally board up and down the corridor three times, and no meal bell rings. A half-hour passes and he returns with another guard calling out every name. "Stand at the bars and answer up when I call your name," he yells, "and lemme see your ugly mugs."

Klyne rolls off his bunk and answers, Mac the same. The guards inspect each cell, and each inmate, individually. Soon enough the count-man will discover which inmate is absent. Probably knew after once actually, and double check per procedure.

Another hour passes, then another. Finally the dinner bells clang one cell block at a time. The meal consumes several hours. Mac and Klyne walk together down the hallway. The guards lined along the way shepherd the inmates into the mess-hall and return them back to the cells immediately after the meal. All cellblocks remain locked down.

The staff determines early on that Alphonse is missing, and a thorough search continues throughout the prison.

Klyne lies motionless on the top bunk, vacillating between sheer delight at his impending departure and grim despair that the government man might ignore him. Of less significance, his worry that the guards will find the corpse before Wings frees him, if Wings frees him. The lights wink out, but the distant sound of guards searching the grounds carries well past midnight.

"Klyne." From beyond the bars, a rough, garbled voice grates his name, his call to freedom. Truly melodic, the lyrics hover about his eardrums, resonating. Angelic, the notes drift aloft, undulating into his consciousness, the symphonic warble of a springtime songbird. "Klyne, get our ass up," the voice sings, "and get your rags on. The warden wants to see you." The sweetest operetta serenades the cozy darkness of a locked down prison cell. The song of freedom fills the room.

Klyne follows the guard along the empty corridors and both arrive at a metal door in the administration wing. The guard produces a key and turns the lock, entering the meeting room where Klyne first met Wings. His eyes roam quickly. No Jonathan Wings. Instead, Klyne faces the warden, his assistant, and two top-ranking correctional officers.

"Know anything about Alphonse disappearing?"

Klyne shows no surprise. He expected the call as soon as the warden figured out Alphonse is missing. He hoped Wings would beat them to it and get him out first, but this late call makes him wonder. Wings might leave him here, which has always been a possibility, and it's apparent the officials failed to locate Alphonse or they would have asked about his death, not his disappearance.

"Didn't know he was missing. He was out part of the day. Sick, Packard said. You guys check the hospital rooms?"

The men alternate, firing questions, the interrogation lasting twenty fast-paced minutes while amateurs attempt a verbal trap with an ex-Army intelligence specialist that almost finds humor in the novice effort. Almost.

Klyne denies any knowledge that Alphonse missed the count, and expresses complete ignorance of any information regarding his whereabouts. "He never came in today. He went to sick call early this morning." The interrogation finally ends and the officer marches Klyne back to his cell.

Concealing his wrath toward Wings and engrossed now in a plot to escape and retaliate, his anger peaks as he walks along the corridor. Never, in any previous operation, has Klyne been motivated by anger, or by revenge. The cell door slams open. Klyne steps inside.

"Guess they didn't find him yet?" Mac's voice sounds in the darkness. "You better hope you're gone before they do."

"What the hell you talking about?"

"Nothing I know for sure, but I can add. Two and two don't make five, it makes a deal," Mac says, then laughs softly. "Shoulda charged ya more." The old convict rolls over and faces the wall.

26

Hallingforth sits behind the same black table when Klyne enters the room, his ankle chains clinking on the concrete floor. Neither smiles, but a tiny grimace creases his face when Klyne recognizes the chubby federal agent. Klyne short-steps across the worn carpeting and settles into the chair opposite the government man. Hallingforth says nothing, just stares at Klyne, bright-eyed. The question shines on his face. The agent radiates nervousness across the table, failing in his effort to appear at ease.

Ignoring the apparent discomfort, assuming it's normal behavior for the man he's only met twice, Klyne stares directly into the darting eyes of his new employer and demands, "Get me out of here. Today."

A brief smile barely curls up the corners of his mouth before Hallingforth contains the reflex. "These papers indicate your willingness to testify for the federal government on a case of national security. This prison need not know why you're leaving, only that you are, and in my sole custody. Immediately." A thin smile appears again and lingers on his lips this time. He brushes it away. A nerve vibrates in his cheek, his left eye twitches above it.

Klyne scribbles his name on the correct line. "Okay. Do it." He maintains the guise of total composure, but a slightly hurried attitude gives a clue to his tension. "I still need nothing from my cell. Let's get on with it."

Anxiety pushes lightly against his patience but Klyne rolls with the pressure, anticipating a difficult end to this operation. He knows this one will not be as easy as the Alphonse assassination.

Hallingforth slides his chair back, walks to the warden's door and raps twice. He enters, leaving the door ajar. Words filter back into the room. "He agreed and signed off on our witness consent. We're ready to leave."

The warden and Hallingforth return. The warden knocks twice and the entry door unlocks and opens. The warden speaks with the guard outside then returns to the table and scans then signs several papers, shakes hands with the Hallingforth.

He looks a Klyne and remarks derisively, "You'll be back, Klyne. This state doesn't allow its felons to go unpunished." Castigation inherent in his attitude, his mouth resembles an upside-down horseshoe hanging on his thrust out chin. The heavy mustache above it mimics its shape, as if all good luck spilled out years ago. The warden turns and strides back through his office door.

Brass keys jingle behind Klyne. The guard approaches and unlocks the steel bindings. The sound of empty chains dropping into a pile on the floor punctuates the removal of a life sentence.

The government agent offers his own set of metal bracelets and locks one around each wrist as Klyne stands passive but anxious. The guard checks the cuffs. Satisfied, he says, "Follow me."

Together, three men exit the room, walk along the hall and down a flight of stairs, unlock another exit door, and step outside. Bright sunlight chased away the morning fog and Klyne stares across the courtyard. Freedom stares back.

Klyne leads the group as they approach the gates, his dancing dream distant from his thoughts. He focuses upon a single item, double barred gates locked tight. "Open the gate," Klyne whispers.

As if responding to his order, the internal gate squeals sideways on a rusted metal track. The group enters a security cage, the gate squeals shut behind them, enclosing all three within it. The watchman presents two green release forms. The agent initials each, and the watchman retreats, scribbling another form inside a small office. The ten-minute sequence from office to gate transcends eternity. An unexpected bang startles Klyne and the exterior gate squeals open. His breath rushes out. He inhales deeply, watching the gates roll sideways. It takes forever.

Hallingforth pulls the handcuffs. Stiffly, Klyne walks past the bars. Expelling gales of rotted breath he sucked into his chest over the months of confinement, he inhales and exhales deeply, again, and again, filling his lungs with the sweetness of free air.

The agent breaks into Klyne's thoughts. "The gray sedan over there, parked against the bushes." Hallingforth points, his fingers maintaining an easy grip on the steel bracelets, reminding Klyne this odd adventure remains engaged.

"Hold on, just a second." Klyne shakes his wrists free, spins about to face the walls one last time. Standing beside the main guard tower, he stretches both hands high in the air. Two middle fingers extend upward. A digital salute aims the ultimate insult at San Quentin State Prison.

The tower guard shifts his rifle across his chest, watches the men climb into the sedan then watches the sedan exit the parking lot, impassively waiting for Friday.

27

In a twelfth floor San Francisco hotel room, Klyne examines information and several items spread across a bed. A briefcase lies open on the floor. The undraped window catches sunlight reflecting off a white ketch motoring between two buoys and several harbor markers, departing the active marina and picking its way to sea.

"They haven't found Alphonse yet. You must have hidden him pretty well," Hallingforth begins.

"Warden won't have any trouble in a day or so. He'll just follow his nose," Klyne says. "That one's behind us. Let's finish our business."

Staring across the bed Klyne inspects Hallingforth, his demanding attitude. But Klyne knows he's totally in command now. "Money." A fluttering of mistrust remains in his actions, but Klyne stands at the ready, fully prepared to earn his freedom or take it. Makes no difference now.

Hallingforth slips an unlabeled envelope out of a side pocket inside his briefcase, hands it over. Klyne begins counting used hundred dollar bills. "Eighty," Hallingforth says, "It's all here, and no expenses taken."

He tosses another envelope on the bed between them. "Twenty-five more. Colombian pesos. Expenses you'll incur in the next phase. You fly to South America tomorrow morning."

Klyne studies the maps, diagrams, and photographs, meticulously committing the drawings and instructions to memory. His plan includes no return visit to San Quentin, nor Seattle, but definitely Los Angeles once he completes the operation.

Hallingforth retrieves a scuffed leather bag from the closet and removes a set of used clothing from it. "Bag, clothes and personal stuff you'll take with you. Nothing new, everything used and worn," he advises. "No sense traveling around in brand new clothes, especially where you're going."

False identifications and passports materialize, three complete sets, with proper photographs and stamped entry dates indicating a variety of recent travels, all very warn and used. "Learn these. Commit everything to memory.

"Stay in this room tonight. It's paid up a month. Your flight leaves tomorrow. Once you complete the operation, return to San Francisco and this room. Don't check in, the room's booked in your name. Just ask for your key by number when you arrive. Unlikely, but if they ask the name, save that Harris ID for last if you can, and use it here if you need it." He offers Klyne a printed card. "After you settle in, run this ad in the Sunday Chronicle under personals. Your contact will follow up on Monday."

"One more very small item."

A strained look on his face indicates the director may have guessed the 'very small item'. A thin film of perspiration covers his body and again, the spastic muscle marks time on his cheek, one eye twitches.

"Payment." The cards belong to Klyne now and he knows it. Confidence radiates off his body and guarantees he will never return to prison. "Fifty thousand dollars, not negotiable. Half deposited in a bank of my choice before I leave the city. Half when we meet again here. I leave, you wait. The operation begins when you deposit the payment. I'll call with the bank and account number within the hour, if you don't answer, I'm gone." Klyne pushes up off the bed, sticks the ID and clothing into the bag. "And you can complete the operation yourself, and track me if you can."

The ICD director's demeanor shifts about, unsure whether Klyne is bluffing or for real. Finally, "Learn a good game of poker inside those walls, did you?" Hallingforth sits back on the bed.

"One hour only, not a single minute more or I'll come after you. If you don't follow up after that, the entire United States government will come after you," he threatens, "and I'll just sit back and watch it happen."

A nervous smile cracks his lips and his tongue flicks in and out several times. His right eye blinks several times and a nerve in his cheek marks time with the eye.

"And remember one more thing. You now have a real murder beef hanging on your tail and I'm the only one in the world can change that."

*

Forty minutes later, Klyne steps out of a bank he chose at random, turns left and walks two blocks, dumps the clothing Hallingforth gave him into a Salvation Army bin then enters a used clothing store on Haight Street near the UC Medical center. Klyne decides if he buys a new old bag and his own second-hand clothes, it eliminates the potential that Hallingforth installed tracker devices. Cheap insurance.

28

On a warm night that requires neither, a heavy coat and a fluffy winter hat drape a stranger sitting on a bus bench across and down the street from the Blue Note.

Pigeons hide among its rafters, silent and resting from morning hunts and afternoon frolics. An early spring evening pushes at the disappearing winter chill, and the night shines clear, the breeze soft and balmy.

Klyne peers out from behind his protection. The unnecessary coat and hat cover his wait with perspiration. A wrinkled leather grip lies at his feet and a two-day growth itches beneath his chin. His coat pocket contains three new deposit books from accounts in three different national banks. Precisely printed in each book, a deposit of six thousand dollars dated yesterday appears. Another pocket bulges with cash and his new wallet contains several sets of falsified identification papers thoughtfully provided by the United States government and the special agent also known as Jonathan Wings.

After waiting and watching more than an hour, Klyne's unsure when or if Sarah will appear.

Earlier, he tossed the ticket to Las Vegas Hallingforth supplied into the trash, and chose a different flight, flew from

San Francisco to Los Angeles, caught a taxi across town, and stepped out two blocks from Sarah's apartment.

Before he left San Francisco two day ago, he located a second-hand clothing store, further outfitting his disguise. He arrived in Los Angeles and caught a taxi, transferring twice to different cabs, and headed toward the apartment, seeking Sarah.

He knocked on her door but received no answer. An anonymous call to the lounge indicated that she's on the work schedule for tonight, but Klyne has not seen her arrive.

At the moment, he remains outside, hidden, hesitant to enter the club unannounced for fear of her reaction in public. Unsure what exactly is going on in his life, he will continue his clandestine behavior until he discovers both the secrets and the answers.

*

Hallingforth had received the call two days before, and funds magically arrived by wire soon enough, almost immediately in fact, deposited to the bank account Klyne named.

Klyne had transferred all funds within minutes, having already opened new accounts in three different banks, dividing the funds equally, and retained several thousand dollars in cash. He signed Sarah as co-owner of all three accounts. He bought his own plane ticket and flew within the hour to Los Angeles.

He divided his remaining cash into three packets of two thousand dollars each, placed the money into three large envelopes addressed to Jake Klyne at general delivery in three different post offices, printed Sarah's return address on each, and mailed them. At least someone he cares about will get the money when the post office returns the mail to sender if he fails to return in thirty days. He kept another thousand in American dollars and all the Colombian bills Hallingforth supplied.

*

No longer confused, he finally has a job. His decision to continue the operation, rather than abandon the mission he based on hard facts and his desire for a comfortable future without looking over his shoulder.

He agreed to serve his country once again in the interest of national security, and furthermore, scampering about the country chased by the federal government for the rest of his life has little appeal. One more not so difficult chore, for which he has been partially paid already, and he can return to the remainder of his life. Klyne has no interest in becoming the government dog, and decides he will decline any contracts once he completes this one operation.

Thoughts of Sarah fill his mind. The heavy oak door finally opens. His eyes snap wide open and hot blood pounds in his head, creating slightly dizzy feeling.

Sarah steps from the dark doorway into a cone of brightness created by the street lamp. His heart thumps, followed immediately by dismay. The red-haired bartender steps out behind her, she takes his arm and they walk together along the quiet streets. The street is nearly disserted, but the warm evening brings enough locals out for a stroll and hides Klyne a comfortable distance behind Sarah and her friend.

Conversation and laughter echo back at a trailing stranger wrapped in a heavy coat and carrying a weathered bag.

Unsure how to deal with this dilemma, disturbed by the apparent partnership, Klyne simply follows the pair for now. In less than twenty minutes, Sarah reaches her door. The man hovers protectively at the entry until she enters, then walks halfway back to the Blue Note, unlocks a station wagon filled with toys, and drives away. Klyne grunts in surprise and relief as the car rolls out into the street.

Klyne approaches the apartment door with caution, and knocks lightly. From inside a muffled voice asks, "Who is it? Barry, is that you?"

It's me, Sarah. It's Jake." His voice cracks, his emotion evident. The door opens and pulls against its chain. Wide brown eyes peer through the slit. The door shuts. The light jingle of a chain reaches his ears then the door swings wide open. Sarah grabs his fingers, but he pushes her hands away and wraps his arms tightly around her waist.

"What are you do ..." she begins, but closes her lips, meeting his kiss, then opens them again and pulls him closer. Eager tongues join and play, artfully exploring the pathways they shared in the past. Sensuous wrestling slips her robe open and the lacey black silk incasing her breasts pushes firmly against his chest. Impatient, his hands slip lower, behind her, and find another silk covered roundness. Light ripping sounds disturb the silence.

Her female scent engulfs Klyne and sends him soaring into a sensual madness he never imagined existed. Pieces of torn black silk float silently to the floor. Klyne eases Sarah to the carpet, fingers, lips, and tongue busy exploring the depths of a fantasy that finally returns to his life.

Sarah filled his thoughts and dreams every day and every night for months, but nothing he envisioned approaches the ecstasy and rapture contained in this moment. He discovers once again her fluid smoothness, warm satiny skin, soft mounds, and moist pulsing valleys, and the woman that Sarah forever embodies.

"Wait, not here ... wait ... we can't ... no ... No!" Her warm feminine breath becomes heated panting, "My children, the kids, my kids ..." she whispers..."are sleeping," ... she finishes, tearing at his belt. The ache that built through months of his desire and dreams explode into her after a few succulent seconds of wildness, her own passions and needs temporarily abandoned. Klyne climbs immediately to an excruciating release too long delayed.

He lies still for a few moments, entwined with his lover and discovers his tears flow freely, joining those of his partner. Tears and smiles now claim both lovers, painting them equally with wetness and giggles.

Then, "I missed you.", Klyne reaches again, sharing another release, and replays the passion previously shared with this lover he will never again forget. Staccato bursts of sexual release and moans carry into the quiet, then both lie still, settling into occasional nibbles. Mutually content this time, both lovers murmur endearments, the hushed whispers filling the darkness as a relaxed sensual harmony encompasses each body.

A lazy smile lies on his face, but falls away when Sarah finally drops a question in his lap, it carries him back to reality.

"So, what are you doing here? How did you get out? Did Jimmy do it?" Sarah half-sits up on a elbow and looks down at Klyne. Her voice races up and down the scale, followed perpetually by her dimples tugging at the smile that almost never leaves her face.

He offers a brief explanation, skips over his deadly act, and obscures the remaining elements. Klyne easily convinces Sarah he gained his release by offering his military skills and working temporarily for the federal government, gathering intelligence in a foreign country.

"Gotta leave in the morning," he says, again wrapping his arms around her voluptuous warmth. Somehow, Jake and Sarah scrambled into the bedroom and up onto the bed during the frenzied lovemaking. "Won't see Jimmy 'til I get back," he adds.

Afraid Dodds might try to talk him out of it, or stop him from going somehow, he continues. "Don't tell him until I'm gone." With little provocation, his tongue stretches out and flicks her nipple. The warm, pink button rises in greeting and the lovers embrace once more.

29

Gusting winds buffet the prop-driven aircraft banking in, skirting the towers, buildings, and suburbs surrounding Las Vegas. The plane flattens out and approaches the black asphalt runway. Its tires chirp as the wheels touch pavement, announcing a perfect landing.

Gaming casinos and fancy hotels rise into the hot, dry air, striking a jagged skyline. Blinking marquees and glitzy rhetoric beg pigeons and marks to visit briefly, feed hard-earned dollars into gaping metal mouths, and then run amuck across the blinding desert, toting satisfied smiles and empty wallets while earnestly believing they just had fun. And true enough, most do, but a few leave everything they own on the tables, and more.

The passenger plane crosses the hot concrete and taxis up toward the boarding gate, bounces lightly, then rolls to a stop near a flashy Lear jet still warm from its recent flight. Whirling dust devils, bits of paper and dry leaves blow across the landing strip.

Klyne waits while other passengers push and shove, emptying the isles, then loosens his seat belt and follows the last of them down the ramp. He confirmed the connecting flight Hallingforth booked to Colombia at the same time he purchased his San Francisco to Los Angeles flight and this one to Las Vegas. The final leg boards in thirty minutes.

Hallingforth included Klyne on a group charter with a group of investment counselors and bankers heading toward Colombia to visit coffee plantations on procurement business. With his false passport and papers in order, and a boarding pass in hand, Klyne searches the blinking tote-boards for his departure gate.

Klyne memorized the procedure. He will board this flight but abandon the group upon arrival in Colombia. Having done what he can to shake off any tails and to accomplish his personal agenda, a night with Sarah, he now follows the plan as Hallingforth detailed it when he met Klyne in the hotel.

Light pressure eases Klyne back in his seat when the aircraft accelerates into lift-off, banks into a lazy turn, then shoots away toward South America, an eight-hour flight ending in Bogotá, Colombia.

A huge white cowboy hat tops a tall, blond man dressed in western clothes and watching the jet glide south out of Las Vegas. He cradles a mouthpiece and says, "Bates here, he's back on track, George, just as we'd reckoned. Side trip to see the woman was personal. Seems he'll continue." Bates listens.

"Yes sir. He took a jet-prop out of Burbank instead." Bates listens again. "Well, I back-tracked across town to LAX to pick up the Lear. No problem though, caught it easily, even landed before his flight." Bates waits another moment, listening again. "Yes sir, I'm leaving now, see you tomorrow afternoon." Bates shuts the phone and retraces his steps to the ICD Lear jet.

30

A glass mug half full of dark beer and a small container of salted peanuts sits on the bar. The lone American tourist dressed in shabby clothing rests his elbows next to it. A scrubby four-day growth decorates his cheeks and chin. Jake Klyne watches the shift change and, according to instructions, waits for Manuel, the relief bartender.

A stout swarthy male pushes a curtain aside and enters from a room behind the bar. The man approaches Klyne. "Greetings senor, I am Manuel," he says. "A refill?"

Klyne declines in Spanish, and says, "You're supposed to direct me to Blind Wings." The last two words he speaks in English. The statement sounds a little odd to Klyne. He has no clue what Blind Wings mean. Surprisingly, he does not think it through and make the obvious connection.

Manuel inspects Klyne for a split second then walks away. He returns a moment later with a refill, collects an amount much larger than the cost of a drink off the pile of pesos beside Klyne. He speaks again in his home language, "Better have another draft while you wait, senor." Manuel wanders away and disappears again into the back room. Five minutes later he returns, but says nothing, works the bar, ignores Klyne.

Fifteen minutes pass, then twenty, then thirty. Klyne waits, his eyes wander around the room. Two men gamble beers over a pool game and a few peasants sip iced drinks and mop sweating brows with colored handkerchiefs. The afternoon humidity simmers in a room nearly empty. A fan with one blade missing revolves erratically above the tables, pushing hot air around but cooling no one. Klyne becomes restless, in a strange country, on a stranger mission.

Manuel disappears into the back room again, and returns after a minute, but still ignores Klyne. Klyne decides to inquire again, wondering briefly whether a new question will cause a bit more money to disappear from his pile while nothing happens.

He stands and stretches. A small hand tugs on his sleeve. A dark-haired native boy of about ten or twelve speaks, "Follow me, senor, for a tour of the Blind Wings. Very cheap, only one hundred pesos." He holds out his empty palm.

"When we arrive," says Klyne, soft enough so only the boy hears.

The boy drops his hand, shrugs then grins.

Music blares from an old jukebox in the corner. The afternoon crowd built slowly, but appears intent on a rowdy evening. Klyne hoists his pack over a shoulder and follows the boy, ducks under the bar behind him and departs through a rear exit.

The boy sets a quick pace, jogging across busy streets, dodging automobiles, old pickups, bicycles and pedestrians. Early evening darkened the horizon, but the heat and humidity remain long after the sun drops behind the hills.

Klyne follows easily, attempting unsuccessfully to hold his breath when the boy turns into a narrow alley and picks a winding trail around litter and debris. The rising stench of uncollected garbage assaults his nostrils. Klyne joins the boy breathing deeply, and a burro bleats at them as they exit the alley. They pick up the pace again and trudge across a mowed field toward the rainforest. A half-moon rises into a clear sky above distant treetops, predicting at least some night light for the trip.

Klyne follows as the boy jogs over winding trails through the thick jungle for more than an hour. Dim moonlight throws ghostly shadows across the path and the bordering vegetation darkens into night. Flat and nearly motionless, an elongated body of water disappears into the blackness, stretching out of sight to the left and to the right, ending the winding dirt path.

Klyne stands on the muddy earth and stares across the black water lapping gently on the other bank.

"Help me, senor, it's very heavy." The boy calls out from beneath a bush. He uncovers a carved wooden canoe, complete with paddles. They push off and quickly stroke a hundred-fifty feet or so to the other shore. The boy promptly ties the canoe to a waterlogged rope attached to a tree branch and twisting down into the water. The boy continues along the trail. Klyne catches his breath and follows.

Two hours later they squat in a clearing, resting on a mound lit by moonlight that barely penetrates the dense foliage. Jagged rocks ring old campfire coals blacken its center.

"Wait here for Blind Wings," the boy directs. "One hundred five pesos, senor," his Spanish pure and clear. He counts the bills individually as Klyne places each one in his palm. The kid breathes evenly. The trail seems hardly a workout for him.

"Thought you said a hundred," Klyne responds, still catching his breath after the fast paced journey.

"Interest, senor. You insisted I wait for my pay." A touch of innocence twists up the corners of his lips, a business transaction in its purest form.

Klyne hands over the extra five and grins.

The boy nods, "Gracias," salutes, and races away into the jungle.

Klyne waits alone, unarmed and unafraid, but curious.

Time passes slowly. Shadows stretch across the clearing and the moon disappears, relegating the clearing to the even dimmer starlight. Klyne stands up and shakes his muscles loose, then slides into the brush, out of sight. He squats, settles in, props his back against a comfortable tree trunk and nods his head, dozing off and on during the night.

A warm, misty dawn transforms the night-blackened jungle into greens, yellows, assorted flowers and leaves. Klyne cracks his eyes open. He listens to the silence a moment, rolls over and rises to his feet, soundless. He freezes, half erect, every muscle tense. He stares at a red bandana wrapped around a head full of black hair streaked with gray that hangs straight and long beside a lined face containing an ice-cold set of gray eyes, one of which sights down the barrel of a vintage M1 carbine and does not blink.

The round black hole where the .30 caliber bullet will exit if the man squeezes the trigger successfully masquerades as a cannon muzzle and points directly at Jacoby Klyne's forehead.

"Come a long, complicated way just to die wondering what the hell Blind Wings mean," Klyne says, his words muffled by the surrounding bushes. Motionless, Klyne stares at a man standing ten feet away dressed in ragged combat fatigues, the sightline filtered through the rich leafy undergrowth, and Klyne's life hovers on the twitch of a fingerprint.

The fatigue-dressed stranger slides the carbine to his side and growls, "Name's Jeremy Blind, Wings must've sent you. He called me Tracker when I worked for him and Bates.

But I don't answer to that one anymore or to them or anyone else in D.C." His voice resembles coarse sandpaper scraping on hardwood. His face remains impassive.

Klyne relaxes. "He never told me your name." He recognizes the password now, but says nothing about it. The stranger continues, "Call me Eyes, everyone else 'round here does. Eyes Blind. Git it?"

He cackles at the nickname, the chortling laughter filtering away into a steamy morning. "Had the best damn eyesight in the whole company," he titters, "maybe, in the whole Marine Corps. Straightening his face, he returns his stare to Klyne and advises, "Two thousand gits you where you're going, and delivers a package Wings sent. In advance." Together, they step into the clearing.

"Half now, half when we get there," Klyne offers, looking into an empty space that a moment ago contained the stranger. Blind had been standing at ease, listening, and in the blink of an eye, disappeared without a sound.

Klyne spins around, but the clearing remains empty. His eyes and ears hunt for the stranger. Nothing, not a sound disturbs the surrounding terrain. Klyne finally brings his eyes back to the grassy spot where the man vanished.

Six minutes pass while Klyne remains immobile, frustrated, and unable to locate the tracker named Eyes Blind. The stubby bush directly behind him suddenly speaks and a gritty voice says, "In advance." Blind steps back into the clearing with one hand held out. "Guess I forgot to say please."

Klyne decides he has little choice, and will follow the lead for now. He squats and counts out a pile of money on the damp turf, respect for the man sliding into his gaze. The pile grows, and Blind reaches down, collects the bills. Blind buttons the brown paper into his pants pocket. "Tell me how you got here."

"A man named Jonathan Wings sent me to Manuel at the bar. I used the *Blind Wings* contact phrase. A young boy showed up at that cantina and used *Blind Wings* too, and told me to follow him. He left me here last night … that's how I got here."

Blind shook his head. "Not that got here. The other got here. How did you get involved in this operation, and why did Wings send you to me?"

Klyne squatted in the clearing. "I don't know any of that, or why I'm here, with you, I mean." He explained some of what happened at the prison, but left out the execution.

He sent you because I turned him down. No matter what happens, watch your back with these guys. And I mean the D.C. spooks too. They owe you nothing, and they don't do much homework on contract ops. So keep your eyes to your six on this one, and watch your own butt."

Blind stands. "Foller me," he grunts and strikes out into the dense foliage, "if you kin." His weird chuckle trails after him, occasionally beckoning when Klyne lags behind.

Klyne follows through the heavy jungle. The bushes seem to part before and fold behind him while Blind leads the way. High, hot sunshine casting almost no shadow hints at the noon hour, as does Klyne's grumbling stomach. Both travelers break into a meadow split by a nearly motionless stream that eventually trickles between the trees surrounding it.

Crouched against the thick, green backdrop stands a thatched cabin with two windows and a front porch aimed at the clearing. Three children romp in the yard and the eldest waves a greeting and laughs. "Welcome to our home, *Gringo*."

The boy who led him the day before waves his greeting and giggles, pointing a finger at Klyne and then at a young girl standing on the porch. He giggles again, removes the money from his pocket and waves it this sister. She grins and claps her hands.

A brown-skinned, brown-eyed woman tends a vegetable garden beside the stream. She straightens up and runs her hand through dark curls that hang past her shoulders. In one sunny corner, a large patch of maturing marijuana plants rises out of the dirt, each about six feet tall with bright green leaves beginning to sprout into sweet golden buds.

"My family." Blind grins, then points at the pot. "My income."

"You already met Jesse." The first real words he has spoken besides grunts and cackles since they left the clearing. The children crowd around, hugging Blind, and he waves to the woman. She gathers her harvest and grabs a carved wooden bowl, serving Klyne the largest salad he's ever seen, accompanied by her smile of welcome. Everyone sits, eats snacks, the adults sip beer and everyone relaxes.

Jesse sneaks a taste of the home-brew once in a while, and his father aims a finger and a thumb a half-inch apart at the cup, indicating 'a small sip only'. An hour before sunset Blind disappears. He returns at dusk with a fat animal, skinned and gutted, and hanging on a stick. Succulent pork chunks and garden vegetables fill his hollow spot once more as Klyne savors the meal, and darkness settles upon the clearing.

Later, the two men sit alone in hand-crafted chairs tilted back on the porch, two sets of feet crossed and resting on the railing. Klyne fills his mug from a jug of home-brew. A soft, melodic and very feminine voice fills the warm evening breeze with native legends as a loving mother tucks her children into bed for the night.

"Lot sweeter flavor than that rot-gut pruno we brewed in the cells at Quentin," Klyne says. He just finished explaining his story in more detail, but still only hitting the high points. Blind passes a hand-rolled smoke. Klyne politely declines. "Working. Need a clear head."

Early in his military tours Klyne discovered a distorted euphoric delight and mental sensitivity falsely influenced his perceptions when he smoked pot, and the sense of well-being and control were extremely deceiving. It had almost gotten him killed once. Since then, he always maintains a rigid discipline in the field, separating work from play. He no longer smokes before or during an operation, and quits drinking alcohol as soon as one begins. He sips his beer, making his second mug last throughout the evening.

"Platoon grunts thought it was a joke," Blind begins his story, "calling me Eyes. But I always wanted the point, that way I depended on myself, not on others watching out for my ass. Knew if I bought it then, least it'd be my own fault. Those enemy soldiers never could sneak around nearly as good as an Apache anyway."

Jeremy Blind had been raised in Colorado by his father, a full-blooded Apache, and his Irish mother, an elementary school teacher on the reservation. He stares off into the distant jungle, his sharp gray eyes fogging a bit. He fills his mug again and sips.

"My father taught me the old ways of hunting, caring for a family," he continues. "Then the Marines used me up. When I got out the intelligence boys came after me. Started operating here in the late eighties, but I don't like how the feds do business, a little back-stabbing when you ain't watching. So I quit, set up housekeeping with Theresa. We bought this place twelve years ago, can't do this kind a living in the states anymore. Jesse came along, then Tina and Marie."

Both men sit for a while, engrossed in the night and lost in personal thoughts. Then, Klyne changes the subject. "How far to my contact point?" He's working, he reminds himself, and anxious to get on with it. The contentment of the Blind family reminds Klyne that he has someone waiting too, in another world.

"Two days, easy trailing. I'll git you there then I'm gone. Don't do operational work no more, don't know nothin' about this 'cept where to drop you."

"Just throw a little information at them, occasionally. Spooks keep my bank account comfortable. Keep asking me, but they got nothing I want anymore. Bout near got me killed on an operation Wings sucked me into a while back."

"Job sounded pretty easy and real good money, so I agreed. Weak intelligence though, missed some protection the boys hired. Turns out, money wasn't so great after all. Wings tried to push me into this one too, but I'm forever done with 'em. Looks like he gits you instead. Shouldn't have any trouble though, this target's real tough when it comes to women and young girls, but pretty soft without his bodyguards. Just git careful when you take him. Then git out quick. Find your way back here. We'll git you stateside."

Theresa appears, carrying a full pack. "Compliments of Mr. Wings," she says, placing it at his feet. "You'll find sleeping pads spread out on the floor inside the door when you get tired."

Pulling the pack closer, Klyne looks it over, but leaves it zipped. He looks inquisitively at the couple.

Blind gets the message, stands, wraps his arms around his wife and kisses her forehead. "Better get myself some rest, we leave at daylight. Be gone four days." Klyne notices the sandpaper voice disappears whenever Blind speaks to his wife. They wander into the cottage, arms wrapped around one another.

As soon as the couple shuts the door Klyne pulls the zippers on the military backpack. To his surprise, he discovers his ancient weapons inside – the tools of his father's work, and more recently his own.

Only for a second does he wonder how Wings retrieved the crossbow and garrote from his storage locker in Los Angeles. And it crosses his mind that the dagger and its leather case, missing since Martinez had been shot in Marin County, materialized along with the other weapons. He ignores those conflicting details for now. After six years in the field and some pretty dicey operations, he's never surprised what the Feds know or do anymore. He's just glad he has his tools.

The pack contains building diagrams and a map, and finally, a new-age weapon. A Beretta M9 shines up at him, and a box of rounds nested next to it. A notation on the box reads: Just in case - JW. Eight days worth of food packs completes the inventory, along with two canteens.

"Looks like plenty of hiking, no transport for this one." Klyne breathes his words into the night, reviewing the map and reading his orders. The target, Dominic Perez. Several maps indicate three places where Klyne might find Perez. Three heavy marks appear on the map, his residence, his main plantation, and an apartment where his current mistress lives. The map highlights eleven minor plantations, where additional crops grow.

A red X marks the initial drop point where Blind will lead him, a hill above the largest plantation. No guessing what Perez grows either, it's obvious. Klyne opens an envelope containing several fuzzy pictures of Perez standing in a field inspecting his crops, and one clear front shot with an extremely attractive young woman next to him, more like a very young girl.

31

"This is crazy Alex, makes no sense," Dodds says. "A drug felon mysteriously dies in prison, choked to death. An agent out of a secret federal office takes Jake away under some weird pretense, and no one knows or admits anything about it." He scratches his head and looks at his boss.

Paar says, "We're checking out that Bates character. He pushed at Jake twice, here and in Panama a few months ago. Could be he's wrapped up in it. No telling where he comes from, but I'll know later today."

His private line dings once, and Paar sticks it on his ear. "Already? Great." He points at the phone, mouths, "Found Bates." Pops a thumb up, smiles at the phone. "These guys are quick."

Paar scribbles on a pad then disconnects, then punches a button on his intercom. "Jennifer, book Jimmy to D.C., first available flight, today if possible." He nods as if she can see it. "Yup. Red-eye overnight's okay too."

He points a finger, "Go grab your hot-bag, Jimmy."

Dodds raises his eyes in question. "What?"

"You're on a flight to D.C. tonight." Paar hands the page across his desk. "Meet with January Hitchcock at this address - she's very no nonsense equipped and will take you to meet Bates. He'll fill in some holes, or she'll kick his butt all the way up the DOD ladder." He looks at the ceiling a second,

"Well maybe not up the ladder, these guys sit pretty far up there already, but she'll kick him off it if she has to."

*

January Hitchcock, a stocky but very fit woman topped with steel gray hair, sits beside Dodds in the federal ICD office. The stare she aims above wire-rimmed glasses sitting on the end of her nose offers Bates no alternative.

"Okay Henry, we put a 'Do Not Touch' order on this ex-Special Forces guy four days ago, and someone's touching him. Officially signed yesterday, but touching's been going on a while. We need to know why. Not tomorrow. Not next week."

Bates reads a document Hitchcock handed him when she and Dodds entered his office a minute ago without knocking or an appointment. He looks across his desk, deciding if it's worth having the legal battle right here. It won't change anything so Bates chooses not, and hands the paper back.

"Where is he, Henry?"

"South America, near Bogotá actually. Accepted a freelance assignment from our division."

"Manipulated into it seems more like it."

Bates stares back, but makes no comment.

"So, how's that happen? Our guy's in prison on a falsified court transaction, and he mysteriously departs with Jon Wings, a cover alias George uses, and now we can't find him. George left with his wife on a four day trip, and he's not calling us back."

Bates tugs at his lip a few seconds, squeezes a black ball in his fist before he speaks. "Whole thing started out whacky, even for one of our Red Ops. For some reason, Klyne executed an inmate after George set him up on a sting. We don't know it all, and thought it was someone in the prison gangs he was after - drug smuggling, or whatever."

"Who's we?" Hitchcock demands, her eyes digging a hole in Bates.

"Nikki ... she knows nothing more about it either. George ran this like any Red Op, closed to everyone but himself."

"After you called, I dug into this a bit. Knew George was acting odd, but figured he was stressed with this Symington issue and losing his ops sequence. Turns out, four drug smugglers worked together on a major deal in Texas two years ago."

"Vicki Hallingforth OD'd on a hot cocktail when she met one of these dudes at a conference in the same hotel. Everyone got a story that she died in a car accident, including her mother. No one but George and I know different. Now, you both know it. No one else." Bates shrugs. "Be nice if you keep it from Margaret, Jan. No sense to her mother knowing at this point."

Bates reaches into a drawer, pulls out a thin file and tosses it across the table.

"George figured it out when some random info he read cross-checked with a DEA operation that snagged one of those dealers, Alphonse, sent up on a murder beef during another major drug sale eighteen months later."

"Martinez, a local drug cop was one of the four. A federal agent named Jack Brighton shot and killed Martinez. Klyne took the hit because he was there, part of the drug deal. George has been really freaked out since he lost Vicki, but no one knew how badly it affected him."

Bates looks away a minute, the emotion welling up in his normally stoic self. Vicki had been like a daughter to him, and Hallingforth his best friend. "George hid it well, Jan. Was worse than I thought though, worse than we all thought."

Hitchcock picks up the files, scans down the lines. "So, he sent you and Nikki to execute the cop and frame Klyne so he could get to Alphonse. That's pretty slimy even for you guys Henry."

She scans quickly, peeks over the file, stares at Bates again. "Jack Brighton, alias twice removed, and a pretend Riley White after the real Riley White got busted in Seattle, and not even his real name either. Sounds like one of your personal fuck ups, Henry?"

Bates says nothing, protecting his alias and his part in the execution.

"Nikki and I didn't know all of it. We worked the Red Op like we always work Red Ops, very tight need to know. George designed the op and ran it, like he always does. We didn't figure it out until we realized Klyne was picked up at Quentin and sent south."

"We thought it was a drug operation gone soft. Especially after we found out that cop - Martinez - was crooked and running pot and cocaine in from Colombia."

"George misled us too, completely. I didn't know it all until I found this file. He lost a little edge with all this happening, and the emotion took its toll. The idea he finally had the chance to revenge Victoria tipped him off a pretty steep cliff."

"Check that last page. Tracker. That's his contact ... one of our retired agents. Go see him, you want to find Klyne. He'll know the set up and the method. Tracker might even be helping Klyne. Our first choice, although he refused the assignment."

*

Two days later, thick jungle bush surrounds Jacoby Klyne and Tracker. The bright evening sun settles toward dusk. Klyne squats in the trees and peers at a marijuana field hacked out of thick native growth.

Over a hundred acres layered up a hillside sprouts into the humid afternoon. Four small farm buildings stand side-by-side on a cut bank beyond the crops. Two houses, a large barn and silo, two blue tractors, three rooting pigs and a flock of chickens complete the scene. A dozen field hands work at various tasks and three heavily armed men wander the grounds, intent on keeping the area private and secure. The residential buildings appear deserted, field workers out for day labor.

"Just so you know. Perez grows the pot here and several other areas, but gits raw coca plants from the surrounding locals, all over the district. He processes it into cocaine at another plant, and transports it to the sellers, primarily in the USA. He's almost never anywhere near that part of the operation, and most often, not around here either. He pockets the rewards, but not the risk."

The ex-agent turns to Klyne and tips his hat, "Don't know why the spooks want him dead, but you can bet it ain't got nothin' to do with drugs."

"This is where I git off." Tracker eases away from the observation spot. He elevates his middle finger and rolls it around a bit, examines it carefully and says, "Give this to Wings for me, raises his other hand, and this one to Bates." He cackles at the thought then melts into the landscape, disappearing without a sound.

*

Two days and nights pass with no sign of Perez or the white Jaguar he drives. Klyne spends the days observing agricultural practices in the backcountry. Busy from dawn until dusk, the farmhands prune, feed, mulch, and carefully tend the crop. The armed lookouts offer no help with farming, but appear extremely capable in different assignments, making a game of target practice to pass the time. Excellent at hitting moving targets, they're absolutely deadly at standing ones, though it might take more skill to miss a standing target with an automatic rifle on full spit.

The wait and the heat wear on Klyne, and he decides to head up-country and check out the residence. The downtown apartment where the mistress lives will complicate his chore and his groceries will only last a few more days. He decides he'd rather catch Perez at this main plantation or at home.

"Looks like thirty miles, day and a half," he grumbles, "if I'm lucky and the road stays flat and packed." He hoists his pack and sets out into the bush, sets his pace at three miles an hour alongside the dirt road that leads away from the farm. Nearly non-existent traffic makes the trip easy and quicker, and Klyne makes good time on the roads. He skips into the forest when a vehicle approaches, but it happens infrequently. He pushes hard and late into the night.

*

At noon the next day, Klyne huddles in a clump of trees, observing the household activities on the Perez estate. The expansive hacienda rises clean and magnificent above well-tended gardens and orchards. Stubby masonry walls decorated with wrought-iron sculpture and statuesque rockwork surround the bulk of the mansion. Manicured lawns and bright flower gardens spread over three acres, fruit trees and shrubs accenting the flagstone pathways meandering throughout.

Replicate security guards guarantee privacy, and Klyne makes note of at least three dogs. A huge Rottweiler and two Dobermans patrol the grounds. The white Jaguar convertible sits beside a new Dodge pick-up truck under a wooden canopy covered with old growth vines. The elusive Mister Perez might be home today. Klyne grins at the possibility.

Across the dirt road, a small red tractor barn and a residential unit of six cottages stand behind a short wooden fence. Several men wander around, some armed but most busy with workday chores. Two lie under the front end of a jacked-up flatbed truck while another replaces a broken window in the barn.

Klyne opens his pack and removes the building plan. He locates the master suite on the sketch and discovers it lies in the sleeping wing directly opposite his approach, but he can circle his way in easily before dark. He retreats into the forest and works his way around until he spies open windows leading into what appears on his drawing as the second floor master bedroom.

Two hours later, Klyne huddles beneath a tree, watching the guard routines. As evening darkens the terrain, Klyne grins, glad there will be no moon. The Dobermans run free on the grounds after nightfall he notes, but the Rottweiler has been absent since dusk. The dog probably stays inside after dark. The guards patrol casually, expecting no trouble.

Klyne reflects on similar situations in other wars and other operations and again applauds the poor discipline that makes his job so much easier. Two armed men wander the grounds in opposing circles, the patterns crossing once per hour near the garage. They spend longer periods visiting each time they meet. The guard changes at midnight.

Zero two hundred hour approaches. The routine remains constant. The house interior darkened thirty minutes ago. The upper bedroom window lights up. Perez pokes his head out and looks at the dark sky then pulls himself back into the room. Four minutes later the window goes black.

Both guards stroll around the perimeter and meet at the garage. Each fires up a cigarette.

Klyne waits thirty minutes and begins his assault with only the stars lighting his way. Slipping quietly up to the rear wall, he peeks between the spikes. He must locate and dispose of the dogs first. The dogs bring a disciplined danger in to the mix, men are simple to deceive and dispose. He throws a pebble at a tree in the small orchard, then another, and another.

A Doberman trots over, investigating the rattle. Klyne throws another pebble. Dancing around under the tree, the dog jerks his head, perks his ears momentarily, and stares into the branches each time a pebble hits. A slight whistle arcs across thirty feet of silence and the brass arrow enters the dog behind its left shoulder. The bolt takes him out with barely a whimper.

Klyne waits. He tosses more pebbles, but fails to attract the other Doberman. He climbs over the fence, seeking the second dog. Rolling over the top as low as possible and distant from the buildings, Klyne slides to the ground and crouches, listening intently. He peers into the blackness for five minutes then slowly eases his way through the orchard. His third step onto a gravel pathway meets a low growl to his left and he barely raises his arm in time.

Soundless, the dog races over and leaps at Klyne, vicious teeth ripping into his forearm. Klyne jams his arm deeper between the jaws and secures a mouthful of hair and skin with his own teeth, biting into the dog's chest to keep it from pulling away and tearing the forearm muscles. Sharp claws scrape along the side of his head, drawing thin bloody ribbons on his cheek and forehead. Klyne fights for a death grip.

His thighs surround the furry flanks, squeezing the air out of its lungs, wrestling for a chokehold. Eighty pounds of writhing muscle continuously growls, attempting to pull away and mount another attack. Klyne keeps the growling subdued with his arm, but the pain's excruciating. His teeth slip away from the dog's chest. Blood and saliva run down his arm, coating the dog's neck and chest with slick residue.

The Doberman tries to withdraw again, and Klyne strains, gripping the muscular throat, but his fingers keep slipping loose, covered with thick slime. Klyne squeezes his thighs together, forcing the air out of its lungs, and finally gains the chokehold he seeks. The esophagus collapses, flooding the lungs with blood. Klyne kicks the dog free and pushes back against the wall, holding his bleeding arm. He listens for sounds of alarm. The night remains quiet.

Struggling back over the wall, he opens his pack and dresses the wound and disinfects the scratches on his face and neck. He flexes the muscle on his left arm. Lucky. No serious damage. The pain makes him dizzy, and he shakes his head to clear it. Bad idea. He sits for ten minutes recovering his strength and settling his nerves.

He rises up and watches the bedroom window. Minutes pass, more minutes pass. Nothing, the window remains black.

"Excellent," Klyne tells himself, and climbs over the wall again, hurries along the pathway, crawls beneath a large bush and eases in beside the house.

He listens.

Silence.

He climbs onto a short wall abutting the house, grabs a corner of the first floor roof, and pulls himself up. Blood drips along his arm and he grits his teeth each time the muscle throbs. The roof tiles curve beneath his feet and he eases his boots down on the supporting edge of each tile to keep it from cracking.

Klyne flattens himself against the wall outside the second story bedroom window then leans over and peers inside. A tile cracks under his foot, popping like a gunshot. Klyne freezes. He rotates his head and scans the dark night.

Nothing.

Slowly, he leans again, staring into the light-less room.

He listens.

No sound, no movement.

He waits ten minutes.

Silence echoes back at him. His eyes nearly useless in the blackness, Klyne slides over the sill. Soft, thick carpeting depresses under his feet. He creeps across the floor and stands beside a massive canopy bed. Barely discernible, an unmoving lump under a silk bed-sheet offers evidence that Perez sleeps alone.

Pausing momentarily, Klyne reaches over his shoulder and a warm tingling spreads to his fingers when he grips the jeweled dagger. Klyne slides the dagger out of its sheath. In a few seconds the game will end and he'll return home, gather his freedom and return to his lover.

Blinding light fills the room.

Klyne blinks at the brightness then squints at the barrel of a shotgun aimed directly at his heart. The patrol guard holds the weapon in hands that know how to use it. The black and tan guard-dog next to him growls deep in his throat, straining at his harness. The Rottweiler curls his lips back over sharp white teeth dripping saliva, and voices his challenge with a deep continuous rumble. He appears extremely eager to greet Klyne close-up.

Wearing a white silk robe, Dominic Perez stands in the doorway behind the guard and dog, a smile plastered on his face. He grips a Glock 17 in his fist and his voice belies the smile. He bites the words off and spits them into the room. "Well, it appears our good friend Mister Hallingforth sent us another guest."

"Welcome, whoever you are. Enjoy our hospitality while you can." Perez looks at Klyne and the bandaged arm, wet with red drippings. "I see you've already met my pets." His smile resembles a flat line beneath a neatly barbered moustache. Perez looks extremely unhappy.

The guard extends the harness and Perez takes it in his left hand and continues pointing the Glock at Klyne. The guard starts across the room, stepping sideways and away from the line of fire.

Klyne says nothing, frozen in confusion. He's never heard the name Hallingforth, nor does he understand how Perez knew he was coming. Wrong about the handcuffs too, Klyne thought he left those behind in California until the patrol guard moved toward him carrying a pair.

"Not again!" A chopped-off whisper slips out of his mouth.

32

The guard buckles the cuffs around Klyne's wrists then pulls him across the room, retrieves the harness and, stepping behind Klyne, barks a command. Still growling, the dog pops to attention, his front legs vibrating with tension.

Klyne stands before Perez and watches the dog.

"Well, my friend, you get to join the last gringo Hallingforth sent," Perez says, rolling the word gringo across his tongue and curling his lips back. "You are a dead man."

Klyne wonders about the name Hallingforth, but holds his questions.

Perez hammers the injured arm and drops Klyne to his knees. Pain shoots up past his elbow and blood oozes through the bandage, a few drops land on the floor.

Klyne glares at Perez, "I don't know any Hallingforth." He grimaces as Perez kicks his arm this time.

"Keep your mouth shut unless I ask you something. Your buddy Symington killed my brother, and you will pay for it just as he did. After you tell me more about this Hallingforth guy, seems that bastard just won't give up."

Raw anger strains his voice. "Looks like I'll have to do something about him. Seems he won't leave it alone."

Klyne says nothing, fearful of another punch. He flexes his arm, but the pain continues. The cuffs keep his hands from rubbing the soreness. Klyne climbs to his feet.

"Why did Hallingforth send you?"

"I don't know that name."

Perez stares at Klyne for a moment. "Symington stuck a knife into my brother and he bled out before we got to him. That agent wouldn't talk either, at first, but he finally blubbered like a sick child when Ricardo sliced off his balls and fed them to the dogs. The not so tough ass gringo died in tears, begging me to put them back." Perez smiles, recalling the incident. "Nobody fucks with Dominic Perez, Mister Special Agent ..."

"Nobody."

"You American spies must think we're stupid, or something. Even after Chico, I could think maybe Martinez was an accident. When somebody killed that sneaky, rat-faced prick Alphonse too then I knew someone would be along again to finish what Symington started. You will find out, my friend, that Dominic Perez is not as ignorant as you believe."

Perez strikes with the pistol.

The barrel splits his lip and cracks a tooth, dropping Klyne to his knees again. The guard jerks him to his feet. Klyne spits a mouthful of blood on the floor.

Anger wells up in Perez once more when a few red drops splash onto his robe. He punches the arm again. Klyne keeps his feet this time, but grunts again as the pain washes over him. He fights off nausea.

A silk bed-sheet drapes the well-defined body of a young and pretty girl who appears behind Perez. Barely in her teens, her nipples push at the thin glossy fabric, her cheek swells with recent bruising, and she stares at Perez with fear in her eyes. Fresh bite marks discolor her shoulder.

"Take him to the basement and lock him to the board, Ricardo. We'll dig out our information in the morning, before we make him squeal." Perez grabs the girl by the arm and drags her back through the doorway, shoves her along the hallway toward the rear bedroom, stalking after her.

Two guards lead Klyne down a stairwell, and one pushes him into a security room located in the basement. Klyne sits on the floor with his hands stretched above his head, while the guard bolts a link of the handcuff chain to a thick block of wood attached to the wall. Blood dribbles along his arm and the torn tissues throb.

The guard exits and slides a flat metal bolt across the door frame. The light winks out, dropping the room into near darkness.

Klyne concentrates and out of the dimness the rectangular outline of a basement window a foot tall, three feet wide, and covered by steel bars six inches apart emerges. The vision jogs his memory back to another room with its own bars. A frown creases his face.

Klyne rests a few minutes, gathering his strength. He tests his bonds, but no matter which way he pulls, the cuffs chafe tighter. The pain in his arm intensifies, and he slumps uncomfortably against the board. He racks his brain. Nothing. No escape.

An attack when they come to question him remains his only option. Recalling his training, he shuts his eyes, forcing himself to rest. He dozes fitfully for a couple hours. The cuffs and injuries repeatedly and painfully jerk him awake whenever he nods off. At least Perez will help him cheat the silver coffin that so often plagues his dreams. Unless Dominic Perez has one of his own. Klyne wonders.

Klyne wakes with a start. Pain jolts through his arm. He stares at the door and watches the metal bolt slowly withdraw. Near darkness still fills the room and the window remains a dim highlight cut in the far wall near the ceiling.

The door creaks open. "Jake." A single word pops into the gloom.

Klyne knows he's dreaming, a disembodied whisper cries his name. But, it sounds exactly like Jimmy Dodds. The voice repeats his name, whispering again from the doorway. "Jake. You in here."

Now Klyne's sure he's delirious. A light beam the size of a pen barrel dances around the room, finally focusing on Klyne hanging from the bolt. A shadow passes through the doorway and approaches, feeling along the wall. Useless, his eyes stab at the night, but he's ready to use his feet if necessary.

"It's me. It's Jimmy," the voice says. Dodds points the circle of light at his face, his face swims out of the darkness, and then his old friend touches the bandage. Klyne finally recognizes Dodds, which startles him even more.

"Jimmy." Klyne grunts, "What are you doing here?"

"Later, gotta cut you loose first." Dodds examines the bolts and the cuffs with the tiny flashlight. "Be right back. Don't go anywhere." Dodds forces a chuckle as he slips back out the door. The eerie silence returns.

A few seconds pass, then a minute. Dodds returns with a wrench, unbolts the handcuffs. "Can't do much about the cuffs right now, but we can get rid of this bolt, anyway."

"What's this all about, Jimmy?" His swollen mouth muffles the words, and his split gums begin bleeding again. He spits a red blob onto the floor.

"Long story, let's just get gone."

Dodds helps Klyne to his feet. Klyne grunts, the pain rips along his arm. Both men creep toward the door and step into the larger basement area. A dog barks on the floor above and the basement door swings open. A shot coughs from a silenced weapon, followed by two more. Bright flashes light the room with each round.

The clatter and thump of a body dropping a rifle and falling down a stairway foils any attempt at stealth from this moment on. Another voice yells through the open door. "Hey, what's going on down there?"

"Damn it." A garbled whisper floats out of the darkness beneath a basement window hanging open. "Kinda hoping we'd git outta here without any trouble, Jimmy."

Klyne doesn't recognize the voice. Dodds helps Klyne move toward the window. The man upstairs switches the lights on, flooding the basement. Sergeant Art Watson crouches near an open window, holding a silenced Beretta M9 in each hand.

Klyne blinks, totally surprised once again.

Watson aims at the stairwell across the room and sends two more shots at the doorway. A man screams and the door slams shut. Watson shoots out both lights, plunging the room into darkness again, and slaps in a new clip.

Dodds shoves Klyne up and through the open window. Klyne rolls clear, Dodds and Watson follow. Both men help Klyne stand and all three men race along the garden wall and out across the brick pathway.

Klyne turns away from the walkway, and yells, "This way," pointing toward the orchard. They sprint down the gravel cart-ways, bending low beneath the branches.

Bright spotlights splash light across the yard. The men race into the shadows and, ten yards from the rear wall, a few bullets spray behind them, accelerating their steps. They hit the wall and roll over just as the adobe sparks alive with automatic rifle fire and they drop to the ground behind it.

"Glad that's not a wrought-iron fence," Watson grunts, breathing hard.

Still handcuffed, Klyne pushes both arms through the straps, lifts his pack, and sprints for the jungle. Dodds and Watson send a few shots at the mansion and follow his trail. All three enter the jungle at a dead run.

Thickening underbrush slows their progress, but they struggle through it, putting thick trees and jungle undergrowth between their backs and the mansion. Random automatic-weapon fire sprays through the vegetation all around them as the guards stand on the wall and empty the clips.

Dodds and Watson pick up the pace, chasing Klyne who twists and turns erratically but makes continuous progress toward the thicker jungle. Suddenly, Watson grunts, grabs his thigh and pitches forward, squirming along the wet ground. "Fuck!"

Dodds yells at Klyne and both men turn back. Dodds kneels beside Watson, opens his knife, slits the fabric wider and examines the wound. The bullet passed through the thigh muscle but missed bone. "Just got meat," Dodds says when Klyne kneels beside him. Each man grabs an arm and helps Watson hobble along the trail.

They make poor time for two hours, and stop to rest.

"They'd never follow us in here," Dodds says, between breaths. All three are huffing heavily. Watson and Klyne are losing a little blood, but the bandages and field nursing work as expected. Both injured men scoot under some brush and hide, resting a few moments.

Dodds works back along the trail, scouting. Ten minutes pass. Dodds crawls under the bush where Klyne and Watson lay recovering. "Nothing I can hear, think they gave it up."

Dodds examines the pressure bandages Klyne had wrapped around Watson's, thigh then checks Klyne and wraps a new pad on his arm.

"Okay, Jimmy. What gives?" Klyne stares at Dodds, his look demanding some answers.

"Jake, you're just not gonna believe this."

A dog howls in the distance, echoed by a second, then a third.

Dodds stands and looks around, then squats again. "Some government spook named George Hallingforth set up a special operation to get four men executed. It's not a federal operation, and we couldn't find out why he did it. Something to do with drug deals and his daughter."

"He sent one of his federal agents, your sweetheart, Alicia Diamond, by the way. Her name's Nichrico Pepperton, a Specialist 909 operative, very high level. She set you up with that bust and Hallingforth somehow got you sentenced to prison so you could execute Alphonse. Martinez, the cop in Bolinas, was on his hit list, along with Alphonse. Perez is the third, but we don't know who the fourth is." Dodds stops speaking.

Klyne suddenly gets it all, his mind quickly connecting the dots. White with anger, his body vibrates with rage. Klyne grunts, "Chico Perez! Dominic had a brother, he's dead already. The fourth man. Another agent killed him, and is also dead. Butchered and castrated according to what Perez told me. Trying to scare me into talking." His voice trails off ... "and Alicia set me up, that bitch set me up. That conniving Bitch!" He screams the words then cuts it off short as he thinks about noise and pursuit.

"And who's Hallingforth? Perez asked me about him too." His voice tight with anger and frustration, Klyne realizes he's been manipulated and lied to, and tricked into killing one man, and almost a second.

Fury floods his mind and he grunts, "What does Hallingforth look like?"

"Don't know. I never met him."

Suddenly, Klyne knows. The short, stout man that freed him and paid him. Hallingforth, not Wings - the false name. But, the why of it all still eludes him. Klyne wrestles with his emotions, curiosity winning out, temporarily.

"How did you get here, Jimmy? How did you find me?"

"Paar finally had some luck, or maybe his hard work paid off. Anyway, he kept pushing at the drug thing with Martinez. It pissed Paar off that a cop was involved in the smuggling, so he kept digging at it until he got his answers."

"Paar called a contact in D.C, Jan Hitchcock, and she forced that agent named Bates into a corner. He coughed up a little bit after he programmed a capture and record program in the main computer. He failed several times, but finally flushed out the details."

He figured out " set this up and then used his agents, Pepperton and even Bates, to his own ends. They don't know exactly why either, but figure Hallingforth couldn't use a regular agent because of the life sentence and the fact he was outside the law for some reason we don't know."

"The Feds are still trying to put together enough evidence to bust Hallingforth. But he's pretty slick, been doing this kind of thing a very long time and he's very good at it. It has something to do with his daughter, Vicki, and how she died. We're pretty sure one of these drug smugglers had a hand in it. We believe one of the Perez brothers hit her with a hotshot, and she overdosed ... not positive though'"

"So he had me sent to prison just so I could kill Alphonse." Low and angry, his voice betrays the rage that rocks his body, and he shakes all over as color floods his face. "But for personal reasons. Simple revenge!"

"Bates doesn't have the whole story, or maybe he just won't give it up. But he told Paar where Hallingforth sent you. Mentioned Eyes Blind, an ex-agent, code name Tracker. Apparently, Bates is pretty tight with Hallingforth and won't help hang him. But he decided you were a victim, in one sense, and knew we were after answers and would never stop. He gave us enough to find you. That's all."

"Why didn't you stop me earlier?"

"Paar sent a message to Blind, but Blind ignored it. Said he has no reason to believe Paar. Blind has little trust for Hallingforth and his buddies. So Paar searched the military and national police force data base and finally found a retired colonel that knew Blind when both were in Special Forces during the Panama crisis. At that time, Blind was another special agent. They called him 'The Tracker' before he quit. The colonel convinced Tracker that Hallingforth had set you up. Jonathon Wings, that's one of his personal code names."

"Although Blind knows Hallingforth and Bates pretty well, he wouldn't give us much. Just told us how to find you. They still pay him for watching some nasty folks in this country, so he waffled a little with us. Pretty confusing to everyone, especially with us trying to figure out where each player fits and whether it's a good guy or a bad guy. Too much code for me."

"The Colombian authorities wouldn't help. Perez is too rich and powerful here, and Paar was afraid to push too hard or Perez might find out and kill you. He damn near did anyway. Paar sent us after you. Blind gave us the location. We tracked Perez here and waited for you, two days. Just didn't see you go in until too late. We were sitting on the opposite side of the grounds, so we had to wait and bust your ass out."

"Guess I forgot to thank you guys for that." Klyne shrugs and finally grins at his friend. I owe you a big one, Jimmy, you too Art." But his anger remains, despite the smile. "And I owe a big one to Mister Jonathan Wings, aka George Hallingforth, government traitor."

Dodds says, "Let the cops handle it. You're in deep enough."

Klyne glances at him, but says nothing.

"Know how to get us back to Blind's farm? Paar can have a chopper fly us out from there. He'll meet us with the guys from the prison. Says you gotta go back there until he gets this all straightened out. Says he'll do everything he can."

"Back to prison?" Klyne says, his voice rising in disbelief. "Uh huh. No fucking way, Jimmy."

"Have to go back, just until they get it straightened out. Paar has no authority over this, and it takes a few days to get the governor moving. Essentially, you are now listed as an escaped felon as well as a murderer. Nothing to do with reality, Jake, just red tape flapping all over this one. We hope."

"What do you mean, 'we hope' Jimmy."

"Well, the nasty fact is, you voluntarily went along on the drug deal. Even if it was a set up. So we have to work through that with the state authorities."

Dodds stares into Jake's eyes. "Besides, you got a second murder beef," pausing a moment, he looks his friend in the eyes. "Alphonse."

"Seems your cellmate MacKlain made a deal. He figured it out and told the warden you killed Alphonse in exchange for a release."

Klyne says nothing, staring at the dirt.

"MacKlain passed the tests three times over the years, and aced the preliminary state exam last time he took it. He'll become a paralegal when he paroles next week. San Francisco Public Defender hired him strictly to research appeals on cases where convicts serving life did not have a good attorney. Claims that's why he lost his original case. Untrue, of course, but MacKlain's out regardless."

"Mac says he'll do your case for free and get you off. Says he owes you one. Says he's sorry, but he told you too many times to trust no one, especially convicts and prison officials."

Klyne stares at his friend for a several minutes, and finally looks away. "Right. Not even my bunkie, I guess."

Dodds speaks again. "Can you find Tracker? ... Lead us to his farm?"

"Yeah, I can find him. About a day and a half, maybe two with Art hobbling." Klyne stands, "Better get to moving. They may get the dogs out after us. Perez won't take it lightly, me getting away, and his men shot up like that."

As if to punctuate his words, several deep howls echoes again in the distance, a little closer than last time. Klyne hoists his pack and heads down the trail. Dodds takes the first shift, helping Watson navigate on a leg and a half.

*

Early in the evening two days later, Klyne and Watson stop on the trail, staring at the business end of an M-1 carbine. Blind points at the cuffs, speaks to Klyne. "Long as these two are friendly we can git you guys fixed up."

"Nice bracelets. You buy 'em local?"

Watson hangs over Klyne's shoulder and the two look nearly dead. Dodds follows behind them and freezes when he sees the carbine.

"It's okay Eyes. It's okay," Klyne says.

Both men drop, exhausted. Blind lowers his rifle. Dodds bends over the men and helps Klyne and Watson to their feet. Then all three hobble along the trail and into the yard and up onto the porch.

Blind works a few seconds with a metal pick and releases the handcuffs, then disinfects and bandages all the wounds. Theresa appears, carrying a bowl of vegetables and a plate of meat chucks in a sauce that smells exceptional. Later that evening, they all gather on the porch, sipping the sweet home-brewed beer. Blind sits beside Klyne and packs herbs into his swollen jaw then changes the bandages once more on the torn arm and treats Watson's leg again.

"Chopper be picking you guys up here tomorrow afternoon," Blind says, "and take you to the airport. Tickets waiting in the name of Paar. Says he'll meet you in San Diego. The state guys will be with him, whatever that means." Blind offers more beers. Klyne declines, claiming the need for sleep. Dodds and Watson accept.

*

The sun creeps above the trees and peeks at Dodds and Watson. Both men stand in the yard, arguing with Blind. Klyne vanished during the night and Dodds wants Tracker to find him.

"Left about three-thirty," Blind offers.

"Why didn't you stop him?"

"Not my concern. Man can go where he wants. Ain't paid to baby-sit."

"We'll never find him. Will you go after him?" Dodds asks.

"Not interested." Blind settles down on the porch and strikes a match. The sweet scent of marijuana drifts across the yard. After a few minutes, Blind wanders through the gate and into the garden. He grabs a hoe and begins helping his wife and children dig and weed and plant. He ignores Dodds and Watson.

Klyne has not returned when the helicopter arrives just after sixteen hundred hours hits. Ten minutes later the pilot lifts off, carrying Dodds and Watson over the wilderness and toward the airport, and a telephone.

Two miles away, along the route to the airport, Klyne crouches under a bush, watching the chopper pass overhead. Unconvinced that the state government will free him after all that has happened. *'Trust no one,'* Mac advised, so now Klyne accepts that as a truth. Klyne waves a hand after his friends and plans a party for two and a dance alone with George Hallingforth writhing beneath his feet.

"Sorry, Jimmy. No way I'm going back to San Quentin. Even for one second." His voice chases the aircraft out of sight. Then, he retraces his steps back toward the meadow and the farm.

*

"Come on, Jake." Blind pushes his way through the bushes behind his home and enters a small clear spot at the base of a tall tree. A thin coaxial cable runs up its trunk to and connects to an antenna sticking above the canopy. He lifts the cover off a metal case topped with a solar charger linked to a heavy duty dual truck battery.

"You didn't show them?"

"Why should I? Those guys might be friends, but they're taking you back to a prison sentence you didn't deserve." Trackers points two thumbs down. "Let them figure it out first."

Blind plays with the phone, dials a number Klyne committed to memory months ago in Panama and recites. Blind hands Klyne the receiver.

The phone line dings twice. "Winston."

"Ambassador Winston, Jake Klyne here. Do you remember me?"

"Of course, Panama. How could I forget? Nasty memory, well except your part in it. Nice to hear your voice. Been a while. I see you're in Colombia this time. Probably in some kind of trouble."

The man chuckles. "And, it's Senator Winston now, Jake."

Klyne stares at the phone a second. Senator Winston? A few steps up from the Ambassador he rescued in Panama. "How'd you know where I am?"

"Simple. As of last month, I'm a United States Senator. I know everything. And so does this phone. You're on a federal secure satellite link, ninety-seven miles south of Bogotá, and you'd not be calling this number unless you're in some trouble you can't handle."

The senator chuckles again. "So, what can I do for you?"

Klyne looks again at the phone, disbelief on his face. He sticks it back on his ear. "Stuck here Senator, need a way back stateside, Texas probably the best entrance. Then an untraceable vehicle for a week. Can't get on a plane stateside for this."

"Want to tell me about it?"

"No sir, prefer not."

"Okay. Go get something to write with. I'll call you back in ten minutes."

*

Twenty minutes later, Klyne wonders if he made a mistake calling. But after thirty-four minutes, the phone dings once and Klyne pushes the link button. "I'm here Senator."

"Let me talk to Blind a minute."

Klyne hands over the phone, and watches Blind nod his head several times, then say, "Yes sir, got it." He hands the phone over.

Jake listens, writes notes exactly as dictated. "Thanks Senator. Will explain this another time, when I have a little more of it." Klyne punches a button and breaks the link.

33

Klyne exactly follows the instructions Senator Winston relayed. Blind drops him at the airport in Bogotá. Over the next several days, he climbs into three separate prop planes and passes over five different countries, the pilots flying low and fast over the trees, jungles, low foothills and mountains, finally landing in Mexico City.

Klyne hops into a Cessna for the final leg and lands on a flat strip of desert outside Matamoros. He hands the pilot his remaining pesos and the Beretta he'd received with his mission package. Per instructions, he leaves his pack and weapons in the plane. The pilot grins at the weapon and slides it under his seat. Klyne disembarks and the small four-seater spins in a circle and lifts off toward the south.

*

Klyne walks across the border and enters Brownsville, Texas. Shows his Harris passport and identification, which passes him easily into the United States. He then catches the next flight to Amarillo, watching for an old friend as he exits the plane.

Aaron Rocho stands and salutes, then grabs Klyne in a bear hug, lifts him completely off the ground. Once again combat buddies meet and prove neither time nor distance lessens the bond that emerges during dangerous missions in foreign lands.

"Got the oddest phone call couple days ago from a senator in Boston, Jake. Guess Ambassador Winston made it big after we carried him out of the bush last year."

"Yup, pretty nice 'thank you'. Paid in full far as I'm concerned. Will give it in person when I'm finished dealing with this mess I'm in now."

Half an hour later, Rocho parks his yellow and white two-door Belair Chevy in front of Rocho Brothers Classics, a car restoration and sales dealership the brothers own in Amarillo, Texas.

"Quite a story, Jake. Sounds like that federal agent needs a lesson in ethics and personal responsibility." Rocho points at a green Dodge parked under a shed roof. Klyne follows Rocho as both men amble over for a look.

Klyne peeks in the window. "Awesome, four on the floor?"

Rocho pulls up a frown. "Nope, all original, three hundred eighteen cubes with three on the floor. Four-speed only comes with the bigger engine. Nice, clean, no one will notice you accept other car buffs. Plates are clean, registered to me, so it won't track to you unless someone knows I gave it to you. And that ain't happening."

Klyne points a finger at his military pack sitting in the passenger seat. "How'd that get here?"

Rocho shrugs. "Just arrived by messenger this morning. I didn't ask, he didn't say. Dropped it here and left."

Rocho pokes a phone at Klyne. Here, take this. It arrived in overnight mail yesterday, and two credit cards and a license. Senator says it's clean, but Feds can trace it within a few days after first call or card purchase, so use it with care and only if you need it."

The next morning, Klyne punches the accelerator and chirps out onto the Interstate, heading east and driving a perfectly restored Dodge Charger. Two days later, he crosses a bridge crossing over the Chesapeake, exits onto Route One, and eventually dead-ends at Constitution Avenue. He turns right, and parks at the Smithsonian. "Federal Services, Intelligence Division," a pleasant female voice states.

"I need an address for George Hallingforth."

"Sorry, can't give you that information. You have to get his approval. I can connect you."

"No thanks." Klyne closes the phone.

He waits an hour and calls again claiming to be a UPS agent with a blurred delivery address on a package to George Hallingforth.

This time, a different operator answered and obliged. Klyne discovers, unfortunately, that the ICD office is located in Baltimore instead of Washington. He drives across the bridges and finds the building easily enough. He sits in the Dodge across the street from the address the operator supplied.

Klyne investigates the area for an hour, then decides he'll rent a room overnight.

34

Klyne sits in a cafe across the street from the Federal Special Services Division building in Baltimore, sipping coffee. He studies the entrance, waiting for Hallingforth to arrive. He had been seeking the agent now for two days. No luck.

The staff checked his credit card and license, but he paid cash for a hotel room, had eaten all his meals at the cafe, and shopped every store within four blocks of the government building without buying a thing. Klyne had located three main entrances, each watched over by a uniformed guard. But no one enters the parking lot without passing another officer in a shack centered in the only driveway in or out, a double exit.

Security personnel check identity cards on every person, even those driving official vehicles. Razor wire coiled along the top of a six-foot chain link fence surrounds the parking areas, reminding him of the 'home' he'd vacated a few weeks ago.

Klyne discovers one other way into the building. A large overhead door secures the delivery entrance at the rear, but it stays locked and barred and behind the gates. He watches the door lift on its rollers. A two-man security patrol unlocks the door, supervises the men unloading, escorts them inside and then immediately locks up afterward, when the men depart.

Suddenly, Klyne stiffens, recognizing the walk. Nearly uncontrollable anger wells up at the sight of Hallingforth, but Klyne forces that emotion to the back of his mind and himself to remain seated. He barely controls his urge to race over and finish the man off right then and there.

Hallingforth speaks with an associate as they exit the building together. The men stop and talk a moment, then part. Hallingforth continues across the parking lot, his gait a little erratic, and climbs into his car.

Klyne watches the dark green Lincoln exit the gate, turn left, and disappear into the evening traffic. He leaves a full cup of coffee on the table and walks back to his hotel.

*

Lying across the bed fully dressed with the lights out, Klyne fingers the remaining identification Hallingforth supplied, tears it up and flushes it down the toilet. The swelling in his jaw has nearly disappeared, but four stitches remain where Blind sewed up his split lip, and he replaces the bandages on his arm daily. The injury is healing nicely, but will leave two jagged scars where the canine teeth shredded his skin.

Klyne awakened this morning as Robert J. Hawkins, with an Oregon license, two credit cards, and a passport, delivered overnight to Rocho when Klyne picked up the Dodge, courtesy of Senator Winston.

Through the fourth floor window, Klyne watches the day emerge, cool and clear. As the sun chases away the final remnants of darkness Klyne rises, grabs his pack, drops his key on the dresser, and opens the door. He wanders the streets again, continuously, circling block after block, until he spots the green Lincoln parked in the lot. Hallingforth arrived during his last circle. The information brings a grim smile to his lips and the soldier circles the block once more on foot and heads into the hotel parking garage.

Klyne returns with his Dodge, circles the block once more and spots the Lincoln still in its slot. He drives up and down the street several times until a pick-up vacates a metered parking slot and slips into it, aimed toward same direction Hallingforth had driven the night before.

Cars and trucks jump the light and race away, while others ignore the yellow and screech to a stop at the last possible second when the signal blinks red. Traffic hustles along the road all afternoon and pedestrians constantly stream by, an undulating mass slithering the packed sidewalks. Klyne huddles behind the wheel, staring at a newspaper as if waiting for someone, but never reads a word. He glues his eyes on the exit, occasionally flicking his gaze toward the Lincoln just to make certain it's still in its spot.

Klyne slumps deeper in the seat and raises the paper. Alone, the stout agent pushes his way through the door, nods his head to the guard, and approaches the Lincoln. He carries a briefcase which he sets on the back seat.

A grim smile settles across his face once more as Klyne twists the key and his pipes rumble beneath the seats. The Lincoln eases into traffic, followed by a Dodge Charger with Klyne at the wheel. The sun drops low in the sky and Klyne shades his eyes as both vehicles head west. Street-lamps click on and brighten the twilight by the time Hallingforth parks beside the ranch-style house situated in a neighborhood full of similar designs.

Staggering slightly, Hallingforth grabs the railing, steadies himself as he steps on the porch. Shades cover the windows, but Klyne watches lights switch on as Hallingforth wanders through the house. "Not much of a home for such a powerhouse," Klyne mumbles.

Klyne has no way to know it, but Hallingforth sleeps at this house only when he works in Baltimore, a few days a month. Klyne's lucky he caught Hallingforth here. Most days when not traveling the director works in Washington, D.C. He and his wife live in Virginia, on a two-thousand acre horse property with its own lake and a lucrative breeding stable – his wife's family owns and has operated the ranch for generations.

Hallingforth also owns a ten-room Colonial in Barnstable County overlooking Cape Cod Bay, a four-bedroom townhouse in California overlooking Santa Cruz harbor, and a penthouse suite in France, eight rooms with a distant peek at the English Channel. Hallingforth likes a water view, has invested well, and owes no mortgage on the properties. And it helps that he'd married a wife with plenty of family money, more than plenty actually. An extremely comfortable retirement looms in his future.

Leaving lights on in the kitchen and bedroom, he walks into the unlit den, settles into his favorite chair, and pours a brandy. He sips, staring at the drapes he had drawn across the double French doors leading outside.

The Charger idles at the curb then slowly rolls to the corner, gathering speed as it circles the streets. Klyne finds no access at the rear. Nearly identical homes line the street, each with a yard fenced, and back up on one another. The homes differ only in landscaping. Each new owner planted a profusion of flowers, trees, and bushes years ago, when these homes were first built, striving for a unique individuality where none exists. He cruises past the house again then speeds away.

Klyne returns on foot after midnight and finds most houses along the road dark and quiet. He wanders along the sidewalk, as if strolling on a warm, spring evening, but his eyes dart about, checking windows for anyone peering out. Teeming with shadows and murk, the neighborhood abounds with late night silence. Klyne slips behind the bushes that border Hallingforth's driveway, eases up to the side fence, and peeks into the backyard. Finding it unlit and empty, he pulls on the top board, testing the fence, then quietly kicks up and drops into a crouch on the other side. Jewels decorating the dagger hanging behind his right shoulder glint in the starlight.

Klyne examines the rear yard. A square redwood table surrounded by chairs and a portable barbecue sit on the patio. Nothing else. He steps on the concrete and edges his eyes around the doorjamb. The drapes block his view inside. Klyne turns the knob, expecting he'd find it locked, but it turns easily in his hand. Surprised, he rotates it completely then eases the door open. Klyne steps into the dark room and sticks one eye to the crack between the drapes, leaving the door open behind him.

A lamp switches on. "Care for a drink, Sergeant Klyne? The doors aren't locked and I deactivated the alarms." Hallingforth sits in an armchair centered in the room, sipping. He sets the goblet down, lifts another and points it at Klyne, and grins. "Brandy?"

The director wiggles in his seat, blinks his eyes quickly several times. "I knew you'd show up, eventually. Actually tracked some of your trip. Harris I.D. is mine, remember. Surprised you used those at all as good as you are in the field. Eventually lost you in Amarillo, when you switched out to another one. I expect you finally got some help from the Senator. Nice play, smart. You sure earned his assistance last year."

"Guess he owed you at least that much. Course, your 'in-the-field' is jungle and back-woods terrain, not pavement and hot-rods. And, I do have some answers for you."

The cheek muscle twitches continuously beneath his right eye and his left eye blinks erratically. Hallingforth drains his glass, pours another for himself immediately, and fills a second glass. The goblet shakes as he extends the drink toward Klyne. His right knee jerks and bounces, then stops, then jerks and bounces, then stops, a continuous nervous reaction to the stress.

Klyne steps between the drapes, but makes no move to accept the brandy. "I didn't come for answers. I came to kill you for what you did to me." He barely whispers, his voice almost hoarse, stretched tight with anger and tension. He takes a step toward Hallingforth.

"Wait. I can explain." Suddenly, a tear rolls down his cheek. "It had to be done. There was no other way." One of the most powerful men in the country whimpers, as Hallingforth sags deeper into the chair. "I'm too old ..." His voice trails off, "just too old ..."

Klyne moves one step closer.

Hallingforth sets his glass down and drops his hand into his lap. When he picks it up again, he grips a Beretta 418 he had hidden beside the pillow, looks like a toy in his hand. His eyes harden, he straightens his spine, and a different person speaks, in charge, in control. "Not another step."

His voice grates, rasping, no longer weak. "One of those bastards is still alive." His hand no longer shakes and the pistol never wavers. "And we still have a deal."

"No deal," Klyne says, but remains rooted, his eyes glued on the gun. "You think that James Bond peashooter will stop me ... not hardly."

"Only eight rounds here, Sergeant, but you can't dodge them all." Hallingforth sips again.

"They're scum, no good, they're rotten. They don't deserve to live. Selling drugs, hurting children. Don't you see?

Don't you see it?" Anger rumbles in his voice. Saliva flies from his mouth and dribbles down his chin.

Then, his voice softens again, cajoling, convincing. "Someone has to do it," he pauses, his chin droops, another tear dribbles. "And I'm too old. I just can't anymore." The pistol settles toward his knee. "Too slow. Can't react."

"You're the only one. We checked." He raises the gun again, the twitching beneath his eye nearly stops, and his voice hardens again. "Symington could have done it, but they killed him too soon," and shows sadness again, "they butchered him," and then shows happiness, convincing once more, "I can show you the pictures." He wipes his mouth with his sleeve and grins. The right knee bounces erratically.

The psychotic agent giggles and sips again, jumping in and out of his depressed state, his mood swinging back and forth, his personality shifting, beyond his control.

"Will that do it? Will you go if I show you the pictures?" Hallingforth babbles on, "Is that enough proof?" His smile remains plastered on his face, sweat covers his skin, but his eyes express nothing but misery.

"Tracker refused. He's pissed at us for last time. Don't know why though, he knows the risks. He's the best. He's the best. He should've done it. But he didn't want to go to prison. But he could have done Alphonse before he was busted. Too slow. I was just too slow, couldn't find him before the cops."

The director giggles again, "We're usually faster than the police, but not this time." Hallingforth suddenly cackles loudly then rubs his eyes. Tears run down his cheeks. He wipes his face with one finger on his left hand, the right still aims the gun directly at Klyne.

Klyne studies Hallingforth, every move, seeking his opening. The gun droops, slightly, but not enough. "Okay," Klyne says, the vague explanation confusing him even more.

"I had no idea these men were so terrible, that they needed killing so badly." Klyne slumps forward slightly, apparently relaxing. "You should have told me. Of course I'll do it."

"Good," the agent says, dropping the barrel another inch.

The kick catches Hallingforth completely by surprise and the pistol flies across the room. A second kick catches him under the jaw when he struggles and half rises.

The chair tips over backwards, with him still in it. Klyne leaps over the chair, aiming his knees toward Hallingforth's chest, attempting to pin him beneath his body, but with surprising quickness, the director rolls away, and jumps to his feet, crouching, his eyes wild and glaring.

Klyne lands hard, his knees skidding on the slick hardwood floor, he collides with the wall. Hallingforth kicks sideways, barely grazing Klyne's shoulder then kicks again. Klyne slaps the foot aside, rolls, and jumps to his feet.

The combatants eye one another, circling in the tight quarters, each seeking an opening. Hallingforth glances at the gun lying against the wall, the tipped chair blocking his way.

"Not a chance," Klyne grunts.

Hallingforth dives anyway, and Klyne punches once, a straight right shot that catches Hallingforth under the chin. He sits down hard and Klyne lands on his chest this time, pinning him and reaching for the dagger. Klyne probes Hallingforth beneath his chin, the point slicing his flesh. Klyne pushes slightly, barely pricking the skin and Hallingforth ceases all movement. Blood trickles along his throat, dripping onto the floor, staining his collar. Beads of sweat roll down his cheeks.

"Don't know what you're talking about," Klyne says, "but if you move, even one fucking twitch, you're dead." Straddling the agent, his knees pressing on his shoulders,

Klyne shakes with uncontrollable rage. The dagger tickles Hallingforth's chin again, aimed directly at his brain.

"Do you have any idea what you did to me, you piece of slime. A government agent? You make me sick, you bastard. You interfered with my life, you made me kill again. You lied to me, used me ..." his voice rises, "... you had me sent to prison on false charges. You made me kill a man! You Miserable Bastard!"

Klyne nearly loses control. The anger, the frustration, the wrath he has held back over the past months surges up, spilling into his veins. He wants his answers first, but indignation finally pushes him over the edge. "You think my life is worth nothing?" Klyne screams the words. "Well, you're dead wrong! I choose, not you! I choose what to do with my life!"

"And I choose to kill you, right now."

Hallingforth shakes his head, quickly, from side to side, and opens his eyes, wide, the eyeballs rolling around. Suddenly, his eyes focus, and he stares up at death staring back at him.

"No-o-o-o," Hallingforth wails. "Don't do it. I'll tell you everything. I'll pay you more," he rattles, "I'll keep you out."

"I'm already out," Klyne growls.

"It's not what you think." A disembodied voice speaks from the patio doorway. Henry Bates pushes the drapes aside and steps into the room with an old Colt revolver in his hand aimed directly at Klyne.

Klyne maintains his grip. As he rotates his body and peers over his shoulder, the dagger pushes deeper into Hallingforth's throat and he squirms, writhing in pain.

"I'll kill him, even if you pull the trigger."

"Maybe, maybe not ... but why bother. He's just a sick old man ... and we can take care of him." Bates waits, his pistol steady.

Klyne flicks his eyes at the Colt.

"Forty-four forty. It'll knock you across the room. And you won't get up."

Klyne says nothing. Both men lock eyes. Hallingforth squirms once again, leaking more blood onto his shirt, but unfeeling in his despair.

"It wasn't the drugs," Bates says, "Not the dealing anyway. The Perez brothers fed a high-grade speed-ball to his daughter and she overdosed. She knew nothing about the drug scene. Dominic Perez met her in Texas, some convention party for the company she worked for. He dated her a few times then invited her to Los Angeles, to meet his friends."

"They were partners, Perez brothers, Martinez, and Alphonse, smuggling high volume cocaine and marijuana into the western United States through Mexico, and by boat into San Francisco. Martinez was a San Francisco cop, and crooked."

"Dominic, as usual, tired of his new girlfriend, and decided to share her with his brother. She wanted no part of it. So they shot her up to get her in the mood, but it was too rich and she overdosed. An innocent victim of sick barbarians."

"They murdered Victoria Hallingforth, a sales recruit for Par-Con Executives on her first solo assignment then dumped her body in an alley. She had just turned twenty the week before. George's only child. It destroyed him once he found the answers."

Klyne held his position, ready to plunge the knife.

Bates continued. "It took George almost two years to find the truth. The stress and pain of it twisted his mind. You can see how he is. He just covered it well. He hired a rogue agent, John Symington, first. Symington got to Chico Perez and stuck a knife in him, but his brother caught him, tortured him for information, then cut his throat and his nuts, and sent pictures to George. It drove him totally off the edge.

"George had to find an operative that didn't know him in case he got caught. He was positive he had to protect his identity and run this as if it were a 909 Red Op. The grief and his paranoia, and the fact that he broke the law, overcame his ability to function. The whiskey didn't help. He became single-minded, motivated solely by revenge."

"He truly believes he did the right thing and that you'd understand and go along with it if you knew the truth. A mental delusion, obviously. His illness manifested, and then superimposed with the secretive nature of his job. So he kept everything hidden, like an undercover operation."

Klyne eases up on the dagger, but maintains his grip. Some of his anger dissolves, listening to Bates. "What about you? You helped him."

"He gave us bits and pieces, and orders. Never got the whole story. We operated just like we always do. Need to know, only." Bates shrugs, as if standard operating procedures excuse everything.

"Your buddy Dodds and his boss in California pushed me in the right direction, well, forced me actually. Your buddy Dodds is a true friend, just so you know."

"I finally cracked part of his code last week and pieced together what he'd done. The rest is probably in his briefcase." Bates hides his emotion, but has been a co-worker and friend for most of his adult life, and embodies an immense respect for Hallingforth.

"He's sick, let me help him. He's done a lot in his life for our country. There may be explanations for the other problems you have, but nothing will save your ass if you do him now. Nothing in this world anyway. Believe it."

Bates places his pistol on the table then raises his hands, palms out. "Think of your woman and her kids, and make your choice."

Klyne relaxes, visibly. He releases Hallingforth and slides the dagger back into its sheath. "I won't go back to Quentin again."

"We'll see about that. You might have to report to the authorities in California, temporarily, at least. I'll do everything I can, as soon as I can. Just so you know it, Nikki Pepperton didn't know anything. She just followed orders. Thought it was legit. She actually likes you, a lot. Admires your sense of duty. And that's very unusual for her."

"Hah, Nikki Pepperton. She's Alicia Diamond, Operation Crossbow, and a damn good agent, even if she is a woman. Very efficient. Very effective." Hallingforth states. He struggles to his feet, retrieves the chair, and sits. "Can we do him now, there's only one left," Hallingforth cackles. A smile creases his face, but his eyes remain dead and another tear spills from each.

Blood stains his shirtfront, still leaking from the laceration beneath his chin. He splashes brandy into his glass, quickly inhales and sips, rolling the liquor quickly around on his tongue. He chugs the rest in one swallow and cackles again. "Thank you Henry, you're always right on time."

"Nikki's not with us anymore. She was shot on a deep-cover operation in China. We got her out, but she didn't make it," Bates says, and looks away, his voice unsteady, expressing the emotions he normally controls easily. Bates picks up the revolver again and pulls a set of handcuffs off his belt. He points the barrel at Klyne.

Klyne stared at the gun. "I don't think so. This whole thing's a mess, and I'm not the only victim. But I'm not going back. No way."

Bates lifts the barrel. "Yes you are. Alphonse is dead. The Governor needs some answers. And, we need to straighten out your problems once and for all."

Klyne turns toward the front door. "I don't believe you'll shoot me, knowing what you know. Not in the back anyway." He opens the door and, without looking back at Bates again, steps out into the night.

35

Hallingforth pulls the wrinkled bathrobe tighter and one fingertip traces the scarred patterns that other patients scratched into the old pine tabletop over the years.

Sitting in the psychiatric ward in Bethesda Naval Hospital, he picks up a plastic cup and pours two fingers of water from a pitcher, then tosses the shot back, and coughs, as if the glass contains whiskey.

He speaks only to himself, and then only in distorted riddles. Even the other patients believe he's nuts. They can't quite understand that he speaks aloud only when planning his new operation, its primary goal, the execution of Dominic Perez. Only that will lay his nightmares to rest, and only then can George M. Hallingforth III, federal spy services wonder boy, begin the healing process.

*

An open-topped jeep rocks to a stop beside a metal hanger at the north end of a well-maintained runway. Dominic Perez climbs out and barks an order. Two male Rottweiler's immediately leap out after him.

"Guard!" Perez commands. Both dogs freeze beside him. Dressed in a freshly laundered khaki jumpsuit, Perez shades his eyes visor-like with his left hand, while his right grips an AK-47. He stares down the runway.

A silver jet with no identifying numbers glides into a flat landing pattern. The dogs remain at attention beside Perez, and six brown eyes follow the jet as its wheels touch, bounce then touch again, and roll toward the hanger. Oddly, the rear cargo door hangs open and the boarding ladder extends, nearly grazing the ground as the aircraft slows, brakes, spins about and begins rolling back the way it came.

His eyes follow the plane, and Perez grins. "Ah, my money. Exactly on time."

The dogs sit, motionless but alert.

Along the opposing edge of the landing strip a few steel barrels sit in random stacks beside several large wooden shipping crates. The jet rolls across his view in front of the containers. A slight movement disturbs the area behind the stacks. Dominic Perez misses that movement, but four black ears perk up and each dog points a black nose at a shadow shifting behind the barrels.

A puff of blue smoke flitters away on the afternoon breeze and the deep crack of a forty-four forty slug echoes along the valley.

The human eye is not sharp enough to track a bullet in flight. Dominic Perez simply twitches. A wet, red dot appears in the center of his forehead, spoiling his perfect tan. His eyes snap open.

Nerves and muscles quiver and jerk, unsuccessfully denying the damage. The back of his head explodes. Unimpeded by incidental contact with bone and brains, the hand-loaded slug tumbles out the back of his head and ricochets off the hanger, disappearing into the bushes. Perez slowly crumbles, a pile of immaculately pressed rags lying in the dirt, convulsing briefly.

"Special delivery from Victoria ... C.O.D.!" Acting ICD Director Henry Bates announces the package. He cradles the polished Winchester carbine in his arms and sprints down the packed dirt runway. He scrambles up the ladder trailing behind the Lear then quickly reels it up. Bates climbs into the co-pilot's seat, his breathing quickly returning to normal.

"Hell of a lot simpler if you just shoot the bastards. Fuck all that spy bullshit," Bates says.

Nikki Pepperton eases the throttles forward. Bright sunlight glints off the wing-tips as the jet banks away, charting a return course to Baltimore and a new desk that awaits Henry Bates in a tenth floor office behind a sweeping panoramic view.

Both dogs remain at attention. Four dark eyes and two brown snouts follow the sleek aircraft as it speeds away to the north. Neither Rottweiler flinches, but both snouts point forward as ordered, each one twitching at the scent of fresh blood. Four brown eyes roll sideways and sneak a glance at the rumpled tan uniform lying in the dirt, bleeding.

*

An office door labeled 'ICD Director' swings open. A maintenance man pulls the door back against knee, pulls a battery-powered screwdriver out of his tool pouch and unscrews a green nameplate that reads George Hallingforth. He places a new plate on the door that reads Henry Bates and re-inserts the screws.

Inside the office, Nikki Pepperton stands at the window, staring down at the parking lot. Bates stands behind his new desk, flipping through a file. Bates lays the open file on the blotter. The left flap contains several color images of an attractive woman dressed in combat fatigues. In one photograph, she holds an automatic weapon and smiles at the camera. Below the photo, red block letters read:

Murder of a Federal Agent
Drugs, Extortion, Kidnapping
Classification: Spec 909 Red - Priority One

SEEK CONTRACT BID
CLASS A-1 OPERATIVES ONLY

Nikki turns away from the window and looks at Bates. "Leave him alone."

"I know where he is," Bates says.

"Doesn't matter. Drop it."

"But, he could do it, and he's already there. We can guarantee he'll get pardoned this time, for everything."

"He'll never buy it. Never in a million years."

"We'll see, Nikki."

"Don't even think it, Henry. I'll shoot you myself."

*

Twenty-four hundred miles south of the ICD office, Eyes Blind stands beside Theresa and three children, and all five stare down the dirt road that enters the farm. A brand new Land-Rover rolls into view and parks in the yard. Klyne sets the brake and climbs out. Sarah and her two children follow. Smiling, the Klyne family approaches the Blind family.

Everyone hugs ...

- 30 -

For additional fiction, documentary works,
and images by Bill Delorey:

Go to:

www.billdelorey.com

Bill remains a lifelong advocate of wildlife and wilderness
protection, and veteran's issues as well as mental health care
and support.

www.ingramcontent.com/pod-product-compliance
Lightning Source LLC
Chambersburg PA
CBHW020332180626
46812CB00001B/161